OASIS ONE

Douglas W. Garlinger

GTS LLC
Fishers, IN 46038

OASIS ONE

Cover Photo used under license from Brian Kinney / Shutterstock.com
Cover Design by Douglas W. Garlinger

First edition
Printed in the United States of America

ISBN: 978-0-9981653-0-1

ACKNOWLEDGEMENTS

The women in my life:
Angela and Kelly, my daughters,
Emma and Lauren, my granddaughters,
Donna, my mom,
Cheryl, my wife.

(It would be good if you skipped over the sex scenes!)

My friends and professional colleagues:
You told me so often, *"you should write a book.."*
This is not the book you expected, and I would remind you,
this novel is fiction!

I would like to specifically acknowledge the five authors
who have influenced and inspired me the most:
Robert A. Heinlein
Mark Twain
Sir Arthur Conan Doyle
Allen Drury
John Grisham

Warning: Mature Content.
This novel contains explicit adult sexual material and language. It portrays incidents of human trafficking in the sex slave industry. It contains graphic descriptions of the heinous practice of female genital mutilation (FGM) common in some third-world nations.

DEDICATION

To the untold millions of young girls and women who have
endured the heinous practices touched upon in this book.
To women who live their lives as property and sex slaves.
To women who are stoned to death for the smallest infraction.

Chapter 1

Callie Grainger stood impatiently in the Florida sun that was not as warm as she had expected. It was early February and, at times, it was downright chilly. Her group had performed their routine flawlessly, but some of the younger girls were having a problem with one of the routines.

The dance coordinator was yelling at them. It was Friday and the Super Bowl was just two days away. There was even talk of cutting the section with the ten to twelve-year-olds. Oasis would not like that; they had billed and promoted this halftime event in all of their clothing stores nationwide since the football season began. Expensive promos were broadcast throughout the NFL football season.

"Perform at the Super Bowl halftime program in Miami" the ads proclaimed. "Spend a week in Florida with fun-filled practice sessions in Orlando, followed by Super Bowl Weekend in Miami."

Each morning the girls practiced the routine at the Citrus Bowl stadium near downtown Orlando. They returned to the hotel for a late lunch and had the afternoon and evening free. Oasis had supplied free admission to Disney World and Universal Studios for the girls and their families.

Five days of practice were not enough. How can you teach 300 giggly girls ages six to sixteen an elaborate routine in so short a time? Most of these girls would be missing six days of school as it was. No more practice than that was possible. The Oasis stores in each state did what they could to find girls with a background that would make this impossible task easier. Callie had been performing for nearly ten years. She joined the Indianapolis Stars Dance Team when she was five and had already performed at Disney World, Disneyland, Busch Gardens, Six Flags, and a dozen other exciting places in her short life.

The dance coordinator was practically screaming now at the ten to twelve-year-olds. One of the girls was from the same hometown as Callie; Susie looked shaken and terrified that their short number might be cut. The coordinator called for a twenty-minute break and stormed off the field.

Callie went over to Susie.

"The bitch giving you a rough time, eh?" said Callie.

"Callie, she's going to cut us, I just know it," her voice went up an octave as Susie whined and tears began to well up in her eyes.

"No, they're not." snapped Callie. She may want to but she can't. Oasis sells clothes for girls age six to sixteen, and that's what this halftime glitz is all about. It's not about the show; it's about girl's clothes."

Susie seemed reassured. One single tear rolled down her cheek. "Are you sure?" said the girl standing next to Susie, her voice cracking with emotion.

"Callie, this is Keisha, she's from Indiana too," said Susie.

"Hi Keisha. I'm Callie. Where you from in Indiana?" asked Callie.

Keisha shuffled her feet in the turf and seemed a bit shy and embarrassed at the attention. Her long, brunette, braided pigtails and deep black skin were in sharp contrast to the blue-eyed blondes that surrounded her.

"I'm from Anderson," said Keisha.

"Well, we're practically neighbors, nice to meet you," said Callie. "Don't worry, I can help you, I know what the bitch wants."

"Oh, will you?" exclaimed Keisha, her eyes widening with delight.

For the next ten minutes, Callie went over the part of the routine that was causing the girls so much difficulty. Some of the other girls joined in, and before long, they all were getting the steps down.

"Way to go, Callie, you show 'em," came a loud, shrill voice from the bleachers. It was Alice, Callie's mother.

"Shut up, Mother," came Callie's response as she saw the coordinator coming back on the field. Alice just laughed. "Callie honey," she said "Oasis should be paying you to choreograph this number instead of wasting it on her." Alice didn't necessarily intend for the dance coordinator to hear her but she didn't care either. Alice didn't know how to whisper; everything she said and did was loud and noticeable.

Miss Rebecca Calloway was the Oasis Dance Coordinator. She was a shapely redhead in her mid-twenties. She once again lined up the ten to twelve-year-olds for their routine. She cued the music and they began. The girls did it much better this time. She stopped them, started again, and the girls did the routine just fine. She had already pushed them too hard and she knew it. She realized she better stop now while she was ahead.

"That was great, Girls," she said. "If you guys can do it just like that on Sunday, you will make your parents and family very proud. You are dismissed."

The coordinator turned and glared at Callie as the ten to twelve-year-olds ran giggling and laughing across the field to the buses. Callie smiled at Miss Calloway, pursed her lips, and softly blew her a kiss.

The coordinator's nostrils flared and she took a deep breath and then just shook her head as she dismissed the rest of the girls. "The rest of you girls can go, too. When you get back to the hotel, you will have two hours to eat and get ready. The Oasis plane for Miami leaves at 7 o'clock. You must be at the bus pick-up at 5 o'clock sharp. To those of you who have parents here, you will say goodbye to them before getting on the bus. There will not be any opportunity to say goodbye at the airport. Please, be on time. If you miss the bus, you will not be allowed to join us in Miami. Do you understand?"

Callie boarded one of the black and gold buses for the twenty-five-minute trip back to the hotel. She sat down next to Karen and Julie. They were her friends from Indiana. They were all freshman cheerleaders from Westfield High School. They had been on the squad together since fifth grade. Karen had almost missed being selected for the freshman squad, but Callie had worked with her for days before the tryouts smoothing out her routine.

There was never any doubt that Callie would make the squad, she and Julie were the two best cheerleaders on the squad and some said they were better than the varsity cheerleaders. Callie enjoyed cheerleading. For the first time in years, she was enjoying what she was doing. When she started with the Indianapolis Stars Dance Team, she was five, right after the divorce. Her mom and dad fought about the money it cost to buy her outfits and send her on trips and pay for the weekly dance lessons. He always said "I pay enough support. If your mother wants you to do this, then let her pay for it out of that money."

Alice would try, but she never was quite able to make the payments on time or scrape together enough money for the cheap airline tickets the Stars always got when they traveled. It was a never-ending cycle; the Stars would try to collect from Alice, and then they would bench Callie. Callie would call her dad. He would grumble and complain and tell her this stuff wasn't good for her, that it was turning her into a "valley girl." At the next practice, she was always off the bench. She knew her dad had paid, but her mom always took the credit. Maybe her mom didn't actually know.

"We're not gonna have anything to eat this week," she would say "but you're still in Stars Punkin'. I gave them this month's payment, and they said if I just pay ten dollars a week, they'll keep you off the bench."

It took Callie years to figure out that her dad and Stars had an unspoken arrangement. He kept them paid but would not sign the membership contract. In return, Alice, who had signed the contract would be periodically threatened by Stars for the payments. Sometimes they would even go so far as to bench Callie. Alice would pay a little bit. Over the eight years Callie was in Stars, Alice actually only paid a portion of the contract. Her dad paid the rest.

Her dad always came through at the last minute for the airline tickets and travel expenses. But he never would buy the pictures. Every year there would be glamour shots of Callie in her new outfit, and her dad would say she looked too sexy for her age and that she had on too much makeup.

Callie's thoughts were broken by the shrill call of her name.

"Callie, Callie," she heard her mother say.

Callie looked out the bus window to see her mother and older sister Annie standing on the curb. Alice motioned her to come with her.

"See you guys later," said Callie, as she hopped up and made her way down the aisle like a salmon swimming upstream against the current of bubbly young blondes pouring onto the bus.

"I'm supposed to ride the bus, Mom."

"What are they gonna do, Take roll? They don't have time to mess with counting you girls now," said Alice.

"Well, if they did take roll, they would get my name wrong," complained Callie "they keep calling me Callie Brooks."

"Honey I'm sorry," said Alice. Brooks was the name of Alice's second husband. They were no longer married, either, but Alice had kept the name.

"I keep telling them that my name is Grainger, but all their records have me as Callie Brooks. They better get it right in the program credits," declared Callie.

"I told 'em too, Callie, I'm sure they will get it straightened out for Sunday," said Alice.

Callie didn't want to ride the bus anyway. Alice had called a taxi on her cell phone when she saw practice was ending. As Callie was getting into the taxi, she shouted to the redhead dance coordinator. "I'm going back to the hotel with my mom."

"The Hilton at Disney World," said Annie to the driver.

They piled into the taxi for the ride back to the hotel. There would be plenty of time to grab a bite to eat now and do some final packing. There were plenty of open tables when they walked into the hotel restaurant.

Alice ordered a salad and Annie got a hamburger and fries. Callie ordered a marinated chicken breast platter. Callie always ordered the most expensive thing on the menu; it was a special gift she had. Her dad had once taken her and Annie to a restaurant that had no prices printed on the menu but Callie still managed to order the most expensive item.

"Girl, you're gonna be the death of me," said Alice.

"What are you worrying about Mom? Oasis is paying for it. This has been a nice family vacation; we all got a free trip to Disney World. Screw em if they can't take a joke," said Callie.

"Watch your mouth," giggled Alice.

"You don't have to take advantage, Callie," said Annie. "They've been nice to us, paid for our airline tickets, the room, our food and gave us all free tickets to Disney, Epcot and Universal."

"Oh, Annie quit your whining. Oasis is getting 300 free performers for the Super Bowl. They probably spent less than $2,000 on each of us girls. That's only a half million bucks for a fifteen-minute performance in the Super Bowl. You know how much a thirty-second spot goes for these days?"

Annie seethed, gritted her teeth and let out a deep sigh; Callie was probably right but it still didn't seem right sticking it to Oasis the way Callie did. Their conversation was interrupted by the simultaneous arrival of their food and dozens and dozens of girls who had just got in from practice on the buses.

Callie just smiled a crooked grin at the girls who were looking at her. Callie already had her food and would be out of here in a few minutes. It would be well over an hour before the other girls had ordered, were served and could get back to their rooms.

Callie looked at her watch. It was 3:00 p.m. She had two hours to do her final packing. That was plenty of time. Everybody else would be lucky to have thirty minutes by the time they finally got their food and were finished eating.

They were just about to get up from the table when a tall African-American man approached their table, "Excuse me," he said.

Callie, Annie and Alice looked up; standing next to him was Keisha and another little girl clinging to his leg. He looked straight at Callie, "I just wanted to express my appreciation to you for helping my daughter back there. She was getting very upset and you made the difference."

"No problem," said Callie. "It wasn't Keisha that had the problem, she's a good dancer."

"I'm Mark Campbell," he said and motioned his hand downward, "and this is my daughter Kara."

Kara clung even more tightly to his leg as her small voice said, "Thank for helping my sister."

"Hi Kara," said Callie.

"Hi Kara," said Annie, as she held her hand out to Kara. Kara slowly held her hand out until she was touching Annie's hand. Annie took her hand and shook it and said, "I am pleased to meet you. My name is Annie."

"Keisha," said Callie, "this is my sister Annie and my mother Alice. Alice nodded her head and smiled.

"Kara," asked Annie, "are you in the Oasis Super Bowl Show too?"

"Yes," Kara said softly."

"And how old are you?" asked Annie.

"Six," replied Kara.

"Kara," said Callie "if you're half as good a dancer as your sister, then you won't have any trouble at all on Sunday."

Both Keisha and Kara broke into a broad grin. Mark Campbell looked at Callie with his face beaming and said, "thank you." Then, he and the two girls started to walk away.

Annie said loudly, "Mr. Campbell, you can have this table, we're finished and you may have some trouble finding one right now." He looked around the restaurant at the tables occupied by hundreds of girls, with no empty tables available.

"I see you're right. Thanks once again," he said, as Annie, Callie and Alice got up. "Bye Kara, Bye Keisha," said Annie.

"Keisha, Break a leg," said Callie as she walked away.

Callie, Annie and Alice went back to the room. Callie began her final packing. Annie had a flight back to Indianapolis the next morning. Annie kept a close eye on her sister as she fiddled with her various outfits. Callie went into the bathroom to pack her backpack. Oasis had supplied a backpack to each girl and that was the only item the girls could take with them on the plane. Annie began snooping through Callie's luggage that was still open on her bed. She pulled out a few items of clothing from the first bag and was going through the second bag when she heard Callie coming from the bathroom.

"Callie, these are my jeans!" scolded Annie.

"Are they?" said Callie, "I thought they were mine."

"You did not. I suppose you thought these socks and this T-shirt were yours too."

"I didn't bring those," said Callie "they must of gotten mixed up with my stuff on accident."

"Some accident. Let's see what you have in the other bag." Annie began tossing the neatly packed clothes out of the second bag and onto the bed. Callie lunged at her just as Annie pulled a gray sweatshirt from the bottom of the bag.

"This is the sweatshirt dad got me when we were in Honolulu. Is that an accident too?" said Annie.

It was hard to tell who swung first this time, but in a few seconds, they were scuffling on the bed, pulling hair and scratching each other.

"Annie you're messing up my clothes," squealed Callie as the bags tumbled off the edge of the bed.

"Well, you shouldn't steal my clothes."

"You take mine," said Callie. "At least I wash yours after I wear them and I put 'em back in your room."

"You only do that so I won't know you wore them," said Annie.

"Annie, you stink. After you wear my stuff, I get it back all smelly and wrinkled."

"You girls, now stop it!" yelled Alice but she just watched. She knew better than to try to break it up right away. The fight would have to run its course for a couple of minutes.

"These are my socks too," taunted Annie, as she picked up several pairs of socks that had fallen on the floor.

"Annie, I need them," Callie was screaming now, and she gritted her teeth and tore into Annie one last time. Annie was almost four years older than Callie, but Annie often came out on the worst end of these fights. Annie didn't mind giving her sister a good thumping but she never really wanted to hurt her very badly. Callie, on the other hand, didn't know when to stop, often drawing blood or leaving Annie with a nasty bruise somewhere.

Alice tried to block Callie's attack and got her hand twisted in with the girls somehow. Alice was screaming now.

"You girls stop it right now! You've broken my damn hand. I don't know why I put up with this horseshit. One of these days I'm just gonna leave. I'm gonna go away someplace and never come back!" screamed Alice.

Both girls stopped fighting now. They had heard that threat a thousand times and, although they knew it wasn't true, it still scared them. When they were little, even before the divorce, Alice used to tell them that. They used to get so upset that they would cry.

"Oh, Lord, why me?" said Alice "You know I do the best I can trying to raise you girls. It hasn't been easy. You girls are going to be the death of me."

Annie glared at Callie. She looked at the clothes strewn about the room and with a grin said "You better get packed. The plane leaves in a little bit and it looks like you haven't even started packing." Annie picked up the socks, the jeans, the T-shirt and her prized Honolulu sweatshirt that she never let anybody wear, not even her mom.

Callie's clothes were scattered all over the room now, and Callie had tears in her eyes. "I can't believe you did this to me, Annie. I'm going to be in the Super Bowl and you did this to me."

"You're not going to be in the Super Bowl. You're not a Quarterback. You're just a little Oasis cheerleader prancing around with 300 blonde airheads during half-time."

"They're not all blondes."

"Yeah, but they're all air-heads." snapped Annie.

"You're just jealous, Annie. You're just another stringy-haired brunette, a blonde wannabe."

Annie just looked at her. Callie was crying now, trying to get her clothes packed back into her bags. She carefully folded each piece of clothing as she put it back into the proper bag. She was always careful to have two pieces of checked luggage, and she packed so that, if one piece were lost, the other piece would still have what she needed.

"Annie, I need your jeans. It's been cold down here."

"It won't be cold in Miami. That's 200 miles south of here."

"Please, Annie, I need them."

Annie just sighed, "Okay, but you give them back to me Monday as soon as you get back."

"Don't you want me to wash them first?"

"Sure, but when I get back from class on Monday, those jeans had better be in my room."

Annie picked up her Honolulu sweatshirt and carefully placed it in her carry-on bag, where she could keep an eye on it until Callie was gone. Annie pretended not to notice when Callie scooped up Annie's socks and T-shirt and put them back in her bag.

Despite all the commotion, Callie was packed and ready to go in short order, and the three left the room. Callie's bags were placed outside the door to be picked up by the bellmen. They found a seat in the lobby while they waited for Callie's bus. Alice had the video camera out as she had all week.

The lobby began filling up with girls and their parents. It was tough on the little ones who had never left their parents before. It was tough on the mothers too. The bellmen were rolling carts crammed with luggage outside to be loaded into an orange twenty-foot box truck marked 'Sunblessed Truck Rentals.'

The parents could stay in Orlando for the weekend if they wanted and the girls would fly back to Orlando on Monday morning. Afternoon flights from the Orlando Airport had been booked for the girls and their families. Very few parents were going to the game. Tickets were hard to come by and Oasis discouraged it by refusing to pay for any return airline tickets from Miami.

The fleet of buses began pulling into the hotel driveway just before 5:00 p.m. Each bus was numbered. The girls' names were called off in the lobby. As each girl answered the roll call, she was given a bus token that was stamped with a bus number. Each girl then gave up the token as she boarded the proper bus. Alice had the video camera going, as many of the girls scrambled around looking for their bus.

The driveway area in front of the hotel was hardly large enough for seven buses. The buses did not park in any particular order, so Callie had to look around for her bus. Each girl carried only her backpack. The rest of the luggage was loaded into the orange box truck parked under the hotel canopy.

Callie stopped at the front of her bus and Alice put down the video camera to give her a hug. "Be careful, Punkin'," Alice said. "I'll be watching you Sunday, and we set the DVR at home to record it for you."

Annie had a forlorn look on her a face and the sisters gave each other a brief hug. "Bye-bye. Love you both," said Callie, as she scurried onto the bus.

Alice picked the video camera up and recorded Callie hanging out the bus window as it started to move. She caught the whole procession of buses followed by the box truck, as they left the hotel parking lot. When the orange van pulled out onto the Hotel Plaza Boulevard, Alice flagged a taxi and she and Annie piled in to go to the airport.

Each bus unloaded the girls at the entrance to the terminal. They passed through the metal detectors and took the train shuttle to the satellite terminal. Oasis personnel kept the group together, as they made their way to Gate 85. Oasis had a special 747 jet to carry the girls to Miami. Each girl had been given a boarding pass with a seat assignment.

When Callie and the other girls got to the gate, her mother and Annie were there.

"How did you get in here?" asked Callie.

Annie rolled her eyes and said, "Mom insisted that we see you off at the gate. The tickets Oasis bought us are full-fare tickets. We just changed them for a flight out tonight. After you leave, we will change them back."

"You guys are crazy," said Callie.

"I know Punkin', but I just wanted to be with you 'til the last possible minute. I'm worried about you going to Miami alone," replied Alice as she started to cry.

"I'm not alone," said Callie as she motioned toward all the other girls. Callie started to tear up and hugged her mom. Annie, who also thought the whole thing was crazy, joined in the group hug. Unlike Callie and her mom, Annie didn't cry, she felt silly.

The 300 girls did not board immediately. When they did start boarding, it took awhile. Annie, Callie and Alice enjoyed their time together. Finally, Callie could wait no longer. They hugged one last time. "Bye, Punkin'," said Alice. "Break a leg," whispered Annie into Callie's ear.

Callie turned and headed to the gate. Callie had 14J, a window seat on the right side of the plane. Karen was seated next to her. It would be a short flight to Miami. It was a big plane and Callie grabbed a pillow and blanket from an overhead compartment.

She sat down, pulled out her ear buds and plugged them into the armrest. She knew there would be no movie on this flight but she thought there might be some music channels. She flipped through the channels and heard nothing but the high-pitched whine of the electric generators. Finally, she heard something on Channel 10. It was the control tower talking to the plane.

She wasn't interested in that. She put the ear buds down and began talking to the girls around her. She spied Susie a few rows back at a window seat on the other side of the plane. They tried to talk to each other across the clamor of the other girls, but it was impossible.

The Captain announced that everyone needed to take their seat, and the few girls remaining in the aisles quickly returned to their seats. As the giant jet backed out of the gate, Callie thought she could see her mom and Annie standing at a terminal window waving at the plane. Callie reached up and switched her reading light off and on a few times and then left it on. It was her mom all right. She could see her jumping up and down, pointing and waving right at her. Callie waved back. Annie had the video camera this time. Callie pressed her face against the window and made a face.

Callie sighed and wished they both could have come with her. They might not always get along, but whenever they needed each other, they stuck tightly together. Alice was Callie's biggest cheerleader. Despite her tough exterior, right now, Callie was missing her mom and her sister.

Callie put on her ear buds and listened to the pilots of the planes lined up on the taxiway talking to the tower. After awhile, she heard the tower instruct Oasis One Heavy to change to 124.3 and contact the tower. Shortly afterward she heard "Oasis One Heavy you are cleared for takeoff on Runway One-Eight Left." The Captain acknowledged and she heard the roar of the engines begin to increase as the plane turned onto the runway.

It was dark when the plane took off, and in just a few minutes, she could begin to make out the pattern of lights that curled around the shoreline of Tampa Bay. She stared at the lights for a long time trying to pick out Clearwater and St. Petersburg. She could see the lights of Sarasota to the south and she even thought she could see the headlights of cars crossing the Bay on the Sunshine Skyway Bridge. It seemed to her that the plane was a lot farther west than it should be to go to Miami. There were probably a lot of extra flights coming into Miami this weekend she thought.

She began talking to the girls around her. After the plane had leveled off, girls started getting out of their seats. There was considerable commotion on the plane with girls milling around in the aisles, giggling and throwing things. Callie got up from her seat and as she did, she could feel the plane beginning to slow down. It would soon begin its descent into Miami International.

She went over to talk to Susie on the other side of the plane. The trip to Orlando had been Susie's first trip on an airplane, but her mother was with her on that one. She was pretty nervous and it helped that Callie had come over to talk to her. When the plane began to bank to the left, Susie grabbed tightly onto Callie's arm.

"See all the lights out there," said Callie, as she pointed out the window. "That's Miami. You can follow the lights all the way up the coastline. There's Fort Lauderdale and West Palm Beach. You could probably see clear to Daytona, if you knew which set of lights it was."

Susie idolized Callie; Callie had been Susie's babysitter in fifth and sixth grade. Callie helped her develop a routine for cheerleader tryouts and Susie had easily made the squad for the last three years. She was in seventh grade now, and tryouts for eighth grade would be coming up in March. Callie was already helping her prepare for it.

The Captain announced that all the girls should return to their seat and they would soon start their descent into the Miami airport. She returned to her seat and fastened her seatbelt. She plugged her ear buds back into the armrest and heard communications that were not in English. She listened awhile and decided they were speaking Spanish. But why?

The plane was going much slower now. Suddenly, it began to descend very rapidly. Some of the girls let out a scream. Callie looked out her window and saw another plane climbing from below, as the Oasis plane continued its rapid descent. The other plane was uncomfortably close, as the two planes passed within a few hundred feet of each other. Other girls had been looking out the window and also had seen the near miss.

The plane leveled off again, and Callie became aware that the lights of the coastline were becoming more distant. This should have been a very quick flight, and here it was almost 8:30 p.m. The lights of the Miami metropolitan area were getting farther and farther away by the minute.

Something wasn't right. She removed her earbuds. She raised up as far as she could in her seat to get a better look out of the windows on the other side of the plane. She could still make out the lights of the coastline on the left side of the plane. She sat back down and looked out her own window. There was virtually nothing now but blackness out the right side. The plane seemed to be going awfully slow. The roar of the jet engines was unusually loud. The sky was clear and she could see hundreds of stars in the sky and, occasionally, she thought she could make out the lights of a ship in the ocean below.

She put her earbuds back on. There was a click and some static and then she heard "Oasis One, Oasis One, this is Miami Approach Control. Oasis One, this is Miami Approach Control."

Oasis One did not respond.

Chapter 2

Just 24 hours earlier, Dan Grainger looked over at the windows on the other side of the plane as the Captain's voice said, "Off the right side you can see the high-rise hotels along the most famous 1-1/2 miles of beach on Earth and the most photographed site in the world - Diamond Head."

There were oohs and ahhs as some of the passengers craned their necks and some left their seats to get their first look at Waikiki Beach. A trip of a lifetime for most of them, but not for Dan; he had made this trip many times. It was a smooth trip, but a long nine hours from O'Hare. Waikiki was not his destination. This time, he was headed for Ka'anopoli Beach and the Sheraton Maui. He was alone as usual.

As the plane made its turns and was on final approach, he looked out his left window and caught a glimpse of the U.S. Arizona Memorial glistening white in the bright Hawaiian sun. He reflected for a moment on the 1,177 lost crewmen still entombed in the battleship at the bottom of Pearl Harbor.

His thoughts drifted to his two daughters, Annie and Callie. Somewhere in Disney World, they were having a good time, he hoped. He didn't know their schedule. At some point Callie would be traveling to the Super Bowl in Miami and Annie would go back to Indiana. Dan liked to take them places. He had taken them to Hawaii and several other exotic destinations. Last summer, it was England and Israel. They were planning a trip to Paris and Italy this summer. Dan's American Airlines Platinum account was loaded with miles and he liked to take the girls on the free tickets whenever he could.

The plane pulled up to GATE 19 and the passengers began to struggle with their over-sized carry-ons in the overhead compartments and under the seat. Dan was sitting near the front of the coach section and was one of the first passengers off the plane. As he entered the terminal area, he began the long walk to the Inter-Island terminal to catch his next flight. After a short time, he came to an open walkway and stopped to take in the warmth and fragrance of the Hawaiian air. It was a delightful mixture of flowers and sea breeze, and then suddenly a whiff of jet fuel filled his lungs. A Delta jet was pulling away from a nearby gate.

He looked at his watch; he had plenty of time. He walked back to the ice cream shop for a Dole Whip. He came back out nurturing the cone and the pineapple-flavored, soft ice cream, and resumed his position on the walkway. He looked around at all the people from all over the world, scurrying about, pulling their little luggage carts, all in a hurry to get somewhere. He looked at the airport control tower looming overhead. He was greeted by the words on the side of the structure "Aloha, Honolulu International Airport."

The Delta jet had taxied away, and the air again was the wonderful fragrance of tropical flowers and ocean breeze. As he finished his cone, he slowly became aware that a young woman was just across the walkway from him. She was a stunningly beautiful, olive-skinned brunette, well-dressed, petite and seemed slightly distressed. She was shuffling papers, looking through her carry-on bag. Finally, she pulled her boarding pass jacket from one of the many pockets in the bag and she let out a sigh of relief.

He watched her, amused, as she looked at the boarding pass and then her watch. She then looked around for a sign, apparently to direct her to her next destination. There wasn't any on the walkway. She had already passed the sign that would have instructed her where to go, and she was another two hundred feet away from the next one.

He could not resist. He was not a pick-'em-up-easy kind of guy, but she was worth suffering a little rejection. "Miss," Dan said, but she did not hear him. "Miss," he said louder. She turned his direction, stared at him for a moment and then smiled a smile of perfectly white teeth and raised her eyebrows. She said nothing.

Dan was no ladies' man. He was neither a party-goer nor the athletic type. He was 5' 10", 145 pounds, with dark-brown hair and a well-trimmed moustache. At age forty-two, he was still winning the battle of the bulge. His only real attribute in a situation like this was his blue eyes. He was nervous.

"Do you need some assistance?" Dan asked as he made his way across the walkway amidst the passing travelers.

"My flight," she said. "My flight leaves in thirty-five minutes, and I am not sure if I need to collect my baggage. I do not recognize the name on this boarding pass."

"Where are you off to?"

"Maui," she said.

"Hawaiian Air Flight 345?" he asked.

Again, she began flipping through her papers, "No, she said, "It's Aloha 114."

"Darn," he thought as he said, "Let me see your itinerary."

She handed to it him; he opened it. It said SFO-HNL-OGG. It read Aloha Airlines 114 Honolulu to Kahului departing 3:15p. His flight to Kahului departed at 3:35 p.m. on Hawaiian. He looked at the baggage claim stubs stuck to the boarding pass jacket and said, "Four bags checked through to OGG, OGG is Kahului, Maui, so you do not have to worry about your bags until you get to Maui."

He was standing directly in front of her now, she was perhaps 5'4" or 5'5", just about four inches shorter than he. Her skin was without a blemish, the aroma of the Hawaiian flowers had been replaced with the subtle and haunting fragrance she had on. It had a Middle-Eastern quality about it. He had smelled it before in the Arab World. He looked at her boarding pass again as he handed it to her. Jasmine Hassan, it said. She was an Arab, but he knew that few female Arabs came in a package like hers, at least not one you could see.

"My Name is Dan, Dan Grainger," he said. "I have a Hawaiian flight that leaves from the same terminal as your Aloha flight. You can walk with me if you wish, and I can show you the way."

She smiled, placed her papers into a pocket of her bag, grabbed the handle of her luggage cart and said, "I am Jessie. Lead the way." He picked up his bag and motioned her to follow.

Walking next to her along the walkway, he didn't really know what to say to her. It was a short walk to the shuttle and then she would get off at Aloha and that would be the last he would see of her. He stammered a moment for words "Four bags," he said, "That's a lot of luggage for one person."

She looked coldly at him for a moment, turned straight ahead and said, "Yes, I am returning to my country. My father is ill."

"I am sorry," he said. "Is it serious?"

"I do not know. I have not been able to speak with him. My uncle says it is so, but my uncle..." her voice trailed off.

"And your country would be…?" he asked.

"You would not know it. It is far far from here and in another place."

He pointed to the escalators. "We can take the Wiki-Wiki shuttle to the terminal if you wish. It's a bit of a walk."

"How long?" she asked.

"Ten minutes."

"We walk.... we walk while I am still free to walk."

He looked at her for a moment; she was not happy. "You do not wish to return to your country?"

"I have not seen my father for five years. It will be good to see him."

"And your uncle?"

"My friend, you ask too many questions. What of your family? What of your wife? Do you make a practice of picking up strange women in airports?"

He could not tell if she was angry or teasing him. "I have two daughters," he said, "ages fifteen and nineteen. I have been divorced for many years."

"Ah, then you do make a habit of picking up women in airports. You must be very lonely. Do you see them often?"

He was uncomfortable with her questions and the tone of her voice.

"Pretty often. Not as much as I would like, but pretty often."

They had made their way to the street, and he turned left toward the inter-island terminal, "Look, Jessie," he said "I have traveled a lot, from Jo-berg to Cairo and Tel-Aviv to Dubai. I would know your country, where is it?"

"Was this direct Tel-Aviv to Dubai?" she said sharply.

He sighed, "You know it cannot be so, I only meant......"

"I know what you meant. You Americans take so much for granted. You have such freedom and you do not know it. You waste it. Freedom is in the air here and all over your country, from Seattle to Miami, from Bangor to San Diego, freedom, especially for a woman, it is in the air you can feel it."

"Was that a direct flight from Bangor to San Diego?"

'You, Mister Dan, are in my country what we call a smart-ass."

"Funny, that's what my ex-wife always called me in this country."

"It is not surprising you are divorced..." she paused, "divorce is not so common in my country. If a husband is sufficiently displeased in his wife, he simply kills her. It is never investigated."

"Well, I can see that saves on attorney fees and child support."

"You are a smart-ass in any country," snapped Jessie.

"Well excuse me, Mizz Jasmine," he slurred out his words with a Hoosier twang.

"There would be no child support in my country, Dan. The father would always get the children. A woman has no rights," she paused. "You are a very helpful smart-ass, and I thank you for showing me to my gate. I think you studied my itinerary a little too closely. I said my name was Jessie."

"How about I call you Pikake? That's the Hawaiian name for the Jasmine flower," said Dan.

"Pikake," she said, as she nodded her head with some approval. "I didn't know that."

It's an especially beautiful name for a flower intended to be given to an especially beautiful woman," said Dan.

"My name is Jessie," she said, with a trace of a smile.

They were at the entrance to the Aloha terminal. She stopped for a moment, let go of the handle of her carry-on cart, and held out her hand.

He took her hand in his, bowed slightly and said, "It has been a pleasure, Jessie. I hope you enjoy your stay on Maui."

She smiled, slowly withdrew her hand and said, "Aloha Mister Dan."

"Look, uh, Jessie," he stammered, "If you need a tour guide, look me up. I'm at the Sheraton Maui."

She took the handle of her luggage cart and walked toward the Aloha Lobby. He watched her for a moment as the automatic doors opened to allow her passage. He waited and watched for her to look back at him. She did not.

"Damn, Damn, Damn!" he thought and headed for his nearby gate.

It was a short flight to Maui, just twenty minutes and as he headed for baggage claim, he began to think of the beautiful Ka'anapali beach that awaited him on the other side of the island at the Sheraton Maui.

He collected his single piece of checked luggage and headed for the Avis Preferred counter. His contract was sitting in the slot. He showed his Indiana driver's license and then, he was off to find his car. It was a red Mustang and only had 412 miles on it. Avis had upgraded him. He pulled out of the parking lot and headed for Lahaina town.

It was a twenty-two-mile drive to the other side of the island. The sun was at that awkward angle, just at the top of his windshield, making it difficult to see the traffic ahead. After a few miles, this was no longer a problem, and he began to appreciate the rich green scenery of the valley. The sky was a deep blue overhead, but just a mile or so to the right, the mountains were shrouded in an ominous mist. He looked to the left, over the sugar cane fields to spot the summit of Haleakala, but the 10,023-foot mountain was completely shrouded in a haze and clouds.

Maui was like a miniature weather system all by itself. The island was just seven miles wide at its narrowest point. He had reached the other side of the island as he passed Buzz's Wharf. The haze had cleared now and before him was the vast expanse of the Pacific Ocean. The road had at times been cut through lava flows that had formed the mountain. Chain-link fence shrouded the walls of the cliffs, rising as high as one hundred feet in some places, designed to keep falling rocks from piercing the windshield of passing motorists. He could have bypassed Lahaina, stayed on Highway 30, and driven straight to the hotel north of town. Instead, he took the coastal road into downtown and drove along the seaside shops. Lahaina had been a whaling town in bygone days. He passed by the 1873 banyan tree with its many vine-like trunks filling a small-town square. Front Street was lined with scrimshaw shops, T-shirt shops, clothing stores, art galleries and even a Hard Rock Cafe. He parked his car on the north side of the strip in a small shopping center parking lot, right in front of Hilo Hattie's. That way, he could remember where he left the car. Now he would only have to remember what color and what kind of car he was driving. He looked at it again. It was a red Mustang. He threw the Avis contract in the back window.

As he walked through the shopping center, he quickly came to Front Street along the ocean. He crossed over to the break wall and walked along the sidewalk toward the downtown shops. His ears were immediately pounded by the sound of rock music coming from the Hard Rock Café. A gathering of teenage tourist types with their beleaguered parents stood in a long line waiting to get in, or maybe waiting to buy a T-shirt, or maybe both.

He continued down the street past several shops and came to his destination - Cheeseburger in Paradise. He walked in, and the host greeted him, "Hey, Mate. Back on Maui again, yeah?"

"Yeah," replied Dan, "How long is the wait?"

"For haoles maybe twenty minutes; for kama'aina maybe two."

"How long for me?" he asked.

He grinned, "Maybe three." He picked up a menu and directed Dan to a table on the makai side of the restaurant. He wasn't kama'aina. He had thought once after his first eight or ten trips that he was but realized after fifty trips that he would always be a haole. Nevertheless, the locals here and on the Big Island seemed to sense he had been here many times and treated him accordingly.

He sat down. It was nearly 6:00 p.m. and the sun was setting out over the Pacific. The golden colors of sunset lit up the western sky. He ordered his cheeseburger with two scoops of steamed rice and sat looking out at the vast Pacific and pondered the serenity of it all. There were many small ships along the coast, some filled with tourists on sunset cruises, some returning from whale watches in the channel between Maui and Lanai. He could see the silhouette of Lanai as the sun sank behind the nearby island. The golden rays of the sun formed a radiant halo around its outline.

It was dark when he finished his sandwich. The sounds of the waves pounding the shore beneath him were putting him to sleep. He looked at his watch, "almost midnight in Indiana," he thought. He walked back to Hilo Hattie's where he had left his car. He couldn't remember what kind of car he was driving. He looked at the Avis key tag, "Oh yeah," he thought, "a red Mustang." He spotted it and the contract in the back window.

The drive to the Ka'anapali Beach and the Sheraton was about ten minutes, and as he pulled into the hotel parking garage, he was looking forward to jumping into the shower and hitting the sack. He grabbed his two bags and headed for the registration desk. He was a Sheraton Gold Club member, and they had upgraded him to a room with a beautiful view overlooking the beach. He entered the fourth-floor room, sat down his bags, and headed straight for the lanai. It was a beautiful view indeed. His lanai and the lanais of the adjacent rooms jutted out an angle that gave a perfect view of the coastline. He could almost make out the forms of people down on the beach and could hear occasional laughter. Several torches burned along some of the walkways and he could see the shadows of people passing by.

He grabbed his carry-on bag and headed for the shower. The spray felt good on his tired body. His hair was oily from the long day of travel. He shampooed it vigorously with the hotel shampoo. The Sheraton always provides excellent amenities. He dried off and looked into the mirror. He brushed his teeth, shaved and trimmed his moustache, and dried his hair with the hotel-supplied hair dryer. He noticed a fluffy white terrycloth robe hanging on the bathroom door and put it on.

He stepped out into the room, and he looked at his watch. It was nearly 2:00 am at home, and he pulled down the covers of the bed. He looked over at the curtains in front of the lanai doors and decided to open the curtains all the way so that the sunlight in the morning could awaken him. He would wake up early his first morning in the Islands.

He stepped out onto the lanai for one last look at the Maui coastline dotted with amber lights and little boats just offshore. The lights of hundreds of rooms were visible in the high-rise hotels along the shore.

"I have been waiting for you," she said.

He was startled when he saw the petite feminine form standing on the lanai. She took a few steps forward, and he took a few steps backward into the room.

He stared at her olive skin, her beautiful face, and her long, dark hair as she stepped closer. His eyes widened "Jessie?" he exclaimed.

"That's Mizz Jasmine to you, Dan," she whispered.

She was close to him, very close to him now. Her Middle-Eastern fragrance had been replaced with the fresh scent of the French-milled, Sheraton-supplied soap. Dumbfounded he continued to back up and she came closer.

"I am very sorry. I was rude to you in Honolulu, and I now wish to properly show my appreciation for your gracious assistance." She reached forward with both hands and untied the half-knot on the belt of his robe. The robe parted open and she dropped to her knees. She stared at him for the longest time. She looked up at him, her brown eyes seductive and irresistible. She wet her lips slowly with her tongue and moved forward toward her target.

He thought of pinching himself to see if he was dreaming. He was very tired. It is possible he had already gone to bed and this whole thing was a figment of his imagination. A moment later he knew it was not.

She engulfed him completely and raised her hands above her head. She ran her fingers across his chest, down the side of his legs, then slowly up the inside of his thighs where she grabbed him firmly at the base and expertly continued her mission. He thought he was going to pass out.

"If this is really happening," he thought, "I don't want it over this fast."

He gently placed his hands on each side of her face. Her skin was soft and he looked down on her jet-black hair. He tried to pull her away, but she held on more strongly. He took her head firmly between his hands and began to force her away from him. As he did so, her strategically placed hands began applying increasingly uncomfortable pressure to his testicles. He got the message. As his grip lessened, hers again became soft and gentle.

She was absolutely and completely in control. He began caressing the side of her face and running his fingers through her silky, soft hair, tracing the shape of her ear with his finger. Then as if she knew before he did, she became more vigorous and moved her right hand down along the inside of his right leg. She slowly traced a path upward along the inside of his leg until she touched and then gently caressed his testicles. He exploded in her mouth and let out a scream that could surely be heard several doors down the hall. A rush came over him and he had to lean forward to keep from falling backward or passing out.

Still, she would not stop, but she was slow and gentle now. She continued to engulf him completely. His heart was pounding. He could have fallen backward; the bed was immediately behind him. He slowly sat down, all the while she remained gently joined to him. He ran his right hand over his forehead and through his hair, pulling it as if trying to relieve a headache. But he did not have a headache.

She slowly pulled back and looked up at him, still on her knees. He placed his hands on her cheeks and drew her up to him.

"You would kiss me now?" she quizzed.

"Yes, Jessie," Dan said softly, "I would."

"No, it cannot be!" she exclaimed and the softness of her face hardened. Dan stood up, went over to the bar and tore off the plastic tie wrap that sealed it. He opened it up and said "What's your pleasure, Coke, Sprite, Evian? You name it."

"Ginger Ale," she said. "I shall have some Ginger Ale."

He hated Ginger Ale. He reached for the can of Canada Dry, popped the top and handed it to her. She was standing now and took a long slow drink. She had a white blouse on with four buttons, as she took her drink, he began to unbutton them. She was not wearing a bra. Her perfectly formed breasts reaffirmed his belief that he was dreaming.

When she finished her first long drink, he took the can from her hand and placed it on the bedside table and drew very close to her. "May I have that kiss now?"

She smiled at him, "If you wish." He began to kiss her, softly at first, then more passionately. She kissed him deeply and fervently. She moaned softly, his arms around her. He felt her body relax, and for a moment, he was in control, or at least, she wasn't. It was short-lived.

She pulled away from him and pushed him back against the bed. She quickly stepped out of her panties and shoved him down across the bed. His legs dangled from the edge of the bed and she turned her back to him, standing directly in front of him she straddled him. She reached between her legs, grabbed him and placed him within her as she sat upon him. He tried to reach her breasts, but she leaned forward and placed her arms to her side at an angle that made it impossible. She had both her feet firmly planted on the floor and began moving up and down, slowly at first, and then more vigorously. He gave up trying to touch her breasts and began to gently caress the sides of her body. He traced her spine from the nape of her neck to the tip of her tailbone.

She was in total control once more. He was forty-two years old and was getting a little too old for these calisthenics. He just gave up and relaxed. As she continued her up and down movement, she reached down with both hands and gently massaged his testicles. He exploded for a second time.

Jessie slowly stood up, turned around and smiled at Dan. Their eyes locked for a moment. She then headed for the bathroom and returned a short time later with a warm washcloth. She carefully and gently cleaned him. He fell asleep.

Chapter 3

The sun was up and had been for a while. He looked out the windows of the lanai doors as he lay in the bed.

"Was it a dream?" he wondered. He got up and headed for the bathroom. There was an ache in his groin that told him he had not been dreaming. He turned back around, looked at the bedside table. The Ginger Ale can was not there. As he stood in the bathroom questioning his sanity, he noticed a washcloth hanging on the shower door. He opened the door. There was a second washcloth wadded up on the shower floor; the one he had used last night.

He took a shower as his mind struggled to analyze the night before. He put on the robe and went out on the lanai. He looked at the breathtaking, golden-sand beach below, with the deep-blue white-capped waves crashing against the shoreline. The morning sun was peeking over the West Maui Mountains. He looked over at the adjacent lanai.

"That's how she did it," he thought. "The surrounding flower sill made it an easy step from one lanai to the next." He went back into the room. He slipped on his sandals and tied his robe in a full knot.

He stepped out into the hall. He took note of the room numbers on either side of his. He went back into the room and opened the bar door. There was a can missing. On top of the refrigerator bar, the bar item menu had been checked next to Ginger Ale and three one-dollar bills were lying on top of it.

He used his cell phone to call the hotel.

"Sheraton Maui," a voice answered.

"Room 4412 please," said Dan.

"The guest's name please?" asked the voice

"Miss Jasmine Hassan."

A moment passed, "I am sorry, that is not the guest's name in 4412, perhaps she has checked out."

"Oh, I am sorry," replied Dan "it is 4410."

"Oh yes, I ring it for you. Mahalo."

As soon as the line clicked, Dan hung up before the ring. It was already afternoon in Indianapolis and only 7:30 a.m. here. He had slept for nine hours or maybe ten, if you count the dream. He was awake now; he had not been dreaming. Jessie was next door.

He went back out onto the lanai. He listened for any sounds coming from her room. He stepped over the railing and onto the flower sill and then over the railing onto her lanai. Her doors were open and he could see the bed. She was not in it. He slipped into the room and could hear water running in the bathroom. "Perfect," he thought.

He went to the front door of her room and slipped into the open closet. A few moments later she came out of the bathroom. Her hair was up in a towel and she had the white hotel robe wrapped around her. She walked over to the lanai and gazed out at the idyllic scene below. She turned to return to the bathroom; her eyes had adjusted to the bright sunlight and the room seemed dark for a moment. She saw a shadowy figure at the foot of her bed.

"I have been waiting for you," said Dan.

"How did you get in?" she demanded to know.

"I might ask you the same question," he replied.

She just stared at him, turned to look at the open lanai door and said, "Oh, I see."

"I am sorry, I fell asleep last night. I thought perhaps I was dreaming."

"Perhaps you were," she said, with a coy smile.

"Well, Miss Jessie, I am awake now, and it was rude of me to fall asleep last night, Now, I would like to properly thank you for the gracious time you spent with me last evening." He stared into her brown eyes, but they betrayed no emotion.

"It was necessary. What is done is done," she said coldly.

He stepped forward and put his hands on her shoulders. She did not move. With his right hand, he stroked the side of her cheek and put his hand on the back of her neck and drew her to him. She moved slowly closer; he kissed her deeply. She responded fervently and began to moan softly. She started to pull away. He was awake now and had his wits about him. As she pulled away, he reached down and loosened the belt of her robe. As the robe parted, she had nothing else on.

He grabbed at the towel turban on her head, unwrapping it with one quick swirl of his hand over her head. Her long dark hair was still damp and fell down her back. She took a step backward. His hands deliberately brushed slightly against both of her nipples as he raised them to caress each side of her neck. He ran his hands across her shoulders, and her robe fell to the floor. He put his arms around her body. He gently ran his fingers upward along her spine to her neck until he was able to grab her long, black hair. He pulled it down sharply.

Her head arched backward and she put her hands against his chest but said nothing. He kissed her again, keeping her head pulled back by his grip on her long hair. She began to moan quietly once more, but she could not pull away. He dropped his lips to the nipple of her right breast and flicked it quickly with his tongue. She arched her back allowing him to pull her head back even farther. He took as much of her breast into his mouth as he could, circling her nipple with his tongue. He quickly turned his attention to her left breast and treated it in the same fashion. She was wiggling a bit now. He continued to guide her down onto the bed until she was sitting on the edge of the bed. He dropped to his knees. He increased the backward pull on her hair, and she began to arch her back toward the bed. She found herself lying on the bed, with her legs dangling, as his had the night before. She could not get up. His lips pressed against her breast and he continued to exert the pull on her hair.

In one continuous movement he slid lower. Realizing what he was about to do, she tried to grab his head, but it was too late. His tongue plunged deeply between her legs. He let go of her long hair that he had held behind her back. He grabbed her shoulders and allowed his hands to slide down to her elbows. His knees were planted firmly on the floor, and his tongue began to explore her innermost recesses. He allowed his hands to slide down her arms to her hands. She held them out to him and for a time they locked their fingers together, as his tongue gently explored every recess of her womanhood. Her body was writhing now. Her hands broke free from his, and she grabbed him forcefully on either side of his face. She made no attempt to push him away.

He stopped for a moment and looked at her. She was moist and her dark, pink skin glistened in the bright morning sunlight. He studied her for a moment, trying to precisely locate the target for his attention. She caressed the side of his face and pulled him closer to her. It was unclear to him whether she did this to stop his study of her anatomy or to regain the pleasure of his exploration. His target remained elusive and hidden from his view, but he knew exactly where it should be, and his tongue began to flick wildly from side to side at the chosen spot. She began to moan more loudly. He felt her muscles tighten. She began a long, slow scream louder perhaps than his of the night before. She had lost her breath but suddenly blurted out "Praise be Allah....Praise be Allah!

Her body had arched up to meet his eager tongue and now she slumped back to the bed. He had thought for a moment that he might have to scrape her off the ceiling. "Scoot back," he said, as he reached down and undid the belt of his robe. He had a little trouble with the full knot, but his fingers worked quickly. He had sprung to life once again. She was lying entirely on the bed now with her head on the pillow at the headboard. Kneeling between her legs he reached an arm around each upper leg and forcefully pulled her toward him and away from the headboard. He did not want her head to be slamming against the headboard. Her eyes opened wide in surprise as a trace of a smile appeared on her lips. He lowered himself against her. She did not protest. Her whole body began to shiver and she held her arms folded tightly across her chest; her fists clenched. She then reached down and gently guided him in. As he penetrated her, she placed her arms around his neck and held on to him tightly.

He did not know if she would kiss him, but as he guided her lips toward his, she smiled and they began to kiss. Dan had never experienced such intensity. It was as if their souls were touching. He looked deeply into her eyes and she returned the gaze. It was a much smaller explosion for Dan, but he was pleased with himself for managing one at all.

He moved from her to her right side. She looked at him with a broad smile. She reached up and grabbed the pillow above her and swung it at him playfully striking him in the head and said, "Get out of my bed, Sir!"

She was shaking her head slightly in disbelief at what had just happened, but the important thing was she had a huge smile on her face and a sparkle in her eyes.

"You are very thorough, Mister Dan."

"Aw shucks Ma'am," he said, with a Hoosier twang and a grin.

"Well, Mister Dan," she said, "is this how you treat all the strange women you pick up in airports?"

He thought for a moment, "Well, yes, Jessie, as a matter of fact, it is!"

She immediately got up and went to the bathroom. She returned with a warm washcloth, a bar of the French-milled soap and a towel. He was lying on his back now. She kneeled between his legs on the bed and carefully washed him and then fluffed him dry with the towel.

She lowered her head and began to kiss him again. She slowly ran her tongue up and down the shaft of his barely erect penis. He could take no more. He wanted her to stop. It was a futile effort, anyway. He was totally spent. She was persistent. She was patient and gently kissed him slowly for a long time. He could not believe it. After a while he could feel it building within him.

She knew it, too, and suddenly became more passionate in her efforts. He began to scream before, during, and for several moments after he came. It was like cresting the hill of a roller coaster ride. She kept him completely engulfed in her mouth.

She then released her hold on him and appeared to be heading for the bathroom.

He sprang to his feet and pulled her back. She stared at him.

"What manner of man is this?" she thought. He clearly intended to kiss her.

Jessie had limited experience with men, but with those few she had been with, she had never been with a man that was more concerned about her pleasure than his own. She had learned long ago not to kiss a man after she had done her duty. But she had learned to enjoy, and was often amused at the power she could hold over men when she pleased them. She could control them. Dan came closer to her and kissed her gently on her tightly closed lips. She then quickly pulled away and looked at him.

"I am twenty-seven years old, and I have never had an orgasm," she said softly. "This is the first time. I did not think it possible. No man has ever tried so hard to please me."

He looked into her eyes. Her lips were quivering, her whole body began to shake, and she began to sob quietly.

"I have experienced pleasure before and a feeling I imagined was an orgasm, but I know now it was not," she said wistfully.

He held her for a moment, but she quickly regained her composure and pulled away.

"Tell you what," he said "Get dressed and I'll take you to breakfast. I'll tap on your door in fifteen minutes."

She looked at him, paused and said, "Make it forty-five minutes."

"You're on." He slipped the robe and slippers back on, opened her door and headed next door to his room. He stood in the hall and stared at his locked door sheepishly. He tapped on Jessie's door; she opened it slightly. The chain lock was already attached.

"That was forty-five seconds, not forty-five minutes," she said.

"Little problem; no key," he said with embarrassment.

"Come in." She had her robe back on now. He headed for her lanai, stepped over the railing, smiled and said "forty-five minutes."

He entered his room and headed straight for his laptop computer. He removed it from the carrying case, hooked up the power supply, turned on the laptop and connected to the hotel Wi-Fi. He looked at his watch and decided to get ready first.

Within twenty minutes he finished his second shower of the morning. He was dressed and ready to step out the door. He had a little time. He went down to the lobby and found a flower shop.

When he returned to his room, he sat down on the bed next to the computer and clicked on the Internet. He selected the online airline reservation system. With a few familiar keystrokes he went to the airport code menu. He remembered most of the rest of Jessie's itinerary leaving Honolulu. It was HNL-NRT-on JAL and HKG-DXB on CX then to BHK but he didn't remember the carrier. The first four were easy. He had been there and had flown those airlines. It was Honolulu to Narita on Japan Airlines, then to Hong Kong and beyond on Cathay Pacific. He selected DXB and up came the airport identifier of Dubai, United Arab Emirates. That's what he thought; he just wanted to be sure. He had only been there once. He then selected BHK; the airport identifier came up as Bukhara, Bukhara.

"Where the hell was Bukhara?" he thought "She was right. He had not heard of it."

He looked at his watch as the minutes had ticked away. He did not have time to search the Internet for information on

Bukhara. He figured it had to be on the Saudi Arabian Peninsula or a short hop from it.

He powered down his computer, took a look in the mirror and combed his hair. He went out onto the lanai and started to step over to her lanai, when he caught a glimpse of her kneeling with her face nearly pressed against the carpet. She was praying to Allah. He quietly retreated into his room, waited a few minutes and stepped out into the hall. He went to Jessie's door and tapped on it. In a moment the door opened, she was all smiles. "You are very prompt," she said.

"I wouldn't want to keep a lady waiting," Dan said.

"Oh," she suddenly became serious, "and after this morning you still call me a lady?" She was not teasing.

"Jessie," he said very sternly "I don't know where you have come from or where you are going. I do not know what has happened in your life that you would judge yourself so harshly. What I do know, is that you are a wonderful woman, with a good and decent spirit about you. I would very much like to spend whatever time with you in the next few days that you will allow. I know the island, I can show you anything you want to see, and I have a car. Forget the rest of the world. You're clearly here to escape for a while, just like me. So, let's escape…Okay?"

She started to say something and her mouth opened, but no sound came out. Whatever she had planned to say she thought better of it. He leaned forward and kissed her on the forehead, held her for a moment and said, "Now come with me, Miss Jasmine Hassan, and I will show you some of the most beautiful sites in the United States of America."

She looked at him with her sparkling brown eyes and still said nothing.

Dan had been hiding something behind his back. He brought his arm around to reveal a beautiful Hawaiian lei made of white flowers. He placed it around her neck.

"Aloha," he said. "Welcome to paradise."

"It's gorgeous," she said. "The fragrance is so light and sweet. It is amazing."

"It is the Pikake blossom," said Dan, "otherwise known as Jasmine."

Jasmine picked up her purse and a slightly larger bag. It was a few steps to the elevator and, as they waited, they had a breathtaking view of the Ka'anapoli shoreline and the hotel pool below. Jasmine kept pulling the lei up to her nose to capture the aromatic fragrance. The pool had opened and some kids were yelling and playing. They entered the elevator for the short trip to the ground floor and exited into the pool area. The early morning sunbathers were already staking out their positions in the morning sun.

They walked toward the hotel lobby and parking garage. As they passed the café he turned to her and asked "Breakfast?" She smiled, shook her head, "No, I am not yet hungry."

"Good," he said, "I'm not really a breakfast person, anyway; we'll get something later in Lahaina." There was an awkward silence for a long time as they walked to the car.

It was a ten-minute drive to Lahaina and this time, he parked the car near the ocean behind the banyan tree. They got out and walked along the docks among the many tourists who were scrambling to get aboard the small vessels for various morning cruises. They walked a block along Front Street and came upon an ice cream shop. "How about some ice cream?" he asked. "I do not think so," she replied.

"Have you ever had shave ice?" he asked.

"What is that?" she quizzed.

"I'll show you. He stepped into the ice cream shop. "I want a lime shave ice, no yogurt. The lady also wants a shave ice." He turned to her, "What flavor?"

She looked at the dizzying array of multi-flavored bottles to choose from. "I don't know," she sighed, as she tried to decide.

"Give her a Special Number 2," Dan told the clerk.

The clerk smiled, "One Special Number 2 coming up." The clerk shaved off a softball size clump of ice and began to form it into the funnel-shaped cup. He took one bottle after another and squeezed a generous portion of multi-colored flavors onto the ice. He added a little pineapple, a little banana, a little margarita flavor, some passion orange guava and a few others. The clerk handed Jessie a rainbow-colored ice sculpture and plucked a spoon-shaped straw into the masterpiece. "A special Number 2," the clerk said, with a grin.

Dan looked at her; her eyes widened. Suddenly, she seemed much younger than her years, as her spoon dived into the ice for her first bite. "This is delicious!" she exclaimed. The clerk handed Dan his simple all green lime shave ice. "Just lime?" quizzed the clerk. "Just lime," said Dan.

The seats just outside the shop were filled with other customers. Dan directed Jessie down the street and under the banyan tree. It was easily a hundred-year-old tree that sprawled for a small city block, with several trunk-like extensions to the ground. They sat on one of the benches. Some of the children were laughing and swinging on the vines until scolded by a large Hawaiian woman.

Dan and Jasmine sat eating their shave ice under the shade of the banyan tree, the gentle ocean breeze occasionally ruffling her long hair, frequently, their eyes met, sometimes for an awkward length of time, but neither of them said anything. She would take a deep breath from time to time, as if taking in the sweet fragrance of the flowers and savoring the moment. She finished her shave ice and looked at her watch.

He looked at her, she was smiling now. The sparkle in her eyes had returned, "How about a walk through town?" he asked. He took her hand and they strolled along the shops for the next two hours. They talked of nothing in particular. Sometimes they stopped at a shop while Jessie looked at clothing. At the far end of Front Street, she went into the Wet Seal. The giant television screens showed a music video, as Dan watched her from the sidewalk. After a while, they began their trek back down the other side of the street.

They went into a bookstore and, while Jessie was looking at some magazines, Dan made his way to the travel section. He opened an atlas to the Saudi Peninsula and looked for Bukhara. He found Dubai and Abu Dhabi in the United Arab Emirates but was unable to find Bukhara. He did find it in the index and turned to the correct page. It was a section of Central Asia just above Afghanistan. He found it. Bukhara was in Uzbekistan, one of the old Soviet Republics. He recognized the capital Tashkent in the northeast and the city of Samarkand in the southeast. Samarkand had been a major trading center in the silk trade a thousand years ago. Bukhara was to the southwest near the Turkmenistan border.

Dan looked at the copyright date on the atlas, it was several years old. He began to look for a more recent atlas. He found one dated last year and opened it to Central Asia, he looked up and saw that Jessie was coming toward him. He glanced quickly at the map. A small section in the south of what had been Uzbekistan was colored as the separate nation of Bukhara. The city of Bukhara was its capital. Both Tashkent and Samarkand were still in Uzbekistan. Dan closed the book and swiftly moved down the aisle to meet Jessie as she approached.

"It is 11:30. Are you hungry yet?" he asked.

"Yes, I am," she replied.

"Well, I know just the place for lunch." They headed out of the bookstore and turned left. They were almost to the banyan tree on the other side of the road when they came to a small shopping center. Dan and Jessie went downstairs and were seated in a small restaurant. The Ohana Blue Lagoon Tropical Café was at the center of the shopping center. Several floors of shops were visible from the table. A female singer was doing her rendition of "*Killing Me Softly With His Song*," and accompanying herself on a tinny piano. She was quite good.

"And so, what do you recommend?" asked Jessie as she studied the menu.

"That's easy. For your first lunch in Hawaii, it should be mahi mahi and steamed rice," replied Dan.

"And so it shall be," she said without hesitation.

The waitress took their order as the singer had changed her tune to "*One Tin Soldier*."

When the waitress had walked off, Dan stared at Jessie for a while as she seemed lost in the lyrics of the music. It was a song about a long-ago kingdom and a treasure buried deep beneath. Finally, her eyes looked over at him, and Dan said, "Your father is in Bukhara?"

She was startled by the name of her country. She shrugged her shoulders and shook her head. "Mr. Dan, you continue to surprise me."

"Aw shucks, ma'am," he said, "I just try to be thorough."

She smiled wistfully and then suddenly her face hardened, "My father has been in the hospital in Dubai. He will be released to return home to Bukhara on the day that I arrive in Dubai."

"And what day is that?" asked Dan, already sensing that he would not like the answer.

"Next Tuesday," she said.

He thought for a moment, today was Friday, she would gain a day on the flight to Tokyo. He tried to quickly figure her itinerary through Hong Kong, but she cut his mental calculations short,

"I leave for Narita tomorrow evening," she said softly.

He pursed his lips, his disappointment was clearly obvious. "Well," he said "whatever of the next thirty-six hours you wish to share, please," he paused, "share it with me."

"I would like that," she smiled.

"You know Jessie, as sad as I am going to be to see you go, you seem just as sad to be going. Do you want to talk about it? Is it your uncle?"

"Oh, yes dear Uncle Nasrullah will just love to see me again," she said sarcastically. "I have not seen him since I was 17 when my mother sent me to Paris to protect me from him. Later, I came to America to finish college and to stay a while."

"You have been in the U.S. for how long?" asked Dan.

"Off and on for six years. I first came when I was twenty-one. I have been living in either the U.S. or Paris since then."

"And before that Bukhara?" asked Dan.

"No, I was born in southern Lebanon, but I am not Lebanese, I am part Arab and part Tajik. My mother and father lived in exile in Lebanon when I was born. It is very complicated to explain." she sighed.

"Jessie, I don't pretend to understand the nuances of the Muslim world, but I do understand much better than most Americans. Give me a chance here. How long did you live in Lebanon?

"When it became bad enough in Lebanon we left. We had family in the Sudan and Tajikistan. I lived in both those places when I was still quite young. Finally, Praise Allah we moved to the United Arab Emirates when I was twelve."

"So how does Bukhara figure in all this? It's a part of the former Soviet Republic of Uzbekistan. When did you live there?" quizzed Dan.

"Never really. I visited it for quite a while about five years ago shortly after Bukhara became independent. My father wanted me to see the Ark before it was restored. I only went after I was assured my Uncle Nasrullah would be out of the country for a while. It is a great historical piece of architecture. I found and explored all sorts of secret passages that are hidden within and beneath the Ark.

"What is the Ark?"

"Dan, it's too complicated. Where do I begin? 2,500 years ago, 1,000 years ago? The city of Bukhara was an important trading center in the silk trade. The Arabs came around the year 90, that's 709 A.D. on your calendar. The city prospered as the "Pillar of Islam, *Bukhoro-I-sharif* or 'Noble Bukhara'." It was the religious and cultural heart of Central Asia. The Ark is the Royal Palace of Bukhara, over 2,000 years old and was still in use until 1920 when the Red Army bombed it, and it fell into near ruin for seventy years under the Russians."

"My family fled the Bukhara People's Republic in the late 1920s when Lenin and Stalin erased it from the map and made it part of Uzbekistan. My family and I are actually Bukhari and lived in exile until the Soviet Union fell apart. Just before the exile, my grandmother's grandmother, also named Yasi Min, was murdered by the men in her family for burning her veil, in a protest at the Ark during the International Women's Day in 1927.

"My grandmother was named after her. I was named both for her and my grandmother. The veil is the symbol of purity for a Muslim woman. Yasi Min and a group of Muslim women known as the Khujum stormed the Ark and burned their veils to show their contempt for the religious tyranny of men over women. Later, almost all of the women were killed by their humiliated husbands or brothers."

"So, your Great-Great-Grandmother Yasi Min was a women's libber?"

"You could say that I guess, but the Khujum protest was a much greater act of courage than the burning of bras by a bunch of spoiled American college students. I tell you it struck at the very heart of men's domination over the Islamic woman. I am so proud of her, and I gladly bear her name and the name of my beloved grandmother. It is a name my uncle despises, and I wear as a badge of honor today."

"I take it your uncle is not proud of your heritage?"

"No, he believes that Yasi Min and the Khujum were Bolsheviks and part of the communist plot to destroy a separate Bukhara."

"Dan, this becomes too complicated. My uncle and my father had different mothers. My grandfather had many wives. My Uncle Nasrullah's mother was from the Sudan, where the family lived for a while after fleeing Bukhara. I can see your head spinning trying to follow. It doesn't matter. All you need to know is I am part Arab and part Tajik."

She continued, "My father and uncle have shared the same dream all of their lives. Their goal was to return to an independent Bukhara, restore the Ark and make Noble Bukhara once again the 'Pillar of Islam' and the pride of Central Asia. They have transformed the city, by building hotels and shopping centers and promoting commerce."

"This is why I must return home. The Ark has been restored in the last four years by father and I must share this moment with him before..." Her voice began to quiver, as she struggled with the last few words ..."before...before he is gone. My mother died four years ago of a broken heart. I did not return to Bukhara for her funeral. I had visited her a few weeks earlier in

Paris. She told me to stay away, but now I must go. I must see my father one more time."

Dan reached across the table and held her hands in his. A few tears rolled down her cheek, as she quickly grabbed a napkin and wiped them from her face."

"Now, Dan Grainger, enough of my story. Tell me yours," she commanded.

"Oh, mine is pretty mundane compared to yours. There were no communist conspiracies or Islamic revolutions in Indiana when I was growing up.

I married my high-school sweetheart when I was twenty, we had two daughters Annie, who is nineteen and Callie, who is fifteen. We got divorced shortly after our tenth wedding anniversary. The girls were around eight and four at that time.

"Do you see your children often then?" asked Jessie

"Oh yeah, I've spent the last ten years just trying to be a dad and having some kind of regular presence in my daughter's lives. I am blessed to have joint custody and I am able to make nearly all of their school activities, sporting events and performances. I travel a lot in the U.S. and internationally for my job and rack up a lot of frequent-flier miles. I take the girls on vacations whenever I can. That's our best times together. I've brought them here four times, but they prefer Waikiki to Maui."

"They are in Indiana now?" asked Jessie.

"Well actually, they are in Florida at Disney World at this moment. Callie is a blonde, cheerleader type and is involved with a big dance production that's performing during halftime at the Super Bowl in Miami on Sunday. Callie goes on to Miami tonight. I think Annie flies home tomorrow, then Callie comes back to Orlando on Monday, and she and her mother fly back to Indiana on Monday afternoon. Actually, I'm not sure.

Annie goes to Ball State and is studying journalism and has to be back in class Monday."

"Is Annie, as you put it, the blonde, cheerleader type also?

"No, actually she is a brunette, plays volleyball and, of course, being from Indiana, she plays basketball. That's pretty much my story. Not much to mine, eh?" said Dan.

"I am sure there is a lot to yours that you're not telling me," Replied Jessie.

"Well Jessie, there's more to yours too, like why did you need to be sent to Paris to protect you from your uncle and what was it that broke your mother's heart?"

Rather than reply to what he had said, Jessie looked at her watch and said, "Dan it is nearly 12:30 and I must have some time alone."

"Noon prayer?" quizzed Dan.

Jessie smiled, "You know, most Americans would not realize that."

"Well, I suspect I made you late for your regular prayer this morning, so I wouldn't want to void two of your prayers in one day. We better go. What time is your prayer?"

"12:41."

"Ooh, it's getting close. You can go ahead across the street beyond the banyan tree to the left there, near the Old Fort ruins. There is a fairly-secluded place just beyond the building," said Dan.

"I need to go to the car first."

He handed her the car keys as they both stood up and suddenly realized the singer had gone on to a different song.… *"I'm Leaving On A Jet Plane."*

For a moment, they both just stopped and listened to her sad refrain. When the singer got to the words *"Oh, how I hate to go,"* a tear rolled down Jessie's cheek, she made no attempt to hide it, she just turned and went up the stairs and headed across Front Street toward the banyan tree.

There may have been a tear in Dan's eye too, but there was definitely a lump in his throat. He motioned the waitress over for the check and handed her his credit card. He sat back down and listened to the singer as she continued her song. The lump in his throat remained.

At 12:45 the singer announced she was taking a fifteen-minute break. Dan got up and headed up the stairs and across the street. He went to the same bench under the banyan tree where he and Jessie had sat at that morning and waited for her. A short time later, he felt her hand on his shoulder. He turned; she was carrying the larger bag with her now.

"Is that your veil and prayer clothes?" asked Dan a little sarcastically as he reached up and brushed some dirt from Jessie's forehead.

"You make fun of me."

"No, Jessie, I'm not. I respect your belief in Allah. After all, he is the same God of Abraham that I believe in but I just have a problem with a religion that has several hundred rules about proper prayer at such regimented times. I don't think that's from God. I think it's from the same Muslim mullahs your great-great-grandmother died fighting against."

She just looked at him but said nothing, she handed him the car keys and they made the short walk to the car. He escorted her to her side and opened the door for her. As he was walking back around to his door, Jessie reached over and unlatched his door for him.

As he got in, he looked at her "You passed," he said, with a big smile.

"What do you mean?" she quizzed

"Very few women do what you just did; you unlatched the door for me. I saw it in a movie once. It means you passed the test as a very special woman, a keeper you might say." He put the key into the ignition and started the car.

Jessie just looked at him in a very disapproving manner and shook her head. "Don't read too much into things," she said.

"What do you think is going on here?" asked Dan.

"You don't know?" replied Jessie "You want a definition?"

Dan just stared at her deep brown eyes as they flashed at him.

"It's sex!" exclaimed Jessie. "We're just two ships that passed in the night and scraped hulls."

"You don't believe that," protested Dan.

"It's what I have to believe," said Jesse, "and that's all it is."

"It's not all that it is," Dan said defensively.

"Believe what you want. Believe whatever makes you feel right about this. If you want to believe that our sordid and sinful encounter has shown me something in myself that I did not know existed, that I did not think could happen, then suit yourself. If you somehow think this makes it easier for me to go into the hell that I will be entering in a few days then go ahead and pat yourself on your back for a job well done. Just be careful you don't fool yourself, Dan. For you it was just sex, and if it seems like more than that now, then it will pass in a few days or a few weeks."

Dan did not know what to say, partly because it was possible that she was right. He put the car in gear and backed out of the parking space.

They said nothing on the drive back to the hotel. As they were walking back to the rooms passing the pool, Dan finally broke the silence, "Jessie, I need to make some calls when I get back to my room. It will only take a few minutes. Would you be interested in going down to the beach after a while?"

"I would like that," said Jessie.

"Okay, it's 1:30 now. How about we meet here at the pool bar at 2:15? I'll find us a nice spot on the beach," said Dan.

Jessie nodded and walked on toward the elevators. Dan walked out onto the beach. There were a dozen or so sun lounges for rent along the beach. There was room enough for two people. They had a shade which could be adjusted to block out the direct sun. Dan found the attendant, "How much are the beach chairs?" he asked.

"The cabanas are thirty dollars a day," replied the attendant.

Dan's eyes widened "I just need it for a couple of hours or so," he said.

"We only rent by the full day."

Dan sighed, "Can I charge it to the room?"

"Yes," said the attendant as he picked up a clipboard. "What is your name and room number please?"

"Grainger, Dan Grainger room 4411."

"Mahalo, Mr. Grainger. You may pick any one you wish, yeah."

Dan picked a location that he liked on the beach, and the attendant helped him move the cabana to give a good view of the cliffs to the right and the Ka'anapoli shoreline to the left. Dan re-positioned the sunshade.

"Hey, Danno," Dan heard and as he turned, he saw the familiar smile of a tall, lean and muscular Hawaiian approaching him. "Make sure you have a good view for the ceremony."

"Kahekili!" exclaimed Dan "It's good to see you. Are you diving tonight?"

"Yes, Bruddah at sunset. You alone?" asked Kahekili.

"My girls are in Orlando. The younger one is practicing for a big Super Bowl event sponsored by Oasis."

"Lani is there, too, Bruddah. What a small world - she's in it, too, at halftime. Her muddah is with her," said Kahekili.

"That's crazy," said Dan, as Kahekili walked on toward the cliffs and gave him the hang loose sign with his hand. Dan returned the gesture.

Dan looked up toward his fourth-floor room. Jessie was there on her lanai. She had been watching. Dan waved his arm and shouted, "2:15 p.m."

She waved back an acknowledgment of sorts and even from the distance he could see her broad smile as he walked toward the elevators.

"Thank you…Mahalo," said Dan, to the attendant.

Chapter 4

Dan tried to call Annie and Callie in Orlando on his cell phone. There was no answer and he left a message for both of them to call him. He wanted to know some more about Bukhara, but he just did not have time.

He found his swimsuit, sunglasses and beach sandals and got ready to go to the beach. He threw on a T-shirt and was ready to go, with a lot of time to spare. He grabbed his computer. He did a search on Bukhara and came up with a couple dozen selections. He searched through the country data; the name Hassan caught his attention. Abdullah Hassan was the Emir of Bukhara, and the Foreign Minister was listed as Nasrullah Hassan.

Dan let that sink in for a moment, "Shit!" he exclaimed, "she's a fucking Princess!"

Her evil Uncle Nasrullah was the Foreign Minister, so Abdullah must be her daddy. Dan skimmed web page after web page of information about Bukhara. He kept looking at his watch as 2:15 steadily approached and then passed.

He knew he had to go. Jessie would already be waiting. There was a knock at the door. He signed off the web and began powering down the laptop. He answered the door. It was Jessie. She was beautiful in her cover-up, bathing suit, hat and sunglasses. She looked stunning with the Pikake lei around her neck.

He just stared at her for a moment. She looked like a Princess. She carried herself with the air of Royalty. Why hadn't he seen it before?

"You know, Jessie," said Dan, "Hawaiian Royalty gave the flower in your lei its name, 'Pikake.' Princess Kaiulani named it after the beautiful peacocks who roamed her Waikiki gardens."

"Really?" said Jessie with great interest.

Suddenly, his phone rang.

"Hello," said Dan, as he quickly grabbed the phone.

"Hi, Dad," said the voice.

"Annie?"

"Yeah, its' me."

"How's Florida, you got a suntan?"

"No," she replied. "It's been kinda cold and windy, but the sun has been shining."

Dan looked a little sheepish toward Jessie. "My daughter," he mouthed quietly. Jessie was enjoying watching him, his voice was different. His whole tone and body language were different.

Is Callie all ready for the big show on Sunday? Is she there? asked Dan

"Yeah, they were practicing all morning. We just got back from the airport. She's on her way to Miami."

"How many planes did they charter?" asked Dan.

"There was just one," she said.

"You're kidding, three hundred girls on one plane?"

"Yeah, I guess."

"It must have been a big plane. They sure must have money to burn," said Dan.

"It was the kind with the deck on top like we flew to Israel," said Annie.

"Oh, that's a 747."

"Well, I don't know. I got your voicemail and was just calling back," said Annie.

"I was just checking in with you guys. I knew if I didn't get a hold of you soon, it would be too late back there and then you'd be on your way back to Indiana in the morning."

"We changed our tickets and now I am flying back Sunday," said Annie.

"Everything's okay, then?"

"Yep."

"Well, okay, I'll call you tomorrow sometime," said Dan.

"Okay, bye, see ya."

"Okay, bye, love ya," said Dan, as he hung up the phone.

Dan turned to Jessie, "Sorry," he said.

"No, that was sweet, to hear your voice so soft with your daughter. I think she has dad wrapped around her finger."

"They both do. That was Annie the older one. Callie is on her way to Miami right now. Let's go," said Dan, as he grabbed his sunglasses and headed for the door.

Jessie stepped in front of him and blocked his exit, put her arms around him and kissed him on the lips.

"What was that for?" asked Dan.

"For being a good dad. It is a noble quality," replied Jessie.

"Yeah, well it's the only one I got, but I'm starting to wonder if you don't have a few noble qualities yourself."

"What is that supposed to mean?" quizzed Jessie.

But Dan didn't answer her as he closed the door and headed toward the elevator. She followed him into the elevator. It was just the two of them. Her hands were full of the items she was taking with her. Her long black hair was tucked up beneath her beach hat exposing the nape of her neck.

Dan leaned behind her and gently kissed the back of her neck. She squirmed slightly. As the door opened an elderly couple standing directly in front of the elevator door stared at them. The old man chuckled and shot Dan an admiring glance as they passed each other. "Come along, Jeffrey," the old woman said, as she got on the elevator.

Dan and Jessie climbed onto the beach lounger. Jessie took a few minutes to become situated. The shade of the lounger blocked the sun from hitting all but the lower part of their legs. Dan put some sun tan lotion on his lower legs in the sun.

They lay next to each other admiring the beauty and serenity of their surroundings. He held Jessie in his arms for the longest time. She rested her head on his chest. A gentle breeze from the ocean kept them cool despite the glare of the afternoon sun. The cheerful voices of children swimming and playing along the beach could be heard. Two little girls were playing in the water directly in front of them. They were laughing and giggling and having a wonderful time.

"You would think these kids should be in school someplace," said Dan, breaking the long silence.

"I suppose," sighed Jessie, "but what a wonderful way to spend your time as a child - carefree, happy, no fighting, enough to eat...her voice trailed off...no tahara."

"Tahara?" asked Dan. "What is that?"

Jessie did not answer right away. Her face was turned from him, and he could not see her reaction. But he could feel great emotion within the length of her body as it pressed against him.

"The tahara," she began, "The purification of young girls, the Arabic term is the Khifad. Those little girls playing on the beach would not be laughing and smiling if they grew up in the places I did. In the west, you call it female circumcision or FGM…female genital mutilation. In my world, it is the purification of young girls, so that they will be fit for marriage. No man would marry an unclean woman. No self-respecting Muslim mother would leave her daughter uncircumcised. That is for the lowest of prostitutes."

Dan didn't know what to say. Jessie's voice had started out soft and weak, but now it was strong and filled with anger as her feelings poured out.

"The grandmothers often do it, using a dirty knife, an old razor blade or even a tin can lid. They don't even know what they're doing. In the Sudan, they just chop and slice away until the entire lips of the vulva are scraped away. Then you are sewn up tight leaving only a small hole for the necessary functions of womanhood. Nothing is left but a scar. They say it keeps you smelling sweet, and your husband will be pleased."

Dan's whole body winced at the thought. He had heard of the practice and had been in some Central African villages that practiced it. He had never heard it described in such graphic detail and with such force of emotion.

"In some countries," she continued "it is not quite as bad. They only cut out the clitoris or snip off the end of it. The holy men of the mosque inspect you and declare you clean or unclean. If they decide you're unclean, then they just snip out a little bit more until you're pronounced clean."

Dan stroked the back of her head with his right hand and his left hand clawed at his own forehead as if he were reacting to the sound of fingernails squeaking across a chalkboard.

Dan's mind was racing with questions. He ventured a small one "How old are these girls? Do they do anything to numb the girls and what about infection?"

She continued as if she had not heard him and yet she answered "Little girls, three or four, some places it's later. And always they check you. Sometimes the holy men would come, and all the girls of the village are forced to lie next to each other on a table or on the ground with their legs spread. They go from girl to girl with the same knife or blade, checking them and if they are unclean they snip some more skin off. The girl screams. My mother and grandmother were always there with me to tell them I was clean.

I am one of the lucky ones. My beloved grandmother took me to Paris, and it was performed by a doctor when I was four or five. I don't even remember, Praise Allah. You can't imagine how lucky I am.

I remember once in the Sudan when I was maybe seven or eight, my Uncle Nasrullah demanded that I be inspected with the other girls of the village. Nasrullah's own daughter, Sirah, was one of the girls. She was lying next to me while the holy man touched me and checked me and pronounced me clean. My uncle objected, claiming I was unclean. He said I was disgusting and hideous to look at. My grandmother was screaming at him. She said it had been done in the form of Sunnah, in the tradition of Muhammed's teachings. The holy man agreed.

Nasrullah was enraged, he grabbed Sirah and said to his mother, Sirah's grandmother "You show them how it is to be done." I could see Nasrullah pinning Sirah to the floor as she screamed and screamed, while the grandmother scraped away at her. I don't know what she was using. Somehow, Sirah found my hand and I held it until they were finished. There was blood everywhere. Then she was sewn up with a dirty needle and pronounced clean. Sirah died a few days later from infection. She was five years old. She was not the only girl that died from the inspections that day.

"After Sirah died, Uncle despised me. Several times over the next few years he would bring a holy man from the mosque to inspect me. Sometimes I think he did it so that he could look at me himself. When we moved to Tajikistan, it happened again. It always happened when my father was away but, Praise Allah, my grandmother was always there."

"I loved traveling with my grandmother. I remember once when I was little, she took my little brother and me to Hong Kong. She loved to travel. She had the most amazing spirit about her. When I was eleven, my grandmother was stoned to death."

"Why?" asked Dan.

"I don't know." said Jessie, "My mother never told me. I had heard it was for adultery, but I do not believe that. It was something else. No one ever talked about it. I think it was her vocal opposition to female circumcision. One of the last things I remember my grandmother telling me was that there was a secret treasure buried within me and one day I would find it."

"Once when I was seventeen, we were living in the United Arab Emirates. Uncle brought another holy man to inspect me again. I remember Uncle Nasrullah's face as I was forced to show myself. He looked at me in a way that I can never forget. My mother saw it in his eyes."

"The next day my mother and father had a terrible argument and she demanded I be sent away to Paris to be safe from Nasrullah. My father loved me so very much. He did not want to be separated from me. I did not want to be away from him or my family. He said he could protect me from Nasrullah but my mother would not give up.

It was very difficult when I left for Paris. I only saw my parents when they came to see me in France. We had many wonderful times in their visits. I never saw Nasrullah again.

Dan did not know what to say. He didn't want to quiz her, but she seemed to want to talk.

"Look, Jessie," said Dan "I was checking out Bukhara on the Internet when you knocked on the door. I know your father is the Emir of Bukhara and your uncle is the Foreign Minister. So, doesn't that, like, make you a fucking Princess or something?

"Yeah, Dan, that's the problem, I am a fucking Princess, an unmarried fucking Princess," said Jessie.

Dan was shocked by her blunt repetition of the f-word but he got the point.

"I am sorry, Dan. I am afraid I have spoiled our wonderful afternoon together by bringing up my problems," said Jessie. "This is such a beautiful place. It's like there are no problems on earth, when you lay here and watch the sun setting in the west and feel the gentle breeze of the ocean…but tomorrow I must leave."

"I understand now why you dread going back," said Dan.

"Do you? I think not. I have no fear of Uncle. I despise him, but he is my father's brother and has been very important to my father's life-long dream of restoring Bukhara to greatness. And it is happening. Five years ago, Bukhara once again became an independent nation. The whole nation is undergoing renovation and being rebuilt. My father was so proud when I came home five years ago. He wanted me to stay and assume my rightful role as Princess. I wanted to stay but I cannot remain in Bukhara for long.

"You are a grown woman now. Can Nasrullah still threaten you?"

"If I remained there, I would be a constant thorn in his side. He has been the force in re-establishing the traditional role of Muslim women. All Bukhari women must now be completely covered in public. Educated women have been forced to quit good jobs and go back under the veil.

I would oppose his little plots. If I was successful in influencing my father, he could simply accuse me of being unclean. If he were able to force an inspection, I would most certainly be found unclean."

"I don't understand." said Dan.

"I am no longer a virgin, I am unmarried, I am unclean, and I would be put to death in accordance with Islamic Law."

"Holy Shit!" gasped Dan.

"Aren't you protected by being the Princess of Bukhara, the daughter of the Emir? Surely, you are not subject to the whim of the Foreign Minister," said Dan.

"To some extent you are correct, but no one is above Islamic Law...absolutely no one, and I am certainly subject to the plots of my uncle," she sighed. "It is not death that I fear. It is bringing shame and humiliation to my father."

"I see," said Dan. He did not know what else to say.

"There are so many superstitions which govern our daily lives. Did you know, many Muslim men believe that if a woman's clitoris comes in contact with a man's penis, it will render him impotent?

"Are you serious?" asked Dan.

"Oh yes, one of many superstitions and beliefs in my world."

"Well Jessie, from what most American women tell me about most American men, there is not too much chance of that contact happening."

Jessie raised her head, turned over to look at him and laughed. "Crazy American," she said, with a hint of a smile.

"It doesn't stop there," she continued "We are told that, during birth, if the child's head touches the uncut clitoris the child will be retarded...the mother's milk will be poisonous...it protects the health of the woman…it prevents her from becoming promiscuous…it's only a little piece of skin…the woman does not miss it. In the Sudan, they say it is done for the beauty of the suture. The parts removed are hideous and disgusting to look at. The tighter she is sewn the more pleasure the husband will have…and it goes on and on."

"Look, I don't know how to say this, but you said you were circumcised. I got a pretty good look at you this morning and believe me, there is nothing disgusting or hideous. You are a beautiful woman in every way."

"I saw you looking at me in the sunlight. I knew what you were doing, and I also know you didn't find what you were looking for," said Jessie.

"Then, how, may I ask, could you have had an orgasm?"

"I don't know," she sighed, "I don't know, it is not possible, maybe I imagined it."

"I don't think so. No one's imagination is that good," said Dan.

"It has never happened before. I am twenty-seven years old and have never had an orgasm. I think I just got carried away with all that was happening…the tension of returning home…I just don't know…I don't want to think about it," she continued. "Can't you understand, Dan? It is not what happened to me that troubles me. It is what did NOT happen to me but has happened to so many of the women and what continues to happen today to little girls all over Bukhara and the Muslim world. My grandmother died trying to stop it. I am not worthy of her name. I must devote the rest of my life to honoring her Islamic faith. I must seek the hidden treasure my grandmother told me about that is buried deep inside me. That will give me the strength to prevail. I am not worthy of the title Princess. I have done nothing the last five years for the people of Bukhara or for the women of Bukhara except hide out in the West."

"That's nonsense." said Dan "I know I will never see you again after we part, but the Lord…" he paused "your Allah placed us together for some reason, I believe that. I believe it was because we both need each other right now."

"You Christians are so funny. You turn things around. You are trying to tell me Allah placed us in bed this morning so that we could defile all that I am supposed to observe? You are crazy…American," she laughed as she said it. "Crazy American."

"I don't know the purpose, Jessie," said Dan, but I believe that the Lord's hand was in this. I believe the Lord can use our mistakes and indiscretions for our own good and to fulfill the plan he has for our life."

"Dan, I used you last night?" said Jessie.

"What?" asked Dan.

"I used you last night, I'm sorry," she said. "The thought of returning to my country made me realize that I may never be with anyone again for the rest of my life. I used you to fulfill my own selfish desires."

Dan did not know what to say. He just held her. Finally, he said, "Jessie, you have a destiny to fulfill for yourself, your country and for all the little girls and women of Bukhara."

"I must not bring shame to my father," she said emphatically.

"There is but one woman in your whole nation that might stop your uncle's persecution of women in the name of Allah," Dan declared "and, I might add in the name of your father. And because you are paralyzed by your own sins…you shrink from your destiny? You know what I say to you young lady? Snap out of it!"

Jessie thought for the longest time. "You give very good advice, my friend. I wish I had the strength to follow it."

The sounds of the beach were suddenly pierced by the sound of a long musical note. Dan and Jessie looked out at the black, rock cliffs and could see several people on top of the cliffs. A man was blowing into a conch shell creating a sustained and very loud, trumpet-like note.

"Ah, that's my good friend Kahekili Kealoha. He is a famous diver on Maui. We should stay until sunset, when they light the torches and recreate a scene from Hawaiian folklore, where a Maui Chief dives into the Pacific from the cliffs. It is a fantastic display," said Dan. "Looks like Kahekili is teaching his craft to some young divers."

They watched for a few minutes as several young men dived into the ocean. Jessie seemed transfixed on the scene. It seemed like forever and the divers did not surface.

"Are they okay?" asked Jessie with great concern.

"Oh, yes," said Dan, "Kahekili teaches his students to hold their breath for an incredible amount of time, five, six even seven minutes." After an eternity, the divers began to resurface. Jessie had been engrossed in the performance and was greatly relieved as Dan just watched her.

Dan looked at her for the longest time. "My God, you are so exquisite. I can't imagine what I have done to deserve even this small amount of time with you." he paused "May I be so bold as to kiss the Princess?"

"NO!" snapped Jessie, "you may not kiss the Princess. It is forbidden!"

"But my friend, for the next twenty-four hours I wish to get as far away from that title as I can. I came here to escape from reality and all the responsibilities I must face soon enough in my life. You may kiss ME, not the Princess. Just ME, the woman you picked up in the airport," and then she stared at him as if it were a challenge.

It was a bit after 3:30 p.m. The sun was getting lower in the sky but still a couple hours from setting. "It would be a shame to miss the sunset," said Dan.

"Oh yes, it would be terrible," replied Jessie.

Jessie and Dan began to gather their things. A moment later they were headed toward the elevator. They burst into Dan's room and shut the door. He picked her up in his arms and carried her to the bed. He frantically removed her clothes and he once again plunged his tongue deep between her legs. He couldn't believe this was happening again. He explored her innermost recesses. Dan Grainger was no stud by any means, but he did have a special talent for this particular activity. Still, he could not find the exact spot, and yet, she responded with moans that became louder and louder and finally ended in a rhythmic crescendo that caused her to scream and sit straight up in the bed.

She whispered, "That's not what I meant when I said you could kiss me."

Dan smiled, "Well it is what I meant, and you did not say where. We needed to find out if what you experienced this morning was just a one-time thing. Clearly, it can be repeated."

Her whole body began to shake. She was smiling from ear to ear. The shaking stopped and, in a few moments, she began shaking again.

"It's after-tremors," said Dan "You've never had them before?"

"No, I have never experienced anything like this," she said, "Never," as another tremor hit and she began shaking again.

"Breathe deeply," Dan said as he held her in his arms and continued holding her, until finally, the tremors subsided.

"This is just not possible, this cannot be," she muttered, as her hand slipped down his side toward his groin. He stopped her. "No Jessie, don't. Believe me, it's just not physically possible for me to do anything more. I don't want to embarrass myself. Let's just consider this afternoon as making it even for last night." She smiled and kissed him on the lips and said, "As you wish."

Chapter 5

As Jessie and Dan lay on the bed in each other's embrace, Dan's cell phone rang. Dan grabbed the phone a little annoyed "Hello," he said.

"Daddy," a voice sobbed.

"Annie, what's wrong!" exclaimed Dan.

"Callie's plane is missing." Annie was sobbing; breathing so fast she couldn't catch her breath.

It was like slow motion for Dan. He heard but he didn't hear. Every sense in his body went on alert. He felt a surge of blood rush to his face "What do you mean? What do you mean?" he blurted out.

"Her plane…her plane," said Annie, with every word an effort as she struggled to speak, "They're saying her plane blew up over the ocean."

"Who's saying that? Where did you hear it?"

"It's all over the news, Daddy, they broke in about fifteen minutes ago," she continued to sob uncontrollably.

"Okay, okay, where are you?" asked Dan as he grabbed the remote and flipped on the TV.

"At the hotel."

"Okay, okay, she's going to be okay, Annie. I will get a flight out tonight. What are they saying?"

"They just said the Oasis plane lost contact with the tower and some fishing boats reported a bright explosion over the water. It just happened a little bit ago, they don't know anything."

"Are you okay, Annie?" asked Dan.

"No."

"She's going to be okay, Annie," said Dan. "I'll call you as soon as I know what I'm doing. I have to get on the phone to get a flight out tonight, and I have to get back over to Honolulu as soon as I can. I love you."

"Bye," a weak and pathetic voice responded.

He flipped the channels searching for CNN or FOX News but did not find them on the hotel system. He stopped at KHON2, the Fox affiliate showing a breaking news story from the network.

The reporter was standing on a dark beach with some harbor lights in the background "Around 8:30 in the evening, witnesses say they saw a bright explosion low in the sky over the ocean just off the coast of Miami Beach. Fishing boats several miles off shore also reported the explosion lit up the night sky and some have radioed that they have discovered debris floating in the area. Air Traffic Control at the Miami International Airport said they lost radio contact with the Boeing 747 just moments before the explosion. The plane had been operated by Oasis and was carrying 300 young girls to the Super Bowl. The Coast Guard is searching the area for survivors. It is dark and there is a report that flames are burning on the Atlantic at the site of the accident. It will be dawn before a massive search effort can be mounted. For FOX News, this is Rafael Garcia."

Jessie had slipped Dan's robe on and stood frozen at the foot of the bed as she watched the events unfold. Dan was now frantically calling the airlines. Jessie walked over to him and placed her hand on the back of his neck. "It is your daughter, Callie? She asked, "She was on that plane?"

"I refuse to accept this, Jessie. This is not happening. She will be okay," said Dan.

"May the peace of Allah be with you," she said, as she sat down next to him and placed her arms around him, as he made the phone calls. She rested her head on his shoulder.

After a few minutes, he realized it was futile. He couldn't get a flight out of Honolulu tonight and even if he could find one, it was Friday, and all the inter-island flights from Maui to Honolulu were booked solid this evening.

He looked at his watch, "Four o'clock," he thought. He turned up the TV again, but they had rejoined regular programming. He flipped around to the other stations, but there was nothing. The hotel's cable news channels were not working. The network newscasts would be on at 5:30. Then he realized, that would be old news, five hours old, tape delayed by the Honolulu stations from the 6:30 p.m. New York or L.A. feed. He had to find out what was going on now!

He couldn't think clearly but was vaguely aware of the soft embrace of Jessie's arms around him. It was calming and he could hear the soft murmur of a Muslim prayer coming from her lips. It was not in English and he did not understand it, but it had a soothing effect upon him, as his mind raced in denial of the looming tragedy. Dan could handle a lot of things. He had already handled a lot of things in his life. But not this. He could not handle it if anything happened to Callie. He would not even let himself think it.

His body began to shake, "Not this," he cried out. "In the name of Jesus, please, not this," and one single tear streamed down his cheek. Jessie cradled him in her arms and continued her softly spoken Muslim prayer.

He searched through his contact list and called a friend that was an Oceanic cable engineer. He quickly found out there was a cable outage on the island. Dan asked if he could come down to their facility and watch feeds on the incoming fiber feed to Maui. His friend was down in Hana and could not get him authorized to visit for several hours. Dan needed to find a way to watch as soon as possible. He needed total freedom to search between cable and network feeds.

He picked up the phone again and called a local number over on the Big Island. Jessie could not hear the other side of the conversation. "Keith," said Dan. "Callie was on the 747 that went down in Florida. Are you able to watch FOX and CNN in Hilo? …Great… Really?... a special at 11:00 p.m. Eastern?... That's great…I need to get into the equipment shed at Haleakala. Is it okay if I do that?"

"The key still in the same place? … right now, I have to get up there before the Special Report begins at 6:00 p.m. …Can I move the dish?…. Okay, Keith, thanks…Yeah, me too, I'll let you know…Thanks, I appreciate that. Aloha."

"Jessie, I have to go," said Dan, "I may not see you again. I don't know what to say; there isn't time." He was packing as he was talking.

"Where are you going?" she asked.

"Haleakala. It's a 10,000-foot mountain over an hour from here. It's a sixty-mile drive. There's a satellite dish up there where I can get news from the mainland. In fact, it's a communication center where I can pick up satellite transmissions from half the world. I can find out what's going on everywhere."

"I am coming with you," declared Jessie.

"No, you can't. I'm taking my bags. I may be up there all night. I might go straight back to the airport in the morning. I may not come back here at all."

"It doesn't matter. You should not be alone right now. If it becomes necessary you can leave me at the airport, and I will make it back here," she insisted.

He looked at her. She was right. He desperately did not want to be alone. "Okay," he said. "Get some warm clothing; it can get chilly up there, especially at night."

"I will be right back," she said, as she headed for the door.

Dan changed his clothes and continued to pack at lightning speed. He always traveled light. He located his National Park Pass and was just closing his bag when Jessie came back in the room. She was dressed and ready to go with a jacket over her arm.

"Let's go," he said, as he stuffed his computer in his carry-on bag and grabbed his other bag. "Here, this is my room key. If I don't come back here in the morning, can you check out for me?"

Jessie nodded as they waited for the elevator. They walked briskly to the parking garage, and Jessie could hardly keep up with him. The first five or ten miles, they were in heavy traffic headed for Lahaina on an Aloha Friday afternoon. When they passed the town, the traffic in their lane thinned out, but it was still heavy in the oncoming lane. It was a difficult road to drive fast, but Dan was heavy on the gas pedal. When they got back to Kahului, Dan turned onto Highway 37 and, oddly enough, a sign said 37 miles to Haleakala. Neither of them spoke, but Jessie watched Dan intently, as he seemed lost in thought. There was very little traffic going up the mountain at this time of day. Several cars and an occasional group of bicyclists were coming down the mountain. There were huge green pastures with cattle grazing on gently sloping hills. Jessie was struck by the large arrays of cactus growing in the fields. At about the 7,000-foot level they entered clouds.

Dan would occasionally look at his watch, as he was racing against time up the mountain. They broke through the clouds at the 9,000-foot level, and the bright blue sky offered a stark contrast to the fluffy, white clouds that could be seen extending to the horizon in all directions.

The land was mostly barren with an occasional silver colored shrub that had taken root in the hostile lava rock. Jessie could see the summit house glistening in the setting sun. Dan drove past the summit onto a service road, and the white dome of the Haleakala Observatory came into view. Dan pulled off the road next to a small equipment shed located next to a short tower with several microwave dishes on it. Next to the tower was a large satellite dish pointed to the east.

Dan turned off the car and opened the door. A cool breeze entered the car. "The air is very thin up here," he said. "Be careful to keep your breath and walk slowly." He did not heed his own advice as he scurried over to the tower and climbed several feet up the tower. He fished around on the tower for a moment and retrieved a key ring. He climbed back down and walked over to the satellite dish and inspected the mechanical arm that moved the dish.

By this time, Jessie had gotten out of the car and walked slowly to the door of the shed. She quickly became aware that Dan's advice about the thin air was true. Dan met her at the door with the key. He was huffing and puffing and could hardly catch his breath as he unlocked the door and stepped in. He flipped on the light and walked over to a rack of electronic equipment and began turning things on. He studied a chart on the wall for a moment and then went back to a satellite receiver in the equipment rack. The color monitor showed a picture, he changed the channels on the receiver and began pushing buttons, and the picture suddenly pixelated and went blank.

He stepped over to look out the door and observed that the satellite dish was moving even farther to the east. A pleased look came over his face. It was the first sign of relief Jessie had seen in him since he had received the call from Annie.

In a few moments a clear picture popped up on the monitor and the dish stopped. Dan turned up a volume control and the sound of the program filled the small shed. "Praise the Lord!" declared Dan as just a hint of a smile came over his face.

"What is it?" asked Jessie.

"It's the East Coast feed of FOX News and I can move it to CNN. Both cable networks were promoting a special recap to be in about thirty minutes. I was afraid the dish wouldn't move and I would have to free up the mechanics. That would have taken a while."

"We have a little bit of time. I want to show you something," Dan said, as he motioned Jessie toward the door. They got back in the car and drove a short distance back down the service road to a parking area. There were just two other cars in the lot, but there was no one to be seen anywhere else on the summit. Dan and Jessie got out of the car, put on their jackets, and walked up a rocky path to a spot on top of the crater rim.

"Jessie, the Haleakala crater has always been a special place to me. I have often come up here to think and to pray." said Dan, "I have never had more reason to pray than I do right now."

Suddenly, Jessie gasped, "It is magnificent! It is so beautiful!"

A panoramic view of a 3,000-foot-deep valley came into view. It looked like a scene you could imagine on the moon. The sun was low in the west behind them and long shadows swept across the lunarscape of the valley below. Multi-colored cinder cones dotted the dark-brown valley floor. The setting sun created a magic of color in the valley, as the clouds on the horizon were a tinge of gold, pink and orange.

"How can such a magnificent piece of the Lord's handiwork be the backdrop for such tragedy in my life? It cannot be so, It is not so!" exclaimed Dan.

"In the name of Jesus Christ, dear Lord, hear my prayers." Dan raised his arms to the sky and looked up to the heavens and began a personal dialogue in his prayer that Jessie had never before witnessed in her life. He lowered his left hand and found Jessie's hand and grasped it firmly.

"Please, keep Callie safe from harm wherever she is and in the face of whatever danger she is facing. Comfort her and let her feel your presence. I ask that Callie and all of the girls be found and be returned safely to their families. Give me the strength to face this challenge as I await further word on this terrible accident. Open up the airline schedules to me, so that I can get to Callie as soon as possible. Help Annie and comfort her. In the name of Jesus, I pray…Amen." Dan finished and continued looking upward at the heavens.

He relaxed his grip on Jessie's hand and turned around to face the west.

"I guess we didn't miss the sunset after all," he said, as she also turned to the west. As though above a field of white cotton, the bright crimson sun slowly descended into the clouds. The couple stood holding each other while the clouds displayed brilliant golden hues. The sun sank from sight. In just four minutes it was completely engulfed by the clouds.

Dan led the way back down the lava rock path to the car. In just a few minutes they were back in the equipment shed. It seemed much warmer now. Dan found a couple of folding chairs in the corner and set them up in front of the rack. In a few minutes, a special report on the Oasis flight began. The anchor was talking about the tragedy looming in the Atlantic.

They re-hashed what little Dan already knew. The plane had taken off from Orlando just after 7:00 p.m. The television graphic showed the path of the plane down the Florida peninsula south of Miami and then to the east out over the Atlantic. The anchor was speaking live with an air traffic controller spokesman who was explaining the procedure. "The last radio contact with the plane was at 8:23 p.m. The plane's last known position was fifteen nautical miles southeast of the Miami International Airport at 6,000 feet. Oasis One should have reported to the tower when it reached the Fowey Rocks Lighthouse located about ten miles offshore. Miami Approach Control attempted to contact the plane with instructions. There was no response. Radar contact with the plane indicated that it rapidly lost altitude and fell off the radar screen into the Atlantic at 8:34 p.m."

The anchor asked, "Was there anything unusual that could give the National Transportation Safety Board clues as to what happened?"

"There were some anomalies on the radar screen that we are studying, but that will take some time to sort out," answered the spokesman.

"Were there any other planes in the area at the time of the accident?"

"Yes," the spokesman continued "There were several other planes in the area. The traffic on this Friday evening was heavier than normal, due to the Super Bowl this weekend. We will be interviewing other pilots who may have seen something."

"Is it possible that the higher-than-normal air traffic contributed in some way to the accident?"

"No, we don't believe so. However, we will conduct a full and complete investigation. As you know, the volume of general aviation traffic is also much greater this weekend."

The anchor replied, "Witnesses we have interviewed at Miami Beach say they observed an unusual number of small planes offshore at low altitudes this evening."

"Many small planes do converge on a city for a major event such as this. By flying above or below the controlled airspace surrounding the airport, these planes are not required to maintain radio contact with the tower."

"Do we know how high Oasis One was when it first ran into trouble?"

"I don't have that answer for sure. That is one of the things we will be determining in the investigation."

"Is it possible one of the small planes we were speaking of could have been at that altitude?" quizzed the anchor.

"I think I would have heard something about that if that were the case. The Class B controlled airspace over the area we are talking about begins at 3,000 feet above the Atlantic and extends to 7,000 feet. No unauthorized planes should have been in that area and if they had been, we would have had a radar indication of their presence. The point you seem to be driving at is a possible mid-air collision. We cannot rule that out at this time, but there are no early indications of such a collision. This happened just three hours ago, and right now we are focusing on search and rescue efforts. We will have plenty of time to sort through the data later. The important thing right now is to find the survivors and to maintain vigilance over planes still in the air this evening."

The anchor thanked the spokesman. Dan and Jessie said nothing as they held hands in front of the monitor. Occasionally Jessie would squeeze Dan's hand.

The next report was from Miami Beach and consisted of the reporter interviewing several witnesses who said they saw an explosion in the southeast and then several balls of flame falling into the ocean. The camera tried to focus on some flames still burning on the ocean way off in the distance.

Then came the worst news for Dan as he tried to remain in denial about the seriousness of the situation. The anchor was speaking to the captain of a small ship near the scene of the fire. The captain was on a cell phone. He had a thick accent and described the flames as burning jet fuel floating on the sea. He said there was considerable debris in the area and that his crew had recovered several pieces of luggage from the ocean.

The Special Report finished the broadcast by saying that the captain had supplied the names of six girls believed to be on the ill-fated Boeing 747. The names had been turned over to the NTSB for verification. The telecast said to stay tuned for the latest on the search and rescue operation.

Dan and Jessie sat there for a while. Finally, Dan broke the silence. "I need to be back up here in a few hours. Let me get you something to eat and I will take you back to the hotel."

"You are coming back here tonight?" asked Jessie.

"Yes, for the Saturday morning feeds of 'Fox and Friends', CNN, 'Good Morning America', the 'Today Show' and the CBS 'Morning News'. There is not going to be any more developments until daybreak in Miami. The equipment up here will allow me to decode local television news feeds from Miami that may not be on the national news. My cell phone is not working up here, and the phone on the wall over there is broken. I need to make some phone calls and check messages back at my office in Indiana."

"Dan, there is no point in you taking me all the way back to the hotel and then driving all the way back up here," she insisted. "I will stay with you. If you need to go back down far enough to find a phone and something to eat, that is fine, but I am staying with you."

"What time is your flight tomorrow?" Dan asked

"8:05 p.m. from Maui," she answered.

"Okay, you win. Besides, I, uh, I would just as soon have your company. We can go down to Kahului to eat, and there is an electronics store in the mall where I can get some things to fix the phone."

"I am going to drive," said Jessie, "We almost didn't make it up here with you behind the wheel. I will drive now and you try to rest."

There were many twists and turns in the drive down from Haleakala. Dan was in no mood to argue with her. Jessie drove.

Chapter 6

All of the girls that had boarded their assigned buses at the Hilton expected to arrive at the Orlando Airport in just a few minutes. They were excited and couldn't wait to get to Miami.

Dan and the rest of the world waited for dawn to break on Saturday morning to aid in the search and rescue efforts off the coast of Florida. On Friday evening, the girls on the red and white bus experienced their own separate horror. Bus#7 never arrived at the airport. The twenty-four girls assigned to that bus found themselves in a sparsely populated area of Florida when the bus stopped.

Kara Campbell clung to her sister Keisha as they made their way down the bus steps with the other girls. They were inside a huge warehouse. The group of twenty-four girls from Bus#7 were directed into an adjacent room and left there. Keisha saw an orange box truck pulling into the warehouse behind the bus. The bus no longer displayed the Oasis logo or bus number. It looked just like any other bus you might see on the highway.

She did not understand. They should be at the airport to board the plane to Miami. Instead, they had driven about an hour to this warehouse area, going mostly east. It was still daylight.

The door was shut and two black men dressed in dirty clothes stood by the door. Keisha smiled at one of them and he smiled back with a grin that revealed most of his front teeth missing.

"Ooh, gross!" exclaimed one of the girls.

The girls milled around for a while. They had no place to sit and were getting restless.

"Where are we?" complained Lani, the 14-year-old Hawaiian girl. "Something is not right here."

"I don't know," replied Gina. She was sixteen and from New Jersey. She was one of the oldest girls.

"Hey Mister," said the Native American girl, Nakota, pointing her finger in the face of the second black man, "What's going on here? Where are all the other girls?" She was sixteen but her long braided black hair and aggressive manner made her seem even older.

The man did not respond to her at all. He just ignored her.

A moment later a tall, white man, badly in need of a shave, came through the door. He spoke with a thick accent, "You girls must remain here for about fifteen minutes. Then, I will come for you three at a time, and you will be taken to join the other girls on your way to Miami. I am sorry if you have become alarmed. There was a problem with the plane, and different transportation has been arranged. Please be patient. I will be back shortly."

Then he left. He walked across the warehouse and opened another sliding door revealing a large airplane sitting just outside the warehouse. It was a dark, camouflage-colored C-130 transport plane. The rear ramp was down at the entrance of the warehouse door. The orange box truck pulled up behind it, and a second white man stepped out. They began unloading luggage from the van and loading it onto the C-130. There were just the two white men and three black men doing the work.

Inside the room, the lone black man kept staring at the girls, one at a time.

In the far corner of the room was a second door. Two of the girls wandered over to it, and the man shouted at them. They stopped and returned to the cluster of girls in the center of the room.

One of the black men returned from the warehouse and said something to the first one in a foreign language. Keisha's face lit up. She answered them back in the same language. The men were startled. The first man came over to Keisha and spoke to her. They began talking and laughing. The other man joined in. They talked for several minutes.

The other girls could not understand what was going on but there seemed to be general relief that someone in their midst could communicate with the men. The first man went to the first door and peeked out at the men unloading the vans. He said something to the second man and laughed.

He then went back to Keisha and motioned her to come with him to the second door. Kara clung to Keisha's leg. At first, the man tried to stop Kara, but Keisha spoke to him and he agreed to let Kara come too.

The three of them disappeared through the second door.

Shortly afterward the sound of airplane engines starting could be heard. The whine of the engines was very loud inside the warehouse.

The second man rounded up three of the girls standing in the center of the room and directed them toward the first door. In a moment, there was a tap on the door, and the three girls were ushered out of the room into the hands of the tall, white man. He motioned the girls up the steps of a platform in the center of the warehouse. It had the appearance of an above ground swimming pool. The platform was about six feet above the floor of the warehouse. The three girls were directed to the edge of the platform and, before they could comprehend what was happening, their arms were pinned at their sides. An elastic strap was slipped around the waist of each girl binding her wrists tightly to her waist. An inflatable rubber tube was placed around their feet. It was quickly inflated tightly around their ankles with an air hose.

The girls were screaming now, but their screams could not be heard over the whine of the aircraft engines just outside the warehouse. One by one they were thrown into the large vat of 6' deep saltwater next to the platform. The inflated tube around the ankles of the girls held their feet above the surface of the water. Each girl struggled in terror to keep her head above water.

When the first black man came back into the room, Keisha and Kara were not with him. About half the girls were now gone from the room. He took up a position at the first door. The second black man then went into the room with Keisha and Kara.

There was a tap at the warehouse door. Three more girls were ushered out the door. After a while, the second man emerged from the room where Keisha and Kara had been taken. He left the door open. All the remaining girls were crying now and huddled in the center of the room. The second man came over to Nakota and grabbed her by her long-braided hair. He stuck his finger at her the way she had at him a few minutes ago. There was a tap on the door. Nakota was forced out the door and into the main room along with Gina and another girl.

This left only Lani in the first room. She could see Keisha and Kara lying on the floor in the other room, naked, crying and bleeding. The first black man went into the room and shouted at the girls in the strange language. There was the tap at the door once again. A few moments later he emerged from the room with Keisha and Kara. They were clothed. Kara was carried by the man and Keisha was walking in front of him. The second man grabbed Lani and forced her into the main room.

They were ushered to the platform in the same manner as the other girls had been. When they got to the top of the platform Keisha saw all the other girls in the vat as the rubber ring inflated around her ankles. Most of the girls were lifeless in the water. A few of the girls were still kicking and writhing in the water and occasionally managed to make it to the surface for some air. Keisha's screams in the language of the black men did no good. She reached for Kara's hand to comfort her. The elastic strap was suddenly placed around her arms and bound them to her waist. She was unable to touch her hysterical sister. Lani understood what was happening and did not cry out as the tube was inflated around her ankles.

In a few more minutes the dastardly deed was completed. The bodies of the twenty-four girls were carefully fished from the saltwater pool and loaded onto the C-130. On the rear ramp now were several skids of airline seats. Each girl was placed in a specific seat and the seat belt was fastened. An un-inflated life preserver was placed over the neck of each girl.

The C-130 took off from the dirt strip and was in the air and bound for Miami. The pilot kept his radio tuned to 124.3, the Orlando Tower frequency. He smiled when he heard the words he was waiting for "Oasis One Heavy, you are cleared for takeoff Runway One-Eight Left," and then the reply of his good friend "Cleared for takeoff Runway One-Eight Left, Oasis One."

The C-130 pilot switched his radio to the Miami Approach Control Frequency. The C-130 remained at low altitude with its transponder set for "1200, the code of a VFR flight. The same code a dozen other small planes might be using in the area.

During the flight the seats which held the lifeless bodies of the young girls were re-positioned. The seats were freed from the skids. A large athletic mat covered the floor of the cargo area under the seats. The seats were in pairs or in threes. Some were turned on the side; some were placed on the back. Every so often the seats would be repositioned. As the blood began to settle into the lowest body part of each girl, there would be no discernable pattern as to the position of the girls at the time of death.   A coroner would be left with more questions than answers if he tried to make a determination.

The C-130 was in position near Miami when the pilot heard Oasis One announce its position and transponder 'squawk' code to Miami Approach Control. Oasis One was being routed south of Miami and then eastward out over the Atlantic and would be brought back in to land on Runway 27. The 747 jet had slowed its speed significantly to prepare for the descent and landing. He was pleased. Of all the plans they had planned, this was the one they preferred. The C-130 pilot set his second transponder to the Oasis One squawk code of 3077. He was careful to leave it in standby for now.

As Oasis One left the coastline, heading slowly east at 6,000 feet, the C-130 was on course to intercept the flight path. To the air traffic controller, two blips were approaching one another separated by 3,500 feet. It was nothing to be concerned about. The Mode C transponders on each plane informed the controller of the altitude of each plane.

A brief exchange and greeting between the pilots of both planes took place on a pre-arranged frequency. The pilot of Oasis One looked at his altimeter and began a rapid descent. The pilot of the C-130 simultaneously began a rapid climb.

Very soon they were nearing the same altitude on a near collision course with one coming down and one going up. As they passed within a few hundred feet of each other, a misleading set of readings continued to appear on the radar screen of the air traffic controller - Oasis One at 6,000 feet, and a VFR flight at 2,500 feet.

On the ground, a team of accomplices generated a wideband signal interfering with Miami's normal radar display for several seconds. It would take days or weeks to sort through the recorded data of the air traffic control radar system. Someone would have to know exactly what to look for to decipher what had actually just happened.

The dangerous maneuver was over in a few minutes, and Oasis One continued its flight out into the Atlantic at 2,500 feet squawking 1200. The blip on the radar screen may have been abnormal for a typical VFR flight, but who was going to notice given the confusion?

The C-130 was cruising now at 6,000 feet squawking 3077, on the course mandated by Approach Control for Oasis One. The C-130 proceeded on course for several more miles and then began to descend. The co-pilot of the C-130 left his seat and climbed down the stairs into the cargo area.

He instructed the four black men to open the rear cargo ramp. The life vests of the girls were inflated. The seats containing the dead girls were thrown into the ocean below. Next, the luggage rained down from the C-130.

He motioned the men to move some of the bales of marijuana from the front of the cargo area to the rear. As they did that, one by one, the co-pilot struck the men in the head with a pipe. He moved the unconscious men to the back of the cargo area and kicked all four of them out the rear ramp.

The co-pilot strapped on his parachute. He picked up a can of aviation fuel and poured it around the cargo area. He took his knife and poked some holes in the can and pitched it out the rear of the plane. He made his way to the rear ramp, removed something from his pocket, pulled the release and threw it into the forward cargo area. The whole inside of the plane erupted into flames. He jumped out.

A few more words were briefly exchanged on the radio between the pilot of the C-130 and the 747.

"Oasis One, this is Miami Approach Control," came the professional, calm voice of the air traffic controller at the Miami Control Tower. There was silence.

"Oasis One, this is Miami Approach Control." the voice of the controller now had a slight tone of urgency about it. There was silence.

A few moments later "Oasis One, this is Miami Approach Control. Say your altitude and position." The sense of concern in the controller's voice was building now. He could see on the radar screen that the altitude of the blip squawking 3077 was dropping fast. The plane had dropped below the 3,000-foot floor of the Class B Terminal control area. "Oasis One, Oasis One, do you read? Oasis One, Oasis One…Oh, Shit!"

On the pre-arranged secret frequency, the C-130 pilot made a final farewell transmission to his old friend in the 747. The 747 pilot returned the greeting and offered his blessing. The C-130 pilot was descending rapidly. He headed his plane directly for the Fowey Rocks lighthouse. Moments before striking the reef near the base of the lighthouse, the C-130 pilot flipped the switch that ignited the fuel in his left wing tank. A gigantic fireball lit the night sky a few hundred feet above the Atlantic Ocean. Witnesses fifteen miles away on Miami Beach saw the fireball streak low across the southeastern sky and come to rest in a fiery inferno on the surface of the sea.

A third voice was heard on the secret frequency. It was the captain of a small ship located near the Fowey Rocks Lighthouse. The pilot of the 747 replied and there was a brief exchange between them. The pilot of the 747 made one final emotion-filled comment and then the secret frequency fell silent.

Several thousand feet below, under the cover of darkness, the crew of the small ship carried out their captain's instruction and began unloading their cargo into the ocean. The Captain surveyed the work of his crew as the flames of the C-130 wreckage burned in the distance.

Chapter 7

The trip down Haleakala to Kahului had been uneventful. Jessie drove slowly back down the hairpin turns that Dan had raced up a few hours earlier. It was almost 9:00 p.m. when Dan directed her to pull into a shopping center.

Dan hopped out of the car and ran to the electronics store. He went to the phone section and grabbed a new phone, some adapters and some telephone cord. After the clerk checked him out, he followed Dan to the door and locked it after Dan left.

"Now that was close," said Dan, as he got back in the car. "Now, how about Italian, is that okay?" Jessie nodded yes.

Dan directed her to Lucci's. They went in and sat down in one of the booths. The waitress appeared immediately to take their order.

Dan sat and stared for a while saying nothing. Finally, Jessie said "I have no children, so I cannot truly imagine how you are feeling. I have lost my mother and my grandmother and my brother. I am sure it is not the same as your own child."

"Jessie, Callie is not dead," Dan said firmly. "I will not accept that until I see her body lying in a casket, and even then, I may not accept it. I will not give up hope, and I will not allow myself to do anything but think positively that some miracle will protect her."

"I understand, Dan," she sighed. "I waited five years with the same hope for my brother and still I hope for a miracle, but I know that the miracle is too late for him."

"What happened to your brother?" Dan asked.

"His name was Adil. He died in an Israeli prison," she said emphasizing Izra-ailee when she said it. "The Jews, they killed him."

"Why was he in an Israeli prison?" Dan asked.

"He was visiting southern Lebanon. The Israeli Commandos stormed a Hezbollah location near the area where he was staying. He was rounded up with them and taken prisoner."

"Was he a terrorist?" exclaimed Dan.

"No. Why is it that Muslims are terrorists and Jews are freedom fighters, when they both fight for the same thing - the land that belongs to them?" replied Jessie. "Five years ago, he was visiting where we were born. We still have family there. I always suspected he had a girlfriend there, but he would never admit that. He never did anything against the Israeli."

'My father and my uncle were able to negotiate independence for Bukhara through some very clever diplomatic maneuvers with the Iranians, Uzbekistan, Turkmenistan and Tajikistan along with the support of the Saudis. They had both Sunni and Shia support. The Uzbek government gave in to the pressure.

After Bukhari independence, Nasrullah and my father attempted to negotiate the release of Adil, my brother, from the

Israeli prison. Some kind of prisoner exchange was arranged with the Hezbollah. My mother and father were so excited. Then word came that Adil was dead. My mother was grief-stricken and she died within the year, I say, of a broken heart. My father, too, I think has never been the same."

"Is that what I have to look forward to?" asked Dan "to die of a broken heart?"

"No Dan," said Jessie, "I believe your Jesus; he will give you your miracle."

"I pray that you are right."

It was around 10:30 p.m. when they headed for the car and the long drive up the mountain. Dan asked Jessie one last time if she wanted him to take her back to the hotel. There was plenty of time. She insisted upon staying with Dan. He drove. There was no hurry now.

It was after midnight when they reached the summit of Haleakala. They parked at the equipment shed. It was pitch dark, the sky was clear; and the Moon had not yet risen. Dan took Jessie by the hand, and they walked across the service road. They stopped and gazed up at the night sky.

"You can see billions and billions of stars from here," said Dan, as he did a bad impression of Carl Sagan. "Have you ever seen so many stars in your life?"

"It has been a long time since I have even looked at the stars," said Jessie. "In Paris, the night sky is washed out by the city lights, you cannot see so many."

He looked for the North Star and the Big Dipper to get his bearing. He found the Big Dipper in the northeast, upside down spilling its milk into the Little Dipper. In the handle of the Little Dipper was Polaris, the North Star, very low in the sky. He turned directly around to face the south.

He stood behind her with his head next to hers. He held Jessie's arm alongside his and traced the ecliptic. "That's Leo, that's Gemini and that's Taurus." His arm continued to sweep to the west, when suddenly he stopped and was quiet for a moment, his voice choked with emotion. "And that," he said, "and that is my old friend Orion, the Hunter."

Orion stood there in all his majestic glory, high in the southwestern sky, as bright and clear as you could ever hope to see him. Even the stars forming the sword of his belt were clearly visible. Dan had stopped speaking now, but Jessie could feel the emotion welling up within his body pressed against hers. "What is it?" she asked.

It was a moment before he responded his voice stronger now. "Looking at the stars like this makes me feel closer to God and closer to Callie. When the girls were little, we used to sit out in the front yard at my parent's house, a hundred miles from Indianapolis. You could see the night sky so clearly. Their grandfather and I would tell them stories about the constellations and the planets and teach them how to find their way at night. Orion was always my favorite, even from when I was a small boy. I used to tell the girls that if ever they got lost, like Orion, I would circle the globe, hunting for them for all eternity until I found them again." He paused, "I had forgotten. It was so long ago and at a time when I was afraid their mother was going to take them and go to another state where I couldn't see them."

"The signs in the sky you point out are well known to me, the Lion, the Twins and the Bull," said Jessie. "You call them by their Greek and Roman names, but they were known in Bukhara long ago. Not far from Bukhara is Samarkand, the site of an ancient Islamic astronomical observatory built by Ulugh Bek in 1420. My father taught me Tajik history, and I learned the names of the stars at his knee, in the desert of the Sudan. Different names, different stories, but the same stars. It is funny, such a long time ago, I was so small and now I remember them and the stories my father used to tell my brother and me. It was a good and happy time with my father."

"Worlds apart and yet we share the simple things in life," sighed Dan.

"Well, there was no electricity, no television and no MTV in the Sahara," said Jessie, "but today, there is satellite TV. I have even seen small dishes on Bedouin tents."

For a long time, they just stared at the stars in the sky. It was chilly, and their light jackets were barely adequate to keep them warm. Finally, they crossed back over the service road and stepped into the warm equipment shed.

Dan adjusted the satellite receiver once again and sat down next to Jessie. At 1:00 a.m. CNN coverage began. The first scene was helicopter video of a 747 vertical tail wing being hoisted from the Atlantic onto a small ship. The video cut to scenes of rescue ships pulling debris out of the ocean. Near the base of the Fowey Rocks Lighthouse, the burned wreckage of a C-130 transport plane was clearly visible. Over it all was the voice of the anchor, "Dawn brought a bitter reality to rescue ships off the coast of Miami Beach this morning. The tail piece of the Boeing 747 carrying three hundred young girls to the Super Bowl could be seen floating near the Fowey Rocks Lighthouse just fifteen miles southeast of Miami Beach."

Debris from the 747 was spread over one hundred square miles of ocean.

"A mid-air collision with a drug-smuggling transport plane is blamed as the cause of the tragedy, CNN's Brian Fletcher reports."

"The wreckage off the coast of Miami Beach has dashed all hopes of finding survivors. The ill-fated 747 was operated by Oasis and was carrying three hundred young girls, ages six to sixteen, to perform in the Super Bowl tomorrow. The plane was flying at 6,000 feet, when it began to rapidly lose altitude about 8:30 p.m. last night. Attempts by the Miami Control Tower to make contact with the plane were not successful. One air traffic controller was reported to have said that the plane just seemed to drop like a rock.

"Flames were seen as far away as Miami, burning on the ocean's surface, one witness had this to say."

An old man popped up on the screen, "I thought at first, it was a meteor or something. It was a ball of fire streaking low in the eastern sky, coming from the south. I didn't know it was a plane until I heard some other people talking about it on the beach."

Then a young couple gave their version of events. "My husband and I were walking on the beach, and I was looking right at it when, suddenly, I saw a fireball passing just over the ocean, then, it stopped and continued to burn in one spot. After a little while the fire seemed to spread."

Brian Fletcher continued, "Witnesses apparently saw the second plane catch fire and streak toward the ocean where it came to rest near the base of the Fowey Rocks lighthouse. The wreckage continued to burn for several hours as the area surrounding the downed plane was covered with burning fuel. The first rescue efforts were hampered by the flames as the Coast Guard attempted to get close to the burning plane. It was thought, in the beginning, that this was the burning wreckage of the 747. It was not until several hours after the crash that the flaming wreckage was identified as a transport plane. Reports began to come in from other ships in the area that were recovering debris believed to be from the 747. The NTSB has confirmed that luggage with nametags, recovered from the sea, match the names of some of the girls. A grisly discovery was made shortly after dawn this morning. The bodies of nine girls were found still strapped into their seats and floating among the debris. There has been no identification of the girls. We spoke with an air traffic controller spokesman about the cause of the accident."

The calm voice of the controller outlined the events "The last radio contact with the plane was at 8:23 p.m. The plane's last known position was fifteen nautical miles southeast of the Miami International Airport at 6,000 feet. Oasis One was approaching the Fowey Rocks Lighthouse located about ten miles offshore. Miami Approach Control attempted to contact the plane with instructions. There was no response. Radar contact with the plane indicated that it rapidly lost altitude and fell off the radar screen at 8:34 p.m."

"The Oasis One 747 was inside the Class B airspace when it first failed to respond to routine transmissions from the control tower. The Class B controlled airspace over the area we are talking about begins at 3,000 feet above the Atlantic and extends to 7,000 feet. No unauthorized planes should have been in that area and, if they had been, we would have had a radar indication of their presence. We are reviewing the radar data from the time of the collision, but we are puzzled by the fact that there was no radar indication of any other planes operating in the area at the altitude of the 747."

The camera came back to Brian Fletcher as he continued "Sources close to the NTSB investigation are speculating that the 747 may have run into some difficulty causing it to lose altitude and plunge toward the ocean. It is possible that the 747 struck the C-130 at a very low altitude. Bales of marijuana have been found in the wreckage of the C-130, leading investigators to believe the C-130 may have been flying very low with its contraband, in an effort to avoid detection of its flight path. It is believed the northbound C-130 struck the 747 in the side at the rear of the plane, tearing off the tail section and dumping luggage from the cargo hold into the ocean. The 747 ripped open at the tail would have sunk quickly to the ocean floor. Divers are on the scene. There has been no signal received from the black box, and the main cabin has not been found. In these shallow waters, it is expected that divers will soon locate the wreckage. For CNN, this is Brian Fletcher."

The report was chilling. Jessie looked at Dan. His face was ashen, his eyes were frozen in a blank stare. Dan switched to Fox News 'Fox and Friends Weekend', and the reports were the same. Jessie did not know what to say to him.

She reached for his hand, just as it was 7:00 a.m. Eastern, and he got up and switched the satellite dish to CBS, then NBC and ABC. For the next hour and a half, he switched from station to station. He found satellite uplink stories from local Miami affiliates including Univision and Telemundo. The visual story was the same in any language. There was little hope for survivors.

It was just after 3:30 now, "I have to call Annie," said Dan. "I should have called her before this." He went outside to the car to get the phone and wires he had bought. Jessie followed him outside. The cool air felt good. He stopped and stared at the night sky. "Well, Jessie," he said "if you believe in omens, there's one for you," and he pointed to a crescent-shaped moon in the eastern sky.

"I believe in omens," she said, "but the Islamic crescent occurs many times each month in the night sky."

She put her arms around him, and he held her close. This was the lowest moment of his life. As he held her, he caught a glimpse of Orion still high in the sky but farther west now. He sighed, and then he saw something in the night sky that did give him a glimmer of hope.

"What about that one Jess? He said softly. "It's there every night, but most Americans never lay eyes on it." It was low in the south but it dominated the sky around it. "The Southern Cross," he whispered, "Can I take that as a sign, do I dare hope this has some meaning, do you have a Muslim name for that one, too?"

She turned to the south and saw clearly the constellation he was referring to. Yes, she knew another name for it, but she was not about to tell him that and dampen his last vestige of hope for an answered prayer.

He stared at it for the longest time. "Please, Dear Lord," he cried out, "show me the way. Show me how to find her. Show me that she is safe. In the name of Jesus Christ, I pray." His body went nearly limp at her side as he turned and walked away. He stopped at the car and got the telephone equipment. She followed him back into the shed.

He quickly hooked up the telephone and called Annie but did not get her. He then called the hotel in Orlando. There was no answer in Annie's room. Finally, the hotel switchboard operator came back on and he asked if they had checked out. They had not.

He dialed his office number in Indiana. There was no cell service along Haleakala, so he couldn't use his cell phone here. He entered the code to retrieve messages. He was not prepared for what he heard.

"Dad, it's Callie. There is something goin' on here on this plane that's not right. Listen." A moment later there was static. Then he heard "Oasis One, this is Miami Approach Control." It was the voice of the controller at the Miami Control Tower. He could hear the urgency in the controller's voice. A few moments later, "Oasis One, this is Miami Approach Control. Say your altitude and position." There was a long pause "Oasis One, Oasis One, do you read? Oasis One, Oasis One...Oh, Shit!"

This was followed shortly by a transmission in another language. Dan could not make it out but it sounded like

Spanish. There was more than one voice. A short time later a third voice was heard speaking the foreign tongue. The signal was breaking up and was filled with static.

"Dad, I hope you got all that. I'm holding the earpiece up against the Cell phone. The plane has turned to the right now, and I can see something burning way down on the ocean." The signal was crackling, I'm losing the cell site signal. I'll call back when I can. Luv ya." The recording was followed by a computer-generated voice "Friday, Eight-Thirty-Four PM."

Jessie didn't know what to think. She could see the reaction on his face and that he was listening intently to the phone. She dared not interrupt him. The next call began "Daddy, Callie's plane is missing." It was Annie and she was sobbing, "It's all over TV. They're saying her plane blew up over the ocean. Call me, I'm gonna try you at your other cell phone." This was followed by the computer voice "Friday, Eight-Fifty-Three PM."

Then the next call took a long time to soak in.

"Dad, there is something screwy goin' on here. I don't know where we're at. This is the first time I have been able to get a signal on my cell phone, since I called you three hours ago. The pilot said there was a problem at the Miami airport with a plane down and that we would have to stay up here until morning before we could land. The tower kept calling us and the pilot never answered them. I think we've been headed the same direction for a couple of hours. For a long time, there were no lights down below. Once in a while, I have been able to see a coastline with lights. It seems like we're going slow; the engines sound too loud. I'm sitting in 14J and I can look right straight out my window and see Orion. I'll call you when I can. Luv ya."

Dan was smiling now. Jessie was looking at him. She didn't know what was going on. Then came the computer voice "Friday, Eleven-Forty-Five PM. That was your last message."

"Praise the Lord!" he screamed! "Praise the Lord. She's alive, she's alive!" He grabbed Jessie and gave her a big hug.

Chapter 8

Dan dialed his own office number back. He let it ring and listened to his own greeting. He looked at his watch. It was precisely 4:14 a.m. When the beep sounded, he said, "This is a test, it is precisely 9:14 a.m. Saturday," and then he hung up.

He then called his office number again and retrieved the message he had just left. The computer time stamp said "Saturday, Nine-Fourteen AM. That was your last message."

Dan was now sure there were no time discrepancies. He dialed another Indiana number. His good friend Mike answered. "Mike, this is Dan."

"Hey, Dan, what's up?"

"I need some big favors today, and I need them fast. They're only next to impossible. Can you help me?" asked Dan.

"Go ahead and shoot," replied Mike.

"I need you to get ahold of Verne at Cellular Indiana and have him get me copies of calls made on one of my cell phones in the last twenty-four hours. It's the one Callie has."

"Say again?" quizzed Mike.

Dan gave Mike the voicemail code for his office number and Callie's cell phone number and then said, "I need you to download the calls from Callie to an mp3 file and send them to me."

"Okay," said Mike.

"I need to know what cell site in the country the calls from my cell phone originated from." said Dan.

"I'll get it. It's Saturday, you know. What if he can't get into the computer records over the weekend?" asked Mike.

"Don't take 'no' for an answer. Have you heard the news out of Miami this morning?" asked Dan.

"Oh yeah, it's all over the news," said Mike.

"Callie was on that plane." said Dan.

"Oh, shit, Dan, I'm sorry."

"Don't be sorry, Mike, just get me that information. And what I tell you now must be kept confidential until I can figure out what's going on here."

"You got my word." said Mike.

"I know that Mike. I also need you to research some information on Boeing 747s. I don't know what model this one was, but the 747-400 is the biggest one I know of. I need you to find out what the maximum range is for a 747 fully loaded with fuel and with a typical load…you taking notes?

"Did you have to ask?" replied Mike.

"I guess not. I also want the range with no cargo and let's say 320 passengers at an average weight of 110 pounds." He paused for a moment. "I guess that's enough for now."

"Where you at?" asked Mike.

"Maui."

"No kidding? You need me to get this for you while you're on your way back?" He asked.

"I don't know. I am having trouble finding a flight back to Indy this weekend. And it's impossible to get to Miami because of the Super Bowl," said Dan.

"Okay, I'll get this for you as soon as I can. I see you're at an 808 number now. How do I get ahold of you?"

"I am staying at the Sheraton Maui, but don't worry about it. I'll find you. You can try my personal cell. It's after 4:00 a.m. now and I have been up all night. I am at the Haleakala Summit and, it's an hour and a half back to the hotel. I'm going to try to get all the sleep I can, then I will call you before I head to Hono."

"Okay, I'll try to get this by then," said Mike.

"Mike, other people try. You succeed."

Mike laughed "Allrightee, anything else?" asked Mike.

"Not for now, Aloha," said Dan.

"Aloha, Bye," said Mike.

Dan began to dial another number. He motioned Jessie to listen. He put the phone on speaker so they both could hear. He re-dialed his office phone and retrieved the messages again. He let her listen to part of Callie's first call, Dan interrupted "Jessie, there is a second language coming up here in a second, I want to see if you can recognize it."

Jessie heard part of Callie's call, and the tower transmissions. The signal was noisy and it was difficult to hear. A brief exchange occurred that was not in English. "Is that Spanish? Can you tell?" quizzed Dan.

Jessie tried to pick it out of the static. Some of the words were familiar but not enough for her to comprehend the message. "No Dan, it is not Spanish, and it is not Italian. It could be Portuguese."

"Portuguese!" he said, "Portuguese?"

"I think so. I am not sure but it is definitely not Spanish."

Dan listened closely again to the rest of the transmissions until Callie came back on. Jessie heard the computer voice announcing the time of the call followed by Annie's frantic message, the computer, and then Callie's second message. The fourth message was from Dan "This is a test, it is precisely 9:14 a.m. Saturday." followed by the computer voice "Saturday Nine Fourteen AM. That was your last message."

"I wanted to make sure there was no time discrepancy," said Dan. He hung up the phone.

"I would have bet my last nickel it was Spanish," said Dan.

"I am sorry, but it is not Spanish. I heard what you said to your friend. Do you really believe the plane could still be flying around out there?" asked Jessic.

Dan tried to do some quick mental math in his head. He was sleepy and was not thinking clearly. "I don't know," he said. "It's been about fourteen hours since the plane left Orlando, yeah, the plane could be in the air another couple hours yet. It depends on the configuration of the plane…it's possible."

He continued, "The thing we know for sure is that three hours after the fire started on the ocean, the plane was still in the air. It could have traveled fifteen hundred to two thousand miles by the time Callie called."

"Dan, you need some sleep, you will think more clearly after you have had some rest. The altitude also is not so good for you. I will drive."

She was right and he knew it. Callie was alive, that was enough to know for right now. He turned off the lights and the equipment he had turned on. He locked the door and placed the key back in its hiding spot on the tower leg. He walked back to the car and got into the passenger side. Jessie backed out onto the service road and headed back down the mountain.

Dan fell asleep before they hit the nine-thousand-foot level.

Jessie was sleepy too, but Dan had been through so much in the last twelve hours that she welcomed the opportunity to help him get some rest. This was her second drive down the harrowing hairpin curves and sudden turns. When she finally reached Kahului she just followed the signs directing her to Lahaina. The eastern sky was just beginning to show the colors of an approaching sunrise as she passed the first turnoff to Lahaina.

"Dan, Dan," she said, as she reached over and shook his arm.

"What is it?" he said trying to open his eyes and focus.

"We are very near the turn off to the hotel, and I didn't want to miss it," she replied.

"Oh, Ok." He tried looking at his watch, but his eyes were having trouble focusing on the numbers.

"It is almost 6:30," she said.

He looked out the windshield and said, "The turn is on up here another mile or so, I think. I'll tell you."

In another couple of minutes, he spotted it, "There it is."

She turned onto the road that took her back along the Ka'anapoli Beach hotels and turned into the entrance of the Sheraton parking garage.

They walked back to their building. The Saturday morning breakfast crowd had already filled the hotel restaurant. They heard the clanging of silverware against plates as they walked past.

They took the elevator up to their room. Jessie stopped in front of her door. Dan gave her a hug. "Sorry, I have kept you up so late," he said.

"Oh, don't worry." she said, "I need to be on Bukhari time anyway."

Dan smiled at her "See you tomorrow, I mean today, well, whenever I get up."

Dan entered his room and immediately called his office number. There were no new messages.

Dan fired up his computer and went online to his reservation service. He checked flight availability from Honolulu to Miami and found some seats had opened up on a flight leaving Honolulu at 9:25 p.m. with a two-hour layover in Los Angeles. It got into Miami at 4:01 p.m. on Sunday. That was probably too late to make it safely to the Super Bowl, or the seats would not have been given up.

He called up American Airlines and changed his ticket. There would be a $125 fare difference and re-routing charge, plus the $200 ticket change fee. All in all, only $325. That was less than he expected.

He rested his head on the pillow for a moment while the computer loaded the latest news. He saw the headline saying the body count was up to eleven. He never read the story. He was out like a light.

He was awakened by a knock on the door. He hopped up and answered it. It was room service, with breakfast, at 2:00 p.m. in the afternoon! The waiter rolled the cart in and set it up by the lanai. Dan grabbed a pen to sign the check. The waiter said, "It has already been taken care of, sir." Dan took another look at the cart. It was breakfast for two.

Dan gave him a couple of bucks and as he was leaving, Jessie walked in.

"I believe you have my breakfast," she said with a smile.

Dan grabbed the cart and wheeled it out into the lanai. Jessie pulled one of the chairs up to the table and sat down. Dan did the same.

As they ate their breakfast they both knew that their time together was coming to an end in just a few hours.

"Have you decided what you are doing yet?" asked Jessie.

"Well, no, I have been asleep. I need to call the airlines and Mike to see what he has found out. What time is your flight tonight?"

"It is at 8:05 p.m. on Aloha. My flight to Narita leaves at 11:30 p.m. and gets into Tokyo at 2:30 a.m." replied Jessie.

"I didn't think JAL had a flight leaving that late. I thought they all left in the afternoon," said Dan.

"Well, I don't know. I have never been to Honolulu before. I have always gone to Europe from America," said Jessie.

"That's 2:30 a.m. Monday morning, correct?"

Jessie thought for a moment, "Yes, it's Saturday here, and I will gain a day, So, yes, it would be Monday morning. Then I catch a 10:00 a.m. Monday morning flight out of Narita on Cathay Pacific to Hong Kong. I may spend the night in Hong Kong. I get to Dubai on Monday night or sometime Tuesday, if I decide to sleep in Hong Kong."

"Wow, so in the next forty hours or so, you will spend twenty-four hours of it on a plane!" exclaimed Dan.

She sighed, "I am used to it."

"Me, too," said Dan, "I have done it many times." Dan looked at her brown eyes and long black hair across the table, "It hardly seems possible that I met you just forty-eight hours ago."

She looked at him and smiled, "I know."

He looked at his watch and then got up for a moment to get the TV remote control. He went over to the set, turned it on and positioned it toward the Lanai. He came back and sat down. He watched a news report on KHON2 but didn't know if it was now or delayed five hours from the mainland.

The hard news had not changed much. They went through the same sequence of events outlined last night on Fox. They had now recovered the bodies of fifteen girls. Search and

Rescue attempts were continuing. Several ships that had been in the area were participating in the recovery of debris. Coast Guard vessels were canvassing the ships in the area, talking to the crew, and taking possession of the recovered luggage and debris.

"Somebody is going to an awful lot of trouble to make the world think all of these girls are dead," observed Dan; "even to the extent of killing some of them. What the hell is going on?

"There is great evil in the world, Dan; more than an American can imagine," said Jessie.

"I would hate to think there's more than I have already seen. I don't know where Callie is right now. One thing is for sure - the plane had to land or go down somewhere, and we know it wasn't off the coast of Florida."

"Do you remember what Callie said last?" asked Jessie.

"I think every word is etched in my memory," he said.

"She said she could see something out her window. Do you remember?"

"Yes, she said she could see something burning way down on the ocean."

"In the second call, in the second call, what did she say?"

Dan didn't know what she was driving at "The coastline?" he asked.

"What did she say she could see out of her window, Dan?" She was like a teacher leading a student to the right answer.

He thought for a moment, ran the call back through his mind. "Orion. She said she could see Orion."

"That's right. Callie said she could see Orion right straight out her window. You don't think that's unusual?" asked Jessie.

"No, not for Callie and not for Annie. They always look for Orion in the night sky."

Jessie was driving at something, and he wasn't getting it. "I guess I am slow here, I don't know what your point is."

She pulled a pen from her purse and said, "If you hand me your napkin, I will draw you a picture?"

She sketched the Florida peninsula on the napkin. Then she tore off a piece of the napkin and sketched a top view of a plane. "Your daughter said she was sitting in 14J." She put a dot on the right side of the plane in front of the wing. "You must learn that every single word is a treasure, everything is a precious piece of a puzzle that fits somewhere. Allah has given us eyes to see and ears to hear. We must use them. Allah does not think for us. We must do that ourselves," she paused. "It is evening in Miami. Where is Orion?"

He looked at her sketch. He raised his right hand to his face and stroked the side of his chin. If I were in Miami at 11:30 p.m., Orion would be in the southwest this time of year. We know that because that's where it was last night for us."

She took the small piece of the napkin with the plane sketched on it and positioned it northbound from Miami. A light went on in his brain. He picked up her pen and made a sketch of Orion at the bottom of the napkin southwest of Florida. He took the small piece representing the plane and drew a line straight out from Callie's seat. "You know," he said, "your field of view out a plane window is maybe 120 to 150 degrees. Let's say 120. He rotated the plane until Callie's window pointed southwest. The plane was headed southeast. He rotated the plane back and forth over a few degrees. "I see what you're getting at, Jessie. Callie's plane had to be heading somewhere between east-northeast and south for Orion to be visible out her window. I am going to have to get the exact position of Orion in the sky. I have a program on my computer that will give me that.

He looked at her with a new appreciation for just how smart she was.

"You know, I think the people of Bukhara are going to be blessed to have such an intelligent and clever Princess," said Dan.

She said nothing.

"I was able to get a flight out of Honolulu at 9:25 p.m. tonight, arriving Miami at 4:01 p.m. tomorrow afternoon. I still haven't made my Hawaiian reservations from here to Hono. I need to do that and make some other calls. I have to check out by 4:00 p.m., so I do not have much time," said Dan.

"I have booked my room for another night, so at 4:00, you can come over to my room after you check out," said Jessie.

"I may do that."

"Well, I am going back to my room to finish my packing," said Jessie, as she stood up.

"Okay," said Dan. He stood up also and they just stared at each other awkwardly for a moment. She reached out her hand to touch his and said "After while," and then turned and walked out the door.

Dan picked up the phone and called Annie. There was no answer. He left a voicemail. "I arrive Miami at 4:00 p.m. Sunday. I'll call later tonight."

He called the hotel in Orlando. There was no answer in the room. He called Mike back in Indianapolis.

"Hey Mike, have you found out anything?" asked Dan

"Oh, yeah," said Mike. "I got about a ten-page PDF file to send you."

"Tell me what you got."

"First off, got the call transferred to .mp3," said Mike, "I listened to them. I understand why you want the phone records. Verne got me the cell phone records for your calls. We owe him big time. Callie's first call was at 8:33 p.m. through the Homestead, Florida cell site. Her second call was at 12:44 a.m."

"12:44," interrupted Dan. "It should be 11:44 or earlier. That doesn't fit." He thought for a moment, "Or maybe it does."

"Oh, it does. It fits like a glove," said Mike. "That's 12:44 a.m. Atlantic Time from the Charlotte Amalie cell site."

"The Virgin Islands!" exclaimed Dan. "I didn't realize Cellular Indiana had a site there."

"I didn't either; probably leased bandwidth," said Mike. "There's more. Verne at Cellular Indiana told me that, typically, a cell phone cannot hit a cell site from a plane, due to the downward orientation of the cell site antennas. There are a few exceptions; if the plane is flying low, maybe up to 4,000 feet, or if the plane just happens to be in a minor lobe of the antenna, which is not too likely."

"So, you're saying the 747 was flying at a low altitude for at least three hours out from Miami?" asked Dan.

"That's exactly what I am saying. It was flying pretty slow too for a 747. I figure about 330 knots. It's twelve hundred miles, max, from Miami to the Virgin Islands. Flying that low and that slow, it would have been burning a bunch a fuel," said Mike.

"So, what do you figure as the range of the plane?" asked Dan.

"Dan, it's hard to say. There are so many variables. I don't know if it was a 747-400 or what. I don't know the engines. I would need to know weather patterns, tailwinds, headwinds. I just don't know," said Mike.

"I understand all that, Mike, whoever planned this wouldn't know the weather for sure, either. So, we just take that out of the equation for now," said Dan.

"Yeah, I kinda figured you would say that. The plane would have enough range to go anywhere in Europe, anywhere in

South or Central America, and anywhere on the western half of Africa, down as far as Capetown."

"Or, it could have turned around and gone to Fiji," said Dan.

"Well, yeah, I didn't really look at that. I have prepared several maps. Great circle maps centered on Miami and they step out in thousand-mile increments. I figure the absolute maximum range is 8,500 miles. Realistically, we know it flew from Orlando to Miami, then three hours or so later it's near the Virgin Islands. It's already been in the air 4 1/2 to 5 hours. I think seven or eight thousand miles is closer to reality.

Do you want me to e-mail this stuff?" asked Mike.

"I am checking out in just a few minutes. You need to send them right away."

"Hold on and I will," said Mike.

Dan could hear Mike's keyboard clicks as he was tapping out the e-mail.

"It's goin' through right now," said Mike. "It's all the calls, the cell phone printout, the great circle maps and some data on 747s. There is also a winds aloft map, showing the wind patterns and winds across the Atlantic at the time after the crash."

"Thanks, Mike, thorough as usual," said Dan. "You listened to all the calls?"

"Yep."

"Could you identify the other language?" asked Dan.

"Nope, I don't have the slightest idea. It's Greek to me?" said Mike.

"Well, I think we have ruled out Spanish. What about Portuguese?"

"Couldn't tell you."

"Okay. One more thing. Could you transfer just the foreign language stuff to .wav or .mp3 files and e-mail them to me?"

"Sure."

"And, said Dan, "could you start the DVR and record FOX."

"Been doing it since you called this morning. Got two machines going; one on CNN and one on FOX News."

"Guess you're ahead of me. That's the second time that's happened in the last half hour," said Dan.

"No, I'm not ahead of you. I just knew you would be asking for it sooner or later. You got a hell of a lot more to think about than I do."

"Okay, Mike, I'm headed to Miami, I'll get there 4:00 p.m. Sunday. I'll call you then."

"No problem. Anything else?" asked Mike.

"Yeah," said Dan.

"What?" asked Mike.

"Thanks."

Chapter 9

It was getting close to 4:00 p.m. He made a last-minute check of the room as his computer was shutting down. He headed out the door with his luggage and tapped on Jessie's door. She opened the door. "Jessie," he said, "I still need to check out and, I need to go down and print some things out. I will leave my bags here and be back in a few minutes. I also have to change my reservation on Hawaiian to tonight."

Dan scurried down to the front desk, checked out and then slipped into the business center. He took out his jump drive and printed out all the documents that Mike had sent him. He marveled at Mike's thoroughness. When he got back up to Jesse's room, he tapped on the door. She opened it.

Jesse had her bags sitting by the door. She was dressed with the beautiful white Pikake lei around her neck. She looked ready to go herself.

"You look like you're leaving," said Dan.

"I am," she paused, "with you. You said you had a 9:25 flight. I changed mine from 8:05 p.m. to 6:30, and I made a reservation for you on the same Aloha flight," said Jessie.

"I always fly Hawaiian," said Dan.

"Not tonight," said Jessie rather sternly.

"Oooh, not tonight," he whined the words, "you sound like a wife," said Dan, as he smiled, winked and looked over at the bed.

"But I am not a wife." said Jessie, "In my country, a wife is not permitted to deny her husband." She also looked over at the bed, looked back at him and said, "Is that what you desire now?"

He looked at her for a moment and shook his head, "No, do you?" he asked.

"No, Dan, I do not. It was a wonderful, wonderful thing. I will always think of you tenderly for how you made me feel. I would prefer to leave it where it is. It would only make our goodbye more difficult."

It was an awkward moment for both of them. "Aloha Airlines it is. Let's go," said Dan.

He picked up his carry-on and then looked at her four bags plus her two carry-ons. "I guess we better get some help," said Dan.

"I have already called the front desk. Someone is coming up. You can leave your luggage here, and they will bring it down to us," said Jessie.

"Okay, you're the boss," he said, as they headed for the elevator.

She checked out of her room while he went to get the car. He pulled up to the hotel entrance and saw Jessie standing with the bellman and the luggage cart. Dan flipped the trunk release and the luggage was placed in the trunk and after that was full, the rest was placed in the backseat. In a few minutes, they were on their way to the Kahului airport.

Dan handed her the stack of printed papers and said, "Your theory is being supported by some more pieces of the puzzle. Look at the cell phone printout."

"Charlotte-Amalie VI." Where is that?" she asked.

"I can't believe there is something you don't know. VI is the Virgin Islands."

"Oh," she said, "U.S. or British?"

He sighed, "United States Virgin Islands and with a cellular phone site that allowed Callie to make the call at 12:44 a.m. Atlantic time or 11:44 p.m. Eastern. Take a look at the maps."

"Oh, yes, this is an azimuthal projection with Miami at the center. Your friend is very helpful," said Jessie. "So, you have a theory now, yourself about Callie's location?"

"Not a theory, just a gut feeling. This little voice I have that gnaws at me."

"And what does your little voice tell you?" asked Jessie.

"It tells me that the plane headed east or southeast and kept on going. It did not go to Europe because if you look at the great circle map, you will note that the plane would have to be on a northeast or even a north-northeast heading to get there. If that was the destination, then why not turn northward a lot sooner than twelve hundred miles out? On the other hand, maybe you're trying to blend in with other Caribbean air traffic as long as possible. So, I think I rule out Europe. How do you sneak a 747 into Europe with all the commercial radar and NATO defense installations?"

"Go on," said Jessie.

"You said, every word is a treasure. I have been thinking about that. The foreign words - what I thought was Spanish, you say is Portuguese. If you are right, and I am waiting for you to be wrong about something, I can rule out all of South and Central America except Brazil. They speak Portuguese and it is consistent with the flight path. Just head out east along the islands of the Caribbean and follow them southeast to Brazil."

'I see. If it's not Brazil, then what?" asked Jessie.

"Africa, if it's not Brazil. Then, it's some obscure airfield in Africa where you can hide a 747 and bribe airport officials to keep their mouth shut."

She looked at him for a moment, "Then why are you going to Miami, if you are so certain she is not there."

"I don't know; to see if I can find out something. It just seems like the place to start. I need to see Annie. She has no idea that Callie may still be alive. She must be going crazy," said Dan.

They arrived at the airport and Dan dropped Jessie off at the Aloha ticket counter and told her to go ahead and check in. He returned the rental car and headed back to the ticket counter with his carry-on bag. Jessie was standing nearby. His single piece of luggage was next to her. He purchased his ticket, checked his bag, and he and Jessie walked toward the gates.

"You know, we shouldn't be talking about any of this on the plane or in the terminal where other people might hear," said Dan.

They walked together to the gate and boarded the plane. It was open seating and Dan suggested that Jessie sit by the window on the right side of the plane so she would be able to see the night lights along Waikiki. It was a twenty-five-minute flight and Jessie had to claim her bags in Honolulu. Dan rented a cart and helped her with her luggage. They walked toward the Overseas Terminal. They came to the international air carriers first. They went to the First-Class check-in line of Japan Airlines. The flight was several hours away, and the line was short. In just a few minutes, she was completely checked in.

"First Class," he said. "I should have figured that. I need to go to the Admiral's Club and change my ticket, then come back out here and check my bag. American is farther down the terminal."

"You have decided then…you are going to Miami?" she asked.

"I can think about it on the plane. I could change my mind in LA and go to Rio," he said. "That will give me a chance to study Mike's info and do some research on the laptop on every place that speaks Portuguese," said Dan.

"And if you are headed the wrong way, you have just lost twelve hours in the search for your daughter."

"Look, young lady, you've got something in that pretty little head of yours that you're not telling me. What is it?" demanded Dan.

"I have a little voice too, and it is not at peace with you going to Miami." said Jessie.

Dan stopped. He looked up at the flight board to see all the flights leaving out of Honolulu in the next few hours. He saw a 10:30 p.m. United flight that caught his attention. He pulled a card folder out of his carry-on bag and went to a telephone. He called United reservations. When he hung up the phone, he was shaking his head. "Now that's interesting. I can leave on United at 10:30 p.m. arrive Orlando 7:48 p.m. Sunday evening, leave on Delta to Rio de Janeiro at 9:30 p.m. and be there Monday morning at 5:30 a.m. I could have Annie meet me at the Orlando airport for a few minutes and then be on my way. The ticket is thirteen hundred dollars. I am surprised it's not more, but that's still pretty salty."

He looked up at the board again and saw a Qantas flight leaving at 12:30 a.m. They had just passed the Qantas counter, and there was no line. Dan walked back and talked to the agent for a while as Jessie stayed with the remaining bags.

"Wow," he said when he came back. "There is a 12:30 a.m. flight to Harare, with a layover in Sydney, and then to Harare arriving 9:20 p.m. Monday night," said Dan.

"You would go Zimbabwe?" she asked. "Why there?"

"First of all, I have friends there at a church in Harare. I have been there, and it's an English-speaking country. It's centrally located in the south of Africa, with easy connections to the rest of Africa. I can get visas to just about anywhere there. If I were going to go to Africa at all, that's where I would want to start. Just one problem," he said.

"And that is?" asked Jessie.

"$4,439 round trip or $4,047 one way."

"That is quite expensive," said Jessie. "What does your little voice tell you about that?"

"I don't know," said Dan.

"Well, you now have three options," said Jessie. "I have always found that when I make a difficult choice, and it is the correct choice, I feel instantly at peace about it. When I make the wrong choice, I continue to be unsettled."

They passed through the metal detectors and Dan pointed out to Jessie where her gate would be. They came to the elevator that took them to the ground level. The JAL first class lounge was right next to the elevator as they got off. They had to wind their way through the Oriental Garden to get to the newly remodeled Admirals Club. When they walked into the lounge, Dan showed his Club card.

"Welcome, Mr. Grainger. It's good to see you again," said Dina, from behind the reception desk. "Are you all set with your ticket?"

"No, Dina, I need to do a change. The reservation is in the system and I need to check this one bag." he said as he handed her his itinerary.

He motioned to Jessie that she could go ahead and find a seat in the club.

He was beside himself. He was racked with worry about whether he was making the right decision. He didn't really have a course of action. He just wanted to see Annie. What could he do in Orlando? How was that going to help Callie? He would just be a third-wheel in the grief of Alice and Annie. They had each other. Annie was already having a difficult time. It would just complicate life for her. He didn't know what to do.

"Oh, yes, I see it, Mr. Grainger. Uh…it looks like that will be $325 dollars. Window or aisle?" asked Dina.

"Wait!" said Dan. "I having some indecision about what to do on this, can I hold off for a little while before I purchase the ticket change?" asked Dan.

"Sure, the flight is not until 9:25. You have an hour and a half to decide, but the sooner the better, so we can get your luggage tagged and on its way."

"Okay, let me think about it?" said Dan

He picked up his old itinerary and went to find Jessie. He sat down beside her. "I didn't do the change yet. Are you surprised?"

"It does not matter what I think, Dan. It is what you think, what you feel that matters? she said.

"I am not at peace in my spirit about the Miami option. But, Jessie, Four thousand dollars! That's a lot of money, that would hurt. What if I turn up in Zimbabwe, when I need to be in Miami or in Orlando with Annie," said Dan.

"What if…, what if…, what if…? You want a guarantee? You cannot afford the four thousand dollars? It is just paper! Money is only important if you do not have it. It is not important if you do," explained Jessie.

"Well, I don't have it. So, it's always important," said Dan.

"You have life insurance on Callie?" Jessie asked.

"Yeah, $50,000 plus another $10,000 rider on my policy," said Dan.

"And how much to bury her?" asked Jessie coldly.

"Uh, $12,000, I guess," he said.

"Well, there you have it, Dan," scolded Jessie. "Four thousand for the ticket, twelve thousand for the burial and you still have $44,000 worth of paper. Does that make you feel better?" she asked.

"You drive a cold, hard point, Princess," Dan shot back at her.

"You have been given a great gift. You may be the only one to whom Allah has revealed the true nature of the challenge. Here you are, six thousand miles from Miami, and you see possibilities that you might not see if you were there. It is the distance that gives you the perspective. There will be time for the grief later."

Her words had the ring of great wisdom. "I just don't know what to do," he said.

"There is but one man in the whole world that might stop this elaborate ruse and save the lives of many girls. And because you are paralyzed by your own grief…you shrink from your destiny?" said Jessie. "You know what I say to you? Snap out of it!"

He remembered his own words. He looked at her "You know, Jessie, you will find that I give advice better than I take it."

He got up and walked over to the counter where Dina was sitting. "Dina, can you make a reservation for me on another airline?" he asked.

"Yes, Mr. Grainger, I can do that. Is this for tonight?"

"Yes," Dan said, as he pulled out the little note he had scribbled. "Qantas Flight 4 leaving at 12:30 a.m. for Sydney connecting with Qantas Flight 63 to Harare, Zimbabwe."

Dina's eyes widened a little bit. She pecked away on the computer. "There are seats available, when would you be returning? she asked.

"I don't know, pick a date; two weeks from now. Give me a price on a one way also."

"Round-trip would be $4,439, and one way is $4,047. It would be best if I made the reservation for you and then you went directly to the Qantas counter to purchase the ticket," she said.

"Okay, if that's the best price you can get? Just make it one way and I'll go get it right now and check in," said Dan.

"Okay, Mr. Grainger, you are confirmed on Qantas Flight Number 4 leaving at 12:30 a.m., arriving Sydney at 6:30 a.m. Monday Morning, connecting to Qantas Flight Number 63, leaving at 9:30 a.m. arriving Harare, Zimbabwe on Monday at 9:20 p.m. in the evening." Dina looked up at him.

"Mahalo!" he said. He walked back to Jessie and picked up his luggage. "I'll be back in a few minutes."

As he was leaving the Club, he noticed Dina on the phone, and she smiled at him from behind the counter as he went out the door. He went to the Qantas counter and checked in. The agent asked to see his passport and Australian Visa. "I'll be in transit," said Dan, "only be there for three hours."

"Oh, yes, I see. Sorry." She tapped at the computer a little while and said, "Round trip, Honolulu to Harare, Zimbabwe connecting through Sydney. That will be $2,812."

"Say again?" said Dan.

"$2,812 round trip," repeated the agent.

Dan knew when to be quiet. He pulled out his American Express Card and handed it to her. She checked his bag clear through to Harare and handed him his boarding pass. "Have a good flight sir. Thank you for flying Qantas."

He checked the itinerary as he walked away. Sure enough, it was correct and it was round trip. A sense of great peace began to come over him. He passed through the metal detector and headed down the terminal to the open walkway. He looked to the south and high in the sky was Orion. He looked up at it and smiled. He prayed a silent prayer and asked for guidance and wisdom and the safety of Callie and all the other girls.

"In the name of Jesus, I pray, Amen," he said to himself. He now had a tremendous feeling of peace about his decision.

He called Mike. It was 1:30 in the morning in Indiana and Mike was sound asleep. "Sorry, Mike," said Dan. "I am not going to Miami after all. In four hours, I will be on a plane to Sydney, Australia connecting to Harare, Zimbabwe. I'm going to need some electronic equipment from the Cellular Indiana repair shop. I know he has some old stuff he can give us. You are going to have to sweet talk Verne to get all the equipment configured the way I need it. You also need to call Leonard in South Bend and get the shipping address of the Rejoice and Praise Church in Harare."

Dan gave Mike a list of things he needed taken care of and then hung up the phone. He walked down to a flower shop and bought one of the most beautiful and colorful leis he could find. When he entered the Admiral's Club he looked at Dina.

"YOU!" he said as he handed her the lei. "You just saved me $1,200 and a round trip ticket to boot. This is a pretty paltry display of my gratitude."

"Thank you, Mr. Grainger," she said as she placed the fresh flower lei over her head, "It is beautiful."

"Here, Dina," Dan said as he handed her five 'Something Special" certificates from American Airlines.

"Oh, thank you again, Mr. Grainger, that was not necessary." said Dina.

"And what you did was not necessary, either, it was something special," replied Dan.

He went over to where Jessie was sitting. Jessie had raised her Pikake lei up closer so she could breathe in the sweet fragrance. "This is so beautiful and the fragrance is exquisite!" she declared. "Thank you."

"No…Thank you," said Dan, "You have brought me to my senses. It looks like I will touch down in Harare about the same time you get to Dubai; unless you overnight in Hong Kong."

"I'll be thinking of you." Her manner was much softer now than it was a short time ago. "I am glad I met you, Mr. Grainger. You have also helped bring me to my senses. I am glad now to be going to Bukhara. I look forward to seeing my father again. I have stayed away too long in fear," she smiled as she looked at him. "It is time. I prefer to be at the gate early for the international flight, in case there are any difficulties."

They got up and left the Club. They walked hand in hand along the sidewalk of the dimly lit Oriental Garden, about as slowly as two people could walk. They came to a bridge and stopped for a while to look at the tropical fish swimming in the pond.

Dan pointed up above to the walkway. "That's the walkway where I first saw you just two days ago. It seems like much longer ago than that."

They began walking again toward the elevator. Jessie turned to him. "I do not like goodbyes. It is better we part here than in the terminal upstairs with all the people. Then I will go on alone."

They put their bags down and held each other tightly for a long time.

She pulled away from him and he gently kissed her on her forehead.

She pressed the button on the elevator and the glass door opened. She picked up her bags and stepped inside. Jasmine turned to face him in all of her royal beauty.

"Godspeed, my Princess," he said. "Go and be a good daughter."

As the door to the glass enclosed elevator was closing, she looked at him and said, "May the Peace of Allah be with you. Now, go and be a good dad."

Her words echoed in his mind as he watched the beautiful Princess gracefully ascend toward the starlit sky.

Chapter 10

Callie was tired. She had not slept for hours. She was fidgety and her legs ached from the long plane ride. Some of the younger girls were crying and calling for their mommies.

Callie looked at her watch. It was 7:00 a.m. That did not make much sense to her, since it had been daylight for many hours. It had been an unusually short night. She looked out her window at the sun high in the sky. They had been in the air now for twelve hours.

She was pretty sure that they had been flying over water for a long time. They were flying very high and there were clouds below them. Every time there was a break in the clouds, she could see the blue ocean dotted with the white caps of the churning waves.

The girls were free to get up and move about the cabin. The flight attendants were courteous and had served soup for dinner and fresh fruit for breakfast. The last word from the captain was that they would be landing in a few minutes. They had all heard that before. Callie wasn't buying any of it. There was something very wrong going on.

The captain came on with another announcement.

"Girls, this is the Captain. Once again let me offer my apologies for this terrible delay that we have experienced. I appreciate the patience you have shown. The Miami Control Tower has instructed us to land at Port-au-Prince, on the island of Haiti, in the Caribbean. This is necessary because we are getting low on fuel. We will land there and let you girls get off the plane and stretch your legs. Please take all of your belongings with you, so the crew can clean the plane. As soon as we refuel, and get the clearance from Miami, we will take off and go directly to Miami. I am sorry for the inconvenience."

The plane began to slow and start its descent. Callie looked out her window and could see the approaching coastline. They had been flying over water for hours and hours. There was coastline to the right as far as she could see. "That's a pretty big island," she thought. "Too big for Haiti."

Then a picturesque little seaside city came into view. She could see a harbor, with ships lined up along the docks. The city center was comprised of many pastel-colored buildings neatly aligned along the coastline. It looked kind of pretty to her.

As they got closer and passed directly over the city, it was like a mirage that suddenly turned into an unpleasant reality. The beautiful pastel buildings were run down, roofs were off some of them. Windows were broken out. Many of the city streets were unpaved and covered with clutter and garbage. The few cars she could make out were run down clunkers.

"Ooh, gross," said Callie. "Look, Karen, at all those kids playing in the mud puddles." Karen was sitting next to her and was in no mood to gawk out the window. "I don't care, Callie," said Karen, "I just want to land and get out of this plane."

Callie had heard about the appalling conditions in Haiti. As they touched down on the runway, a huge cheer erupted from the girls. The little ones had stopped crying now in the excitement of the landing. The 747 rolled down a cracked taxiway and up to a dilapidated terminal. There was a large white Air France jet parked close to the terminal. Callie knew they spoke French here so that seemed to fit.

The Oasis One 747 did not pull up to the terminal but continued down a taxiway to a separate ramp area where Callie could see several military camouflaged transport planes parked. The 747 pulled up near them and stopped. The engines were shut down. A fuel truck drove up to the side of the 747 and two black men hopped out and began fueling the 747.

The flight attendants told everyone to remain in their seats, until the girls in the upper deck exited the plane. Callie could see the girls beginning to gather outside the plane on the ramp. All the girls had their Oasis-supplied backpacks with them. In a little while, the front section of the lower cabin began to exit. Callie and Karen got up and grabbed their things.

There was no jetway. There was a huge roll-around staircase next to the door. She heard the girls in front of her oohing and ahhing as they stepped on the stairs. When she stepped out the door, she did the same "Oh, Geez!" exclaimed Callie, "It's a blast furnace out here!"

It was humid and hot and must have been a hundred degrees.

"Oh, shit, I can't stand this crap," said Callie. The afternoon sun beat down on the girls, and the pavement was hot enough to fry an egg. Callie had only been outside for a few minutes, and already sweat was rolling down her forehead and into her eyes. The girls jockeyed for a position in the shade next to the plane.

Several black men came out of a nearby hangar, carrying boxes of water bottles. They began handing a water bottle to each girl. The girls were happy to get it, and soon there were dozens of girls guzzling the water from the bottles.

When Callie and Karen were handed their bottles, Karen started to open hers. "Hold it," said Callie. She took the bottle from Karen and looked closely at the lid to see if it was sealed.

"Looks okay. My dad always says, 'when you're in a Third-World country, don't drink the water. Keep your fingers out of your mouth and out of your eyes," said Callie.

She looked carefully at the label on the bottled water. "My dad says bottled water is okay if it's from the U.S., Israel or France, otherwise, don't drink it," said Callie. "Hey, this says Bottled in France."

She gave the bottle back to Karen. She opened her own bottle. It wasn't very cold but it was wet. The girls were milling around the plane laughing and giggling. Callie looked up at the plane and could see that there were many girls still on board. She looked at the staircase and no one was coming down. She looked at the group of girls on the ground and estimated it was about half the group, maybe 150 girls. A bucket truck had pulled up to the rear of the plane. Two workmen were raised into the air and began peeling the Oasis logo off of the vertical tail wing.

Callie looked back at the Oasis staircase and watched as two Middle-Eastern men escorted Miss Calloway, the dance coordinator, down the stairs and across the tarmac to a corporate jet. She didn't look happy. Miss Calloway kept looking over at the girls with a helpless look on her face. Her long red hair was blowing in the wind. Callie suddenly felt very sorry for her as she watched Calloway forced into the small jet.

A group of soldiers in dirty dark green uniforms was approaching. They carried some type of automatic weapon with bayonets on the end. The soldiers spread out and began to herd the girls toward several transport planes. The soldiers were shouting at each other and at the girls in some foreign language. Callie thought it sounded a bit like Spanish, but she knew it was not French. She didn't know where she was, but she knew it wasn't Haiti.

Some of the girls were screaming as the bayonets were poked in their direction and the guns were pointed at them. Some of the girls fell down. Callie stopped and helped one little girl who was still calling for her mommy. "What's your name?" she said.

"Amy," the little girl said weakly.

"You stay with me, Amy," said Callie, as she grabbed Amy's hand and walked toward the transport planes. Callie looked around at the soldiers. Many of them were very young and very, very black. About one-fourth of the girls were herded up the rear ramp of one of the planes. More girls were herded into the second plane.

The cargo area was cramped and there was no place to sit down except on the hard floor. There were about seventy girls crammed into the cargo area like sardines. A basket was handed around that contained packages of foam ear plugs. A few moments later the rear ramp was raised and the engines started. It was deafening inside the plane. Some of the girls put their hands over their ears to try to block out the noise. Others struggled to get the packages open and place the ear plugs in their ears.

In a few minutes, the plane began to move and many of the girls were tossed to the floor. Callie was holding on to a pipe along the wall on one side of the plane. She was also trying to keep Amy from falling down. Soon the plane was in the air and ascended rapidly. Callie finally blurted out loud what she had known for hours. "We've been kidnapped!"

"What?" said Karen as she tried to hear "What?"

"We have been kidnapped!" screamed Callie.

It was no use, Karen could see Callie's lips move but she couldn't hear her. The sound of the engines made conversation impossible. Callie helped Amy with her ear plugs before she put in her own. There were little girls and big girls crying and screaming all over the plane. But you couldn't hear them. Some were nursing scraped knees from falling on the floor. In a short while, the plane leveled off, and it was possible to stand without holding on to anything.

After a little while, the girls found they just could not stand any longer and one by one they assumed an uncomfortable sitting position on the hard floor of the cargo area. Minutes turned into hours. Callie kept looking at her watch. It was hot and stuffy in the plane and there was little ventilation. Sometimes it was hard to breathe. When the plane finally began to slow down and descend, they had been in the air nearly four hours.

Callie felt the plane touch down on a very rough landing surface. It taxied for a while and finally came to a stop. When the ramp was lowered, the blast of hot, fresh air from outside was a relief. The girls were ordered down the ramp and out of the plane. Callie looked around. The sun was low in the sky but still maybe an hour from setting. She saw a second transport plane coming in for a landing. She could see the runway now. It was just a dirt strip that had been cleared by some bulldozers. The bulldozers were sitting not far away.

She looked around at the strange surreal surroundings. They were in a clearing of a forest. The trees were broad-leafed and jungle-like in appearance. It was not a dense forest and the trees were spaced from each other. It was beginning to get dark now. In a few minutes, the last two transport planes circled the clearing and landed on the dirt strip.

There were now four transport planes sitting in the clearing. Callie surveyed the situation. There were three metal Quonset huts near the side of the clearing and there were two footpaths leading away from the clearing. Eventually, all of the planes were unloaded and the group of girls stood helplessly in the center of the jungle clearing. A small contingent of black men in dirty, dark-green uniforms stood near the planes.

A tall, thin, white man came forward. He was carrying an automatic weapon in his right hand and a megaphone in the left. He fired several bursts of gunfire into the air. Pandemonium broke out. Girls were screaming and yelling and running everywhere. Callie yelled to Karen "Get down!" and they both hit the dirt. Callie pulled little Amy down with her.

The gunfire had stopped but the girls were in complete disorder. Some had run to the edge of the clearing but had stopped when they reached the beginning of the uncleared jungle. The noise and crying of the girls had begun to subside when one group of girls began screaming at the top of their lungs.

Callie raised her head up from her prone position and looked over at the girls. They were running from a spot along the edge of the jungle. An ugly-looking creature emerged into the clearing. It was more frightened than the girls. It was the size of a pig and about as muddy. It scurried around the clearing in a clumsy trot with its tail standing erect as a flagpole. A small clump of hair at the end of its tail even looked like a small flag as the creature darted down one of the footpaths.

The white man laughed. "Girls, girls," he said, "perhaps, you would like to chase our little friend down that path to wallow in the river with him. Feel free to do so. He would make a fine pet, but do watch out for the crocodiles along the river."

The girls had become quiet. The man fired into the air once again. A few of the girls screamed. Many did not.

"Excellent," he said. "You are learning. You can scream all you want; as loud as you want. There is no one to hear you. There is no one to even understand your language."

Callie held Amy and was patting her on the back trying to calm her.

He fired another burst into the air. A few girls let out a short scream.

"You can all get up. It is safe, you have nothing to fear. Look around you," he said, pointing toward the three metal buildings, "For the next few days, this will be your home, and after that we will be taking a journey."

He walked over to one of the older girls and stared directly at her. "You Americans are spoiled. You are soft. You must be taught to live like the rest of the world lives. You must be toilet trained and learn not to make a mess in your own nest. We have no extra-soft Charmin for you to use. You must learn to use what you have available to you. This woman will assist you in your training." He motioned to a white woman in a white uniform that had stepped from one of the metal buildings.

One of the older girls darted from the clearing toward the other footpath. A soldier threw down his gun and raced after her. He tackled her bringing her to the ground. "No, No, No!" yelled the white man, "Do not harm her," and then he added a phrase in another language.

He walked over to the girl and helped her up. Her knee was bleeding. Other soldiers had gathered around.

"Are you all right?" the white man asked the girl. She didn't say anything. "Let me apologize for the clumsy actions of my subordinates." The soldier that had tackled the girl stood at attention next to her. The white man handed his gun and megaphone to the white woman. He picked up the soldier's gun from the ground and slammed the butt of it into the soldier's gut. The soldier bent forward in agony. The white man raised the butt hard into the face of the soldier and knocked him backward. The soldier fell writhing and bleeding on the ground.

He threw the gun down and took his gun and megaphone from the woman. He continued to walk among the girls and spoke into the megaphone. He would stop once in a while and stare at one of the older girls. He walked over to one of the younger girls that was sobbing quietly. He placed his hand on her cheek. "We do not want you girls to become ill. Your health is very important to us. There are many things here that can make you sick."

He motioned to the soldiers and said something in the other language. The soldiers began to herd the girls into one large group. The white man walked around the group and then separated them into three groups of approximately the same size.

"That will do," he said. "I want each group to go into their own building and get settled. There is insect repellant that you must put on and plenty of bottled water to drink. Now go!"

Like sheep, the girls were herded into the three buildings. There were fans blowing through the building, and it was clean inside. There were not any beds or cots. But a large section of the floor was covered with a soft mat. In the corner of the building were several small pots. There were about a hundred girls crammed into the building. It was hot but the fans supplied a welcome breeze.

In a few minutes, the white woman came into the building. She walked around the room surveying each girl. A few of the girls had some scratches on them from hitting the dirt outside. The woman stopped, cleaned their wounds and put some medicine on them. "It is best to let the air get to it," she said. "There is water over there." She pointed to one end of the building. Some of the girls had already noticed and were drinking the bottled water. Bottles were quickly handed around to the rest of the girls.

"Girls," the woman said. "Girls, in order to prevent illnesses during your short stay here, it is necessary to give you a vaccination. Now I want you to form a line over here, and we will get this over with as quickly as possible."

The soldiers set up a small table, as the white man entered the room with his weapon and a notebook. He sat at the table with the machine gun at his side and the notebook opened to a list of names. The woman positioned herself next to the table with her medical supplies and prepared a hypodermic needle. As each girl came forward, there was surprisingly little resistance. Some cried and screamed like stuck pigs when they received the shot. A clean needle was used for each girl.

The woman rubbed a damp cloth lightly over the exposed skin of the girls. "It was insect repellant," she explained. It smelled bad and the girls cringed when she put it on them. The process seemed to calm the younger girls who were screaming the loudest from the shot.

Each girl was asked her name. The man at the table searched the list until he found the name and checked it off. A plastic medical type ID bracelet was placed on each girl's wrist. The bracelet had the girl's name on it.

Callie was in line and thought about trying to resist the shot. She didn't know what she could do in the face of the armed soldiers and the small confines of the building. As she approached the table in line, she could read the names upside down on the list. She tried to find her name but the first page did not go all the way to "G." She looked under the "B's" for Brooks and, sure enough, it was there.

As her time for the vaccination got closer and closer she tried to decide what to do. There was something deep within her that told her that keeping her true last name to herself might be best. She struggled with the choice. When the man asked Callie her name, she said "Callie Brooks."

Karen was standing right behind Callie and started to react, but Callie reached back and softly pinched her. Karen remained silent. The man checked Callie Brooks' name off of the list. When the pinprick of the shot came, it wasn't that bad. Amy told her name to the man and began crying. Callie held her and comforted her when Amy received the shot. Amy let out a yelp and began crying even louder.

And so it went, until all the girls had been checked off the list, given shots and covered with insect repellant. Callie, Karen and Amy had sat down on the floor mats. Some of the girls were still crying. Many of them were all cried out and just stayed quietly on the mat. Some of the girls had gone back outside.

"I hope that shit they gave us was on the level and not some kind of crazy drug."

Amy had fallen asleep on the mat. Callie decided to go outside. She picked up her belongings and headed for the door. Karen picked up her stuff and followed Callie outside. There were some dim amber lights strung up forming walkways in the clearing. They were similar to a string of Christmas lights. The girls were free to walk outside and go into the other buildings. Callie peeked inside one and it looked identical to the one they had just come from. It was pitch dark outside and the stars were shining very brightly in the night sky.

Callie looked for the Big Dipper and the North Star but couldn't find them. Then she spotted Orion, or, at least thought she did. It just didn't look quite right. It was too high in the sky. Callie started twisting and turning her neck to get a different view. Karen looked at Callie "What are you doing, Girl?

"I don't know. The stars look different," said Callie.

Karen looked up at them. "They look the same to me," she paused for a moment. "Callie."

"What?" said Callie.

"How come you told them your name was Callie Brooks? That's your mom's name," asked Karen.

"Well, I kept trying to get that straightened out with Oasis and they never did get it right. I just decided that the less these people know about me the better."

"What do you think's going to happen?" asked Karen.

"We've been kidnapped," said Callie, "I don't know who all is in on it, but the pilot definitely is. He didn't answer the control tower in Miami, he lied to us for hours when we were in the air, he lied to us when we landed, and he gave these people the passenger list."

"Do you really think so? Callie, I'm scared?" said Karen.

"I'm scared too. Whoever planned this has been planning it for a long time and has gone to a whole bunch of trouble to pull it off."

"Where do you think we are?" asked Karen.

"Well, it ain't Haiti," said Callie. "Haiti couldn't be more than a couple of hours different than Miami. By my watch, it's still the middle of the afternoon in Florida. It's been completely dark here for several hours."

Callie continued to look at the night sky. She turned her head one way and then the other as she and Karen talked.

"What do you think's going to happen to us?" asked Karen, her voice starting to crack with emotion.

About that time, a small beeping sound could be heard from Callie's backpack. "Oh shit!" said Callie as she fumbled to get her cell phone out of her backpack and stop the sound it was making. She pulled the cell phone out of her backpack, pressed a button and looked at the display screen.

"It's a low cell, I need to charge the battery," said Callie.

"What's the point?" asked Karen "Who's going to call you out here? What would you do anyway, call home on your shoe?" sneered Karen.

I can't allow the batteries to run down. The phone will keep searching for service and run down quicker." Callie switched the phone to vibrate and muted all the alert tones and then turned it off. "I have got to find a way to charge the battery. It's our only possible means of communication." When she bent over to put the phone back in the backpack she looked up at the sky from a different angle.

"That is Orion!" squealed Callie "and there's Gemini." Callie stood back up and looked at the stars again. "That is Orion. He's above Gemini. He should be below it, and he's upside down."

"Who is Ryan? What you talking about?" demanded Karen "How can you be so calm, stargazing like we're on a Girl Scout trip. We've been kidnapped and you've taken up Astrology?

"You mean Astronomy," said Callie. "I have to stay calm and use my head until he gets here."

"Who?" asked Karen. "Do you mean Ryan?"

"No," said Callie, "My dad."

Chapter 11

Annie could not understand why she had not heard from her father. It was Sunday morning and he had left a message at 9:00 p.m. last night that he would call. Annie had not slept much.

Alice was not doing well. Part of the time she sobbed, the rest of the time she just stared. She had finally fallen asleep and Annie wanted to let her sleep as long as she could. There was a briefing scheduled for the families at 10:30 a.m. in one of the meeting rooms.

The phone rang and Annie darted for it, hoping it was her dad.

"Annie Grainger, please," said the male voice.

"Yes, this is Annie?"

"Annie, this is Mike."

"Yeah, Mike, how come you're calling me?" she asked

"Your dad called me last night about 1:30 in the morning and asked me to call you this morning," said Mike

"Yeah, he's coming into Miami at 4:00 p.m. We've been trying to get a rental car and get down there to meet him. I guess you heard about Callie's plane?" said Annie.

"Yes, I have. There's been a change in plans, Annie. He's not coming."

"What do you mean not coming? Is he coming here, or is he going to Indy?" asked Annie.

"Neither. Now, I just need to tell you exactly what he told me to tell you."

"Mike," Annie said suspiciously, "What's going on. Where's my dad?"

"Annie, listen. I'm sorry about the situation with your sister," said Mike.

"Situation?" she said, "What do you mean, situation?"

Mike sighed "Let me start over. I have a message for you from your dad. He told me to tell you to keep this to yourself."

"You mean don't tell Mom," Said Annie.

"Well, I suppose. I don't know," said Mike.

"Well, just get to the point," said Annie.

"Your dad is on a plane to Sydney," began Mike.

"Sydney!" exclaimed Annie. "Why is he going to Australia?"

"He's not really. That's just the fastest way he could get to Harare, Zimbabwe," said Mike.

Annie wanted to react. She looked at her mom. She didn't want to wake her. "Why did he go there, Mike?" but already her mind was leaping to a conclusion. There was nothing that would have kept her father from coming straight to Florida. Nothing except…"

"Your dad has a theory. More than a theory really, that Callie is alive and well; that the entire plane has been hijacked and flown to Africa," said Mike. Mike paused. He had not realized how crazy the whole idea sounded until he actually spoke it.

Annie started crying, with joy at first, but then she started thinking about the seventeen girls they had found. She wanted to believe. "Mike." she said, "How can that be? They have found some of the girls."

"Annie, I am sorry. I haven't handled this too well," said Mike. "It is vitally important that you keep this confidential. No one must know we suspect anything until we figure out who is behind it."

"Tell me how my dad came up with this idea? What does he know?" demanded Annie.

She was her father's daughter. She was zeroing in on the problem and was not going to let go until she got a straight answer.

"Okay, Annie," said Mike, "Callie called from the plane and left a message on your dad's office voicemail at 8:34 p.m. Friday night. Then you called about twenty minutes later with the bad news."

"Yeah," said Annie trying to remember the time frame.

"Callie called again at 11:44 p.m. and left a message. This was three hours after the plane supposedly crashed into the ocean. I have the voicemail. When you get back you can listen to it."

Annie didn't know what to think.

"What about the girls they found? What about them?" asked Annie.

"Your dad thinks that they were never on the plane, and that they were deliberately killed as a decoy. He believes the luggage and wreckage are all part of an elaborate scheme to kidnap the rest of the girls."

"This is unbelievable," said Annie. "When do you think he will call me? asked Annie.

"I don't know. He gets into Harare on Monday evening late."

"Okay, anything else?" asked Annie.

"Yeah, don't tell anyone," Said Mike.

"I hear you." said Annie.

"Okay, bye."

"Bye," said Annie.

She hung up the phone.

"Mom, Mom!" she screamed. "Dad thinks he knows where Callie is!"

Alice was groggy but the excitement in Annie's voice caused her to immediately become alert. "What is it, Punkin'?" she said.

Annie told her the whole story. Everything Mike had said and everything her dad had said in the message.

"I sure hope your dad's right," said Alice.

"Oh, he's right," said Annie. "He wouldn't go running off halfway around the world if he didn't really believe it was true."

"I don't know about that," said Alice "I have seen him do some pretty stupid shit."

"I don't want to hear it, Mom." said Annie.

The briefing is in a little over an hour. We need to get ready. Dad's theory is the only hope we have, and I'm clinging to it and that's all there is to it," said Annie. "You make sure you don't say anything to anybody about this."

"I won't Punkin', I won't," promised Alice.

A large meeting room had been set up on the second floor. When Annie and Alice stepped off the elevator there were hundreds of parents milling around in the hall. A table had been set up for name tags. Annie and Alice each filled out the tag and stuck it on. Oasis had supplied coffee and donuts.

People were standing around in groups, munching on donuts and talking about the accident.

Annie and Alice hadn't eaten. They helped themselves to some donuts. Annie didn't drink coffee so she just had water. They talked to some of the other parents. Everyone was nervous. Some had clearly given up hope and imagined that this was going to be the official announcement that all the girls had died. Others prayed in small groups.

Annie's optimism about her dad's theory was beginning to dwindle in this sea of despair.

"Hello, Annie," said a deep male voice "How are you holding up?"

Annie turned around to see two tall African-American men standing near them. "Mr. Campbell," said Annie, "Okay, I guess, I don't know."

Mark Campbell motioned toward the young man standing beside him. This is my son James. He drove down from Atlanta yesterday. James extended his hand to Annie "It's Jimmy," he said, as he shook her hand. His nametag also said Jimmy.

"Hi, I'm Annie Grainger and this is my mother, Alice Brooks."

"Hi," Alice said and forced a small smile.

"Hi," said Jimmy, as he shook Alice's hand.

"They have one young lady on the plane. Callie, the young lady I told you about. She helped Keisha the other day."

"Oh, yeah," said Jimmy, "I remember. I talked to Keisha right after that on the phone. She certainly thought a lot of your sister; of Callie."

Their conversation was cut short by an announcement that everyone should take their seats. The four of them walked into the meeting room. Mark and Jimmy found a couple of seats on the aisle toward the back of the room. Alice wanted to sit closer to the front and they found seats farther down the aisle.

A man in a suit stood at the podium waiting patiently for everyone to be seated. Several women in business suits were roaming around the room, looking at nametags, as people were being seated. Once in a while, they would usher someone out of the room.

In a few minutes, most of the people had settled down and the room was becoming quieter. The man at the podium seemed satisfied to let the crowd settle down on their own. Finally, one of the women who had been roaming around the room came up to him and said something to him.

"We would like to get started," he said. "I am deeply sorry for the tragic circumstances which have brought us here today. You have been asking a lot of questions and we at Oasis have done our best to work with the families during these difficult times. We have had very little information ourselves, but we have tried to share what little we knew."

"At 5:00 p.m., there will be a press conference in Miami. Officials of the FAA and National Transportation Safety Board will be answering questions surrounding the accident. We are not equipped here this morning, nor are we qualified, to answer many of the questions that you may have. We have been authorized by the FAA and NTSB to make an announcement regarding search efforts and the status of the passengers of the plane."

"It is my sad duty to announce to you that no survivors have been found, and it is believed that all the passengers and crew aboard the plane have perished."

A gasp went out from the family members in the audience. Many began to cry and sounds of grief permeated the room. Alice began sobbing loudly but she had cried so much already that the sounds she was making quickly subsided. Tears rolled down Annie's cheeks as she tried to comfort her mother. In a few minutes, an eerie calm came over the room. The man at the podium began speaking again.

"On behalf of Oasis, I want to extend our deepest condolences over the loss of your loved ones. We will do everything we can over the next few days to help you and assist you in every way we can. The remains of seventeen passengers have been recovered. Search and recovery efforts are continuing. Seventeen of the girls have been identified."

Shortly, demands came from the audience for the identity of the girls.

"The family members of the seventeen girls have been informed and have been taken to another location," the spokesman said.

"Still the crowd clamored for the names."

"We do have the names and pictures of the girls which we supplied to the FAA. If you will be patient, we will get those."

A few minutes passed and then a woman brought a stack of paper into the room and placed it on a table near the podium. She took one of the papers and handed it to the spokesman.

"We have about a hundred copies of an information sheet that have been prepared for the press. It contains the names and pictures of the seventeen girls. That is not enough for everyone to get a copy; I will read you the names. He began rattling off the name, age, and hometown of each girl. Each name was greeted with a reaction in some part of the room.

Annie sat motionless as each name was read. Each name made the tragedy more real, more unbearable. Her father's theory seemed less believable with every name that was read. Then the spokesman said the names "Kara Campbell, age six and Keisha Campbell age eleven from Anderson, Indiana."

Annie turned around to look down the aisle. The seats that Mark and Jimmy had been sitting in were vacant.

After reading all the names, the spokesman once again offered the condolences of Oasis. He told the somber audience that several members of the clergy were on hand to offer counseling to the families. The meeting ended with a simple non-sectarian prayer.

Annie immediately scooted up the aisle and grabbed a few copies of the handout. She looked at the faces of the seventeen girls. Many of them she recognized from the last few days of practice. She hadn't known their names. Then she stared at the little faces of Kara and Keisha. It was almost more than she could bear.

"What was worse?" she thought to herself. "To see Callie's face on this sheet or to still have hope for a miracle?"

She decided she would choose to cling to her father's belief in a hijacking.

It would postpone her loss of sanity for a while. She and her mother went back up to the room. There was a news conference scheduled for 5:00 p.m. in Miami. Annie had press credentials from the Ball State school paper. She wanted to go.

She began calling rental car agencies again. Everyone she called had the same story. She was too young. She had to be twenty-five years old. Some required just twenty-three. She had to have a major credit card. She had a VISA with a small credit limit, but she still wasn't old enough. Alice did not have a major credit card, so she couldn't rent the car either. The only way was to put down a three-hundred dollar cash deposit. They didn't have that.

She flipped on the news. Most of it was the same old, same old story. They were reporting that family members in Orlando had been told not to expect any more survivors. There continued to be interview after interview of witnesses who had seen the flames over the ocean. They had video shots of watercraft of all sizes participating in the search for bodies and debris. Search efforts were being hampered by choppy seas.

They were interviewing Coast Guard officials, small boat owners and ship captains. There was a report that four men had fallen overboard Friday night while trying to recover debris from the plane. They were feared drowned. They had an interview with the captain of the ship "Lobito." He did not speak English well, and an interpreter translated what he was saying. He was the captain of the ship that had lost the four men. There were cutaway shots of the mostly black crew members working on the ship and the ship's cranes. There was a large pile of luggage, the vertical tail wing and other plane debris on the deck that the Lobito had recovered from the accident site.

The captain of the Lobito explained that they saw the fiery explosion in the sky on Friday evening and departed from their course to see if there was any aid they could offer. They found some debris and bodies as soon as they were on the scene. In the excitement and confusion of the recovery efforts, four of their crewmen were swept overboard. The bodies of the crewmen had been recovered. The Coast Guard and NTSB had boarded the Lobito to inspect the recovered items. They took custody of the remains of the girls and the four crewmen and transported them to the Dade County Coroner's Office.

They now had pictures of the seventeen girls on the screen. One by one, they went through the name and age of each girl and identified her hometown.

There was Gina from Brooklyn; the Native American Nakota from Arizona; and of course, there were Kara and Keisha Campbell, the two sisters from Anderson, Indiana. Annie watched them display a full-color picture of each girl on the screen. It was only seventeen girls, but the list seemed agonizingly long. They were from every region of the country, every race, color and creed. What a cross-section of America they represented.

Annie turned the volume down on the TV. She called her dad's house again. There were no new messages. More and more it kept nagging at her to go to the press conference. She decided to try calling the bus station.

After a little thought, she discarded that idea. Even if she could get to Miami, how would she get to the news conference? How would she get back to Orlando to fly back to Indiana with her mom? She was getting hungry. She had not eaten since the donuts.

She woke her mother up long enough to see if she wanted to eat. Alice did not. Annie went down to the hotel lobby. She wanted something light. All the restaurants were crowded. Then she remembered the snack shop by the pool.

The snack shop was not crowded, and it felt better to be outside, anyway. It was warmer today than it had been. Tomorrow, it was back to the Indiana winter. She bought a newspaper and sat down at a table in the far corner. She ordered the soup and sandwich combo and sat in the corner reading the Miami Herald Sunday paper.

Once in a while, she would look at the people playing in the pool. Just a few days ago, it was Callie and her together in this same pool. She wondered if this is what it was going to be like without her. Everything she did, every place she went, reminded her of her sister.

She looked up again at the pool area, her eyes tearing once again. There was a young black man getting out of the pool. He saw her, picked up his towel and came over. "Annie?" he said.

It was Jimmy Campbell. "Hi," said Annie. She didn't want to be rude, but she really just wanted to be alone.

"Do you mind if I join you?" he asked

"What could she say, No?" she thought. The man had just lost two sisters.

"Sure," she said. "Have a seat. Jimmy, I'm sorry about Keisha and Kara. I don't know what else to say."

"I know," he said. "My dad is being flown to Miami right now for a positive identification of the bodies," he paused, "Any word on Callie?"

"No, you heard what they said," she sneered "They don't expect any more survivors."

"Well, you can't give up hope," said Jimmy. "There isn't any left for us, but I wouldn't give up until they find her, if I was you."

"Now, that's something my dad would say," said Annie.

"Is he here?" asked Jimmy.

"Nope. He's, uh, well, he's been in constant contact with us. There is nothing he could do here. He and my mom are divorced; have been for a long time. He was going to try to make it to Miami this evening, but it just didn't work out."

"Miami? Why?" he asked.

"Well, knowing my dad, he would have wangled his way into the news conference and asked some really tough questions. You know, stuff like that."

"Divorced, huh? Did you see him much when you were growing up?" asked Jimmy.

"Oh, yeah," said Annie. "How's your dad doing?" she asked.

"It's hard to say, retired Marine and all; never shows his true emotions," said Jimmy. "Identifying the bodies is going to be tough. I know he loved those little girls. It's going to be very hard for their mother and sister."

"How old is their sister?" asked Annie.

"Well, their natural sister, Kima, is fifteen. She's back in Indiana. Keisha and Kara were my step-sisters. My mother died several years ago. Dad raised us himself for a long time. He got moved around a lot in the Marines. I have a real sister, a couple of years younger than me. She's in college now. There were times when he sent us to live in Atlanta with our Granny. He didn't want us changing schools so much," said Jimmy.

"Did you get to see him often?" asked Annie.

"Yeah, quite a bit, except for when he was stationed overseas," said Jimmy. Then one day he came home with a new wife and three new daughters. We weren't too happy about that."

'I can imagine," said Annie.

"It took us a while to get used to it. But you know, we were always busy with school. I don't know why it mattered so. I have never seen him as happy as he's been these last three years…now this." He began to choke with emotion.

"It's just not fair. He's a good man and deserved better than this." His eyes filled with tears and he stopped trying to speak.

Annie didn't know what to say. She was trying to deal with her own grief. She had her mother to deal with. She just wasn't in the mood to be comforting somebody else.

"So, when you guys going back to Anderson?" asked Annie.

"Well, my dad's flying back in the morning." They are doing an autopsy tonight on Keisha and Kara, and they are being flown back to Indianapolis first thing in the morning. We don't know about the funeral yet," said Jimmy.

"And what about you? When do you go back to Indiana?" asked Annie.

"Not until the day before the funeral, whenever that happens. It's just awkward being up there with the new wife and all. Good woman, but I think my dad needs his space with her and Kima. I'm just going to hang out here in Orlando the next few days."

"Here?" asked Annie "At this hotel?"

"Yep," said Jimmy, "I will drive the truck back to Atlanta and then fly to Indianapolis for the funeral."

He seemed so callous about it, thought Annie. "So, you going to Disney World or what?" said Annie a little sarcastically.

Jimmy picked up on the tone of her voice. "Look, life goes on, Annie. Don't look at me that way. I feel bad for my dad. I just didn't know those two little girls well enough to…It's not like you. Callie was your real sister."

The word hit her like a ton of bricks. "Was!"

"I refuse to accept that," said Annie. "Callie is alive and that's all there is to it. We're going to find her."

"I'm sorry," said Jimmy, "I didn't mean to upset you."

"That's OK," said Annie, "I need to be doing something to help instead of just sitting here and crying in my beer."

"Uh…that's Coke," said Jimmy.

"Whatever," said Annie, "If my dad was here, I know he would find a way to get to Miami. He would go to the briefing. He would go to the crash site. He would be nosing around everywhere looking for any clue that might help him find Callie. I'd do that too if I could, but I'm too young to get a rental car, so I just have to sit in my hotel room until we go home. I just sit there waiting and wondering."

"I'm sorry," said Jimmy, "I didn't mean to…"

"It's OK, I am sorry about Keisha and Kara. I am sorry that there is no hope left for you, but there is for Callie and I won't let go of it."

Annie got up, looked at the check and placed a ten-dollar bill on the table to cover the check and tip. She picked up her paper and went back up to the room.

Chapter 12

Once Annie was back in her room, she set the video camera up to play into the TV set in the room. The video started with them waiting to get on the plane in Indianapolis last week. There were some shots on the plane, the arrival in Orlando and all the places they had been. It was a documentary of the last few days. It showed the practice sessions. It showed the red-headed dance instructor having trouble with the ten to twelve-year-olds. It showed Callie helping Keisha and Susie with the steps they had trouble with. It showed the scramble for the buses and the procession leaving. The last shot began with the Oasis logo on the vertical tail wing of the plane, as it was leaving the gate area. As the camera widened, a light was flashing on and off at one of the windows. The camera zoomed in to reveal Callie waving out the window and then making a face. You could hear Alice's voice, as she was jumped up and down making a commotion. "There's Callie, there's Callie."

Every picture of Callie had been torture for Annie to look at, but still, she had watched the entire two hours of tape until the screen went to black. It was after 4:00 p.m. now. Annie flipped the set to FOX News. The press conference would be on soon. She woke her mother up.

Alice sat up in bed. Her eyes were puffy from all her crying and her head was stopped up. Annie had some ice water for her. Alice picked up the newspaper Annie had bought and began looking at it. On the front page was a big picture of the recovery efforts. The OASIS logo was clearly visible on the vertical tail wing of the plane, as it was being hoisted aboard the ship.

Alice threw down the paper. "Annie," said Alice.

"What?"

"Where's that flier you picked up that showed the faces of those seventeen girls?" asked Alice.

Annie went to her purse and got one of the fliers and handed it to her mother.

"Wonder how long it'll be before they hand one out with Callie's picture on it," she said.

"Mom, don't say that?" scolded Annie.

"Shit, they need to put my picture on one of these, I feel like dying right now," said Alice.

Annie said nothing.

"So, your father thinks she's still alive someplace, huh?" chided Alice.

Well, I sure hope to hell he's right. It's about time he got something right."

"Mom, please," said Annie.

"Where is your father anyway?" asked Alice not really expecting an answer.

"He went to find Callie, and he is going to find her," said Annie.

"Well, I hope you're right," said Alice "You know what I don't understand Annie?

"What's that Mom?"

"These girls. These girls in the pictures," said Alice. "You got a redhead, you got an Italian, looks like maybe an Eskimo, a couple of Asian girls, an Indian, some Hispanics and a few Blacks. I can't even pronounce some of these last names."

"Yeah, so what's your point, Mother?" said Annie.

"No blondes," said Alice. "No blondes. Hell, most those girls were blondes. Sometimes, I couldn't even pick my own daughter out of the routines 'cause they all looked alike."

Annie just stared for a moment. She went and grabbed the flier out of her mother's hands.

"You're right!" she said. "You're right." Annie went back over to the TV set and reconnected the video camera. She searched the video until she found one of the routines where all the girls were on the field. Alice was right. There was a sea of blondes. Maybe ninety percent of the girls were blondes. The other twenty or thirty were mostly brunettes. She only saw five black girls on the tape. Three of them were pictured on the flier.

Annie didn't have any idea what this meant, but she was sure it was important.

The phone rang. Annie hurried to get it. "Hello," she said.

"G'day Mate," came the male voice on the telephone.

"Daddy!" squealed Annie "Where are you?"

"I am in Sidney, Australia where it is already early Monday morning. How are you guys holding up?" asked Dan.

"Daddy, they had a meeting for the families a little bit ago. They handed out pictures of the seventeen girls they have recovered so far."

"How's your mom doing?"

"Not too good," said Annie.

"What did she say about me heading off to Africa to look for Callie?" asked Dan

"Mike said to keep that quiet and not tell her," Said Annie.

"I know he did, I told him to. Now, what does your mother think about me going off to Africa?"

"She thinks you're nuts," said Annie.

"And what about you, Annie?" asked Dan.

"I don't know…I want you to be right," she said, "but the TV…they have pictures of the tail of the Oasis plane being pulled out of the ocean. They have identified luggage from a lot of the girls, and they have seventeen bodies. It's kinda hard to hold out hope."

"Look, call Mike and have him play the voicemail for you. I am telling you that there is absolutely no way that the tail wing of the plane came off at the supposed crash site. Callie was alive three hours later and over one thousand miles east of Miami when she called. The luggage was never on the plane. The dead girls were never on the plane. It is all a part of a very elaborate ruse."

"I hear you," said Annie.

"Yeah, you hear me but you're not believing," said Dan.

"Mom noticed something in the pictures of the dead girls. I think it could be important," said Annie.

"Yeah, what?"

"Dad, almost all the girls were blondes - blue-eyed blondes, in fact. I mean like ninety percent of them. I even checked the video I shot in the last few days to be sure," said Annie.

"Okay," replied Dan.

"But every single one of the girls they've found has been a brunette or red-head. No blondes at all. Don't you think that is odd?" asked Annie.

"I sure do." said Dan, "You know somebody once told me that every single piece of information is a treasure. It is part of a puzzle that fits somewhere. How much video did you shoot?"

"Quite a bit," said Annie "We even have the plane taxiing away from the gate."

"Really? Did you get anything of them loading luggage into the plane?"

"I never thought to look. I got them loading the luggage into the truck at the hotel."

"What do you mean?" asked Dan.

"Well, the luggage was all set outside the rooms and brought down on carts by the hotel people. I saw them loading it all into the back of a truck," said Annie.

"And how did the girls get to the airport?" asked Dan.

"In buses. There were seven of them," said Annie.

"Now, that's interesting. There are luggage holds in the bottom of those buses. But they chose to use a separate truck. Look at the video again. See if you can identify the buses that the girls they found were on," said Dan.

"I don't like to look at it. It's hard seeing Callie and then; once in a while, you see a girl that you know they have found," said Annie.

"I understand," said Dan. "When do you fly back to Indy?"

"We leave in the morning. We get to Indy around 11:00 a.m.," said Annie.

"Okay, take the video to Mike right away and have him look at it. Tell him what we are thinking about the blonde girls and the truck and the bus," he paused. "You know if we could find that truck and the drivers of that truck and the bus, we might really have some proof here that things are not as they seem."

"Okay, I'll take it to Mike tomorrow." said Annie.

"One more thing Annie," said Dan.

"What?"

"I want you to call John Kosten when you get to Indy."

"The attorney?" asked Annie.

"Yes. His office is on the north side. You can get the number from the internet. Explain to John everything that has happened, including my hunch, and where I am. Take Mike with you and all the video and voicemails. It's important. We are going to need him," said Dan.

"Okay. I'll call him from the airport," promised Annie.

"I will try to call him from here and leave a message on his voicemail to expect your call. I am going to have to go now. I am in the transit lounge for another couple hours. Call Mike and listen to the voicemail."

"Okay, maybe I'll do that," she said.

"Do it…then you will believe."

"Dad, even if she is alive, she must be in great danger. We still may never see her again," said Annie.

"I love you, Annie, it's going to work out. It has to," said Dan.

"Okay, bye."

"G'day," he said, in his attempt at an Australian accent.

Dan dialed information for the 317-area code and got John Kosten's office number. His home number was unlisted. He called and got the answering machine. "John, this is Dan Grainger, I am very sorry to bother you, but I need your help and your prayers. My youngest daughter, Callie, she's fifteen, she was on the Oasis One plane that went down in Miami," his voice started to crack. How could he explain what he was thinking? It sounded unbelievable even to him. "John, I believe that Callie and all the others girls may have been kidnapped and this crash is part of an elaborate ruse to hide the kidnapping," he paused. "My oldest daughter, Annie, is flying from Orlando to Indianapolis tomorrow. She gets in at 11:00 a.m. I have instructed her to set up an appointment with you and to bring you some voicemails and other evidence that you will find interesting," he paused again. He didn't quite know what to say. "I was in Honolulu when I heard the news. I am in Sydney, Australia, now, and I am on my way to

Zimbabwe…Annie will explain. In the meantime, please pray for Callie and the other girls."

Dan hung up the phone, picked up his carry-on bag and headed for the transit lounge restroom. He noticed a Qantas agent asking passengers if they were on Flight 63. Dan mixed in with the group of passengers that had assembled to hear what she had to say.

"I am terribly sorry," she began. "Qantas Flight 63 will be delayed significantly as the result of a security concern."

"How long?" asked one of the passengers.

"We cannot answer that question at this time, but we expect it to be at least four hours, perhaps longer," she answered.

Dan did a little quick math in his head and realized that would put him into Harare after midnight and that was no good for him. He listened a while to the whining and complaining of the other passengers. Then he went over to another gate agent and said. "Excuse me, I am an American and am on the delayed Qantas Flight 63 to Harare."

"Yes," replied the agent.

"I am very tired from the long flight from Honolulu, Is it possible for me to get a visa issued and spend the night in the city and then take tomorrow's flight to Harare," asked Dan.

"That may be possible. May I see your passport?" she asked.

Dan handed her his passport from the zippered pouch of his carry-on bag. She took it and started typing into the computer. "There are seats tomorrow," she said, as she looked closely at the passport and typed some more. "You have entered Australia before I see."

"Yes, several times," replied Dan.

"Officially, you have not entered Australia yet, and are still in Immigration. We can do it. The fee for the Electronic Travel Authority visa is Australian twenty dollars, and will take a few minutes. I will arrange it for you and page you when it has been processed. I will not change your ticket until the visa has been issued. I will hold on to your passport and ticket until then."

"Thanks. I appreciate your help."

"No worries," she said.

Dan did not notice that a tall, thin man had been watching him as he had been talking to the agent. Dan picked up his bag and headed for the restroom. The man was talking on a cell phone in Arabic.

"I don't know his name," the man said. "He is an American. I followed him from Honolulu. I do not know his final destination. I had to buy a ticket on to Hong Kong. I didn't have an Australian visa and they wouldn't sell me a ticket just to Sydney. My flight leaves in a few minutes."

The man listened for a moment. "Yes," the thin man said "He was with the Princess just before she left. She was with him the two days in Hawaii. He has been talking to a flight agent here, and it looks as if he is about to leave the transit area. I won't be able to follow him." He paused again to listen.

"You have the proof?" asked the voice on the cell phone.

"Yes, I have proof," said the thin man.

"Kill the American and find out who he is," the voice said. The thin man hung up the phone and walked toward the restroom.

Dan was sitting in one of the stalls. He was tired. He wanted to get to Harare as soon as possible, but landing there in the middle of the night was not a good thing. A shower and a good night's rest in a Sydney hotel would be a blessing. He had gotten very little rest on the plane, and a clean bed was a temptation. He double-checked all of his papers and travel documents. He felt uncomfortable to be without his boarding pass and passport. He checked the cash he had with him. It was distributed between his wallet, his carry-on, and some bills were tucked into his sock and wrapped around his ankle. His carry-on bag was sitting on the floor beside his left foot. As he stood up and fastened his belt, he caught a glimpse of the tip of some object moving his direction along the floor from the next stall. He felt pressure on his ankle as it struck him.

In one mighty leap, he moved his foot to the top of the stool, grabbed the top of the stall divider and hurled himself across the top and down into the next stall. He came crashing down on the occupant; who was down on his hands and knees and had been poking the device into Dan's stall.

Dan's knees landed on the upper back of the culprit, slamming the man's head against the hard floor. The man lay motionless on the floor of the stall, knocked unconscious by the force of Dan's fall. Dan removed the object from the man's grip. It was a collapsible pointer of some type like a speaker might use when giving a sales presentation. He examined the extremely sharp tip. At the other end, he found a trigger-like mechanism. When he released it, a fluid shot out the tip.

"Oh Shit!" exclaimed Dan. Dan looked at his ankle where the man had poked the tip. He pulled out the wad of fifty-dollar bills that was wrapped around his ankle. There was liquid dripping out between some of the bills. He examined the bills and discovered a puncture through some of the bills that had not penetrated them all. "Thank you, Ulysses," he thought. "This is a bummer."

He did not have all that much cash and he didn't know what the hell the stuff was on the bills. He sat the moist ones aside. At best this guy was trying to disable him. At worst maybe even kill him. He sat the guy upright on the stool and searched his pockets. He found his passport and itinerary. He also had a transit boarding pass. Dan studied the itinerary. The man had been on the same Qantas flight from Honolulu. The ticket had been purchased at the Qantas counter on the day of the flight. He was continuing on to Hong Kong.

Dan took a good look at the passport. It was a French passport. The guy didn't look French. He opened the passport. The picture matched. He appeared to be a Middle-Eastern or North-African man. His name was Al-Qadir Ravshan. He made a mental note of the man's height and weight. He would have to do the metric conversion later. "What was this guy's deal?" wondered Dan.

The man had quite a few U.S. one-hundred-dollar bills in his wallet. Dan looked at them for a moment. He should have had no reservations about taking them. Dan decided to take them but replaced them with the moist, contaminated fifties. He searched through the man's bag and found nothing unexpected. Then, in a side pocket, he found two rolls of undeveloped 35mm film. The film had been shot, but he could not find a camera. "Who shoots film these days?" Dan wondered.

He grabbed the film. He also took the man's passport and boarding passes. He reached over to the adjacent stall and retrieved his own carry-on bag. He tucked the film into one of the side pockets of his carry-on. He listened to the sounds in the restroom. He carefully unlocked the door and peeked out of the stall. He saw a man quickly finishing a small bottle of liquor and then pitching it in the trash as he left. When he was confident the room was empty, he opened the stall and positioned the unconscious man's bag against the door to hold it closed.

The restroom was empty. He stopped to comb his hair and straighten his clothes dand then walked out into the transit lounge. He checked the monitors and found the flight to Hong Kong was now boarding.

He was trying to think clearly. There was a man unconscious in the restroom. Dan had his passport and boarding passes. There was nowhere to run and nowhere to hide. They would soon know a transit passenger was missing. The passenger had to be in the lounge somewhere.

Dan walked over to the refreshment area. Passengers were milling around, talking, eating snacks and drinking. Containers of unfinished drinks were sitting around. It gave Dan an idea. He ordered a coke and calmly drank until the plastic cup was nearly empty. He then began moving around discreetly finding unfinished and abandoned alcoholic drinks. He poured what remained in the coke cup until it was nearly full.

He took the cup back into the restroom and waited in front of the mirror, combing his hair and washing his hands until the room was empty. He pushed open the stall door. Dan threw the passport and ticket jacket to the floor of the stall. He poured the alcoholic concoction into the man's mouth and over the man's chest. He dropped the cup by his side. The stall reeked of alcohol. He again propped up the man's bag to hold the door closed as he left. He picked up the instrument of death and placed it in the trash can. He pushed it to the bottom. He left and found a seat in the transit lobby, while he pondered the meaning of what had just happened.

In a few minutes, the PA system was announcing the last call for passengers to Hong Kong. There were several gate agents and a security guard looking at the computer. In a few minutes, he saw several security men walking around the lounge announcing the Hong Kong departure. Methodically, they combed one end of the lounge to the other until; finally, one entered the men's restroom. A short time later he scurried out and summoned some assistance. In a few minutes, more security personnel came and entered the restroom.

His observations were interrupted by an announcement on the PA system "Passenger Grainger, Passenger Grainger, please come to the service desk."

Dan walked over to the smiling Qantas agent. "Your visa has been approved. Here are your passport and new ticket on Qantas Flight 63, leaving for Harare tomorrow at 10:30 a.m. You can pick up your checked baggage at the baggage carousel in customs."

"Why thank you Ma'am," said Dan as he took the papers from her.

"Enjoy your stay in Sydney," she said.

Dan headed down the corridor toward international arrivals and customs, as he saw several men emerge from the restroom carrying a man on a stretcher. He walked right next to them for a few steps. The Middle-Eastern man lay face up and was unconscious. The odor of alcohol filled the hall, as he was carried out of the transit area. Dan turned to look at the Hong Kong departure gate. It was closed for boarding.

Dan claimed his checked luggage and cleared customs with no problems. He wandered around the terminal for a few minutes and then placed a telephone call to a local hotel. He purchased a twenty-dollar ticket on an airport shuttle service to downtown.

The driver threw Dan's bag into the back of an old Toyota van. "Sheraton Four Points at Darling Harbour," said Dan, as he was the first in. In a few moments, others came, and before long, the van was crammed full of passengers. All appeared to be European of various nationalities. At least one of them could have really used some deodorant. The last passenger was a young female that spoke English and appeared to be Mediterranean. She squeezed in between some of the passengers and sat next to Dan. She positively reeked of garlic. It was quite warm in the van, and Dan's eyes watered from the sting of the garlic. As bad as it was, it was still an improvement over the odor of the other passengers.

Dan sat quietly looking out the window and taking shallow breaths through his mouth. In a few minutes, the driver stopped at hotel after hotel dropping off his passengers. Finally, Dan saw the monorail from Darling Harbour, and he knew the hotel was nearby. The driver turned on Sussex Street and parked beside the hotel. He got out to get Dan's bags. Dan slipped him a couple of U.S. dollar bills as a tip. Dan entered the lobby and checked in.

Chapter 13

Dan's room was on the corner of the fourth floor. He stepped out onto the balcony, which revealed a beautiful view of Darling Harbour. He could see the National Maritime Museum and the Sydney Aquarium.

He didn't bother to unpack or even take a shower. He lay down on the bed and was out like a light.

He awoke a few hours later and looked at the clock. It was almost 2:00 p.m. He needed to get up or he would be all screwed up later when it was time to go to bed. He realized he was quite hungry. He got up and quickly showered. While in the shower, he recalled how much he had always enjoyed his visits to Sydney. He had often told people that Sydney Harbour might well be the most beautiful place on the face of the earth.

As he left the hotel elevator, he noticed the lobby was filled with young Japanese girls, many of them quite small. He couldn't help but think of Callie and all the missing girls on the Oasis flight. As he left the lobby, he turned to the right and took the stairs and walkway that took him over the western distributor lanes of a busy highway. The stairway ended at the harbour dock just in front of the Aquarium. Once again, he noticed dozens of Japanese girls milling around the harbour area.

He bought a ticket on the Rocket Ferry and waited for the next one to come along. In a few minutes, the small ferry docked and a few people got off and a few got on. He was one of them. The ferry left the dock and began its journey around the harbour. In a few minutes the ferry turned right and, as it went under the Sydney Bridge, the world-famous Sydney Opera House came into view. He never failed to be impressed by the beauty of the harbour. The rays of the bright February summer sun produced deep-blue water contrasted with glistening white caps. He wondered for a moment how a world filled with such beauty could also produce such evil. His mind filled with thoughts of Callie and what she must be going through. He just stared at the blue harbour water and the Sydney skyline as the Rocket Ferry rounded The Rocks and docked at the Circular Quay.

He stayed aboard as most of the passengers got off. There was another group of Japanese girls that got on. They were giggling and smiling and doing the silly girlish things that the young do. They were taking pictures of everything. He found that he was getting a great deal of enjoyment watching them. Somehow it made him feel closer to Callie.

The Rocket Ferry departed the Circular Quay and made a short trip around the Opera House and docked again. All the Japanese girls disembarked and walked toward the Opera House entrance. Dan remained on the ferry until he reached his destination; He stepped off onto the wooden dock and made his way up to Doyle's on Watson Bay.

He got a table with a great view of the harbour, and he simply enjoyed his meal as he watched the sailboats dotting the harbour. It was still early afternoon and the restaurant was not busy. He noticed a table of Japanese businessmen and thought that it seemed the Japanese were everywhere in Sydney today. When they left, he watched them walk along the dock and sit for a while on the benches. They took turns taking pictures of each other with Sydney Harbour and then the restaurant as the backdrop. Finally, they boarded a private yacht and cruised toward Sydney.

Dan finished his meal and walked out along the dock also. It had been almost an hour since he had been dropped off, and the ferry would be along soon. He sat at the same benches where he had watched the Japanese businessmen. Then he noticed a briefcase leaning up against one of the legs of the bench.

He looked around for a moment to see if it might belong to someone nearby. It did not. So, Dan picked up the briefcase and began examining the contents. There were several CDs along with many documents in Japanese. He thumbed through the documents and came to a stack of flyers in English.

The flyers promoted a Japanese Dance Troupe performing at the Sydney Opera House. He looked at the dates and noticed the first performance was tonight at 7:30 p.m.

There were other fliers in other languages promoting upcoming appearances in cities throughout Asia and Europe. He searched through the pockets of the briefcase and found a Japanese passport. He opened it and recognized the picture as one of the businessmen that had been seated at Doyle's. Tucked in the passport was an Australian Visa issued to Mr. Hiro Toguchi. There was also an Australian entry card like he had filled out himself only a few hours ago when he cleared customs. The card listed the ANA Hotel as Mr. Toguchi's address while in Sydney.

There were a lot of things he could have done, and he sure had more important things on his mind. To lose a passport is a serious thing, and he couldn't help but consider how distressed Mr. Toguchi would be when he realized his loss. As the Rocket Ferry arrived, he considered what he could do. It would be a simple matter to drop the briefcase at the ANA Hotel. It was not that far of a walk from his own hotel, or he could take the ferry on to the Circular Quay where the ANA Hotel was nearby. Dan picked up the briefcase and boarded the ferry.

The trip back was beautiful. Dozens of sailboats dotted the harbour seascape. Their sails billowed in the wind. As the Sydney Opera House came into view, he was reminded that one of the inspirations for its design was the sails of the ships that brought the early settlers and convicts to the Land Down Under. Other locals suggested the Opera House looked more like a group of turtles in heat.

There were a few quick stops on the trip back before Dan could disembark at the Aquarium dock. As the ferry passed Sydney Cove, Dan caught a glimpse of the ANA Hotel on the Sydney skyline. He returned to his hotel and once again found the lobby bustling with young Japanese girls. He went up to his room and looked up the number for the ANA Hotel.

He dialed the number and the hotel switchboard answered.

"The room of Mr. Hiro Toguchi," said Dan.

"Thank you," replied the operator.

The phone rang once and was answered in Japanese.

"English, English, speak English?" said Dan very slowly.

"Ah, yes, Hello," said the male voice.

"Hi, I am looking for Mr. Toguchi," said Dan.

"Who I say calling?" asked the voice in a thick accent.

"Tell him it is the guy that has his passport and briefcase," said Dan.

He heard the man's voice become very excited and, in a moment, there was a great commotion and murmur of Japanese voices. In a few seconds a voice came on the line in very good English, "Hello, I am Mr. Toguchi."

"Mr. Toguchi, my name is Dan Grainger, and I found your passport and briefcase at the dock by Doyle's on Watson Bay."

"Ah, yes, I remember now. Thank you, Sir. I am very grateful that you have recovered my belongings. I must come immediately. Where can I find you?" asked Mr. Toguchi.

"Well, I am at the Four Points Sheraton," said Dan.

"Oh, the Hotel Nikko," said Mr. Toguchi. "I know it very well. I must come immediately."

"Mr. Toguchi, it is not that far. I can bring it over to you in a little while."

"Sorry," said Mr. Toguchi. "Very important. Must have immediately. You have CDs in case?"

"Yes, there were several CDs in the briefcase," replied Dan.

"Very good, Very good. I come immediately," said Mr. Toguchi.

"Okay," said Dan. He gave his room number and said he would be in his room for a while.

Only a few minutes had passed when there was a knock at the door. Dan opened it and there were two young Japanese men at the door.

"Mr. Grainger," asked one of the men.

"Yes?" replied Dan.

"Mr. Toguchi send us."

"Just a second and let me get his briefcase." Dan closed the door a little distrustful of the men at the door and retrieved the briefcase from the room. He opened the door and offered the briefcase to the men.

"No, you come. You bring and give to Mr. Toguchi. He come soon and will meet in lobby," said one of the men.

Dan shrugged his shoulders. "Sure," he said, and closed the door to his room and accompanied the men down the hall and into the elevator.

One of the men selected the Lobby button and said, "You do Mr. Toguchi great favor. He very grateful."

"It is a bad thing to lose your passport. I am glad to help."

"No no, passport can be replaced. You have CDs. You have music and lighting control data for tonight?"

"I don't understand," said Dan.

"Tonight is opening performance of Japanese Dance at Opera House. The music that girls dance is on CD and lighting controlled by data file on CD. Director of Music lose CDs and Mr. Toguchi have backup set. Mr. Toguchi lose backup set. No CDs, no performance. Prime Minister be there. Everyone be there tonight. Very embarrassing. No CDs no performance. Everyone disappointed, Mr. Toguchi disappointed, girls disappointed. We try to get files transferred over Internet but there not time. Mr. Toguchi ready to cancel performance. You call. Everybody happy! You see?"

"Well, I guess so," said Dan although he didn't entirely.

The doors to the elevator opened and they stepped out onto a sea of young Japanese girls. This time, they were not giggling and carrying on. They stood very quietly and respectfully, smiling as the three men walked toward the doors. At the door, just inside the lobby, stood a single Japanese gentleman. He was dressed in a finely tailored suit. He wore glasses and smiled as they approached. Dan recognized him from the passport photo.

"Mr. Grainger, I am Mr. Toguchi. I am very pleased to meet you," said the man, as he bowed slightly in Dan's direction.

Dan bowed slightly also, matching the bow of Mr. Toguchi and extended his hand. Mr. Toguchi extended his and they shook hands.

Dan was carrying the briefcase in his left hand and offered it to Mr. Toguchi. Mr. Toguchi took it from Dan, again with a slight bow and said, "I owe you great debt, Mr. Grainger."

"No problem. I knew you would want your passport back but I had no idea the importance of the CDs. I am glad to have assisted you."

"You are American?" asked Mr. Toguchi.

"Yes, from Indiana" replied Dan.

"Ah yes, Indianapolis 500, Bobby Knight, Purdue, Notre Dame," said Mr. Toguchi.

"Yes, you know Indiana then?"

"Yes, I was Hoosier," said Toguchi.

Dan didn't know what to think of that remark. Dan just smiled and nodded his head.

"You do not believe I was Hoosier?" asked Mr. Toguchi with a smile. "Many year ago. I was young man and attended Indiana University in Bloomington for one year."

"Oh, I see," said Dan. Well, I am from north of Indianapolis ten kilometers."

"That is good. You are visiting Australia long?"

"No, I arrived this morning. My connection was delayed and I am flying out tomorrow morning," said Dan.

"Then, Mr. Grainger, you must come tonight and see our performance," said Mr. Toguchi.

It was more of a command than a request. "Well," began Dan "I will think about it. I have never seen Japanese dance before, and it would be quite interesting, I am sure. Maybe I'll get a ticket and decide to go later."

"You will be my guest. I owe you great debt. Limousine will pick you up here at 6:30, okay?" said Mr. Toguchi.

"I don't want to inconvenience you," said Dan. He didn't want to go but Mr. Togucci had a commanding presence that made it difficult to say no.

"No inconvenience," replied Mr. Toguchi, "We have many girls and staff staying here. This hotel was Japanese Hotel Nikko. We still stay here."

Dan had nothing else to do except sit in his hotel room and have his mind filled with thoughts of Callie. Yet, it didn't seem quite right to go to an entertainment event. The notion of watching several hundred young girls who were also dancers seemed pleasantly appealing. He had done Mr. Toguchi a great favor, and to decline his hospitality would be considered rude.

"Very well, then, Mr. Toguchi," replied Dan, "I would be pleased to attend tonight.

"Thank you, Mr. Grainger," he said as he made a wide sweeping motion with his arm and applause began behind and throughout the lobby. Dan turned around to see dozens of young Japanese girls applauding and smiling with approval as Mr. Toguchi said, "Mr. Grainger save performance and tonight he is our honored guest at Opera House."

Dan turned back around and shook Mr. Toguchi's hand. The two parted. Mr. Toguchi headed out the door to a waiting limousine and Dan down the lobby toward the elevator. Throughout his entire walk he was greeted with young Japanese bowing to him. He bowed back each time and felt a little bit like one of those toy dogs with a bouncing head that you sometimes see in the back window of a car.

He went back to the room and realized it was almost five o'clock, and he did not have that much time to get ready. Worse yet, what the hell was he going to wear?

He looked in the hotel directory and found a tuxedo hire listed in the basement floor of the hotel. He shaved and freshened up. He went down to the basement shops and, sure enough, there was a tuxedo rental shop at the bottom of the escalator to the basement. He walked in and explained his problem.

"No worries, mate," was all the clerk said.

In a few minutes, Dan Grainger left the store fully decked out in a tuxedo and shoes well suited to the occasion. He carried his other clothes in a plastic bag back up to the room.

It wasn't long before there was a knock at the door. He looked at his watch. It was 6:25. The same two Japanese men from earlier were there.

"Mr. Grainger, your limousine is here."

The two men escorted Dan down the corridor to the elevator and through the lobby to the waiting car. Dan got in and the two men joined him. It was a fifteen-minute ride to the Opera House, and he could see many people arriving by foot, taxi, bus and limousine. The two men ushered Dan into the mammoth Opera House seating area. He was taken over to a seat that was down front and center stage. The view of the stage was magnificent. It was nearly 7:30 and everyone was trying to find their seat. In a few minutes, an entourage of businessmen led by Mr. Toguchi approached the area. As the group looked for their seats, Mr. Toguchi came over to Dan, bowed slightly and shook Dan's hand.

"Mr. Grainger, I am so pleased that you could join us this evening," said Mr. Toguchi.

Mr. Toguchi sat down next to Dan. Dan didn't really know what to do or say. He sat somewhat uncomfortably in his seat for a while. He chastised himself for coming at all. His daughter's fate was unknown, and his mission was to find her. Yet, here he sat at the Sydney Opera House waiting for a performance to begin.

Fortunately, in a few minutes, the lights dimmed. The music started and the stage was soon filled with hundreds of young girls fully dressed in traditional Japanese garb.

Dan had never seen this kind of dance before, other than for a few seconds as he surfed past it on a cable channel. He didn't understand it and, at times, it was quite boring. At other times, people laughed and the laughter was contagious. He did enjoy seeing young girls dancing. His thoughts drifted to Callie and the hundreds of other missing girls that were in their present circumstance because they were dancers. As Dan watched the various styles of Japanese dances performed on stage, he realized he was enjoying himself as much as could humanly be possible at this point in his life.

The finale of the dance act included hundreds of the dancers dressed in kimonos and other traditional Japanese dress. They moved around the stage in an incomprehensible choreography that seemed haphazard. It ended in a magnificent light display. The dancers took their last bow and left the stage.

Everyone rose to their feet to applaud and after a while, the applause died out and people began filing out of their seats toward the exits.

Mr. Toguchi turned to Dan "You enjoy?"

"Yes, Mr. Toguchi, it was very entertaining. I enjoyed it."

"Car take you back to hotel," said Mr. Toguchi.

"If you don't mind, Mr. Toguchi, I will walk over to the Quay and take a ferry back. This is my only night here and the harbour lights are magnificent at night."

"I agree. Travel on water is better. You come with me," said Mr. Toguchi.

Dan followed Mr. Toguchi out of the main auditorium. He would stop occasionally and greet businessmen and Australian government officials. In a few minutes, they had made their way through the crowd and outside. Mr. Toguchi directed Dan to the left, over to a small dock area at the side of the Opera House.

A private yacht was waiting at the dock for Mr. Toguchi. The only passengers to get on were Dan and Mr. Toguchi. The yacht pulled away from the dock and began its journey through the harbour. The Sydney skyline at night was breathtaking. Mr. Toguchi pointed to the right of the skyline. "You see All Nippon Airways Hotel just to right. We fly ANA for Australia tour. For our Asian tour, we will fly Japan Air Lines. It is good that business be shared between Japan businesses.

"Times have been very difficult for all of us," said Dan.

Mr. Toguchi turned to face Dan, standing squarely in front of him.

"You have children, Mr. Grainger," asked Mr. Toguchi.

"Yes, two daughters, ages fifteen and nineteen," replied Dan.

"Beginning to blossom?" said Mr. Toguchi.

"Yes," said Dan.

"This is good. Daughters bring great pride and happiness to father," said Mr. Toguchi.

"Yes," said Dan nodding in agreement.

"Ah yes, we have hundreds of young ladies, all like daughters, all beginning to blossom."

"I understand. My youngest daughter is also a dancer. She, uh…" his voice trailed off.

"I sense great sadness, Mr. Grainger," said Mr. Toguchi.

It was not Dan's nature to spill his gut to strangers. The pleasant summer evening, the tranquility of the Harbour and Mr. Toguchi's decent manner lulled him into speaking. "My youngest daughter was on the plane that went down in Miami. She was going to perform in the Super Bowl. They have found no survivors, but I have not given up hope," said Dan.

Mr. Toguchi reached out with both of his hand and grasped Dan's shoulders. "I know of this tragedy. Mr. Toguchi burn incense tonight and say prayer to Buddha that your daughter be safe."

"Thank you, Mr. Toguchi," replied Dan.

"Hundreds of young girls very difficult to take care of and move them. They have so many needs and require great care and planning. Mr. Toguchi not understand why use plane to go such short distance from Orlando when bus is more efficient."

"I have wondered that myself," said Dan, as he shook his head. "All the trouble they went to chartering a 747, I suppose it was all about image and public relations. I don't know."

"Very expensive flight," said Mr. Toguchi, "and now perhaps priceless."

The yacht pulled into the dock at Sydney Aquarium. Mr. Toguchi went to a drawer on the yacht and pulled out a miniature Buddha and handed it to Dan. "You take with you, it bring good fortune to you in your journey," said Mr. Toguchi.

"I, uh, I can't do that Mr. Toguchi, I am sorry," replied Dan.

"You Christian?" asked Mr. Toguchi.

"Well, not a very good one, but I try," said Dan.

"We all try to please our Master," said Mr. Toguchi, "I understand. I keep for you. Blessing of Buddha very powerful. Can bring you good fortune if I keep. I place next to heart." He placed the small Buddha in the pocket of his suit jacket over his heart. He then placed the palms of his hands together in front of his chest, he took a very deep breath, closed his eyes and exhaled slowly.

He looked directly into Dan's eyes. "May the Blessing of Buddha travel with you in search for daughter. May the Blessing of Buddha be with daughter until safe with father."

"Thank you, Mr. Toguchi," said Dan, as he bowed slightly.

"I owe you great debt," said Mr. Toguchi.

Dan turned and stepped onto the dock. He headed for the stairs. At the top of the walkway, he turned and looked back at Darling Harbour. He watched the yacht move along the Harbour until it was lost within the myriad of lights that dotted Sydney Harbour.

Chapter 14

It was unbearably warm. The fan tried to circulate some air in the room.

The girls were restless. There were about a hundred of them in the first group. It was early in the morning, and the day had just begun.

Two uniformed men stood at the entrance to the door when a bearded man and a woman wearing a white uniform entered.

The girls were ordered to remove their clothes from the waist down. They were told they would be examined, and that it was for their own good.

The younger girls started crying for their parents. They were told to be quiet, that yelling would do them no good. The uniformed men looked on, their weapons at their side. The bearded man opened a notebook and began to jot some things down as if he were taking notes.

"Girls, girls, settle down," the woman shouted.

"This is for your own good. Do not be alarmed, you will not be harmed." she said.

Some of the girls began to comply with the instructions and removed their clothes. Some tried to leave their underwear on but were told they must be removed. Even the oldest girls were crying and screaming "No, no, please don't!"

The first girl was asked her name. The man holding the notebook searched for it in the list and checked it off. The girl was told to lie down on the mat and spread her legs. The woman in the white uniform kneeled beside her and spread the lips of her vagina apart. The bearded man got down on one knee between her legs and took a closer look. "Okay, next," he said.

The second girl refused to spread her legs. Two women came over and kneeled on each side of the girl. They forced her legs apart. When the woman touched her, she tried to wiggle and get free but she couldn't. Once again, the bearded man kneeled between her legs. He had a small flashlight and pointed it at her vagina. He instructed the woman to re-position her hands. The girl began screaming uncontrollably and breathing deeply. "Relax," said the woman, "It will be over in just a moment. We are just concerned about your health and welfare."

You can put your clothes back on as soon as the examination is finished. Finally, he said "Next," as he made an entry in his notebook.

The third girl was more cooperative. "Next," the man said. The woman in white put a new pair of latex gloves on for each examination. The old ones were discarded into a special container for waste. The woman in the white uniform touched every girl.

Some girls cried and sobbed. Others just stared blankly until it was over. A few urinated on the mat. The mess had to be cleaned up, and the area sprayed with disinfectant before the process continued.

Finally, after nearly two hours, the entire female student body of Mr. Campbell's high school classes had been examined for signs of sexual abuse. Here in the United States of America, in the State of Indiana, such a monstrous thing had just happened. Shirley Merriman was the Director of Madison County, Indiana Child Protection Services. She was proud of her morning's work. She removed the last pair of gloves and sprayed her hands with disinfectant. She turned to the man with the notebook.

"Thank God that none of the other girls was molested in the same way by this monster," she said while turning to see a man with a business suit enter the gymnasium. It was Steve Foulke, the Prosecuting Attorney of Madison County. "It's about time you got here," she snapped at him.

"Well, you should have notified me in advance," he replied. "You're going to hear about this from the parents. You were supposed to notify the parents today and conduct the physical examinations tomorrow. Each girl should have received a thorough explanation and given her permission to be examined."

"I have the court order signed by the judge," Merriman said tersely. "I have the legal authority and that's that."

"Look, we are going to nail this guy for what he did to his own daughters," said Foulke. "I guess we can let the deputies go now," he motioned to the uniformed men that they could leave.

"Did you properly inform each girl that she had a right to refuse the examination at this time and report to a medical professional's office to have the examination performed?" asked Foulke.

"Ms. Merriman," repeated Foulke, "did you inform the girls or not? I am going to check into what the judge ordered."

"It sure is hot in here," she said, as she stared at Foulke and ignored his question.

"Yeah, I know. I think there is something wrong with the heating system. It's on full blast all the time," said Foulke.

"Let's step out in the hall where it's cooler," Merriman said, as she headed toward the door. The bearded man and Foulke followed.

"What's with the white uniform?" asked Foulke. "You're not a nurse."

Once again Merriman just ignored Foulke's question.

The bearded man walked up and interrupted, "There were a couple of those girls that looked like they had some problems. I noted them here in the log."

Merriman looked at the names of the girls. "Yes doctor, sad cases. They both have a history of abuse from their step-fathers. Unfortunately, we know them well."

"Just like Campbell," said Foulke. "Are those two girls related?" he asked.

"No, two different families," said Shirley. "We get it all the time. Usually, it's the step-father or the boyfriend."

"It just makes you sick. I'd like to lock these guys up and throw away the key," he said with disgust.

"We're getting them one at a time," she said. "It's a slow, frustrating process, but we get them." she paused, "Now, what about Campbell's other two daughters?

"Well, one of them is his natural daughter and she is away at college someplace," replied Foulke "We don't know where yet. The other girl is a freshman in high school. She didn't go to school today. We know she is at home with her mother. We are picking her up at 11:00 a.m. and bringing her to your office for the examination."

"What about Campbell?" she asked "Do we have him yet?

"He is due in any time now. I have a couple of Madison County Deputies waiting for him when he gets off the plane in Indianapolis. Of course, some Marion County Sheriff Deputies and the Indiana State Police are there to actually make the arrest," said Foulke.

"What then?" she asked.

"We're transporting him to Anderson and we will hold him until the results of our own examination of the deceased girls," said Foulke, with a trace of a smile.

"What time we checking the daughter?" asked Merriman.

"1:00 p.m.," he replied.

"What about the two dead girls?" asked Merriman.

"They arrived at the airport early this morning and have already arrived at the county coroner's office."

"Do you think it's as bad as Dade County said?" she asked.

"I think so," said Foulke, "they said it was a nasty case of sexual mutilation. Our county coroner, Larry Crawford, was in Miami for the Super Bowl and he stayed over to be on site at the Dade County Coroner."

"And they got semen samples?" she asked.

"Oh, yes, plenty from both girls," he said solemnly.

"When can we see the bodies?" she asked.

"Soon as we are finished at the high school," he said. "I told them to expect us about 2:30. I told the coroner I wanted him there, too." He paused and took a deep breath. "I am absolutely going to nail this son-of-a-bitch Campbell to the wall," declared Foulke

"And when is the news conference?" she asked.

"It's set for 5:30 p.m.," he said, "I expect it'll be live on some of the stations. Two satellite trucks have already shown up over at the courthouse."

"Okay, Mr. Celebrity Prosecutor," she said, "I'll see you later at my office." She left the gym and went to lunch.

Kima Campbell had been looking out the window hoping to see her father pull up. She knew it was too early, but she kept looking anyway. Her mother had been crying most of the time, since she heard the news about Keisha and Kara. When her father arrived they were all to go down to the mortuary for the sad task of selecting a casket. They had decided to bury the girls together. Little Kara would never be separated from her sister Keisha again. Kima started crying as she thought about it.

Life had been so good for her mother and the three sisters, since coming to America from Bissau three years ago. Her stepfather, Mark Campbell had met their mother at a Christian Church service in Guinea-Bissau, while he was stationed at the U.S. Embassy in Bissau. He married her and brought the four of them back to America. He legally adopted all of the girls. It seemed like a fairy tale come true, until now. Now, both of her sisters were dead.

She was still looking out the window when she saw the Sheriff's car pull up. Two deputies got out of the car and came to the door. Kima answered the door. "Is this the residence of Mr. Mark Campbell?" asked one of the deputies.

"Yes," said Kima.

"Are you his daughter?" he asked.

"Yes sir." said Kima.

"We would appreciate it if you and your mother would come with us downtown," said the deputy.

"I don't know. We are waiting for my father to come home. My mother very rarely goes out, especially in the winter. She prefers not to speak English," said Kima.

"I'm sorry, Miss, but I'm afraid we will have to insist," said the deputy, "Your father will be downtown. We will pick him up from the airport."

Kima's eyes widened. She turned to her mother standing behind the door. Her mother shook her head yes.

"Okay," said Kima. "We will come. We need just a few minutes."

Kima closed the door. She helped her mother put on her winter coat. Her mother had never adjusted to the cold Indiana winters. In a few minutes, they were ready and walked out the door. The deputies accompanied them to the car and opened the rear seat doors for them.

It was a short drive to the Anderson courthouse. The sheriff's car was parked in front of an office building not far from the courthouse. The deputies escorted Kima and her mother into the building. They accompanied them to the office of Child Protective Services.

"Mrs. Campbell, Kima, my name is Shirley Merriman. I am the Director of Child Protective Services for Madison County," said Merriman. "This is Steve Foulke, the Madison County Prosecutor."

Foulke nodded and said, "Mrs. Campbell, I am so sorry for the loss of your daughters. It's a terrible tragedy."

"Thank you," the mother said, in clipped English.

"We need to talk to you about something for a minute while Kima waits outside," began Merriman.

"No," said Mrs. Campbell. "Kima stays."

Kima interrupted "My mother does not speak English so well unless she gets mad, I may need to translate."

"Really?" said Merriman. "I did not realize that. What language does she speak? Where is she from?

"We are from Guinea-Bissau in West Africa," said Kima. "We speak Crioulo."

Foulke's eyebrows raised. This was a new wrinkle.

"How long have you been in this country?" asked Foulke.

"Three years," said Kima.

"I see, and, your sisters, they were from…from…uh," she couldn't remember the name of the place. "From Africa too?

"Yes," said Kima.

"And your stepfather? He is an American?" asked Merriman.

"My father," Kima said proudly, "was a Sergeant in the United States Marines."

"And he met your mother in…"

"In Guinea-Bissau," snapped Kima. "Perhaps it would be easier for you, considering your age if you referred to it as Portuguese Guinea."

"I'm sorry, Kima," said Merriman. "And then he married your mother and brought all of you here to America."

"Yes," said Kima,

Kima's mother said something to Kima in Crioulo.

"My mother says to tell you that you ask too many questions?"

Merriman looked at Mrs. Campbell, who was staring at her sternly. Merriman shot a concerned glance toward Foulke and nodded her head toward the door. They both stepped outside into the hall.

"Steve, this fits a classic pattern," said Merriman in a hushed voice.

"What do you mean? This is really not my area of prosecution," said Foulke.

"An American serviceman goes overseas, marries a woman with young girls and brings them back to America where he can molest them at will. The mother or children can't complain because they are told it will mean deportation if the husband goes to jail."

"What are we going to do? We can't question the mother without the girl to translate," said Foulke.

"Well, Kima, is going to find out soon enough anyway. I guess we just tell 'em," said Merriman.

"Okay," replied Foulke, as they stepped back into the room.

"Mrs. Campbell, Kima, I am afraid I have some more bad news for you. There is a warrant for your father's arrest," began Foulke.

Kima's mother erupted in a burst of the foreign tongue.

"What for?" demanded Kima

"For sexual abuse of your sisters," said Merriman.

"No," said Mrs. Campbell.

"It is not true!" said Kima. "My father would never hurt them. How can you know this?" screamed Kima at Merriman.

Foulke answered, "The Dade County Coroner called us Sunday morning and reported certain physical findings he made during the autopsy. The Madison County Coroner happened to be in Miami and went over and saw for himself."

Mrs. Campbell stood and stared directly into the face of Merriman.

"What is it that you want with us?" said Kima.

"Kima, I know this must be very upsetting to you. You must understand that we are only trying to help," said Merriman, "Tell your mother that we need to examine you."

Merriman no sooner got the words out of her mouth when the swift right hand of Mrs. Campbell struck Merriman across the left cheek and knocked her to the ground."

"No, it is evil! This is America," exclaimed Mrs. Campbell in perfect English as she pulled the winter glove from her right hand to reveal a grisly two-pronged mass of flesh. Mrs. Campbell pounced on Merriman and clamped her neck like a vise with the powerful appendages of her right arm.

Two deputies came bursting into the room and grabbed Mrs. Campbell by the arms and pulled the two women apart.

"Let her go," said Merriman, as she picked herself up.

The deputies looked at the prosecutor. Foulke nodded.

The deputies let go of Mrs. Campbell and stationed themselves at the door, still inside the room.

"Kima, you must come with me for the examination," said Merriman, as she straightened her clothes and tried to regain her composure.

"I want to see an attorney," said Kima.

"I am afraid that is not possible," said Merriman.

"My mother will not give her permission," said Kima.

"I am sorry to hear that," said Merriman, as she picked up a piece of paper from her desk. "This is a court order signed by a Madison County judge, placing you in the temporary custody of Child Protective Services. It orders the examination to be performed immediately."

"I will not submit," said Kima, as she bolted for the door and slid past the deputies. They gave chase and quickly cornered Kima at the end of the hall. They marched her back into the office with one 220-pound deputy holding each arm of the small frightened fifteen-year-old."

Kima was crying now as she was taken into a small examining room adjacent to Merriman's office.

"Merriman," said Kima's mother, "in my country, it is the Religious Police, just like KGB or Gestapo, and here it is you, the CPS, a despicable lot, all of you."

Merriman stared at her for a moment and then turned and went into the examination room. The mother tried to follow.

"You can't come in here," said Merriman.

"I will be with my daughter, or I will be dead," said Mrs. Campbell, as she held up her grisly right hand again toward Merriman. 'The Religious Police did this to me. They chopped off my hand for the crime of carrying a Holy Bible. An old German doctor took pity on me and fixed me up with this Krukenberg hand. It is very powerful."

Merriman stared at the radius and ulna of Mrs. Campbell's lower arm. It had been separated and covered with flesh to form a lobster-like pincher. She looked at Mrs. Campbell's determined expression.

The two women glared at each other for what seemed like an eternity.

"Very well," said Merriman.

Kima was instructed to slip into an examination robe. A screen was provided for her to stand behind while she changed. When she emerged from behind the screen, she was told to lie down on the examining table and place her feet in the stirrups. The same bearded doctor from the morning's events conducted the examination.

Foulke and the deputies stepped out of the room.

Kima was crying. She had been forcibly examined before, but she never dreamed it could happen to her again in America. Her mother went to her left side and cradled Kima's head in her arms and began softly singing to her in Crioulo. The doctor sat down at the end of the table and his eyes widened with disbelief. Merriman was looking over the doctor's shoulder and she turned white as a ghost. She snapped several pictures with her phone and even took a short video.

In a few minutes, it was over. A somber doctor and Merriman came walking out of the examination room. Merriman put the phone in front of Foulke's face and the video showed in living color and great detail the condition of Kima's privates.

Foulke was a hardened prosecutor that had often seen many gruesome pictures. He had seen actual murder victims at the scene that had been sexually brutalized. Merriman's video caught him off guard. Foulke took one look and bolted into Merriman's office but didn't make it to the wastebasket. He could be heard as he threw up all over Merriman's office.

The doctor stopped and asked Foulke if he was okay.

"I don't know, I just ate lunch…I…God, what's been done to that girl?" he asked.

"I have never seen anything like it in all my forty years as a doctor. Some monster has mutilated her," said the Doctor.

"I need your report as soon as possible. I can't hold Campbell very long without charging him," said Foulke as he continued to wipe his lips with a tissue. "We need you to look at her deceased sisters, too."

"You will have my full report, complete with all the pictures," said the doctor.

Merriman came into her office and her eyes widened as she saw the mess Foulke had made. "Couldn't you have hit the wastepaper basket instead of the top of my desk?" exclaimed Merriman.

Foulke, still pale, just used his napkin to wipe his lips.

Merriman stepped back into the hall and went back to the examination room.

"May we go now?" asked Kima weakly.

Merriman looked at her. Actually, CPS had custody of Kima now, but with Mark Campbell soon to be in custody, she would be safe at home. She decided Kima had been through enough for now. She could take physical custody of her whenever she wanted.

"Kima," began Merriman, "I am going to release you for now into the custody of your mother, but we will have to talk again soon. I am so sorry for what has happened to you. We are only trying to help you. You need to try to understand."

Mrs. Campbell stared coldly at Merriman and said, "It is you who needs to understand, you are like a blind child."

Kima and her mother went out into the hall and refused the ride home offered by the deputies. The deputies watched out the window as Kima and her mother began the two-mile trek toward home in the cold Indiana February weather.

It was nearly 2:30 when Foulke and Merriman arrived at the coroner's office. Merriman drove and Foulke sipped on a 7-Up.

There were two examining tables, each with a white sheet covering the small bodies. Foulke could hardly bring himself to look. The Coroner raised the sheet to reveal the tiny little frame of Kara. There was a look of terror on the six-year old's face. The condition of her genitals was shown to the prosecutor. The process was repeated for Keisha. Semen samples had been taken from both girls after the bodies had arrived. The Dade County Coroner had also provided samples of semen and seawater taken in Miami.

Foulke looked on. He knew what to expect this time, He did not turn white. Somehow, it was less troubling to observe on a corpse than on a living breathing fifteen-year old girl. These two girls were lying here dead because of a terrible tragic accident. But they had been living a heinous existence with Campbell.

"Have you determined the cause of death?" asked Merriman.

"Yeah," said the Coroner. "They drowned just like Dade County determined. There was saltwater in their lungs. We have samples."

"So, they were alive when the plane went into the ocean?" asked Foulke.

"Yeah. They had life jackets around their necks when the bodies were recovered. These two were still strapped in their seats, floating in the Atlantic."

"No wonder they looked so terrified," said Foulke.

Apparently, several of the girls were recovered floating in pairs of seats still bolted together. My report will show that the blood in these two pooled in various portions of the body. That indicates the body was changing position shortly after death. That's consistent with being tossed around in the ocean.

"Did any of the other girls recovered from the accident show signs of sexual abuse?" asked Merriman.

"Well, the last I heard the body count was seventeen. So, it's too soon to say for sure. But, in the first eleven, Dade County said none of the other girls showed any outward appearance of sexual abuse.

"Okay," said Foulke, "I need a preliminary report from you soon.

"You'll have it," said the coroner.

Merriman started to leave. Foulke said "You go ahead. I will get a ride from somebody. I need to go home for a bit to freshen up before the news conference at 5:30." Merriman left.

Foulke turned to the coroner and said, "Larry, she always seems so damned sure of herself."

"Steve," said the coroner, "you know I never cared for her. She runs that office like the Gestapo. I don't like her…never have…never will."

"Strange you should say that." said Foulke "You're the second person that's said that about Merriman today and the other person had just met her."

"One of these days someone's going to take her down a notch, and I hope I am there to see it." said the coroner.

Chapter 15

The Indianapolis Leadership Prayer Breakfast was held at 7:30 each Monday morning in downtown Indianapolis. John Kosten was introduced to lead the opening prayer. A very nice-looking man with light brown hair and wearing glasses stepped up to the microphone. He was dressed in a dark blue suit.

"I am sure you have all seen the Indianapolis Star this morning." He held up the newspaper headline for everyone to see the Super Bowl results. "Now, I suppose this is an important story. We are all interested in the Super Bowl and I am sure many of you watched the game last night. In between the million-dollar commercials and the replays was the halftime performance. If you watched the game, you will know that there was supposed to be a performance by a group of three hundred young girls, arranged by the Oasis Corporation that is based just right up Meridian Street in Carmel. We know that at least five of the girls were from Indiana."

"Those three hundred girls didn't make it for that halftime performance. This event was supposed to be the most exciting thing in the lives of those young girls. Instead, it may have been the catalyst for the loss of their lives. We never know how much time we have on this earth or when we will be called to leave."

"Last night, during the half-time show, they observed one full minute of silence in honor of these young girls. Now that may seem like a lot of time at one million dollars per minute but, I could not help thinking that was only two-tenths of a second per child. Five girls a second, three hundred girls for the whole minute…What a tragedy." He paused and turned the paper to below the fold and said "300 dead," and pointed to the smaller headline."

"It says here that three hundred girls died in the crash in the Atlantic Ocean. Their plane plunged into the ocean, after it was struck in the tail by a drug-smuggling plane flying at low altitude. They have recovered the bodies of seventeen of the girls, and they now say there is no hope of finding any more of the girls alive."

"Yesterday, the headline said "300 feared dead," he held up the front page of the Sunday Star.

"What has happened in twenty-four hours that this headline has gone from '300 feared dead' to '300 dead'?"

"I'll tell you…just one thing…a loss of hope…lost faith that any of these girls can still be alive. The daughter of a friend of mine was on that flight. I received a call on my voicemail this morning asking that I pray for his daughter and for all the girls that were on that flight. And I would like to do that just now if you would all please rise."

Those in the room stood up at their tables as John began, "In the name of Jesus, Lord, we come to you and ask that you comfort the families of these three hundred girls and help them to know your love and that you care about them. Help them cope with this tragedy. Give them strength to carry on in the troubled days ahead." Some in the crowd began to agree and some shouted, "Amen" and "Praise the Lord!"

John continued, "We know that you have the power to do all things and we ask that, if there is just one girl alive out there, that you help her hold on. We have not lost hope. We have not lost faith."

A chorus of "Amen" and "Praise Jesus" could be heard in the room.

"We believe she can be saved," John said loudly. "Give her strength if there are two or a dozen or a hundred or three hundred that have somehow survived this tragedy…we ask that you protect them and bring them back safely to their families. In the name Jesus, we pray. Amen."

John left the podium and returned to his table.

Eight hundred miles away in Orlando, Annie and her mother had boarded the plane Monday morning for the two-and-a-half-half hour flight back to Indianapolis. It was an uneventful flight, and the two did not talk much. Annie stared out the window, thinking of Callie, wondering and hoping her dad was right. She was thinking of her dad in far-off Africa. She wondered if he was there yet.

The plane landed and pulled up to the gate. As Annie and Alice entered the main terminal, they walked into a commotion of bright television lights and a crowd of cameramen, reporters and sheriff's deputies. Their path to the baggage area escalator was blocked. Annie stood up on one of the seats to see what was going on.

A black man was handcuffed and being led by several deputies. There were camera flashes going off all over the place. The swarm of television cameramen and reporters were shouting questions. "Campbell," one of the voices shouted out. "Campbell, did you molest your daughters?" The handcuffed man remained silent as he was deliberately paraded past the line of cameramen and reporters.

"That's Mr. Campbell!" exclaimed Annie.

"Who? Who is it?" asked Alice.

"It's Mr. Campbell, from Orlando. Mark Campbell. You remember, Keisha and Kara's father?" said Annie.

"What's going on?" asked Alice as she tried to see over the top of the crowd.

"They have arrested him. He has handcuffs on. I don't know what they're doing."

Annie watched as Mark Campbell was led through the terminal hallway by the deputies. The throng of reporters and photographers followed. In a little while, the terminal cleared enough that Annie and Alice could make their way to the baggage claim.

As they waited for their bags, she looked up the number of John Kosten. She called the office and was put right through to John.

"Mr. Kosten."

"Annie," said John, "We are praying for your sister and your mother and your dad."

Annie was taken back by his kind words. "My, uh, my uh, dad said I should call you when I got back to Indianapolis."

"Are you at the airport?" asked John.

"Yes," she said.

"Do you have transportation?" he asked.

"Yes."

"If you want you can stop by here on the way from the airport and we can meet?" said John.

"I guess we can do that," replied Annie. "There are some things I need to bring to you. Some of them I do not have with me."

"It is up to you," replied John. "We can make it later."

"What time?" asked Annie.

"I will be here until late this evening. How about 4:30? Will that give you enough time?"

"Yes, it will," she paused. "Is it okay if I bring a friend of my dad's who has some of the things you may need to look at?"

"That will be fine, Annie. See you at 4:30."

"One more thing," said Annie.

"Yes?"

"We just arrived at the airport, and the police were here to arrest a man we know from Orlando who lost two daughters on the plane. They were little girls - Keisha and Kara Campbell. Their bodies have been recovered, and I know Mr. Campbell went to Miami yesterday to identify the girls. He seemed like a real nice man; Mr. Kosten and the TV reporters were shouting nasty things to him about molesting his daughters. I just thought you ought to know because it all seems very strange to me."

"Well, what do you think about that Annie?" asked John.

"I just don't know. I know you can't always tell about these things, but if they are talking about Keisha and Kara being molested by him…I just can't believe it. He was too kind. They both adored him. It just doesn't make any sense to me," said Annie.

"I see. Well, it's time for the noon news. If TV cameras were at the airport to cover the arrest then they were tipped off by someone in law enforcement. There should be something about it on the news in a few minutes. I will be sure to watch.

"Well, okay, then I will see you at 4:30." said Annie.

"Bye, Annie," said John.

"Bye," said Annie.

Annie pulled her phone from her purse and looked up Mike's number and called it.

"Hello," answered Mike.

"Mike, this is Annie. We just got into the airport and are waiting for our bags."

"Hi, Annie, what's up?"

"We, that's you and me," she began "have an appointment to see John Kosten at 4:30 p.m. We need to take all the voicemail files and everything we have for him to look at. I need you to help me explain it all. I don't think I can."

"You're talking about John Kosten the attorney?" asked Mike.

"Yeah, you know him. He is a friend of my dad's."

"I know who you mean now, I have seen him on the TV news once in a while," said Mike.

"I will gather everything I have so far. What about you, Annie? What do you have?"

"All I have is the video I shot and a handout showing the pictures of the girls they have found so far."

"You know where I live. Can you drop off the video and handout on your way home? I want to make a copy of everything and preserve the masters. John Kosten may want copies, and I don't want to give up the originals."

"We can do that," said Annie.

"I will see you in a few minutes then."

"Okay, but there is one more thing." added Annie.

"Shoot," said Mike.

When we got off the plane, they arrested a man named Mark Campbell. He wasn't on our plane, but he must have come up from either Orlando or Miami the same time we did. He is the father of two of the girls they have recovered. The TV reporters were here, you might want to watch the news at noon to see what's going on. It didn't sound too good."

"I will run a DVR on all the news stations and see who has what. Anything else? asked Mike.

"No," replied Anne. "I will see you in few minutes."

"All-rightee," said Mike, and he hung up.

Annie saw her mom coming from the baggage carousel with the bags on a luggage cart.

"Did you get them all?" asked Annie

"Sure did," replied Alice. "Here is your coat, Annie. You better put it on. It looks pretty cold out there."

Annie and Alice made their way out of the terminal to the shuttle bus that would take them to Annie's car. It was cold and there were several inches of snow on the ground.

Annie and Alice stepped off the shuttle bus and found Annie's car covered with snow. They struggled to get the trunk open and place the luggage inside. They got in the vehicle and Annie started it up. As they waited for the car to heat up, they both scraped snow and ice off the car and windows.

When the windshield was finally clear, they got in and headed for home. Annie drove past the exit she should have taken to go home.

"Where you goin' Punkin'?" asked Alice.

"I need to drop off the video camera card off at Mike's house. He is copying it for Dad," replied Annie.

"Where is your dad anyway?" asked Alice.

"Well, it's just after noon here, so I suppose he is just a few hours away from landing in Zimbabwe."

"Your father," sneered Alice "I sure hope he knows what he is doing."

"Me, too, Mom, me too."

Annie pulled into Mike's driveway, and Mike was standing at the door. Annie got out of the car to get the tape from the trunk, as Mike came outside to meet her.

"Hey, Annie," said Mike. "Hi, Alice."

"Hi, Mike," said Annie. "Here is the video card, the Miami Sunday paper, and the handouts we got from the Oasis briefing."

"Okay, Annie. Thanks. I watched the news about Campbell. They were saying some pretty bad stuff about him molesting his daughters that died. He is being taken to Madison County and they are going to have a press conference at 5:30 p.m. to talk about what they got on him."

"It just doesn't seem possible. I just...he was so nice. The girls loved him," said Annie.

"You knew those girls?" exclaimed Mike.

"Oh, yeah, Kara and Keisha. They were both little. You will see them on the video. They are pretty easy to pick out," said Annie. "What else did they say about him?"

"They just said he was a former Marine and now was a school teacher in Anderson. They said the Dade County Coroner suspected the abuse during the autopsies of the girls. They said some of his students had been questioned this morning. Not much else," said Mike.

"This is so bizarre...I just can't believe it. But, hey, what's one more unbelievable thing in a sea of unbelievable events?" said Annie.

Mike just shook his head and then said, "I will see you at 4:30 p.m. at Kosten's office."

Annie got back in the car and backed out onto the street. Mike turned and went inside to make a copy of the video.

Annie and Alice arrived home. Some of Callie's things were scattered around the room of the trailer that they lived in. Her pictures were everywhere. They just sat down on the couch, held each other, and cried for a while.

Alice fell asleep and it was as if Annie was all alone.

She thought for a very long time about all the events of the last two days. She was all cried out and, at the moment, there were no tears left.

She picked up her house landline phone and dialed the Orlando hotel. The desk clerk answered.

"The room of Campbell please...Jimmy or Mark Campbell," said Annie,

In a moment the phone rang.

"Hello."

"Jimmy."

"Yeah," he said.

"This is Annie Grainger."

"Annie, what's up?" he asked sensing that something was wrong.

"Have you heard from your father, Jimmy?" she asked.

"No, he flew up to Indianapolis this morning. He has hardly had time to get home and get settled. I don't expect to hear from him for a while anyway."

"Jimmy, Mom and I saw him at the airport. He was arrested by the Madison County Sheriff."

"Arrested!" he shouted. "Are you nuts...what for?"

"Look, Jimmy, all I know is what I heard at the airport and what they said on the news. It's all over the news up here. They said he molested his daughters."

"You're not serious...that's a lie. He would never do that. That man is as straight an arrow as they come...God, Country, Duty, Family...No, this can't be happening!" screamed Jimmy.

There is a news conference at 5:30. I can call you this evening and tell you what they are saying but I just thought you should know if you hadn't already heard," said Annie

"Yeah. Annie, thanks for letting me know, I need to call my sister. Annie, listen to me...you can take this to the bank...My dad would never do what they said. Never?"

"I believe you, Jimmy, I believe you," said Annie. "I will call you later. Bye."

"Yeah, I'll see ya. Bye," said Jimmy.

Annie looked at the clock. There was just enough time to freshen up and get to Kosten's office by 4:30.

John Kosten was seated in his first-floor corner office when Annie walked up to the building. John smiled and waved at her as she headed for the entrance. Mike was standing in the lobby waiting for her with a briefcase full of various items.

They walked into the office and were immediately greeted by John Kosten. He smiled and shook the hand of Mike and introduced himself. He then put his arms around Annie and said, "Annie, I have been praying for your sister and for you, your mother and your father."

Annie thought she was cried out, but she began to sob in his arms and he held her for a while in a way a father would hold his own daughter. In a few moments, she regained her composure and the three went into John's office and sat down.

Mike pulled out his computer and turned it on and positioned it on John's desk so John could see the screen.

"Okay," said Mike, "let's start with the voicemail files and the log of calls made from Callie's cell phone. I have prepared a timeline of events that you can follow, as I lay out Dan's theory for you."

"I am impressed already Mike," said John, as he began to look at the chronology printout.

"I have to tell you, Mr. Kosten, some of the pieces fit very nicely together, but right now, some of it is going take a little faith."

"Well, Mike," said John, "you have come to the right place, I have no shortage of faith."

Chapter 16

John Kosten listened intently for nearly an hour to the information that Mike had compiled. There were maps showing the possible range of the 747-400 aircraft. There was an analysis of wind directions and very-impressive proof that a call was made on the Virgin Island cell site three hours after the plane should have been at the bottom of the Atlantic.

He had seen heartbreaking video of Callie and the other girls and Callie with Annie and their mother. There were some very troubling things to digest here. But the unfortunate truth was that all they really had was the phone call from Callie, referring to the fire she could see through the plane window, and the Indiana cellular printout placing that call at 11:44 eastern.

They were going to need a lot more than that and John knew it. He looked at his watch, it was nearly 5:30 p.m.

"I think we better take a break and see what they have on the news from Anderson," said John.

John picked up the remote and flipped the TV to the local station. He quickly tuned through the local stations, and all of them were covering the live news conference from Anderson. The Madison County Prosecutor, Steve Foulke, began to speak. He was clad in a finely tailored suit with an off-white shirt - perfect for television. Every strand of his medium-brown, blow-dried hair was in place.

"At 11:30 a.m. this morning, the Madison County Sheriff's Department, accompanied by officers of the Marion County Sheriff's Department and Indiana State Police, placed Mark Campbell under arrest as he stepped off a plane from Miami. Mr. Campbell is the stepfather of Keisha, age eleven and Kara, age six. Both of these girls lost their lives tragically in the crash of the Oasis 747 off the coast of Miami. The bodies of both girls were recovered and taken to the Dade County Coroner's office for examination. Our office was informed of the results of that examination and our own county coroner, Larry Crawford, was in Miami to personally view the autopsies. Based on that information, we arranged for the immediate transfer of the bodies to the Madison County Coroner. Larry Crawford, our Coroner, has conducted a second examination of the girls and the results confirm the disturbing suspicions of Dade County. These girls not only died tragically. They lived their life in tragedy. Our worst fears were confirmed when the Madison County Child Protective Services conducted an examination of the fifteen-year-old sister of Keisha and Kara. She too has been sexually molested in the same fashion. Normally, the identity of the sister would remain confidential, but in this case, that will not be possible."

"The nature and scope of the sexual abuse these girls have been subjected to is beyond my ability to convey in words. I thought I had seen it all. I have been physically ill since being present at the autopsy and learning of the condition of the fifteen-year-old. Both the Dade County Coroner and the Madison County Coroner have extracted semen samples from the bodies of both girls. Preliminary DNA testing has indicated that the samples are consistent with an African-American male. We are holding Mr. Campbell on suspicion of sexual molestation of his daughters, pending confirmation of a precise DNA match. We intend to formally charge Mark Campbell. There will be a full Coroner's Inquest conducted into the circumstances surrounding the cause of death for the two deceased daughters."

Some of the reporters began asking questions of Foulke, but the station cut away to another reporter who did a story on Mark's background in the Marines. He had finished his military career as an embassy guard in various locations in Africa. Mark was credited with saving the lives of several embassy employees and the U.S. Ambassador to Guinea-Bissau, when it came under attack from Islamic extremists. When he left the Marines, he settled in Anderson and was a very popular teacher in the local high school. Quick sound bites from other students and teachers described him as a popular and well-liked teacher. They showed pictures of him in his Marine uniform and from the high school yearbook. The piece ended with video of Mark Campbell being led through the airline terminal in handcuffs.

John muted the sound. "What do you think, Annie? he asked.

"Mr. Kosten, I don't know what to think, but I don't think he did it. If he did, then I am no judge of people at all. Those two girls loved him and clung to him. I can't imagine he would ever hurt them," replied Annie.

"Annie, the strong implication here is that both girls were sexually molested shortly before they left their father to go on the plane," said John.

"I was with them," said Annie. "I saw the girls all morning on Friday. I met them Friday just after noon, and I saw them at a late lunch. They were happy and giggly and dancing around all day. It just doesn't seem possible they could have been molested that morning. There were only a couple of hours between lunch and leaving for the airport. I saw them just before they left. They seemed fine. There is probably some video of them just before they got on the bus for the airport."

"Really? Can we find that?" asked John.

Mike fast-forwarded the video to the girls running around looking for their bus. "Do you see that?" said Annie. "Almost all of those girls are blondes, and you can't see it on the video, but they all have blue eyes, including Callie. There they are!"

You could clearly see a tall, black man comforting his little daughter and directing them both on to a red and white bus. He hugged them both one last time, and then they hopped on the bus. Annie had been operating the video camera and panned the camera along the windows, as Keisha and Kara found a seat midway to the rear of the bus. They both waved to their dad and were smiling.

"See what I mean!" shrieked Annie "There are no blondes on that bus. Look at it. I recognize some of the girls in the windows from the handout. Look at it." She picked up the Oasis handout and shoved it toward John.

John picked up the flyer and asked Mike to re-run the video several times, as he studied the video and the pictures in the handout.

"I see what you mean, Annie. You know, Mike, I don't think Dan's theory requires so much faith after all. There is something very wrong going on here. I can feel it in my spirit. We just have to figure out how to prove it in court. If Dan is right, then those girls on that bus never made it onboard the plane."

"Annie, how old are you?" asked John.

"Nineteen," she said.

"Good," replied John. "I can represent you in a civil case against Oasis. The corporate headquarters is here in Hamilton County. With your permission, I will file a civil suit against them tomorrow for negligence, child endangerment or something, to buy us some time and get something on file. As Callie's sister, you have the legal standing to make that charge."

"I don't have any money to pay you with and I just don't know right now. I think I need to talk to my dad and my mom, what do you think, Mike?" Asked Annie

Without a moment's hesitation Mike replied "Annie, from halfway around the world your dad contacted this man for help, John saw us immediately and was willing to listen to our crazy story based solely on his knowing your dad. It's your decision, but I know what your dad would say if he were here."

Tears filled Annie's eyes as she looked at John. "You're hired," she said, as her voice cracked.

"You are officially a client now. I will need you to come by the office tomorrow morning and sign some papers. I will file the suit in Noblesville tomorrow afternoon. Then I can file a Motion for Discovery on Oasis and try to uncover information about the selection process that favored so many blondes over other girls."

"My phone!" said Annie as she reached for her purse. She took out her phone and looked at the screen. "It's my mom. She's texted me with an '811'. That means it is very important."

Annie called her mom.

"Mom?" said Annie when Alice answered.

"I am sorry to bother you, but it's that Jimmy from Florida. He's called our house number three times and said he has to get a hold of you right away," said Alice.

"Jimmy Campbell?" asked Annie.

"Yeah, I can give you his number at the hotel."

"No, I have it. I guess I will call him," said Annie.

"I didn't know what to do, he was so insistent, I'm sorry."

"It's okay, Mom. I'll call him."

Annie hung up the phone and said "It's Jimmy Campbell, Mark Campbell's son. He wants me to call him right away in Orlando. He has already called three times."

"How old is he?" asked John.

"Mid-twenties I guess, I don't know."

"Annie is this the same hotel room in Orlando where his father stayed?"

"Yeah, why?"

"Well, it may not be a good idea to talk to him, the police may be checking phone records and could even have him under surveillance or the phone line tapped," said John.

"I already talked to him once today," Annie said sheepishly.

"What about?" asked John.

"I called him to see if he knew about his father's arrest. He didn't."

John thought for a moment. "You have already called him once, he has called your home three times, so the police may already have a connection to you. Go ahead and call him. It probably won't hurt anything at this point."

Annie picked up the handset and dialed the hotel and asked for Jimmy's room.

"Jimmy, it's Annie."

"I am coming up there tomorrow to see my dad in jail. I called my sister in Atlanta, and she will be there as soon as she can. I talked to my dad's wife and Kima, the full-blooded sister of Keisha and Kara. They don't know what to do. We need to find an attorney fast. Do you know any up there? Kima and her mother won't be of any help. Kima is scared to death and her mother hardly speaks English. You are the only other person I know in Indiana that could or would help."

"Just a second," said Annie, as she put her hand over the phone. "He is flying up here tomorrow to see Mr. Campbell and he has to find an attorney right away and wants to know if I know any."

"Let me speak with him," said John.

"Jimmy," said Annie, "there is someone here with me that I think you should talk to." Before he had a chance to answer she handed the phone to John.

"Mr. Campbell," said John.

"Yes," said Jimmy.

"My name is John Kosten, I am Annie's attorney. I think you need to be aware that your phone may be under surveillance and the records of all of the phone calls you make may be subpoenaed by the Madison County Prosecutor."

"No shit!" said Jimmy "Well, I need an attorney or rather, my dad does, and he needs one right away and I don't care if the whole damned police force knows it. My dad has nothing to hide. I just want to get him out of jail."

"Annie says you are flying up here tomorrow. If you will call my office when you get in, I will give you the names of three attorneys in Anderson that could handle the case," said John.

"I don't want no attorney from that red-necked town Mr. Kosten. I hate that town. I am already worried some of the locals will show up in white sheets and lynch my dad. I want somebody from Indianapolis. I want a big city attorney that can take on them jackasses in Madison County. Where you from, Mr. Kosten?"

"I live in Hamilton County same as Annie, but my office is on the north side of Indianapolis," said John.

"Sounds good to me," said Jimmy. "Will you meet with me tomorrow when I get in?"

"I don't think so," said John, "I am currently representing Annie in a cause that could conceivably be a conflict of interest. I would have to think about it."

"Well, you just think about it Mr. Kosten," sneered Jimmy, "but you and I both know ain't no black man going to get a fair shake in that town. He would have a better chance in Alabama than that part of Indiana."

"I understand your concerns, Mr. Campbell," began John.

"Call me Jimmy."

"Okay Jimmy, I hear you, I understand what you are saying, things are much better over there than they used to be."

"Look, my dad needs an attorney right away. A good one. His wife can hardly speak English, and Kima, my stepsister, was forcibly examined by Child Protective Services today against her will and against the will of her mother. They took custody of her by court order."

"Where is the girl now?" asked John.

"Well, they let Kima go home with her mother, but they made a point of saying they could come and get her any time they wanted," replied Jimmy.

Kosten pursed his lips. He seemed more intent now. "Do you know the caseworker's name?" he asked.

"Yeah, it's Merriman," replied Jimmy.

"I know her. Shirley Merriman is the Director of Madison County Child Protective Services. I have had some dealings with her in the past," said John.

"You said the mother does not speak English. What language does she speak? asked John.

"She and the three girls speak Portuguese. The girls have learned to speak English pretty good since they have been here. Their mother understands English but does not always speak it very well."

"Portuguese," replied John, "Where were they from?"

The west coast of Africa, my dad met them when he was an Embassy guard in Bissau. It's actually a bastardized form of Portuguese Creole. I don't remember the name of the dialect."

"Jimmy, I am interested in your dad's case. I am familiar with some of the circumstances. I am going to have to consider the possible conflict of interest problems that could arise. I would have to meet with your dad before I would take the case. I will go ahead and put together a recommendation for three Anderson attorneys and three Indianapolis attorneys. Call me tomorrow."

"Okay, I will do that. I get into Indy at 10:00 a.m. and will call you then. Can I speak with Annie?" asked Jimmy

"If you insist, yes, but my advice is that you wait until you get here before you talk to her again, and remember, you may be under surveillance. Watch what you say on the phone to anyone," warned John.

"Okay, I will take your advice. One more thing - don't worry about the money. We don't have much but my sister said she will find the money to pay you," said Jimmy.

"We can talk about that later," said John. As he hung up the phone, he was clearly troubled.

"Are you going to take Mark's case?" asked Annie.

"It is problematic," said John. "There is an uncomfortable relationship between the two cases. One is civil, one is criminal. I can't help thinking that my potential subpoena powers under a criminal case would be greater and more compelling than under a civil case against Oasis."

"What was the deal on Portuguese?" asked Mike.

"Well, it turns out that the native language of Mark Campbell's wife and the three girls is a Portuguese dialect from West Africa," said John.

"Remember what Dan said?" asked Mike "He identified the other language on the voicemail as Portuguese. Does that fit somehow?"

"Your guess it as good as mine. I don't know but it is surely a curious coincidence," said John.

The conversation was cut short by Annie. The video had been running the whole time they had been talking and was now up to the part where Oasis One was leaving the gate and Callie was flicking her light on and off.

"Stop the video!" cried Annie. "Pause it I mean, where's the newspaper you had Mike?"

"Which one?" asked Mike, as he thumbed through the stack he had collected.

"That one, the Miami Herald," she said, pointing to a large front-page picture of the tail section of Oasis One being hoisted from the Atlantic onto a recovery ship.

"Look at the position of the Oasis logo on the tail in the photograph. Back the video up a little bit and look at the tail on the tape." Mike reversed the video back a little bit and then paused it on the shot of the tail section as it was taxiing away from the gate area.

"See?" exclaimed Annie "It's not the same. The Oasis logo on the tape is closer to the front of the wing and higher up than it is in this picture."

"You're right, Annie, you're right," said Mike. "It's as obvious as hell once you see it. The logo is about the same size but it is not in the same place on the tail. It is much closer to the leading edge of the vertical stabilizer on the video. It's like somebody just didn't match the correct placement of a decal on the vertical stabilizer. The tail section of the plane in the newspaper is not from the same plane in the video. Holy crap! You know what that means?"

The three of them sat silently for a moment until John Kosten softly whispered, "Praise the Lord!"

Chapter 17

Yasi Min Hassan looked out the window upon a magnificent nightscape of high-rise buildings reflected in the Persian Gulf. The plane was on final approach to the Dubai International Airport. The flight from Honolulu to Narita and Hong Kong had been long but without incident. Here she was embarking on the mission of her lifetime - to complete her beloved grandmother's legacy and create a new day for women in Bukhara.

She pondered her unworthiness and thought too often of her lurid sexual encounter with the American in Maui. He got what he wanted she thought, what every man wants from a woman. At least, he was polite and gentlemanly, unlike most she had been with. Still, a trace of a smile came across her lips when she thought of him and how he had made her feel. It was like no other she had ever had, in fact, given what had been clipped from her body when she was younger, it was not possible.

She had gathered her carry-on and was proceeding down the jetway. She wondered what Dan must be doing now and she felt great sorrow at the circumstances his daughter was in, yet she also felt hope.

"Princess," she heard a deep voice say as she snapped back to the present. A man in a Bukhara military uniform was looking at her. He was flanked by two Dubai Security Guards. She looked at him startled.

"Your uncle awaits and he is with your father. Please come with me. We will collect your luggage."

As he led the way, Jasmine followed and the two security guards positioned themselves behind her as they walked through the airport. She was dressed elegantly in a long-sleeved, light-blue Islamic dress. A beige hijab covered her head and was draped around her neck and shoulders. Her face was fully visible.

Many of the travelers in the terminal stared as she walked toward the gate guarded by another group of Dubai Security Guards. Jasmine entered the gateway alone and walked to the open door of the waiting 767. "Welcome aboard, Princess," a loud and gruff voice proclaimed as she set foot on the plane. Jasmine stared coldly at the man in white with the traditional Royal headdress. "Hello Uncle," she said coldly "Where is my father?" Nasrullah stepped to the side revealing a customized hospital bed in what had been the first-class section of the plane.

"My child," a frail, male voice cried out. "Father," she said, as she scurried to his bedside. He held out his hand and she clasped it firmly as she leaned over and kissed him on his forehead. "Father, it has been so long and I have missed you so," she said.

"Well, you are here now, my child," uttered the weak voice of her father. "We have much to talk about," but the old man fell asleep before the plane taxied to the runway. Jasmine fastened her seatbelt in a luxury recliner next to her father, she needed to get some sleep. She had a big day tomorrow.

The plane took off from Dubai, traveled across the Gulf, and entered Iranian airspace. They traveled the entire length of Iran south to north. Jasmine heard her father stir and came to his side. They spoke of Jasmine's mother, of Jasmine's time in Paris and in the United States. Jasmine had never had a conversation like this with her father in all her years. Abdullah even spoke of his own mother, Yasi Min. Jasmine's beloved grandmother. She had been stoned to death when Jasmine was eleven. Her father had never spoken to her of Yasi Min before. He said Jasmine looked so much like her. His sadness grew even greater when the conversation turned briefly to her brother Adil. "Damned Israeli's. Damn Jew bastards. They killed my son!" exclaimed Abdullah. "One day I will exact revenge in the name of Allah on those who took my son, even if it is the last thing I do."

Abdullah was quickly calmed by the soothing voice of his daughter. As the old man looked into his daughter's eyes, he said, "You have your grandmother's eyes and your mother's smile." The plane began to descend into the Bukhara Airport. Once on the ground, Emir Abdullah Hassan, bed and all was wheeled out to a waiting jetway and lowered to the ground where he was placed into a Red Crescent ambulance. Jasmine was by his side at all times and rode in the ambulance to the Ark. This was the ancient fortress of Bukhara. Originally built in the Fifth Century A.D., before there was a Muslim religion and destroyed and rebuilt many times. It was a massive stone structure covering nearly ten acres of the city. It was a small city within a city. Jasmine had not seen it in nearly five years. The restoration in the last five years was breathtaking. It was clean, and the intricate blue, white and gold mosaic patterns gleamed in the sunlight. The massive walls along the perimeter of the citadel loomed fifty to sixty-five feet into the air. Two eighteenth-century towers stood on either side of the Ark's main entrance doorway. Above the doorway, a terrace connected the two towers and overlooked the newly rebuilt Registan Square.

The ambulance stopped at the ramp in front of the main entrance of the Ark. Her father's bed was quickly removed from the ambulance, and the attendants began rolling him up the ramp to the main doorway.

Jasmine looked up the ramp and at the terrace above the main entrance. A lone figure dressed in royal garb stared down at her and the events unfolding around her. She immediately recognized him as the man she most despised after her uncle. It was her cousin Alim Hassan, the son of her Uncle Nasrullah. Their eyes locked for a moment and he smiled an evil smile before she turned from him. She began to follow her father up the ramp.

"No, Princess," came the voice of her uncle standing behind her. "You will join your father shortly, after he is settled in the Royal Chambers. For now, you must remain with me, as I have things you must learn about."

A customized, bullet-proof, black Mercedes G-Class SUV was waiting behind her uncle. It had a very simple box-like appearance and yet it exuded elegance. Two chrome exhaust pipes were visible just below the rear passenger door. A uniformed officer opened the door. Nasrullah motioned for Jasmine to get in the back seat. She complied and slid into the luxurious, leather-upholstered, rear seat. Nasrullah climbed into the middle seat and sat directly across from Jasmine facing her. The door closed and Nasrullah motioned the driver to go.

The Mercedes slowly circled the entire Ark as if the uncle wanted to remind Jasmine of the sheer magnitude of the fortress. There had been much new construction in the vicinity of the Ark. They circled all the way back to the front where a small crowd had gathered.

A woman was standing flanked by two Bukharan military men. The Mercedes pulled up about fifteen feet away. Another uniformed man opened the rear passenger door of the Mercedes, giving Jasmine and her uncle a clear, unobstructed view of the woman.

Nasrullah's booming voice declared, "This woman was caught in the very act of adultery. She is the daughter of a no-account day laborer, and her life is of no value. But she must receive the punishment prescribed by Sharia law."

Nasrullah paused as if waiting for a reaction from Jasmine. She looked at him with contempt and their eyes locked. She did not look away.

Jasmine then watched as the woman was forced to step into a blue sack that engulfed her entire body. The drawstrings of the sack above her head were pulled tight by the two military men who then immediately stepped away.

Jasmine's eyes searched the crowd and there she saw a huge pile of fist-sized stones. She closed her eyes. She had witnessed this scene before, but she tried desperately not to remember the drama she knew was about to unfold before her eyes. But she did remember. She could not help but remember. She knew the crowd would soon begin hurling the stones at the woman who could not even see them coming. After many long minutes of unbearable torture, she would drop to the ground. One of the men would open up the sack to see if she was still alive. If she was, he would close the sack up again and the crowd would continue to throw the stones until, finally, her body was lifeless.

Jasmine looked around Registan Square. It was surreal. This heinous act had become commonplace. The crowd was not large. Many people went about their normal business. Along the wall of the Ark, men and women played chess and backgammon while sipping tea. Merchants sold their wares, seemingly oblivious to the scene that was unfolding.

Nasrullah continued "This woman has sinned against Allah but in today's Bukhara we must not prolong the suffering of this evil woman unnecessarily. Her life is an example to no one."

Suddenly, she heard the sound of machinery and looked over to see a large yellow and black front-loader approaching the woman. Its bucket was high in the air and was filled with heavy rocks. The front-loader stopped at the side of the woman and tilted its bucket downward. In a moment, over a thousand pounds of stone came crashing down on the woman compressing her into a lifeless heap. The crowd cheered in approval as the front loader turned and left as quickly as it had arrived.

A tear streamed down Jasmine's cheek much to the amusement of her uncle.

The silence was broken by Nasrullah's gruff voice. "Unfortunately, Princess, this more humane method of dealing with an adulteress is reserved for those who are not required to live their lives as an example to other righteous women."

"You call that humane, Uncle?" Jasmine said as she spat out the words.

"It's all relative, Princess," said Nasrullah. "I imagine you would beg for such a quick and merciful punishment if you as a Princess were found guilty of adultery."

Nasrullah motioned in the window and a group of soldiers parted to reveal a beautiful young woman in white garb perhaps twenty-two years old or even younger. A black sash just above her waist bound her arms to her body. Her face was fully exposed to the crowd. She was escorted several feet and forced to step down into a pit that had been prepared for her.

She stood in the pit as the soldiers quickly filled in the dirt around her legs and nearly up to her waist. Her arms were bound to her body just above the elbows.

"This young woman is the daughter of our Deputy Foreign Minister," said Nasrullah. "She had a duty to live her life as an example to all the women of Bukhara. She must pay the price for her sin in the full public view of the people she has betrayed."

A man in cleric's garb pronounced some words over her as he faced her. He then turned to the crowd about fifteen feet away. The young girl was helpless before the angry crowd, with her long dark hair hanging down well below her shoulders. The first man hurled the first stone and it crashed against her left shoulder causing her body to lurch backward. The young woman regained her composure and made herself as erect as she could. Her face betraying no sign of the pain she had just endured. The young woman in the pit glared at the crowd. A second stone was handed to a man. He immediately threw the stone with great force striking the girl in the center of her forehead. Her head lurched violently backward. Another woman in the crowd threw up her hands in approval and cheered, as a young boy next to her watched. The girl was bleeding now from the wound in her forehead. A small trickle of blood traveled down her forehead and between her eyes; down her nose, across the center of her lips onto her chin and dripped onto her white outfit. Her eyes were closed now and she began to sob. A man in the crowd shouted "Allahu Akbar!" Her head tilted forward now as she cried. The crowd cheered. Somehow, she raised her tortured face toward the crowd and looked at them once again. The third rock pelted her in the head so hard she fell fully back against the ground. Blood was streaking everywhere. She again brought herself to an upright position. Her face was now covered with blood and her white garb stained all over in blood splatters. Her long dark hair was now matted to the blood on her face. She gasped in pain. Her hands just above the surface of the ground also covered in blood tried to desperately to do something to help She leaned forward now sobbing uncontrollably. A woman in the crowd cried out in some kind of protest and was quickly escorted from the deadly scene by a group of men. The protesting woman threw herself to the ground and began to wail. Then the crowd let loose with hundreds of stones. Nearly every deadly stone found its target on her head and upper abdomen. Those that missed and fell short all seemed to ricochet off the ground and strike the girl in an upward motion. Her body was swaying in all directions reacting to the striking force of the stones coming from so many in the crowd positioned around her.

In what seemed like an eternity to Jasmine as she watched, the stones continued to come. Even after the girl's broken and mutilated body lay in a crumpled mass of blood and dirt, the crowd continued to cheer and throw the stones. After a while, the crowd finally stopped and began to slowly dissipate. One man in the crowd walked up to the lifeless corpse of what just a few minutes before was a beautiful young woman. He came close and spat on her body and kicked her in the head.

Jasmine closed her eyes trying not to reveal to her uncle how deeply disturbed she was.

"And that, Princess, is how we punish the evil adulteresses in our society. I trust the Princess understands that if it were ever to be proven that she had sex outside of marriage that she would face the same justice."

"Yes, Uncle," began Jasmine, in a defiant voice, "I understand completely that you arranged the death of two women today. Believe me, I understand exactly what you are capable of. You have just reenacted *The Stoning of Soroya M* for the sole purpose of making your point to me. You are evil,

Uncle, and with my father's help, I will end your barbaric distortion of the Koran. I will end your influence in Bukhara."

"Your father awaits, Princess," said Nasrullah, surprised by her defiance. He motioned Jasmine out of the Mercedes. A soldier escorted her up the ramp into the Ark and accompanied her to her father's royal chamber.

Chapter 18

Qantas Flight 63 touched down in Harare, Zimbabwe right on time at 9:20 p.m. on Tuesday evening. There were no jetways into the terminal gate. The passengers made their way down a large stairway that had been rolled up to the door of the jet.

It was very hot when Dan stepped onto the concrete of the ramp area. February in the southern hemisphere was the middle of summer. The passengers were loaded on several buses for the short ride to the terminal and immigration.

It took Dan almost an hour to collect his one piece of checked luggage, fill out the necessary forms and then clear customs and passport control. It took several minutes of persistence to obtain an entry visa on the spot. Dan always carried extra sets of passport pictures with him tucked in his carry-on bag for visa applications. He explained this trip was personal, but he had visited Zimbabwe in the past when he was affiliated with a humanitarian relief agency or Non-Governmental Organization. Someone affiliated with an

"NGO" as they were called, was often able to get a little extra leniency in the application of the rules. Dan was relieved when he finally made his way through the process.

As soon as he entered the main terminal outside customs, he was mobbed by a group of people wanting to help him with his luggage. One man even tried to take the luggage out of Dan's hand as he walked.

"No," Dan said sternly. "I can do it."

The man remained insistent for a short time but finally gave up. Then the chorus of "taxi…taxi," began, as a group of taxi drivers competed loudly for the next fare. One of the drivers began walking along with Dan. "Taxi, sir? Need a taxi?" he asked.

"Do you know where the Rejoice and Praise Church is?" asked Dan.

"Oh yes, I know it, my family goes there, you need taxi?"

"How much to the church?" asked Dan.

"Oh, that's a long way, fifty dollars," said the driver.

"How much in U.S. dollars?" asked Dan as he continued to walk amidst shouts of "taxi…taxi" from other drivers.

"Fifty dollars U.S," replied the driver.

"NO!" said Dan, "Ten U.S. dollars."

"Ten U.S. dollars. No, my friend it is very far, ten dollars is to the hotels nearby." The driver paused and smiled, "For you, my special friend, a special price - thirty dollars," and the driver reached for Dan's bag and tried to take it out of his hand.

Dan stopped "Twenty dollars U.S., no more," said Dan, as he showed the driver the American twenty sticking out of his shirt pocket.

"Okay," said the driver, as he reached for the twenty.

"Dan cupped his hand over his shirt pocket and said, 'After we get to the church. I am in a hurry."

The driver picked up Dan's bag and they headed out into the poorly lit parking lot. The cab was a run-down Toyota mini-van with the seats ripped and the stuffing sticking out of the seats.

The driver put Dan's luggage in the rear compartment and tried to take Dan's carry-on from him.

"I will keep this with me up front," said Dan, as he walked around to the right side of the van and opened the door. "Oops," Dan said, as he stared at the steering wheel on the right side. The driver smiled and said, "You want to drive?"

"No, I don't think so," replied Dan, "but I do want to sit up front." Dan went around to the left side of the van and got into the passenger seat. The drive into town took some getting used to. Dan had driven on the left side many times in his travels but he always found it disquieting.

"So, you attend the Rejoice and Praise church?" asked Dan.

"Oh yes, for five years now," said the driver.

Dan wasn't sure he was telling the truth. "You know Pastor?" asked Dan.

"Oh yes, I know Pastor."

"No, I mean his name. Do you know his name?" asked Dan.

"You mean Pastor of the whole church?" asked the driver, "It is a big church with many Pastors."

"Yes, I know," replied Dan. "Pastor Doyle, Do you know Pastor Doyle. Is he still the pastor of the church?"

"Oh, yes, Pastor Timothy. Pastor Timothy Doyle. He is the pastor of the whole church."

"Is there a Tuesday service tonight?" asked Dan.

"Yes, every night, we have a big service," said the driver,

"Why every night? What's going on?

"We are having a big revival; a camp-meeting. We have guest pastors from all over Africa here. Big revival," said the driver.

'No kidding," said Dan, as he leaned back in his seat to relax a little bit for the first time since arriving in Zimbabwe. It was almost 11:00 p.m. when the driver pulled up to the church. Dan could hear singing and clapping coming from inside the building.

He stepped out of the minivan, as the driver removed Dan's luggage from the rear. Dan handed the driver the twenty and then reached into his side pocket and pulled out another ten. Can you help me with the bag?"

The driver smiled. "Sure," he said, and he picked up Dan's bag and tried to take Dan's carry-on."

"No," said Dan, "I can carry this one."

They walked up the steps into the church. It was a beautiful building, and, as he looked around, he saw a sea of people, black and white, on their feet and singing to the Lord. There were two large TV screens on either side of the pulpit, and the words of the song were on the screen. A bouncing ball guided the entire congregation as they sang

"Shout to the Lord all the Earth, let us sing
Power and majesty, praise to the King."

It was a very familiar tune to Dan, and he felt suddenly at peace. He and the driver made their way along the far aisle of the church and down to the area where a group of pastors was sitting to the right of the pulpit. The driver was right. Dan recognized the faces of many of the men assembled here as a veritable Who's Who of Charismatic and Spirit-filled pastors from all over Africa. He did not remember many of their names, but he recognized them just the same.

He stood next to the wall for several minutes as the singing continued, and people were standing and many were jumping up and down with their hands held high into the air. There were white and black businessmen in suits, finely dressed women as well as women in casual western dress, and many black women attired in brightly colored traditional African dress. Whole rows of people with eyes looking upward and arms outreached were swaying back and forth and singing.

"My comfort, my shelter
Tower of refuge and strength."

The irony of this particular song was not lost on him. He looked up at the large screen on the wall and saw in very large words "Shout to the Lord." It was a praise and worship song written by Darlene Zschech from the very nation he had just left - Australia.

He stood there for a while and could not help but sing along.

One of the men seated in the front row with the pastors noticed Dan. For a moment he smiled in recognition, and then suddenly, his expression became very serious. He immediately leaped to his feet and came over to Dan.

"Dan! Dan Grainger! What on earth are you doing here?" the Pastor said as he opened his arms up and embraced Dan, and gave him a big hug. "Why didn't you tell us you were coming?"

Dan was never very comfortable with these physical displays and he stiffened slightly as the Pastor tightened his arms around him.

"Pastor Doyle, it's good to see you," said Dan. "I wasn't sure the service would still be on this late."

"Are you kidding? We will be going strong till midnight, Praise the Lord!" He paused. "What's wrong, Dan? asked the Pastor. "I sense great tribulation within you."

"If that was a word of knowledge, Pastor, you're right on the money. I need help, a lot of help. My youngest daughter's life is in danger," blurted Dan.

The pastor maintained his arms around Dan and patted him on the back. When he let go he motioned to some of his aides and said, "Let's go to my office." The pastor's aides picked up Dan's luggage and Dan's carry-on and accompanied Dan and Pastor Tim to a door at the side of the sanctuary.

Dan and Tim sat down in the office chairs in front of Tim's desk. "Okay, Dan, tell me about your daughter, Callie, isn't it?" said Tim.

"I can't believe you remembered her name, but I guess that should not surprise me. Remembering people is one of your great gifts." Dan continued, "Pastor, a lot of people believe she is dead, but I refuse to accept it. I am holding out hope that she has been kidnapped along with about 280 or so other young girls."

Tim's expression did not change. "Go on," he said.

"You have heard of the plane crash in Miami with three hundred young girls on their way to the Super Bowl last Friday?" asked Dan.

"Of course, it's all over the news especially CNN International."

"Callie was on that plane. I have reason to believe that the plane never crashed as reported but that there is an elaborate plan to kidnap the girls." Dan took the next ten minutes to detail his suspicions and to share what little evidence he had to support it. He did not mention Jasmine nor the incident in Sydney. Tim listened without comment until Dan finally ran out of things to say."

"Where are you staying tonight?" asked Tim.

"I don't have a place yet, I thought I would try to get in touch with you first and then see if I could get a room at the Hotel Meikles," said Dan.

"Nonsense," replied Tim. "You will stay in my house tonight. It is right next door and we have plenty of room." He motioned to one of his staff. "Would you go over and tell Mrs. Doyle that we will have another guest tonight and to have a room prepared.

"Pastor Doyle, I was hoping to enlist the help of some Flying Doves pilots. I have some things being shipped here to the church from Indiana. I am hoping they will come tomorrow. I hope that was okay," said Dan.

"That's fine. Whatever we can do to help we will. Do I have your permission to share your story with other members of my staff and with some of the other pastors?"

"I place my total confidence in you, Pastor. You can tell anyone you think can help. Africa is such a huge place, and I have so little to go on. The plane may not even be here," said Dan with a deep sigh.

"That, Dan, is a negative confession and we do not permit that here. You have far more to go on than you realize. Africa is not nearly so large as you would think. There are not that many airports where a 747 can land. There are far fewer flights each day in the whole continent of Africa than at O'Hare in just a few hours. It may reassure you to know that many Flying Doves pilots are here in Zimbabwe this week because of our conference."

The pastor's words were reassuring to Dan. He knew if anyone could help him find Callie and the girls it would be Pastor Doyle or someone Pastor could put him in touch with. Dan suddenly realized how tired he was. He had gotten very little rest on the flights. The last seventy-two hours were a complete blur, and he had been in the air for much of it.

Pastor Doyle looked at Dan and said "Dan, you need to get some rest. We can talk further at breakfast in the morning."

Tim motioned for one of his aids. "Please take Mr. Grainger and his luggage over to the guest room."

They all left the office and went back into the sanctuary. It was during altar call. Dozens and dozens of the faithful had flocked to the front by the pulpit. All of the pastors were on their feet now and wading into the crowd. They were laying hands on the foreheads of the people that had come forward and were praying for them. Many of the faithful were then falling backward onto the floor. Church staff members were trying to keep up with the pastors by standing behind the person being prayed for. They tried to catch the person when they fell backward, lowering them gently to the floor to break the fall. Often, they covered the person with a small cloth. The congregation was aroused into a fever pitch with many speaking in tongues and asking to be filled with the Holy Spirit.

Several of the women dressed in traditional African clothing were making a loud, high-pitched trilling sound from their mouths, with their tongues rapidly going from side to side. It was a traditional African ululation sound often made at joyous occasions. Men and women lay strewn around the floor as if it were a battlefield. Some were lying calmly and peacefully and some gyrating violently in spasms and crying out.

Dan just stood in amazement at the scene unfolding before him. He had seen it before but was never able to be comfortable with the great outpouring of human emotion that was taking place. He never knew quite what to think.

Pastor Doyle had made his way through the crowd to the pulpit. He began to join in the prayers for the congregation.

"I have a friend who has just arrived from America tonight to join us," began Pastor Doyle. "We need to lift him up in prayer and ask the Lord to guide him in the work he has come here to perform."

The entire congregation joined in with thunderous applause and praise. Tears began to form in Dan's eyes. He had just traveled halfway around the world on a mission that no one could easily believe. And yet, Pastor Doyle believed everything he had to say, and now thousands of Christians were praying for his success.

How could Dan fail with allies like these? Dan's faith had been fed and his doubts had been starved. Dan could not help but believe that the Lord was going to guide him to save Callie and all the other girls. Dan was overwhelmed.

He looked around and saw a staff member with his luggage.

"You are ready now, Sir?" asked the staff member.

"Yes," Dan said softly, as he nodded, barely able to speak.

"Then follow me to the guest room. It is prepared for you."

Pastor Doyle had picked up the hand-held mike and was walking back and forth across the stage, leading the whole congregation in another rousing musical chorus.

It was another song particularly meaningful to Dan. It was originally written and performed by a fellow Hoosier, the late Rich Mullins. Dan was at peace.

"Our God is an awesome God
He reigns from heaven above
With wisdom, power, and love
Our God is an awesome God."

Chapter 19

Dan awoke to the sounds of birds chirping outside his window and the morning rays of the sun slipping through the louvers on the window. He looked at his wristwatch. His early morning eyes would not focus on the face of the watch. The numbers remained a blur. He looked over at the clock on the dresser. It said 7:30 a.m. A large ceiling fan turned slowly over his bed providing a pleasant breeze.

He had only slept for seven hours but it felt like ten. He got up and opened the louvered shutters on the windows. He had a beautiful view of a neatly manicured garden area with strange-looking broadleaf trees and shrubs all about.

"Good morning." Dan heard a voice from somewhere in the garden. He looked around and finally noticed an area where several people were seated for breakfast.

"Good morning, Pastor," replied Dan.

"Come on out and have breakfast with us Dan," said the pastor.

"I just woke up and need to freshen up a bit first," said Dan.

"The bathroom is down the hall to the right. Please hurry, there are some pastors here I would like you to meet before they leave. What do you want for breakfast?" asked Pastor Doyle.

"Whatever you have is fine," replied Dan.

"Eggs, bacon, ham, toast, rice, juice…you name it," said the pastor.

"Fine," said Dan. "Eggs over medium, ham, toast, rice and orange juice. I'll be out there in fifteen minutes," said Dan.

"Good. We will see you in fifteen minutes, by the way, there is no hot water this morning," shouted Pastor Doyle.

"TIA," shouted Dan, back to the group at the table.

"Ah, you remembered T-I-A, This is Africa and welcome to Harare!"

Dan pulled a change of clothes out of his luggage and put on a robe hanging in the room. He picked up his carry-on and headed for the bathroom. A nice, long, hot shower would have been great, but the short, cold, one woke him up. He quickly washed his hair and showered. He fumbled in his carry-on for his hair dryer. He looked at the outlet on the wall and switched the hair dryer to 220vac. He searched around in the bottom of his bag for the correct adapter.

He plugged the hair dryer in and turned it on. It ran a lot faster and got hotter than usual but it worked. He finished dressing and dropped his carry-on back at this room and made his way out to the garden area.

"Come sit over here," said Pastor Doyle, as he motioned to the chair next to him just as someone appeared from the kitchen with Dan's breakfast. Everyone stood up as Pastor Doyle introduced Dan to all of the men seated at the table. It was a dizzying array of names. He knew he would not remember them no matter how hard he tried. He nodded his head and shook their hands and then sat down.

"Dan, we will give you a few minutes to get started on your eggs, then we will get down to business.

Dan sat down in front of his breakfast and suddenly realized how hungry he was, but he paused awkwardly for a moment not sure what he should do next.

Pastor Doyle took him off the hook, "Lord, Bless this food for Dan and help restore his energy for the trying days ahead. Keep him safe and keep Callie and the other girls safe from harm. In the name of Jesus we pray," and then the others joined in with a chorus of "Amen."

The pastors talked of the camp meeting and how it was off to a good start on Sunday. Last night's meeting was great for early in the week. They looked forward to the meeting continuing each night and then culminating in a great service next Sunday night.

Some of the pastors had just come in on Monday, and some would be leaving on Saturday. Many pastors felt that it was unwise to be away from their own church for two Sundays in a row.

After a few minutes when Dan had a chance to finish most of his breakfast, Pastor Doyle turned to him and said "Dan, I have filled in the pastors on your incredible story. We are all impressed with your faith. While most men would have run back to Miami or home to Indiana, you had the strength to follow what the Holy Spirit has revealed to you."

"I don't know that I thought of it that way," said Dan, 'I was just following a hunch. The whole thing didn't feel right, and this little voice inside of me kept telling me to come to Africa. I didn't feel peace until I did that."

'Call it what you wish," said the pastor, "Those of us sitting here at this table understand that 'little voice' as you call it.

"After breakfast, with your permission, each of these pastors is going to call home and ask someone in their church to physically go out to the airport and look for a white 747 sitting on the ramp. They are going to discreetly ask if any was seen over the weekend and they are going to inquire about canceled or delayed flights."

"That's great. Thanks," said Dan, as he looked around at the faces of the pastors. "One of the reasons," continued Dan "maybe the main reason that I came to Africa was the connection we made to Portuguese on the voicemail. I am not positive it was Portuguese, but I am reasonably sure it was.

"You have no idea what was said on the recording?" asked Pastor Doyle.

"No, but I sure would like to find out if one of you can help me?" Said Dan,

"We would like to hear it," said Pastor Doyle. "There are several nations in Africa that speak a form of Portuguese. Some of the Pastors here speak Portuguese, and I am sure one of us can translate it for you."

"There is a computer system in the audio visual lab, Dan' You are free to use it," said the Pastor

"I have my laptop," said Dan.

"Well, you can use yours if you want," replied the Pastor, "but it may be difficult hearing the audio out here, and we will not all be able to see the display."

"Okay, I'm convinced," said Dan. "I will just use your system.

Pastor Doyle rose from the table. The other pastors and Dan got up also. Several of the pastors made a point of shaking Dan's hand and offering any assistance they could. The group of pastors then headed down the hallway.

Pastor Doyle motioned for a staff member and said, "Please take Mr. Grainger to Audio Visual and get someone to help him with the computer system."

"Pastor Doyle," said Dan, "one more thing."

"Yes."

"The Flying Doves. I need to get in touch with the Flying Doves," said Dan.

"That is no problem," replied the Pastor. "Most of the pastors and guests from outside of Zimbabwe were flown in on planes from the Flying Doves."

"I hope I have some electronics coming in today to the church. It is possible I can track Callie's cell phone. I need to get these units into the air and travel some routes where we think the girls could be held."

"Later today," replied Pastor Doyle, "several of the pastors are going up to Lake Kariba for a three-day seminar and will be back here later on Friday. They are going in my plane and many of the Flying Doves' planes. You are welcome to go along and then go on to Victoria Falls tomorrow. The Flying Doves squadron commander and most of the pilots will be there until Friday. We can get you a room at the Makasa Sun right on the Zambezi River and next to the falls."

"I may just do that, but I need to check my e-mail and maybe even call home if possible. My phone won't work here in Africa."

"There is a phone in the audio visual department next to the computer."

"Thank you," said Dan.

Dan went back to the guestroom and picked up his laptop. He then accompanied the staff member over to the church and into the audio-visual department. One of the aids in the room showed Dan how to access the projector screen and audio system. The room had Wi-Fi.

He checked his e-mail. Most of the messages were his routine correspondence. There was one from Annie that simply said that she had met with John Kosten Monday evening.

There was an e-mail from Mike that said that he and Annie had met with Kosten. He suggested that Dan call him, no matter what time, to discuss some of the more sensitive legal aspects of the discussion. Mike had his own secure FTP website and had uploaded several audio clips, video clips and some still pictures and documents to the site.

Dan linked to the site and entered the password. Mike had been a very busy man. There were the .wav files from the voicemails. There were several short video clips showing some of the video that had aired on various networks. Mike had scanned in the handout from Oasis showing the pictures of the seventeen girls that had been recovered. There were some front-page articles from the Miami Herald and the Indianapolis Star and a list of the names and hometowns of all the girls on the flight. There were also some news stories from the Indianapolis Star website that told of the arrest of Mark Campbell in Anderson.

Dan didn't know what that was about but he was sure Mike had some reason to include it. There was additional information about the possible range of a 747-400 and a great circle map centered on Miami showing the airline distances to other parts of the world. Dan downloaded everything even the stuff he already had. He printed out all the documents on the church's color printer. It took quite a bit of time.

As it was printing, he was able to scan the documents. The most encouraging piece of evidence was the position of the Oasis decal on the tail of the plane. Mike had carefully scanned the picture of the Oasis tail wing recovered off the coast of Miami. Dan vividly remembered seeing that picture on the opening of Good Morning America last Saturday morning.

Mike had skillfully captured the video Annie had shot of the Oasis tail wing as the plane was leaving the Orlando gate. He matched the two pictures to the same size and placed it all on one document. When Dan printed it out, he ended up with one sheet of paper with two full-color photos that showed clearly that the position of the Oasis decals on the tail wing did not match. It was a beautiful piece of craftsmanship.

Dan just looked at it for the longest time. Relieved, he realized this was the first real corroborative evidence he had in addition to the time of the phone call.

Dan ended up with a whole stack of papers that Mike had put together.

Dan transferred everything to a USB jump drive. To check it out Dan ran one of the .wav audio files. It was Callie's first phone call to him. He also viewed the video clip of the Oasis plane pulling away from the gate. He could hear the reaction of Alice and Annie. He suddenly realized this was the last moment that anyone had seen Callie. The tears welled up in his eyes and there was a lump in his throat.

He looked down at the picture of Callie on the front page of the Indianapolis Star and, for the first time, saw that she was identified as fifteen year old Callie Brooks of Westfield. "Shit," he muttered. "Wonder how that happened?" He picked up the complete list of the girls. There was no Callie Grainger listed. Sure enough, it was Callie Brooks. He just shook his head and whispered. "I'm going to find you, Girl."

He looked at his watch. It was almost 11:00 a.m. He could call Mike, he was always up early. Dan felt like he was up to speed just by reading the material and decided to call him at a more reasonable hour. He wanted to find Pastor Doyle.

He roamed around the church for a few minutes looking for the pastor. He was not in his office. Then Dan saw him in the sanctuary. "Pastor Doyle," said Dan.

"I would like to show you these," and he handed the printouts to the pastor. He explained the discrepancy in the tail wing decal.

"Excellent, my boy. Excellent," said the pastor. "Can I copy these and take them with me on the plane. You are coming with us to Lake Kariba, aren't you?"

"I would like to come, but I would like to check on the package from Indiana," said Dan. "I downloaded the tracking number."

"Don't worry about it, Dan," replied the pastor, "The package is at the airport. DHL called a few minutes ago. They cannot clear it through customs. We can pick it up at the airport before we leave. We have to check with customs anyway. It is not out of the way."

"Well okay then. If I have those radios, then my next step is the Flying Doves," said Dan.

"Well, you should go get packed," said Pastor Doyle, "We will leave right after lunch. What about the printouts? Can I make copies of these for myself and the other pastors?"

"Certainly. I just want to find those girls safe and sound. You do whatever you think will help."

"Lunch is at noon in the garden," said the Pastor

"I will see you then," replied Dan.

Dan returned to his room and repacked his bags. He fired up his laptop and looked at the information again that Mike had sent him. He carefully read all the materials and still did not understand the connection to Mark Campbell. A few minutes before noon, he shut down his computer and put it back in his carry-on. He picked up his luggage and headed for the garden area.

Dan sat his luggage down near the table and took a seat among the pastors. Some he recognized from breakfast, but there were some new ones he had not seen before. They introduced themselves to Dan and shook hands.

Pastor Doyle appeared and sat down. He had several manila file folders.

He handed one to Dan and said "Here are your printouts." He turned to the other pastors and said, "I have here a folder for each of you. You are all familiar with Dan's situation. I would like you to look over the material on the flight to Kariba, and we will discuss it this evening. Dan will be staying with us at Lake Kariba tonight, and then tomorrow Dan will be going over to Victoria Falls."

The staff was bringing food to the table from the kitchen. The pastor gave thanks for the food and the conversation remained on church related matters. At about 1 o'clock, Pastor Doyle said, "Our drivers are here."

The pastors got up and headed for the driveway. The staff had already collected their luggage and loaded it into the rear of the vehicles. Dan kept his carry-on but a staff member had picked up Dan's other piece of luggage. In the driveway were several Mercedes automobiles. The Pastor motioned Dan to get into one of them with him.

As the caravan of Mercedes pulled out of the church compound, the stark realities of life in Africa were suddenly apparent to Dan. The streets were dirty, and many of the side streets were unpaved. There were open sewers running along the main road and directly in front of the houses. Little children played in their bare feet near the open sewers. The houses were simple small concrete structures with faded paint. Brightly colored clothes hung on clotheslines. A wide dirt sidewalk along one side of the road was filled with people. Women walked the sidewalk with large pots on their heads. Some had bags balanced on the top of their heads. Dan recognized the bags as forty-pound bags of corn meal or flour. Women had small infants in papoose type arrangements on their back.

They passed many sidewalk shops and open markets. Once in a while, there would be a small structure selling soft drinks painted bright red and sporting the familiar Coca-Cola logo.

The buses they passed were crammed full of people and there were large crowds standing at the bus stops waiting for the next bus to come along.

The number of people along the side of the road became less and less as they reached the airport. All of the vehicles pulled up to the hangar area where several small planes were waiting. There were several Cessna high-wing, single-engine planes. Dan thought they were a Cessna 206. There were a few low-wing Piper Archer, single-engines and a dual-engine, low-wing. Dan thought it was a Cessna 410.

The pastors all got out of the cars and their luggage was collected and placed in the planes in no particular order. They informally decided who would go in each plane. The dual engine was Pastor Doyle's plane. The pilots took down the names of the passengers in each plane, Dan and Pastor Doyle headed across the ramp to customs.

Once inside the customs office, the pilots gave their aircraft registration number and passengers list to the official. He stamped the document, and gave them back a copy.

Pastor Doyle asked about the DHL package. They had it behind the counter as had been requested by Pastor Doyle. The package was addressed to Dan. It had been opened and they wanted to see Dan's passport.

"These are your radios?" asked the customs official

"Yes."

"For what purpose have you brought them to Zimbabwe?"

Dan hesitated for a moment, "For radio communication between my colleagues."

"I see," said the official "and what of this telephone?"

"That is a personal telephone," said Dan.

"You will be taking them with you when you leave Zimbabwe?"

"Yes," said Dan.

"Very well, said the official," and handed Dan the cell phone.

"What is the price of each radio in U.S. dollars?"

"I don't know," said Dan "$200 each, I guess."

"There are ten radios at a declared value of $2,000 U.S.," said the official, "Please fill out this form with all of the serial numbers of the radios."

Dan began filling out the declaration form. He took each radio and wrote down the serial number on the form. When he finished the customs official stamped the document and gave it back to him and said, "That will be $1,000 U.S. please."

Dan's eye widened. "What for?" asked Dan.

"Fifty percent import duty on electronic items," said the official.

"No, No, No," said Pastor Doyle. "These are for the church.

"It makes no difference. If they stay in Zimbabwe, you must pay the import fee." said the official.

"I will be taking them with me when I leave," said Dan.

"Very well," said the official. He asked Dan for the disembarkation form he received when he arrived in Zimbabwe. Dan reached into his carry-on side pocket and pulled it out and gave it to him. The customs official looked it over and then turned it over and meticulously copied all of the model number and serial number information to the form. The man documented each power cord and antenna. After several long minutes, he gave all the forms and passport back to Dan.

"You must have the radios with you when you leave Zimbabwe, or you will be taxed the $1,000 before you can leave," said the official.

Dan just looked at him and said, "Okay."

Dan picked up the box with radios and they all headed out to the planes.

"That was fun," said Dan.

"Don't worry about it, Dan," said the Pastor. "He gave you all the copies of the paperwork. He didn't keep a copy. There is no record of this except what you have on you. Just fill out another disembarkation form without the radios listed and throw the papers he gave you away."

"Are you sure?" said Dan.

"We have forms on the plane. It is not a problem. They only stamp the form if items were declared. You can just fill out another one and put it with your passport when you leave the country."

"Don't they realize that people can do that? Asked Dan.

"You know the answer to that," said the pastor with a bit of a grin.

"Oh," said Dan, "T-I-A."

"That's right," said Pastor Doyle. "This is Africa."

Chapter 20

The pastors had been milling around the planes in the hot afternoon sun, waiting for the pilots, Dan and the pastor to return from customs. When the pilots arrived they opened the doors and the pastors began climbing into the planes.

Dan and Pastor Doyle stepped on the wing of the dual-engine Cessna 410 and took their seats. The pilots took their time moving the luggage around from plane to plane to get the weight and balance correct for each plane.

The pilot of the dual-engine plane started up its engines first and received clearance to taxi from the tower. The Cessna 410 taxied to the edge of the runway, and the pilot performed a quick run-up on the engines to check the tachometers and gauges. Another brief radio exchange, and the plane lined up on the runway, and the pilot moved the throttle full forward. They were airborne in a few moments and on course to Kariba in the northwest.

They flew right over the city center. Dan looked out the window as they passed over the rows and rows of small run-down shacks that people called home. Many of the residential streets were unpaved. Dan just shook his head at the conditions.

"Dan," said the pastor, "Harare is actually very nice compared to most major African cities. If it were not for the drought in this nation, I think Zimbabwe would have made much more progress by now."

"Yeah, I know," said Dan, "but when I think that just a few days ago I was in Maui, the contrast is very stark." He paused, "How long is the flight?"

"It's only 150 to 175 miles," said Pastor Doyle. "Not long."

Dan continued to look out the windows at the vast savanna and grasslands. He could see the effects of the drought. They passed over several small rivers that failed to come up to the banks of their normal path. It was a big continent…huge! How could he ever find Callie in this place? He hardly knew where to start.

Dan saw a pretty-good-sized lake on the horizon as the plane began its descent. "What's that?" asked Dan.

"That is Lake Kariba," answered the Pastor. "It is where the Zambezi River widens for over a hundred miles to form the lake. Victoria Falls is another two hundred miles upstream to the west."

"The pilots do not like this airport," continued the pastor, "especially for low-wing aircraft."

"Why is that?" asked Dan

"It's unpaved, very rough. It's really just a dirt strip. It is easy for small rocks and debris to be kicked up and dent the wings," answered the Pastor.

"It looks like we have a little problem," said the pilot as he pointed to the runway. Dan craned his neck to get a view. The pilot was on final approach and there were four, very-large elephants wandering around on the runway. The pilot came in low and slow and held the plane about twenty feet off the runway. As he passed over the elephants, he revved the engines. The elephants, startled, by the sound, began scurrying out of the way. The plane made another go around to land, but one of the elephants was still on the runway. There were men running toward the elephant, trying to get it off the runway. The pilot continued his second approach.

Finally, the elephant was persuaded to leave the runway and join the others. The pilot came in very low and slow. He kept the plane off the runway as long as he could. When the plane touched down, Dan could hear the dust and debris hitting the flaps and the wings. The pilot raised the flaps as quickly as he could and brought the plane to a crawl. He taxied slowly over to the area where several other planes were parked.

When they got out of the plane Dan spotted other planes in the traffic pattern preparing to land. Dan looked around at the land. It was dry and a brown grass grew sparsely. Trees dotted the landscape but many had few leaves and the bark of the trees was parched.

In a few minutes, the rest of the planes had landed. The Kariba staff collected all of the luggage and the entire group was directed down the path to the resort area. They passed by a large shelter area that was nothing more than a large thatch roof supported by some poles.

Pastor Doyle said 'Now, Gentlemen, in a little bit we are going to meet here for an important meeting. Please identify your luggage and after you find your cabin, please return here at 6:00 p.m."

The area was dotted with many small huts with thatched roofs. Dan pointed out his luggage and the box of radios. Dan picked up his carry-on with his computer inside. The staff member picked up Dan's other piece and the box of radios. Dan followed the man toward the cabins and was told to take his pick. He chose one at the edge of the compound next to a clearing. He stepped inside. There wasn't much to see. A bare concrete floor, one small bed, and a place to set your luggage up off the floor. There were two small windows that opened to the outside. There was no glass in the windows, just several vertical sticks that gave the appearance of a jail window. The entire area of the hut was less than one hundred square feet. Above the bed was a huge net that could be lowered and draped around the bed. After a moment, Dan realized it was a mosquito net. There was no electricity, no lights and no water.

It did not take long to get settled. The staff member then directed Dan down the path to the restroom and showers. Dan wandered around the compound for a few minutes. He noticed these huge dirt mounds several feet in diameter and six to ten feet tall dotting the landscape. They did not look like natural formations, and there were dozens of them. Finally, he asked what they were.

"Oh, those are made by the ants," said the guide.

"They're ant hills?" asked Dan.

"Well, not exactly," said the guide. "The ants live underground in huge colonies that generate great heat. In order to keep the colonies cool, the ants build these huge structures as part of a ventilation system to cool the subterranean colony."

"That is amazing," said Dan

It was getting close to 6 o'clock, and Dan made his way to the shelter house where many of the pastors had assembled. There were several bulletin board displays set up on easels. Many of the documents Dan had printed out from Mike were tacked to the display. There was a large map of Africa positioned in the center of the display.

Dan and the pastors sat down at the tables near the display. Pastor Doyle entered the shelter and picked up the microphone of the PA system.

"Welcome, Gentlemen," said Pastor Doyle. "Dan, did you bring the radios with you?"

"I left them in the cabin," replied Dan, "but I do have my laptop with the audio files and a jump drive."

Pastor Doyle motioned to one of the staff people "Would you go to Dan's cabin and get the cardboard box of radios?"

The staff member headed toward Dan's cabin as the Pastor turned to the people seated in the shelter house "Let us pray," he said.

"Lord," the pastor began his prayer, "we ask today that you give us special wisdom in our efforts to determine the location of Callie Grainger and the rest of the children. We ask you to keep them safe until they can be found and returned to their families. We ask that you guide us in our efforts to find them, in the name of Jesus we pray," and the rest of the pastors joined in "Amen."

"Has everyone had a chance to review the material I gave you regarding the kidnapping?" asked the pastor. A nod of general agreement came from the other pastors. "Dan," continued Pastor Doyle, "we have pastors here from twenty different African nations. Some have had experience in several nations. I have had a chance to discuss this with several of the Pastors and I suspect we are all in agreement as to the motive," said Pastor Doyle.

Dan looked around at the somber faces of the pastors.

"What have you come up with?" asked Dan cautiously.

"Dan, there are three hundred young American girls missing in this terrible tragedy. I believe you said they were ages six to sixteen, correct?" asked Pastor Doyle.

One of the other pastors interrupted "Dan, I am Pastor Albert Svenson. My home church is in Sweden. We have seen incidents like this before on a smaller scale with young blonde girls from Eastern Finland, Estonia, Latvia and Lithuania. They have been kidnapped by the FSB and more recently the Russian Mob."

"Dan?" asked Pastor Doyle, "you said most of the girls on the flight were blue-eyed blondes?"

"Yeah," said Dan. "My oldest daughter believes that virtually all of the missing girls are blue-eyed blondes. None of the bodies recovered have been blondes as far as I know, but my information is a bit outdated. I need to call Indiana for the latest information."

"Dan," said Pastor Doyle, "we might as well get straight to the point. These girls have been kidnapped for the purposes of white slavery; to be used as sex slaves. Typically, they are sold to powerful men in the Middle East, Southeast Asia and East Indies."

Dan just sat there for a moment and let it sink in. It had crossed his mind before but he had dared not dwell on the possibilities.

"This is not a new thing for us," said Pastor Doyle, "Each of us here has known of entire villages of young girls taken and sold into slavery to another tribe. In the worst cases, village chieftains have sold off their own young women to get hard cash. The slave trade throughout Africa is hundreds of years old and continues today."

"Do you have any idea where the plane could have landed?" asked Dan.

"Dan, we do not know. There are dozens of places throughout Africa where it is possible. Some are more likely than others. Some airports that could handle a 747 have only two or three international flights a week. However, the bright side is that a white 747 is going to be remembered if it is or was sitting on an airport ramp somewhere."

"There is one airline that serves many airports in Africa that flies such plainly marked, white planes," said one of the other pastors. "It's Air France."

"Their planes are just a basic white, nothing fancy," added Pastor Doyle, "It would be easy to add an Air France decal to a white plane if you were trying to hide it. One thing for sure, you cannot hide a 747, even in Africa. It has to be sitting out in full view of someone. That is, if it is still in Africa."

"You think it could have flown on to the Middle East, or Asia?" asked Dan

"Yes, that is possible too, but if it did, it would need clearances to fly across many of the African nations. That would leave quite a paper trail. The other possibility is that a regularly scheduled 747 flight of some other carrier was canceled and the Oasis 747 flew their route at their normal time and took the girls out of Africa that way."

"So, what are you saying?" asked Dan.

"We are just exploring the possibilities Dan," said Pastor Doyle.

"Dan," began one of the other pastors, "if the girls arrived in Africa on that 747, we think it is still here. It is one thing to fly over the South Atlantic, undetected, on an overnight flight. But to move that plane around Africa would require the collusion of too many people in too many different places."

"I can't believe you could manipulate a canceled flight out of Africa to provide cover for the plane. It's too risky. There would be hundreds of passengers involved and ground personnel at the airport. There would just be too many questions."

"Now, it is possible that they could have landed in the Sahara region of North Africa," said another pastor. "The plane could have refueled and taken off again across the Sahara. The problem is that would require the cooperation of several Arab governments. I can tell you that most of those nations would not be prone to such approval."

Another pastor added, "That route brings you in the vicinity of Israel, so the Israelis are going to be monitoring that closely, not to mention the Egyptians. NATO would track flights across North Africa and American AWACS out of Saudi Arabia would monitor all air traffic coming into the Middle East from that direction."

A Catholic priest added "The plane must have landed on the West Coast of Africa someplace and the girls unloaded. The circle map of your friend seems to support that too. They will be smuggled out of Africa by ship, down around the Cape, and then to their final destination somewhere across the Indian Ocean."

"They don't have to go around the cape," added another Pastor. "They could be smuggled overland by truck or train, although that is riskier, but it does take a couple of weeks off the trip around the Cape. There are pretty well-established cargo routes and slave trade routes that could be followed."

"Give me some cities. Give me some countries," said Dan, as he stood up and went up to the map of Africa."

One of the pastors got up also and went to the map. "Well, when it comes to the plane landing," he said as he pointed to the map locations, "I believe you can rule out South Africa, Namibia, Zimbabwe, Zambia, Tanzania, Kenya, Uganda, Ghana, Senegal, Nigeria and the Ivory Coast. These airports are too busy and too controlled, and you could not bribe everyone you needed to."

Another pastor joined in, "Two real suspects would be Bujumbura, Burundi and Kigali, Rwanda. There is no doubt you could pull it off at either of those airports, if, and it is a big if. If you could get the plane across Zaire in the first place."

"From Burundi," added one pastor, "It is a simple train or truck ride to a port city on the Indian Ocean."

"Okay, okay," said Dan, "If they were going out by ship, where would they leave from?"

"Well the answer there," replied one of the pastors "is any port. If the girls have been smuggled into shipping containers then they could make their way into any cargo hold of any ship in Africa without being inspected, if the container papers were in order."

"But back to the Portuguese thing for a moment," said Dan. "We would just be talking Mozambique or Angola, right?"

"That's right," answered one of the pastors, "but Mozambique is not a very likely place for the plane to have landed. It would have flown over Zambia, Zimbabwe or Tanzania to get there. If a ship were leaving from Beira, Maputo or one of the smaller ports, the girls would have to be smuggled overland through Zimbabwe and down the Beira corridor. If, however, Portuguese is an important part of this puzzle, they could have landed in Bissau in West Africa near Senegal."

Another pastor added, "And if it's Angola, then they could have landed in Luanda or Lobito and been transported to the port within a short time. The ship could already be underway around the Cape."

"Dan, you said you had the phone calls from Callie on your laptop? Can we hear that?" asked Pastor Doyle.

"Sure," said Dan. He had brought his laptop to the meeting. He turned it on and went to the .wav files. "If you have the right cable, I can put it into the PA system."

The pastor motioned to a staff person, and in just a few minutes, he produced a rolled-up audio cable that plugged into the back of the PA system and gave the other end to Dan to plug into the computer.

Dan located the file and said "I am first going to play the three messages for you as they were left on my voicemail in Indiana" He hit the audio Play button

"Dad, it's Callie. "There is something goin' on here on this plane that's not right. Listen. Oasis One, this is Miami Approach Control." A few moments later, "Oasis One, this is Miami Approach Control. Say your altitude and position." There was a long pause "Oasis One, Oasis One, do you read? Oasis One, Oasis One…Oh, Shit!'"

Then there were several transmissions in another language that were difficult to make out. There were several voices. The signal was breaking up and was filled with static.

"Dad, I hope you got all that. I'm holding the earpiece up against the cell phone. The plane has turned to the right now and I can see something burning way down on the ocean." The signal was crackling. "I'm losing the cell site signal. I'll call back when I can, Luv ya." And then there was a computer-generated voice, "Friday, Eight Thirty-Four PM."

The next call was from Annie, it began

"Daddy, Callie's plane is missing It's all over TV, they're saying her plane blew up over the ocean. Call me, I'm gonna try you at your other cell phone."

This was followed by the computer voice "Friday, Eight-Fifty-Three PM.

The third call was Callie again

"Dad, there is something screwy goin' on here. I don't know where we're at. This is the first time I have been able to get a signal on the cell phone, since I called you three hours ago. The pilot said there was a problem at the Miami airport with a plane down and that we would have to stay up here until morning before we could land. The tower kept calling us and the pilot never answered them. I think we've been headed the same direction for a couple of hours. For a long time, there were no lights down below, but I have been able to see a coastline for the last half-hour or so. It seems like we're going real slow, the engines sound too loud. I'm sitting in 14J and I can look right straight out my window and see Orion. I'll call you when I can, Luv ya," followed by the computer voice "Friday, Eleven-Forty-Five PM.

The Pastors listened intently and somberly to the audio.

"Now," said Dan, "I am going to play for you just the non-English portion of the tape. My friend Mike has edited it out of the tape and digitally processed it to remove much of the noise and static." Dan hit the play button and the precious few seconds of the unknown language played. It was remarkably clear. A significant portion of the noise and static crashes had been removed.

"It is definitely not Spanish," said one of the pastors.

"I know what it is," said one Pastor. "It is Portuguese."

Chapter 21

"There is no doubt about it," said the pastor, "It is Portuguese and there are at least three different voices. There is something at the end that I do not understand. I don't think it's Portuguese. Let me hear it again."

Dan played it again.

The Pastor tried to translate the best he could "The first voice is saying something like 'Our cargo or packages of twenty-four and four have been delivered. Reveal your position'. A second voice then says 'The signal is flashing and we have you in our sights.' Then, the first voice says 'I see you and the lighthouse. Well done.' The second voice then says, 'Goodbye brave warrior or something like that.' Then, the first man says something in a language that is not Portuguese. It is followed by a third voice that is also not Portuguese. I can't make it out."

Dan was transcribing the Pastor's translation into his word processor, The Pastor went over it a few times, until Dan got it typed.

Dan pulled up the voice editor and said, "Can you identify for me when the other language begins?" He played the audio slowly near the end of the Portuguese.

"There," said the pastor.

"Here?" asked Dan, as he manipulated the start of the next audio phrase.

"Yes, that is the beginning," said the pastor.

Dan performed an audio edit copy and paste and created a new .wav file of just the other language. He then played it again.

None of the pastors understood the language.

"I think it's a Middle-Eastern language," said one the pastors. "It is not Arabic, but it could be Farsi."

"Farsi?" asked Dan.

"I speak a little Arabic, and it is definitely not that. I have also spent some time in Teheran, and it sounds like it could be Farsi, I just don't know."

"Well, at least it gives me a new lead to go on. I will just have to find someone who knows Farsi or is familiar with Middle-Eastern languages," said Dan

"I think we need to stop all of this conjecture," said one of the pastors. "Actually, hearing Dan's daughter on the audio breaks my heart and really causes me to feel a great burden. We all have made phone calls this morning. Later today, we can get the reports back from a couple dozen airports. Let's see what information that uncovers or may lead us to. It is not doing Dan or those girls any good for us to sit here like a bunch of old women gossiping about what might or might not be. Let's pray about it and see what we can uncover as hard facts."

"Well, I agree," began Pastor Doyle, "but I think it has been valuable to run through some of the possible scenarios for Dan's benefit. Now, Dan, can you explain what your plan is on the radios?"

Dan picked up one of the radios from the box. "It is really quite simple," said Dan. "Each of these radios can simulate a cell phone site. Callie has a cell phone. If her cell phone is still on and we fly near her, the phone will think it's entering a cell site and will ping the radio."

Dan held up a cell phone. "This is just like the one Callie has, and they have been cloned from Callie's data to respond to the same transmitted data information. I will program these special transmitters to send out a text to her cell phone. If it's received it will be acknowledged, and the radio will record the time and any data that might come from her phone."

"Very clever," said one of the pastors. "How did you get the information to do this?"

"I have friends inside the Indiana company that supplied the cell phone that Callie has with her," replied Dan.

"I see," said Pastor Doyle, "and this is where the Flying Doves come in?"

"That's right," said Dan. "I have ten radios, I am hoping to get ten planes in the air, to travel along routes we suspect as landing sites, and to use these radios along the flight path. They can be used out the window with the small attached antenna, or if possible, we can connect them to an existing antenna on the aircraft to get better coverage in all directions. My plan is to fly at high altitude first, which will cover a great area. If we get blessed and get a return signal, we can zero in on it with a directional antenna or by flying at a lower altitude."

"Excuse me," came a voice from the back of the shelter.

"Yes," said Dan.

"I am a Flying Doves pilot, and I can speak for them when I tell you it will be no problem getting their cooperation on this. Most of the squadron are over at Victoria Falls right now."

"I am so glad to hear that," said Dan.

"Another thing," said the pilot, "time is of the essence here. I suggest you let me take one of those radios over to Victoria Falls tonight. We have a Learjet headed for Dakar that is leaving out in the morning. We can have him get clearance for a flight path along the entire western coastline of Africa from Namibe to Dakar. It will be a much longer flight that way, but it will sure get this project off to a great start. He will be at a very-high altitude and can cover a lot of territory along the coast and several miles inland."

"That's a great idea brother," said Pastor Doyle. "How soon do you want to leave?"

"I'm good to go now," said the pilot. "I can give the fellows a heads-up over there to be ready for Dan when he shows up tomorrow."

"I need a couple minutes to program one of the radios. I can do that right here with my laptop."

"Let's do it," said the pilot.

Dan fished one of the radios and a cable out of the box. He connected the cable from the computer port to the radio. There was a jump drive in the box that Mike had sent containing the programming software. Dan loaded the software into his computer. Mike had already programmed Callie's cell phone information and authorization codes into the software file. Mike had also set up the sequence for cell phone interrogation. Dan only had to modify the test message sent to the phone.

He suddenly realized he needed to be careful about what he said in case the message fell into the wrong hands. Yet, it had to be a message that Callie would clearly understand and know who sent it. It needed to be short. He thought for a little longer and then began typing.

"ORION HUNTING FROM ABOVE FOR SHAMROCK CHEERLEADERS LOVE AND PRAYERS KEEP CELL

PHONE OPEN TO SKY AND AWAY FROM METAL SHIELDING."

Dan looked at the message. Callie would instantly recognize the message as coming from her dad. The Shamrocks were the name of the Westfield High School team. He thought about it for a while and decided he could make no improvements.

He hit the connect button on the software and sent the message to the radio transceiver. He then picked up the radio and activated the programmed sequence. After a couple of transmit cycles, he picked up the cell phone and turned it on. Within a few seconds, the cell phone alerted with the sound of a received text. Dan picked up the cell phone and checked the message. Sure enough, on the screen was the message.

"ORION HUNTING FROM ABOVE FOR SHAMROCK CHEERLEADERS LOVE AND PRAYERS KEEP CELL PHONE OPEN TO SKY AND AWAY FROM METAL SHIELDING."

Dan looked at the cell phone. The display indicated a text had been received.

He checked the radio display screen and hit the "History" button. A display came up on the window indicating several cycles of transmission with negative results and then a positive contact reading on the cell phone on one cycle.

"It's all set," said Dan to the pilot. Let me show you how to operate the transceiver. There is nothing to it." Dan spent the next few minutes instructing the pilot how to clear the entries, start over and operate the unit. He also explained how to connect the radio to the plane's antenna, if possible, for better and more, uniform coverage. It turned out the pilot was also an avionics technician and very little explanation was required.

Dan walked with the pilot to the runway. The pilot shook Dan's hand and climbed into the Cessna 206. Dan watched as he taxied slowly down the dirt runway to the far end and turned, performed his run up, and then came back down the runway and took off.

It was getting quite dark now, and Dan made his way back to the shelter. The pastors were discussing church matters and he noticed a supply of flashlights on one of the tables. He picked up one and headed for his hut. Along the way, he passed another shelter where they were preparing food for dinner. He was a little concerned about eating the food prepared here. He wandered through the shelter and decided he would probably skip dinner. If he changed his mind he determined it would probably be safe to eat the rice and the bread. They had a supply of soft drinks and he picked out an Orange Fanta.

He could hear the sound of a small electric generator that was apparently supplying the lights and electricity for the two shelter houses. He used the flashlight to find his way to his cabin. He looked up at the night sky. Out here in the middle of nowhere, with no city lights to wash out the sky, there were thousands of stars.

He tried to orient himself without the Big Dipper, which was not visible from here. He found the bright star Sirius and Orion the Hunter. He stared at it for a long time and thought of all the times he, Annie and Callie had spent looking at the stars on clear nights in Indiana.

Orion was upside down from the way Dan was accustomed to viewing his old friend. Dan had been in the Southern Hemisphere before and it was not a new experience. He looked around and found the Southern Cross. He said a silent prayer for the safety of Callie and the other girls and asked for wisdom and guidance in his search for them.

One of the pastors happened by and asked Dan if he was going to eat dinner. He said "No" and asked the pastor to tell Pastor Doyle and the others that he was going to try to get some sleep. There wasn't anything else to do in the compound except go to bed anyway.

By the light of the flashlight, he tucked the mosquito net in around the mattress and took the things out of his pocket. He took off his shoes but kept the rest of his clothes on and crawled into bed. He kept the flashlight by his side. In a few minutes, he had fallen asleep in the pitch black of the darkened cabin.

There was no way to know how long he had been asleep when he felt some sort of creepy crawly thing going across his back. He jumped up startled and flipped on the flashlight as he brushed at his shoulder. He didn't feel anything with his fingers and a complete check of the bed clothes did not produce any bugs or other uninvited guests. He finally decided he had imagined it, or the mosquito netting had brushed his shoulder as he slept.

He was almost back to sleep, when it seemed like the whole cabin was shaking. He flipped on the flashlight once again. The mosquito netting was bouncing around, and the entire roof was shaking. There was a great commotion outside and some men were yelling. He jumped out of bed and scrambled to put his shoes on. He stepped cautiously outside to find himself staring straight into the face of a giant water buffalo. The giant beast seemed oblivious to Dan as he scratched his back on the overhanging corner of the thatched roof. The animal's long horns were swinging around like giant daggers. Dan ducked back into the hut and peered out the window.

There were at least a dozen of the water buffalo wandering through the compound and bumping into the other huts. Occasional screams and yells were heard from the startled occupants. In a few moments, Kariba staff members appeared, making great noise and herding the bewildered animals out of the compound.

The staff made rounds and announced an all clear and that everyone could go back to sleep. He heard one of the pastors yell out "What happened, what were those things?"

One of the staff answered back, "It was just a herd of water buffalo that wandered into the resort by mistake. We will post some men at the edges of the compound and it will not happen again. You can go to sleep."

Another voice shouted out "T-I-A."

Dan removed his shoes and went back to bed. The adrenaline had been pumping and it took some time for him to settle down. In a little while, he was sound asleep.

Morning came quickly. He looked at his watch, it was 6:30 a.m. He had managed to get plenty of sleep, even with the interruptions. He gathered a change of clothes and the things he needed and went to the showers. It was just what he needed, another cold shower. There was no hot water in the compound. This time, there was no way to dry his hair. He dried it with a towel the best he could and combed it using his hand mirror. He returned his old clothes and other things to the hut.

He decided that the shoes he had been wearing were the wrong ones for this environment. He searched through his luggage for the pair of rugged shoes he had planned to use while hiking Haleakala's rough terrain on Maui.

He packed his luggage and was all prepared to leave whenever the opportunity presented itself.

He walked over to the shelter where they were serving breakfast.

There was a lot of small talk and exchanging of stories from the water buffalo episode of the night before. After everyone was finally seated, one of the pastors said the blessing over the food. Dan was seated next to Pastor Doyle.

"Dan," began Pastor Doyle, "I don't know if I actually introduced you to our pilot yesterday, but this is Dave Brume."

Dan and the pilot shook hands and then Dave sat down next to Dan.

"Pleased to meet you," said Dan,

"Likewise," replied Dave, in an accent that sounded a little like Australian.

"Dave was born in Zimbabwe and knows the southern portion of Africa as well as anyone. After breakfast, he will fly you over to Victoria Falls where you can meet with the Flying Doves squadron."

"Thank you, Pastor. I am looking forward to getting these radios into the air as soon as possible."

"Well, Dave will take one of them. You can have the full use of our plane for a couple of days and longer, if necessary," said the pastor. "Incidentally, the churches and friends that the pastors called were instructed to e-mail a report of their findings to the Rejoice and Praise Church in Harare."

"How many airports do you think we can expect to hear something about?" asked Dan.

"You would be amazed," said the pastor, as he walked up to the map on the easel. He pulled a slip of paper out of his shirt pocket and began to rattle off the names of major African airports as he pointed to them: Dakar, Bissau, Freeport, Monrovia, Abidjan, Accra, Lagos, Kanos, Douala, Yaoundé, Libreville, Brazzaville, Kinshasha, Pointe-Noire, Luanda, Lobito, Benguela, Lubango, Namibe, Walvis Bay, Swapokmund, Windhoek and Cape Town. That is nearly every major airport along the west coast of Africa."

"This is remarkable!" said Dan. "This is like having your own private network throughout the entire continent."

"No Dan, it's just that we are all here for the same Great Commission. Sometimes we work together better than others. This one is easy. Everyone everywhere wants to help. The Lord's timing in this surpasses all understanding. The fortuitous circumstance of having so many key Pastors assembled in Zimbabwe for our camp meeting and the entire Flying Doves meeting at Victoria Falls is truly one of God's miracles. Otherwise, we could not possibly have pulled this kind of effort together this quickly."

"Praise the Lord!" exclaimed Dan.

When breakfast was over and the conversation was winding down, Dan looked at the pilot and asked, "How soon are we leaving?"

"I am ready now," said Dave.

"I am packed and ready to go. I'll just go and get my bags," said Dan. He stood up and said his goodbyes to all the pastors. Several of the men hugged him. Pastor Doyle came up and put his arms around Dan and said, "If those girls are in Africa, we will find them, the Lord will lead you to them. Dave here is the best bush pilot in Africa and he has the very best co-pilot. You are in very good hands."

"Thanks." Dan hated long goodbyes but he felt a deep and abiding sense of gratitude for these men and the tremendous effort they had put out for him. He didn't really know what to say.

Pastor Doyle gave Dan a hug and then placed his hands on Dan's shoulders and said, "Godspeed, Dan Grainger, Godspeed."

Dan and Dave walked over to Dan's hut to pick up the luggage and radios. Dave carried the box of radios as they walked to the plane. The luggage was stowed in the side compartment, and Dave walked around the plane performing his pre-flight inspection of the aircraft. He stopped to look at the underside of the flaps. "This bloody runway is dreadful on the paint job," said Dave with disgust.

Dave was of medium build and about 5' 10" in height. He was dressed in the traditional khaki-colored, two-pocket shirt and pants. They were neatly pressed with sharp creases in the pants leg that extended just above the knee. He wore Ray-Ban aviator-style sunglasses. He looked every bit the part of a pilot.

The two men climbed into the plane and got settled for the short flight to Victoria Falls. Dave started the plane and taxied slowly to the far end of the runway.

"This is really not good practice," said Dave, "but I am not going to do a full, pre-flight run-up on the engines. It kicks up so much dust and debris that it can chip the paint on the wings."

He pushed the throttle forward and held the brakes for a moment until the engines revved up. A dust cloud sprang up and you could hear the dirt particles hitting the plane. He abruptly released the brakes, and the plane lurched forward and was in the air very quickly.

As soon as they were airborne, Dan saw a vast herd of water buffalo wading at the edge of the lake. There were a half dozen elephants in the area also. The wildlife was amazing.

"Impala," said Dave, pointing to a large group of the animals sprinting across the countryside. A herd of zebra grazed at the edge of a clearing and one lone wildebeest galloped along the edge of the trees. The shores of the lake were lined with flocks of birds of many kinds. This splendid African morning was teeming with life, and Dan felt optimistic that things were moving in his favor faster than he could have imagined.

Dave narrated the journey, talking about the river and the wildlife and some of Zimbabwe's history. Then he pointed up ahead at one of the eight wonders of the world. A magnificent spray of water and mist extended hundreds of feet into the sky.

"It's the Falls," said Dave. "When the water goes over the edge and drops over one hundred meters, it lands with such force that it splashes up hundreds of meters. Much of the water is in the form of a mist that settles back down over the area around the falls and has created a small rain forest. It rains here all the time and never stops.

Dave dropped down low and flew along the river at the edge of the mist. A quaint nineteenth-century vintage railroad trestle spanned the gorge just a few hundred feet downstream from the falls. The river was very narrow and had cut a serpentine trail through the African jungle. The falls were magnificent beyond description and as the plane passed over the western cataract, the river was suddenly very peaceful and meandering. The Zambezi was over one mile wide just before its plunge down the falls.

"The center of the river is the border between Zambia and Zimbabwe," said Dave. "We have had some terrible drought conditions, and the falls is just a trickle compared to its normal condition."

"That's just a trickle," said Dan with amazement, as he surveyed the large quantity of water flowing over the falls.

"Quite right," said Dave.

Dave banked the plane to the right to circle the falls. He pointed to a small town across the river "That is Livingstone," said Dave. "It is about ten kilometers from the falls and is the major city in the south of Zambia."

The plane had crossed over into Zambian airspace and was approaching the falls on the east end. "Look, Dan," said Dave.

"The water is so shallow on the Zambian side that you can hop the rocks halfway across the river to Livingstone Island."

Dan looked down to see a few brave or foolish souls navigating carefully from rock to rock as they traversed the river just a few feet from the three-hundred-foot drop of the falls. One misstep and they would be swept over the falls in a second.

'They must have a death wish..." began Dan, when he was interrupted

"It's bloody MIGs at ten o'clock!" shouted Dave.

Dan looked to the left to see two Russian MIG fighters approaching the small plane at a high rate of speed. "What the hell!" exclaimed Dan.

"It's Zambian MIGs," said Dave, "They have taken offense at our unauthorized entry into Zambian airspace. As the two MIGs continued their approach, they split, one to the right and one to the left and sped past the small plane on either side.

The wake of the planes buffeted the Cessna as Dave struggled to keep the plane under control. He banked to the right and crossed back over the river into Zimbabwe. "The bloody bastards!" screamed Dave. "They were just hot-dogging. They didn't need to do that."

"What was the problem?" asked Dan as the MIGs headed upstream just right of the river's center remaining in Zambian airspace.

Dave began laughing "They were just having some fun at our expense. They probably had come from Lusaka and just happened on to us as we circled the falls."

Dave picked up the mike and requested a direct approach into Sprayview Airfield about one and a half miles from the falls and on the other side of the small town of Victoria Falls.

As the Cessna 410 touched down, Dan could see dozens of small planes and small jets lined up along the runway and in the ramp area.

"This is a busy airport," said Dan.

"It's the Flying Doves," said Dave. 'Virtually the entire squadron is here."

They taxied over to customs and waited as the officials checked Dan's passport against the passenger list. Dave explained that they had just come from Kariba, where he had picked up Dan and dropped off some other passengers.

The official studied Dan's passport and his declaration papers.

"Where are the radios?" asked the official.

Dave opened the cargo door and pulled out the box of radios for the official to examine. After a few minutes of examining the radios and looking at the papers, the official said, "There are only nine radios. Where is the other one?"

Dave answered. "One of our colleagues flew it over last night from Kariba, and it left early this morning on a Learjet flight from here."

"Oh, yes, I remember the Learjet this morning," said the official, "Do you know the destination?"

"I believe it was Dakar," replied Dave.

"That is correct," said the official. "Very well, you may proceed." He handed the passport and papers back to Dan.

Dave put the radios back in the plane, and they taxied over to a parking spot along the taxi strip and lined up with the other planes. They collected their luggage and placed it in the car that had been waiting nearby. It was a short drive through town to the Makasa Sun Hotel.

"This is where we will be staying," said Dave as he pointed to the hotel, "but we are going down the street to the Victoria Falls Hotel where the squadron is waiting for us."

The car stopped in front of a beautiful, colonial-style hotel. Dave told the driver to wait for them. Dave picked up the box of radios and headed for the courtyard. Dan grabbed his carry-on luggage that contained his laptop computer. There were dozens of pilots milling around the hotel courtyard and sitting at tables. The scenery behind them was a breathtaking and beautiful site. A deep gorge had been cut by the river below, and the Zambezi Bridge spanned the magnificent gorge linking Zimbabwe and Zambia by train.

The pilots immediately gathered when they saw Dave approach. They had been completely briefed on the details of the Oasis 747. Small talk was exchanged before one of the pilots came up to Dan. "You must be Dan." He said, "My name is Walter. They shook hands and Walter turned and said, "Dave, I will be your co-pilot in your Cessna 410. We will remain here in Victoria Falls for now while we send eight planes out from the airport. We plan to use high-wing planes to allow a better signal coverage from the hand-held radios to the ground. We have sixteen pilots ready to leave as soon as we familiarize ourselves with the operation of your radios.

Dan instructed the pilots in the use of the radios. It was a simple and straightforward operation; second nature to men accustomed to the operation of their own avionics equipment. Soon the pilots began leaving the courtyard and heading for the airfield.

Dan and Dave returned to the waiting car and told the driver to return to the airport. In a few minutes, they were back at the airstrip. The group of pilots was congregated near Dan's Cessna 410. Walter smiled as they approached. They all formed a circle and held hands as Walter said a quick prayer about the mission and the hope of finding the girls safely.

A chorus of "Amen" concluded the prayer and the group broke up in pairs as they headed for their planes.

Walter, Dave and Dan watched as the pilots did their preflight checks and taxied to the end of the runway. It was a small but impressive air force that took off, one after the other, until all eight planes were in the air. It sent chills down Dan's spine just to watch this miracle unfold before his eyes.

It was high noon as the planes each picked up their carefully chosen flight plan that would search the vast African sub-continent. Dan reflected for a moment on all those who pitched in to help him since his arrival. Without a moment's hesitation, these men had pledged their time and money on a desperate father's hunch. Dan thought for a moment how his hopes of finding Callie were riding, quite literally, on a wing and a prayer.

Chapter 22

On their first day of captivity in the jungle, the girls were up at the crack of dawn. They were given bottled water and some kind of disgusting granola bar.

Callie chomped on her granola bar as she sat with Karen, Susie and little Amy. Most of the girls were cried out now and offered little resistance to the orders of their captors. At first, this simple meal was refused by some of the girls. Later in the day, they were glad to get it and ate quietly. None of these girls had experienced real hunger in their entire lives until now. These girls were spoiled by all the freedom America had to offer, but now they were at the complete mercy of their captors.

The girls quickly began to develop cliques and separate groups that encouraged rivalries. One of the older girls had become obnoxious and fancied herself and her group as the leaders of all the girls. This particular group of girls immediately began bullying the other girls, often ridiculing and shoving the younger girls. They would make them move from where they were sitting when the shady spots moved throughout the day. They were a menace to all the other girls.

Their leader was a loud-mouthed sixteen-year-old and she had decided that she and her close group of friends would be running the show. That delusion ended abruptly when she picked on Susie.

Initially, Callie had remained low-key and avoided confrontation. She preferred to remain quiet and bring no attention to herself. It was not long before Callie had enough. Susie was being shoved around by the sixteen-year-old as her mean friends began to circle Susie. Callie forced herself past the other girls to stand at Susie's side. They were completely surrounded by the mean girls. Hundreds of other girls looked on from a safe distance away. Susie was knocked to the ground by the sixteen-year-old.

There were sharp words exchanged between the sixteen-year-old and Callie. The sixteen-year-old pushed the smaller Callie out of the way and again stepped toward Susie, who was trying to get up. Years of Callie's physical struggles with her older sister were unleashed with a vengeance. Callie tore into the sixteen-year-old, thumping her unmercifully and leaving her on the ground in tears. The mean girls just stood there watching in disbelief as their leader was taken down in a matter of a few seconds. Callie did not stop. She continued to pound the girl until the girl pleaded for mercy. Cheers erupted from the girls that had been watching. At that moment, Callie became the de facto leader of all the girls.

The girls grew accustomed to using the primitive bathroom facilities, with toilet tissue rougher than a cheap paper towel. The only western luxury was the sanitary napkins given to the girls that needed them. The girls could take a crude shower with cold water. Some of the girls had reacted to the shots and were a bit ill that first day. All of the girls seemed to be in pretty good shape physically.

There was nothing to do, and the 276 girls just milled around at the edge of the clearing. They tried to stay out of the intense sun during the mid-day hours. Several of the girls got nasty sunburns the first day. The white woman gave them ointment to relieve the pain.

Callie took the lead in teaching all the other girls to play simple games they had never heard of. These girls were accustomed to smartphones, computers, iPads and electronic games.

Each September, Callie and her sister had gone to visit their grandparents for a very special weekend in a small Indiana town with a population of three hundred. An annual festival, "Loblolly Days," was held in honor of its founding. Here, Callie and Annie learned to play the low-tech games of the pioneers and simpler times.

Callie taught the girls to play these simple games that required little more than exercise and imagination. The girls laughed and giggled in playing shadow tag, hopscotch, drop the handkerchief, cat's cradle and red rover red rover. At times, you could hear them singing the Hokey Pokey.

The area was always guarded by a contingent of the black soldiers. There were several run-down military vehicles parked at various spots around the clearing. Even the ones that ran looked like they shouldn't. Some looked like they would never run again. Some of the girls played on the old trucks and jeeps to pass the time of day.

Callie, Karen and Susie watched one day as one of the soldiers tried to start one of the jeeps. The engine made a loud clicking sound but did not turn over.

The soldiers raised the hood and fiddled with the engine for a while. The jeep continued to make the clicking sound and would not start.

One soldier pointed to a jeep in even worse condition parked next to Callie. The old jeep had three flat tires. Two of the soldiers brought their tools over to the jeep and raised the hood. One soldier got in and turned the key. The engine cranked a few seconds and then started right up. The soldiers were all smiles.

They shut off the jeep and began working on the engine. In a few minutes, they had removed the starter and carried it back to the first jeep. They began removing the starter from the jeep but were having a great deal of difficulty. One of the soldiers began beating on the side of the engine with his wrench. The loud clangs filled the clearing, causing everyone to look over.

Callie watched the unfolding events with great interest.

The soldiers had stopped pounding on the jeep engine. They finally got the old starter loose and began to install the starter they had taken from the other jeep. Callie handed her backpack to Karen and said, "Stay here."

Callie casually walked over to the jeep with the flat tires and scanned the instrument panel. The vehicle was an ancient jalopy, but Callie spied what she was looking for - the socket for the cigarette lighter.

She looked over at the soldiers. They had completed the installation of the starter now. One soldier got in the driver's seat and turned the key. The jeep immediately purred to life. The soldiers laughed and patted themselves on their backs. They all hopped in the jeep and sped off across the clearing.

Callie came back over to the other girls. "Let's go play in that old jeep," she said.

"Why?" asked Karen.

"Just follow me and shut up," said Callie, as she picked up her backpack and headed for the jeep.

Callie got in the driver's seat; and Karen hopped in the other side. Susie and Amy stood at the side. Callie reached into her backpack and pulled out a cord. "Ta-dah," she said. She plugged one end of the cord into the jeep cigarette lighter jack and the other end into her cell phone. She tried turning on the cell phone but still had a low-battery icon on the screen. She reseated the plug in the jeep a couple of times with no success. When she tried it again, the whole adapter pushed through the dash. The hole was poorly cut and didn't look like a factory job.

"Jeez, I hope I didn't break it," said Callie. She carefully removed her plug and the jeep socket dangled from the jagged mounting hole by two wires. "I think it's okay. I didn't break any wires."

"It's not working or maybe the connection is too corroded," said Callie. "Do you have your phone and charger cord back at the building?

"Yes," said Karen.

"Go get it and bring your charger cord," said Callie.

While Karen was gone, Callie kept trying to re-seat her plug in the cigarette lighter jack, but her phone never showed charging. Karen returned with her phone and charger cord. Callie took out fingernail clippers and a BAND-AID from her backpack. She cut off the end of the USB plug and stripped the four wires back with the clippers.

"All four wires are the same color. I don't know which is which, Karen, I may burn up your phone," said Callie.

"What does it matter? The battery is almost dead. It doesn't work here. Do it," said Karen.

Callie methodically touched two wires at a time to the terminals dangling from the cigarette lighter. Karen watched her phone. Finally, after several wrong combinations were tried Karen exclaimed, "It's charging, Callie, it's charging!"

Callie clipped off the two wires she didn't need and carefully wrapped the two remaining wires around the terminals on the cigarette lighter, she had to twist them tightly to get them to stay. She then cut the Band-Aid into several pieces with the clippers and wrapped the Band-Aids around the wires to hold them in place.

"How do you know how to do this?" said Karen.

"You know my dad. He made Annie and me build a crystal radio when we were little. We grew up watching him do this stuff. It's no biggie," said Callie.

"The soldiers are coming this way," whispered Karen. Callie slid both phones under the seat as the soldiers walked by without paying the girls any attention.

Callie pulled her phone back out. She closed her eyes as if to say a little prayer and carefully plugged in the makeshift charger cord. The battery icon indicated "charging," and Callie flipped on the cell phone with a big smile.

"The only way I can charge it is to leave it here, plugged into the jeep," said Callie.

"What if it rings when a soldier is here?" asked Karen.

"Oh man," said Callie, "Wait, I can fix that."

She took the phone and selected the menu feature that muted all the alerts. She placed the phone on silent. "That will take care of that," she said. "You know this is tricky. If I take the phone back into the shed tonight, then it won't receive anything. If I leave it here, it may be found."

"What is the point?" said Karen. "It's not like anyone is going to call you out here. There is no service."

"This is our only link to the outside world, Karen. My dad is coming for us and this is the only way he can find us. He's done it before. When I was little, I got lost in the woods at my grandparent's house in the country. I had my phone but there was no service and it was getting dark. My dad slapped together a radio direction finder and found me in no time.

"How did he do that?" exclaimed Karen.

"I don't know how he did it. All I know is that was what needed to be done and he did it. The cell phone is useless unless it's recharged. It is just a piece of hi-tech junk," said Callie. "We are going to have to leave it here until it is charged."

"What if we get caught?" said Karen "Then they will know. They might see the wire connected to the dash and figure out what's going on."

"Shut up and let me think," said Callie. Callie sat there for a long time, looking around at the jeep and out into the clearing at all the other girls and the soldiers guarding them.

"Okay, here's the deal," said Callie.

"What?" asked Karen.

"Just never mind." Callie carefully placed the dangling cigarette lighter jack behind the dash and arranged the charging wire out of sight as she routed it to the floor.

There was an old burlap sack on the floor. Callie placed her cell phone under the burlap sack and positioned the wire so it could not be seen."

"That's all I can do," said Callie, and she gave Karen back her phone.

Callie checked on the phone from time to time during the day and realized she just had to leave it there overnight. It would never receive anything inside the metal hut and it would continue to search for a cell site until and the battery ran down.

It was hard for her to sleep, knowing the phone was out there to be discovered. She kept telling herself that the starter had been removed and it had three flat tires. There should be no reason anyone would be poking around the jeep now.

Everyone was up early the next morning but Callie could not get to the jeep right away. Callie, Karen and Susie approached the jeep cautiously and got in and pretended to play.

She looked at the phone and the display indicated a text message waiting.

"It says I have a text message!" exclaimed Callie. She scrolled down to the text feature and selected it. Up popped the message.

"ORION HUNTING FROM ABOVE FOR SHAMROCK CHEERLEADERS LOVE AND PRAYERS KEEP CELL PHONE OPEN TO SKY AND AWAY FROM METAL SHIELDING."

"Praise the Lord!" exclaimed Callie.

"What is it?" asked Karen.

"It is from my dad. He's searching for us and he's close. Look," said Callie, as she handed the handed the phone to Karen and the Susie.

"Does he know where we are?" asked Karen.

"No, silly, read the message." said Callie.

"Well, how did your dad do that anyway? There are no cell sites out here, that's for sure," said Karen.

"I don't know; maybe from a satellite," replied Callie, "but what difference does it make? He is looking for us, and the cell phone is our ticket out of here."

There was a commotion in the center of the clearing. Callie quickly hid the phone under the burlap sack.

The thin, white man was standing in the clearing, as the soldiers began collecting the girls and herding them into the center of the clearing.

"Our journey is about to begin," declared the white man. "Return to your building and gather all of your things." The girls were ushered back into the Quonset huts. The soldiers stayed outside. The white woman went from building to building and instructed the girls to strip and throw their clothes on the floor in a pile in the corner of the building. They were also instructed to throw all of their belongings into the pile except for their shoes and socks.

Callie didn't know what to do. She removed her wristwatch and placed it under the mat. She looked over and saw another girl a few feet away hiding something under the mat also. For a moment their eyes locked. She was one of the older girls too, but Callie did not know her. Callie removed her clothes and placed them and her backpack into the pile.

In a short time all the girls were without their clothes. A few minutes later, the white woman came back in. She walked around the building inspecting the girls. She motioned the girls to the back of the building and told them to put on the outfits in the boxes.

She stood there as the girls complied. There were several boxes of long pants and long-sleeved shirts but no underwear. The outfits were of various sizes, and all of them were bright orange. They put on their shoes and socks and waited for the next thing to happen.

Soldiers burst into the building and rounded up thirty of the girls and marched them out the door. A few minutes later the soldiers returned and rounded up another thirty girls. While this was going on, Callie retrieved her watch and slipped it into the top of her sock.

She saw the girl who had hidden something under the mat being rounded up in the second group. Callie peeked under the mat. The girl had hidden a small Bible there in a plastic baggie. Callie picked it up and stuck it under her shirt, as she too was rounded up in the second group. There was mass confusion as the thirty girls were marched out into the clearing. Fortunately, Susie, Karen and Amy were all in the same group. They were instructed to put on insect repellent.

The girls were marched across the clearing and down one of the paths into the jungle. This was the path to the river that the white man had warned them about. It was a narrow footpath. The broadleaf branches of the jungle trees hung over the path in many places. Occasionally when a girl moved past a low hanging branch, it would swing back and smack the next girl in the face. The girls learned quickly not to let that happen.

There were frequent shrieks, as the girls would spot the various creepy crawly things on the ground or in the branches. An occasional scream signaled that a creepy thing was on one of the girls. The bright sun was largely blocked by the canopy of the jungle trees above them. Strange birds made strange noises that now seemed routine, after several nights in the jungle. The smaller girls could not walk so fast, and the caravan of orange-clad girls proceeded at a snail's pace through the jungle.

They came to the river in a very short time. There was a small clearing along the river, where several boats were waiting on the shore. Callie had seen these types of boats on a whitewater rafting trip to Colorado. The first group of thirty girls was already aboard the first boat, and it was leaving the launch site as Callie's group arrived at the clearing. Shortly after the boat left the shore, there was movement in the bushes at the river's edge. Two crocodiles slipped into the water in the direction of the departing boat and the girls screamed.

There were several white men operating the boats. They were all thin with dark hair and a stubble of whiskers on their face. They spoke to each other in a language that Callie did not recognize.

One of the men began shouting to the girls. "Do not even think of trying to escape. Your bright orange clothes will make an easy target for us in the jungle, and if we don't catch you, the lions or the crocodiles will. Now, put these life jackets on. We also have sun lotion. You will have a very miserable week if you fail to protect yourself from the sun today."

The men handed out bright-orange life jackets and tubes of sun lotion. As the girls were putting on the jackets and lotion, Callie slipped the Bible out of her pocket and looked at it. It obviously was not the King James Version. Callie turned the first page and saw an inscription: "To Ilsa with Love. Enjoy your time in Jerusalem." It was dated and signed "Father." Callie realized this was the Torah. Callie made her way through the maze of girls over next to the girl who had hidden the book. "Ilsa," whispered Callie. The girl turned and looked. She had long, blonde hair and her blue eyes betrayed no emotion. "Yes," replied a bewildered Ilsa. "I'm Callie, Here, take this."

Callie slipped the Torah to Ilsa's side and whispered "shalom" in Ilsa's ear. Ilsa looked down briefly to see the holy book. Ilsa quickly slipped it under her shirt. She looked directly into Callie's eyes, smiled briefly and said, "May the Lord bless you and keep you safe." She said it with such strength and authority that it startled Callie.

"I pray we are all kept safe and get out of this mess soon," replied Callie.

"We are all in grave danger, I more than you. Those men speak Arabic. If they find out I am Jewish, I will be of no value to them. I will be expendable," said Ilsa.

"What kind of value are you talking about?" asked Callie, not wanting to hear the answer.

"White slavery as sex slaves in some Sheik's harem," said Ilsa coldly.

"Callie's eye widened "You are not serious!" she exclaimed. "This is the twenty-first century. That kind of stuff doesn't happen anymore."

"The evil in the world never changes," said Ilsa

"Look, Ilsa," began Callie "There are people looking for us, people that know we are still alive. My dad will come for us."

Ilsa replied, "I place my faith in the Lord. On this earth, I cast my lot with the crocodile rather than the jackal."

The conversation ended abruptly as the soldiers and the white men directed the girls onto the boat. The ID wrist bracelet on each girl was examined. The girl's name was then checked off a list as she boarded. There was room for the thirty girls, two soldiers and one of the white men. One of the soldiers piloted the boat. The engine was started and the boat was pushed away from shore. The pilot allowed the boat to float out into the current a few feet and then revved the engine. The boat sped off downstream. Even Callie shrieked when she saw another crocodile slither off the shore into the muddy waters of the river.

The sun was beating down on the exposed skin of the girls. Callie was seated next to Amy. Callie checked Amy and added some suntan lotion to Amy's skin. Callie yelled out to all the girls. "Check the little girls for suntan lotion." A few girls sitting close by heard her. The roar of the engine and the rush of the wake drowned her words out.

Callie held up the tube of lotion and motioned toward Amy. She put some lotion in her hand and began spreading it on Amy. The older girls got the hint and started doing the same for the young girls seated next to them.

The boat moved along the winding river at a good clip. Sometimes the boat cruised in the center of the river;

sometimes the boat would weave over very near the shore. The growth of trees along the river had diminished significantly. The banks of the river were edged in a brownish grass in some places and thick, green grasses in other areas. It was a swampy marsh in some areas. A group of hippos languished along one shore as the boat sped by. The number of crocodiles visible along the shoreline had diminished.

Occasionally, Callie would catch Ilsa's eyes. Ilsa was on the other side sitting near the edge of the boat. Callie noticed that Ilsa was holding the Torah and was moving her upper body back and forth. Her eyes were closed as she clutched the Torah to her chest beneath the life vest. Her head was bobbing back and forth at an increasing rate. Ilsa moved the plastic bag with the Torah to between her knees and slowly unfastened the life jacket. Callie's eyes remained fixed on her.

The boat made one of its frequent swerves toward the shore. Suddenly, Ilsa's eyes popped open, she threw off her life jacket, clutched the Torah and leaped backward off the side of the boat just as it began to swerve away from the shore. Callie stood up and screamed "ILSA!"

Callie saw Ilsa disappear in the wake from the boat. Many of the girls began screaming and crying. The white man scurried up to the soldier piloting the boat and frantically grabbed his shoulder. The boat did a wide U-turn in the river and sped back to the location of the fall. The two soldiers and the white man searched off the side of the boat looking for signs of Ilsa. In a few minutes, one of the soldiers retrieved Ilsa's life jacket from the river. Ilsa was nowhere to be found.

Callie scanned the shoreline not far from where Ilsa jumped. The river bank was lined with tall, green grasses. She saw no signs of Ilsa anywhere. Callie hoped and prayed for a miracle as she held tightly on to Amy.

The trip down the river had seemed like an eternity now, but in fact, it had only taken a few minutes. The bright sun was beating down on the boat and the air was like a hot sauna. Up ahead, Callie could see another boat that had stopped along the shore and was now launching back the way they had just come. It was the first boat that had left with the first thirty girls. The girls were not on board as the two boats passed.

The boat the second group of girls was in slowed and came ashore at the point the other boat had just left. There were a group of men there that tied the boat and placed a ramp from the shore to the boat. The girls were herded off the boat by the soldiers and directed up a path away from the river.

Waiting for them were two flatbed, semi-tractor trailers. Each flatbed had a large, white shipping container as cargo. The containers were open at the end. Callie could see that one of the containers was filled with the orange-clad girls from the first boat. Callie watched as the door was swung shut and a metal strap was crimped onto the door handle. In a few minutes, the truck began moving down the unpaved road.

One of the white men shouted in English to the girls, "If you need to use the bathroom, you may wish to go now." He pointed to an area off to the side of the remaining truck. "If not, you can use the facilities in your new home."

Callie took advantage of the offer and helped Amy. Karen and Susie went with them.

"Did you see that poor girl fall overboard?" asked Karen.

"I saw her go overboard," said Callie, "but she didn't fall."

"You mean she jumped on purpose?" quizzed Karen.

"Yep, she picked up her Bible and did a back flip into the river," said Callie.

"That girl's crazy," said Susie.

"Maybe, maybe not," said Callie. "Maybe crazy, like a fox."

Callie heard another vehicle approaching. Another flatbed semi was driving into the area. It also had a white, shipping container on it.

The girls were rounded up and told to climb up the ramp onto the bed of the trailer and into the open shipping container. When all twenty-nine girls were inside, the door was shut. Callie could hear them crimping the tag on the door.

The girls were remarkably calm. It was not dark inside. There were some lights along the center of the ceiling, but they were not on. There were several louvers along the sides of the container that allowed plenty of light in. The louvers were covered with a fine-mesh screen. At the far end of the container was a crude toilet. Callie walked up and peeked into it. It was open and Callie could see the ground below.

There was a bench along each side of the container. The floor and bench were padded with a gray, plastic mat similar to the ones used in gym class.

The container was tall enough that Callie could stand upright in it. It was about eight feet wide and maybe twenty feet long. There was a supply of bottled water, soap and various paper products located on shelves by the toilet.

Some of the girls had sat down. The trailer lurched forward slightly and knocked a few of the girls to the floor, and several of them let out a shriek. The rest of the girls sat down on the benches or the floor as the truck began moving.

Callie sat down in the corner and was able to position herself to look out the space between the louvers. It was difficult, but if she held her head just right, she could see out the screen between the louvers. She could see more girls coming up the path from the river. From her seat, she could see out the side and the back of the container. The truck did not go very far until it turned left onto a better road. Callie could see several more trucks with white shipping containers lined up along the road as the truck turned. After the truck was on the road, she could see one of the waiting trucks begin moving down the dirt road toward the river.

The road they were on was still not so great, and it was a bit of a rough ride for the girls. After several minutes the ride got suddenly smoother. Callie peeked out the louvers to see that the road was nicely paved. The land was very flat, almost like Kansas. In the distance, Callie could see patches of broadleaf forests. The truck began to slow down and Callie could see they were driving through a small village. She could see some roadside stands selling fruits and vegetables. She saw a gas station that said "petrol." It slowly dawned on Callie that most of the signs in the village were in English. A sign on one of the larger shops said in English "Caprivi Strip Novelty Shoppe, The Golden Highway's Finest."

The sign told her nothing, and yet, it told her a great deal. Callie had known from the position of Orion that they were in the Southern Hemisphere and she suspected they were in Africa. The sign in English told her they were in a former British colony. As the truck began to pick up speed, it became uncomfortable to continue looking out between the louvers. A welcome breeze passed through the container as the truck moved faster. Callie looked around at the girls lying on the benches and floor. Some were holding each other. Some were trying to comfort the smaller girls. Callie reached out and put her arms around Amy beside her. Amy snuggled closer to her.

Callie had to be strong. The other girls depended on her. If she lost it, the other girls would fall to pieces. She began thinking about Ilsa and wondered if she had survived in the river. Callie's thoughts were haunted by Ilsa's words. "White slavery as sex slaves in some Sheik's harem." Ilsa was willing to die trying to escape rather than accept that fate.

She looked around at the container's metal sides and metal roof. Callie had seen the big container ships in Honolulu Harbor and the Port of Long Beach, California. The girls were being transported in a shipping container, and that meant they were headed for a seaport somewhere. How could her dad ever find her now, without the cell phone? For the first time, she became truly frightened. She began to sob quietly as she prayed for a miracle.

Chapter 23

Rebecca Calloway, the girl's dance coordinator had been separated from the girls when they first landed. She had been transported by corporate jet across Africa. They had stopped three times for fuel. She worried about what was going to happen to her, but she worried more about the girls. When they finally landed, it was in an Islamic country. She was transported through a city with many mosques. She was taken into a large Muslim building and escorted to very-nice room.

Other women were there and they immediately attended to her. They removed her clothes. She was bathed and carefully cleaned. She was shown to her bed, and the lights were turned out and she slept.

The next morning the process was repeated. The attendants bathed her again taking great care in her hygiene. Resistance was futile. She allowed them to put lipstick on her, and they dressed her in a thin flowing gown. She was then lead down the hall and into another room.

There was a tall Middle-Eastern man dressed in a long white thobe with a white, ghutra headscarf and a black, agal cord. He had a manicured, stubble growth for a beard and a moustache. He looked like Saudi royalty.

"Good morning, Miss Calloway," said the man.

Rebecca had no idea what to do or say. At least, he spoke English. Out of habit or custom or whatever, she replied, "It is a pleasure to meet you."

"The pleasure will be all mine, Miss Calloway," said the man as he stepped very close to her. He smelled the perfume on her neck. She was uncomfortable but did not move. She was petrified.

"Ah, my favorite fragrance," he said as he grabbed her and pulled her against him. She resisted but he was very strong.

"Ah, you American women. You always resist in the beginning," he said with a smile.

He held her firmly as he pulled the sash on her garment and it opened up to reveal the front of her body. With one yank to the back of her garment, it fell to the floor and she stood in front of him completely nude.

She tried to cover her privates and breasts with her hands.

"Such modesty, Miss Calloway. You will soon get over that."

"Your life as you knew it is over. Your sole purpose in life is to please me or whomever I offer you to."

"I will never," she said. "I'll die first."

"That rarely happens. The time will come, and soon, that you will willingly serve me. It is the only thing that will bring you happiness," he said.

He stepped toward her and began to touch her. She slapped him across the face as hard as she could.

He rubbed his cheek where he had been struck. Looked at his hand to make sure he was not bleeding. He walked over to his bed and rang a buzzer. Two men immediately appeared.

"Bind her and prepare her for me."

The men were very strong. She was taken into an adjoining bedroom and strapped to the bed. Her legs spread. The bed was a few feet from the wall and had no headboard. The two men left and the man appeared. He removed his clothes and raped her. He then got up and walked to the head of the bed, tilted her head back and forced himself down her throat. He left her lying there sobbing when he was finished.

He returned again later and repeated the process. Each time attendants appeared to clean her and take her to the bathroom. She was then strapped down again for the man to return. This happened over and over again throughout the day and night.

The next morning, he appeared one more time and raped her again. The attendant cleaned her up again. She was left naked, standing before the man who had raped her so many times.

"American redheads always bring a premium. I should do very well after you are trained. He turned to a man that had entered the room and said, "place her in the accelerated program. I have buyers coming soon. She must be ready."

A leash was placed around her neck, and Rebecca Calloway was led through the halls of the building totally naked. Numerous uniformed men gazed at her as she passed. They entered an elevator and it began to lower. When the door opened, Rebecca saw a sight she could have only imagined in her worst nightmares. There were bright studio lights and television cameras everywhere. Every few feet there was a different studio set with a bed, or maybe it looked like an apartment with a couch. Men and women of every race and ethnicity were having sex. The women seemed to be eagerly participating in the sexual acts without hesitation. The cameras were capturing it all. She was led along a row of jail cells with nude women in each cell. There was a large, open area that the cells faced. A woman was being tortured and she was screaming. Other women were bound in various ways and were being raped.

Rebecca was thrown into a cell and left alone with only a small hole in the concrete for a toilet. There was no bed, just a concrete floor. Later, a man walked along the cells pushing a large pot with wheels and two handles, somewhat like a wheelbarrow. The man filled a small bowl from the pot. The bowl was slid between a horizontal opening in the bars. Rebecca took it. Whatever it was, it smelled horrible. She dipped her finger into it and tasted it. It tasted worse than its odor. She set the bowl down. She was hungry but not that hungry. She would never be that hungry.

Constantly, in the area outside the cells, one woman after another was being raped. There seemed to be an endless supply of men dressed in sharply-tailored military uniforms that showed up to participate. Her cell was suddenly opened and she was taken out to the same area. She was forced to lay down on her back and was strapped to a horizontal board. Her legs were raised over her head and placed in a stockade-like device. Her rear was fully exposed. At the other end of the board there was not enough horizontal board to support her head. Finally, after several minutes, she let her head fall backward where it was supported at a forty-five-degree angle. It made her a little bit dizzy but she became accustomed to it. Above her was a large mirror tilted so that she could see herself lying there. She closed her eyes.

Suddenly, without warning, she was penetrated between her legs. A large man was raping her. She could see it happening in the mirror. When he was finished, a second man came and repeated the act. Suddenly, a man was at her face and penetrated her mouth, shoving his penis down her throat. She threw up when he came and nearly choked to death. The process was repeated, as one man after another continued the unimaginable acts. All of the sordid events were captured by an ever-present photographer with a camera.

She was on her back. She could not turn over. She wanted to die. She learned very quickly that she had to swallow or she would choke to death. After several hours, she was returned to her cell. She was not cleaned up but was left to wallow in her own waste and the residue of the countless men who had used her. The next morning, she was cleaned up, and the whole process was repeated. Rebecca lost all track of time. When again the unappetizing bowl of swill was slid through the horizontal opening in the bars of her cell, she consumed every drop.

After several days she was bathed and taken into a different room. There was a table with a mat. She was strapped down to the table facing the ceiling and her legs tightly bound together. Padded clamps at her ankles and wrists prevented her from moving. Her feet extended over the end of the table.

As Rebecca looked around the room she could see several television cameras. They were operated by remote control. A microphone hung from the ceiling.

An old woman entered the room. "Rebecca my darling," she said, "I am so sorry you must endure this, but you must be trained to serve your master without hesitation. You must learn to anticipate his every desire and please him to his satisfaction."

Rebecca could not help but think she would willingly do everything the Middle-Eastern man wanted of her, if she never again had to endure what she had now endured for days.

The old woman picked up a cane and showed it to Rebecca. "This is the cane," the old woman said. "You are a beautiful woman with beautiful, lovely skin. You must not be scarred. It would affect your price." She turned to the men holding her down. "Hold her tight."

Rebecca heard a whistling sound and then felt unimaginable pain on the soles of her feet, as the cane was brought to bear with all the strength the old women could muster. Rebecca screamed in agony.

A few moments passed and again the whistling sound came and the intense agony was repeated more strongly than the first stroke. After the third stroke, Rebecca lost all control of her bladder and her bowels. She lay there whimpering not knowing when the next stroke would come or how many there would be.

"My child, I am so sorry, but you must learn," said the old woman. "There came the whistle of the cane for the fourth time and the pain came. Then, immediately afterward, a fifth time.

Rebecca cried out, "Please stop and I will do anything you ask. I will do anything the master wants. Rebecca did not even stop to consider that she was giving up all pretense of resistance. She just wanted it to stop. She had surrendered completely to the pain and her fate.

"I know, my darling," said the old woman, "but you will say anything now to stop the cane. I have seen this many times. Your defiance and resistance will return. It is best that you endure this now and never be subjected to the cane again. Believe me, my darling, this is in your best interest."

"We are halfway through the training," the old woman said as the sound of the cane came again.

"Oh, God, help me. Please help me," cried out Rebecca. She could not possibly stand four more strokes. She prayed to die, but she did not.

There was a long pause and Rebecca actually fell asleep. She did not hear the sound of the seventh stroke, but the tremendous pain woke her up and she screamed. The eighth and ninth came again in rapid succession and the pain intensified.

"My child," said the old woman with a soothing voice. "You will be asked to do many things to please your master. He will ask you to please other men of his choosing. You must never hesitate. Do you understand?"

"Yes, yes, I do. I will do whatever Master wants, anything," cried out Rebecca.

"I know you will, my dear, I know you will," said the old woman. "But we must make sure you never forget the cane so that you never experience this again. Just one more, my dear. One more. The master wants you to ask for the last stroke."

"Will it please the master?" asked Rebecca.

"Yes, it will please the master?"

"Please cane me to please the master," said Rebecca.

"I'm sorry. Dear, I didn't hear you," said the old woman.

"Please, I want to please Master. Cane me," screamed Rebecca.

Rebecca heard the whistling of the cane, and she cried out in agony for the last time."

The cane was hung from the ceiling and was left for her to see every time she opened her eyes. She was left to lie in her own urine and waste for the rest of the day. She didn't even care. The caning had stopped.

She was awakened by a group of female attendants. She could not walk; the soles of her feet were very tender and in great pain. She was carried to a clean room with a real bed and mattress. It actually had a stool and a lavatory. It was painful to get to the stool but she could do it. Later food, good food was brought to her and she ate it feeling blessed.

The next day, attendants appeared at the cell door with a wheelchair. She was bathed and helped into the wheelchair. She was wheeled along the cells until they came into the bright lights of the studio. She was wheeled to one of the film sets and helped onto the bed.

The old woman appeared. "My child, I trust you rested well in your new quarters,"

Rebecca said, "Yes, I did. Thank you."

"I would hope that you will not displease your master," said the woman, "and have to be returned to your previous quarters and endure the cane."

"I will please Master," said Rebecca.

A man was standing beside the old woman. "This is the director of a scene you will appear in," she said. "He will tell you what to do. The teleprompter will have your lines and will also tell you what to do."

"Do you understand?" asked the old woman.

"These other men are actors, too, and they will be in your scene," said the old woman.

Rebecca understood completely. "This will please Master when I obey?" she asked.

"Yes, the master will be very pleased," said the old woman.

The scene began and Rebecca eagerly and without hesitation, did everything asked of her, and more.

Chapter 24

Annie Grainger and her mother Alice Brooks sat in the Hamilton County court room next to their attorney, John Kosten. As the judge entered they all stood until he was seated. John Kosten had sued the Oasis Corporation in the deaths of Callie Grainger and the three other girls from Westfield - Julie, Karen and Susie.

The parents of Julie, Karen and Susie sat in the front row behind Annie, Alice and John Kosten.

There was little interest from the local news community in this particular inquiry. One TV station did have a reporter in the court room and a live ENG truck outside to report on the events. The local newspaper, the Noblesville Ledger also had a reporter present.

There was only one item to consider during the hearing today. The Oasis Corporation had been served with a Motion for Discovery. The Oasis attorneys were claiming that some of the interrogatories were totally unnecessary, "a fishing expedition" as they put it.

Kosten rose to speak. "Your Honor," began John, "the Oasis Corporation has indicated their refusal to answer some of the interrogatories in the Motion for Discovery. They have filed an Objection to the Production of Documents. We are seeking the detailed criteria for the selection process of the girls who were chosen to participate in the Super Bowl program and we want the names and physical descriptions of all the applicants in the country who sought a place in the program."

"Your Honor, we object," came the voice of the respondent's attorney. "This is a fishing expedition. We at Oasis are heartbroken over the loss of all the girls. It is a tragedy of unspeakable proportions and the Oasis Corporation intends to be as compassionate as humanly possible in this matter."

"Overruled," said the judge. "I have read your Objection to producing the documents Mr. Kosten has requested, I don't need to hear you outline it for me again. We are here to determine why Mr. Kosten believes you should produce those documents."

The attorney for Oasis sat down next to an Oasis executive wearing a smartly tailored suit.

Kosten continued, "It is our belief that the nature of the selection process may have had certain specific criteria that, if revealed, could be shocking in its nature and explain a great deal as to why a certain segment of young girls may have perished while in the trust and care of Oasis. If our suspicions are shown to be true it will be very troubling."

The judge spoke "Mr. Kosten, you are speaking in riddles. I have known you a long time, so get to the point or I will rule in favor of Oasis. It is late in the day."

John Kosten walked over to the judge and handed him a document, walked over to the Oasis attorney, gave him a copy and provided a copy to be marked into evidence.

"Your Honor," began Kosten "This is a list of all three-hundred young girls believed to be on the Oasis 747, along with their descriptions and pictures. My office has gone to great lengths to obtain pictures of the girls by studying press reports from newspapers and online sites around the country. Kosten paused as the judge thumbed through the document, and he watched as the Oasis attorney studied the document.

"There are two troubling statistical anomalies in these documents, and we want to drill down to find an explanation for them," said Kosten.

Again, he paused for a long time. At the back of the room, one of Kosten's legal aides handed a copy of the document to the TV reporter and the Ledger reporter.

Kosten continued very deliberately, "Of the three-hundred young girls that have been lost, it appears that approximately ninety-one percent of the girls were blue-eyed blondes."

The Oasis attorney looked a bit dumbfounded, as he quickly turned page after page. Slowly, he rose to his feet. "Your Honor, I object. I don't know what kind of stunt Mr. Kosten is pulling here but it is ridiculous. What is he suggesting? I don't think even he knows."

"Mr. Kosten, Where are you going with this?" asked the judge.

"I don't know where I am going with this unless Oasis responds to my interrogatories, so that we can learn how such a statistical imbalance can exist. We need to know if there was some specific discriminatory bias in the selection of the girls that went beyond each girl's performance ability at the tryouts. A bias that was not disclosed at the time of entry that made it unlikely other qualified girls would be chosen even if they had successful tryouts," said Kosten.

"Objection overruled," said the Judge, as he looked at the Oasis attorney.

The Oasis attorney was now smiling smugly as he stood up and waved the very document that Kosten had provided the Court. He had a page open to pictures of African-American girls.

"Your Honor," he began, "one need only look at this document to see that there was great diversity among the girls selected. I reject Mr. Kosten's assertion and ask that the Court grant our Objection to the Production of Documents that we have filed."

The judge raised his eyebrows in seeming agreement and looked squarely at Kosten for his response.

Kosten looked at the judge somberly; he turned to look at the spectators in the court room and turned back to the judge, being careful to catch the eyes of the opposing counsel. "Your Honor," said Kosten, "this very-accurate observation by legal counsel for Oasis has highlighted an even greater and more-tragic statistical improbability. The attorney for the respondent has correctly pointed out great diversity in the section he is now looking at. This is a section showing the physical descriptions and pictures of all the girls that have thus far been recovered from the crash location off the coast of Florida. The only girls who are known to be dead and the only girls that have had their bodies recovered are minorities and Caucasian girls that are not blonde."

There was an audible gasp in the court room.

Kosten continued "It is inconceivable that ninety-one percent of all the girls were blue-eyed blondes and yet, one-hundred percent of the girls who have been recovered are not blue-eyed blondes. I ask that you order Oasis to answer all the interrogatories, so that we can get to the bottom of this perverse and diverse tragedy."

The judge rapped his gavel to silence the murmuring of the spectators in the court room. "I will take this matter under advisement. Adjourned," snapped the Judge, as he rapped his gavel one last time. He rose and left the court room.

John Kosten, Annie and Alice made their way to the back of the court room and exited into the hall. They gathered their coats and made their way down the wide stairway and out into the chilly air of the courthouse steps.

The TV reporter and the Ledger reporter began peppering them with questions. Kosten answered calmly and said, "We just want to get to the truth and we need the cooperation of Oasis. The Oasis Corporation has been good for Hamilton County and provides a lot of jobs. We are just asking them to share with us all they know, so we can make try to make some sense of this tragedy."

Annie nudged her mother and Alice began to speak as if on cue in her loud voice. "My baby is gone!" screamed Alice, "My beautiful Callie. Oasis knows something. Oasis is hiding something. A mother knows these things. How can a 747 be right there in the ocean and nobody can find it? How come there is no emergency signal? There is something sinister going on here and I'm gonna find out what it is if it's the last thing I do." Alice sobbed when she said it.

It was all caught on camera and was aired on just one local TV station during the evening news. It wasn't even repeated on next morning's early news. The story was not repeated locally and gathered no legs. It did appear in the Noblesville Ledger that evening in a small article at the bottom of Page 1.

Some of the morning cable and network news shows picked up Kosten and Alice's comments the next day. One of the commentators opined about the mother's loss and the seeming irrationality of suggesting there were sinister forces behind the tragedy. The news commentator was very empathetic as she mentioned she had young children of her own and could feel the mother's pain.

There was a brief panel discussion after that and a clip of the Oasis attorney standing outside the courthouse saying "We at Oasis are heartbroken over the loss of all the girls. It is a tragedy of unspeakable proportions, and the Oasis Corporation intends to be as compassionate as humanly possible in this matter."

The network then did a special report on recovery efforts off the coast of Florida. The shallow waters had been choppy and were hampering attempts at recovery of bodies and aircraft debris. The Coast Guard and NTSB had rendezvoused with the ship, Lobito, to take custody of the remains of the girls the Lobito had recovered. The body count had remained at seventeen for many days. They also took custody of the remains of the four Lobito crewmen that had been swept overboard the night of the accident. Their bodies had been recovered by the Lobito the next morning.

The NTSB inspected the remnants of the 747 that the Lobito crew had been able to recover. This included the vertical tail section that had been seen on all the news reports the morning after the accident. The parts were inventoried, but a comprehensive analysis of the plane fragments could not be made until the Lobito docked at Miami.

A large warehouse had been designated near Homestead, Florida to piece together the wreckage as debris and plane fragments were recovered. Divers had located and retrieved many small pieces of the wreckage from the reef in the vicinity of the Fowey Rocks Lighthouse. Everything recovered had been transported to Homestead for analysis and verification.

Despite the best efforts of the divers in the choppy seas, the major components of the plane's fuselage, wings and engines had not been located. There had been no signal detected from the "black box."

This was very puzzling since the ocean was relatively shallow in this coastal region of the Atlantic. One person interviewed suggested that the cockpit voice recorder and flight data recorder may have been located near the tail of the 747 and suffered damaged by the collision with the C-130.

When this report ended, an Oasis spokesperson joined the panel session on the news set. She explained that Oasis had reached out to all the families and were paying the entire cost of funerals and memorial services all over the nation.

The news commentators generally agreed that the whole episode was tragic. They expressed understanding that Callie's mother, Alice, wanted to blame someone. An Oasis spokesperson was present to repeat the heartfelt sorrow of the Oasis Corporation and to point out what a great corporate citizen Oasis was for Hamilton County, Indiana and for the hundreds of cities around the nation that were the home of Oasis retail outlets.

John Kosten watched the report at home as he ate breakfast. He was always concerned that the world would be skeptical of the truth. The Oasis public relations operation was skillful. He did not expect to win his Motion for Discovery with the Hamilton County Court. This concern strengthened his belief that his representation of Mark Campbell would one day give him an opportunity to subpoena Oasis records as part of a criminal case. Then, Oasis would have to comply. He prayed quietly for several minutes and then left the house.

John Kosten began the forty-minute drive to Anderson, Indiana. The morning traffic was heavy on I-465. After he turned north on I-69, the traffic was much lighter. He parked in front of a well-cared-for residence and walked up and knocked on the door.

A smiling African-American woman in traditional African dress answered the door.

"Mrs. Campbell?" asked Kosten.

"Yes, Mr. John Kosten, I have been expecting you. Jimmy has told us all about you," she said. "My husband and I believe Jesus has sent you to us. Praise the Lord!"

Chapter 25

Dan had checked into his room at the Makasa Sun. It took him a few minutes to get settled. He went through his luggage, sorting his clothes and trying to place things in some semblance of order.

He shuffled various papers he had accumulated in his carry-on luggage pockets. He had carried this stuff halfway around the world. He searched through it to see what he could throw away. Tucked into one of the zippered pockets of his carry-on, he found two rolls of 35mm film. He thought for a moment about the guy that tried to rob him in Sydney. He had no time to find a way to develop the film now, but he was too curious to throw them away. He tucked them back in the zippered pocket.

He came across a receipt from the Ohana Blue Lagoon Tropical Café in Maui. It was from the lunch he had shared with Jasmine in Lahaina. It seemed like a lifetime ago. He looked at the crumpled piece of paper as a feeling of great despair came over him. It was the first time he fully realized that he would never see Jasmine again. Earlier, that thought had not bothered him so much, but now it was nearly devastating.

In the few hours that he had been with her, she had made him feel in a way that he had not felt in years. She had stirred emotions and a depth of feeling in him that he had believed for years that he was no longer capable of feeling. Now she was gone. He had met her in a fairy tale moment in a Pacific paradise. His mind was filled with the images of their good times together - the café, the shops along Front Street, her laugh and her smile, the way Jasmine tossed her head, and the way she could catch his eyes and make eye contact that pierced deeply into him. He thought about the moments when he held her in his arms, and he savored the feeling he had deep inside his soul when he held her. It all came rushing back to him as his despair deepened.

He could have cried but he didn't. Instead, he marveled that he could have feelings this deep for someone he had known so briefly. He thought back to the last moment he had with her at the airport, and he could close his eyes and relive the moment she stepped into the elevator and ascended from the Oriental Garden to the second floor of the Honolulu International Airport.

He started to breathe deeply. He was afraid that he was going to lose it. He was not sure what a panic attack was but he was afraid he was having one. The more he breathed, the more overwhelming the feeling of despair became.

He chastised himself for thinking of her at all. Jasmine was right. They would never see each other again and the encounter would become meaningless with the passage of time. Thinking of her did get his mind off of Callie and his real problems. The stark reality was that his real problems and his real despair remained. He continued to try and catch his breath,

Here he was, in the middle of Africa, thousands and thousands of miles from home. Did he even know what he was doing? What the hell was he thinking to be traipsing off halfway around the world, when he should have gone home to be with his daughter, Annie? Then, he thought of Callie.

He sat down on the edge of the bed and tried to maintain control. If he could not keep it together, how could he expect Callie to? "My God," he thought. "If she is alive…what must she be going through?" Then he realized that he had just thought the word "if."

It was more than he could bear. He began to recite the Lord's Prayer. Over and over, he recited the start of it but did not seem to be able to get through it. He did not seem to be able to remember how to pray a prayer he had said a thousand times.

He quickly fumbled through the pockets of his carry-on and pulled out a small NIV New Testament. He opened it to Matthew, Chapter 6, Verse 9, "This, then is how you should pray:" it began, and he read the prayer through in a strong voice.

He closed his eyes and began to overcome the great despair he had felt. He held the small Bible in his hands, as he tried to control his emotions.

A loud knock on his door pierced his concentration. "Dan, come quick," shouted a voice at the door. Dan opened the door to find Walter, the co-pilot.

Walter had been knocking on Dave's room across the hall at the same time. Dave opened the door "What is it?" asked Dave.

"You guys get down to my room right away," Walter said, as he took off running down the hall. Dave and Dan followed Walter down the hall, as he burst into his room and picked up the phone.

"Just a second," Walter said into the phone and handed it to Dan. "This is the pilot from the Learjet that took off this morning. They stopped at Cabinda on the Congo for fuel.

"Hello, this is Dan."

"Dan, I need to ask you a question about the operation of the radio," said the voice on the phone.

"We took off this morning and I placed the radio on the dash next to the windshield. I inadvertently left it on. We climbed to 28,000 feet, and I didn't give it any thought until we got near the coastline. When I picked it up to start our search, it was already on and indicated that we had a return."

"You're kidding!" said Dan.

"Well, I am not sure," said the pilot. "I thought it was some anomaly in the start-up of the radio. We set down here in Cabinda and I have had some time to play with it some more and I just thought I should call."

Dan and the Learjet pilot talked for several minutes. Dan carefully explained to the pilot how to step through the menus and retrieve the history of the transmissions and returns. Dan's voice became increasingly urgent and excited as he talked to the pilot. "Are you sure?" said Dan. "Can you read me the number back from the list?" Dan grabbed a pen and paper from the desk and began writing. "Thank you, thank you, thank you," said Dan, as he hung up the phone.

He sat down on the bed and took a deep breath. His uncontrolled despair of a few minutes ago was gone. Dan looked up at Dave and Walter and calmly said, "We have a positive return from Callie's cell phone early this morning."

"From where?" asked Dave.

"Well, we need to get to a map to plot the location," began Dan, "but the pilot of the Learjet says he was flying a 277-degree bearing from Victoria Falls to Namibe, Namibia and that the radio return occurred at what he believes was around 250 kilometers into the flight."

"Well, let's get to the airport and plot it," said Dave.

The three men rushed from the room to find a car and driver. In a few minutes, they were at the airport in the pre-flight planning area. A large aeronautical map covered an entire wall. The Victoria Falls airfield was marked with a protractor and a string fastened at its center.

Dave plotted the bearing to Namibe and measured 250 kilometers along the course. "It is the general area of the Sioma Ngwezi National Park or perhaps the Caprivi Strip," said Dave.

"What's that?" asked Dan

"Caprivi is a narrow corridor that connects Namibia to Zambia and provides a commerce and transportation link to the Indian Ocean. It separates Zimbabwe from Angola.

"You have your radio, Dan?" asked Dave.

"I do; here in my bag," replied Dan.

"And your passport and papers?" asked Dave.

"Yes."

"Then let's go," said Dave.

They walked over to the Cessna 410 and soon were in the air on a westerly heading.

"The Learjet was climbing to 28,000 feet and still in the early part of its journey. It would have covered the 250 kilometers in a very short time. I asked for clearance for 8,500 feet," said Dave.

They had gone only a few miles when the squelch of the communication frequency of the plane's radio was broken by a transmission from a Flying Doves pilot. "We have a positive return from a cell phone interrogation. Our course is 270 degrees. We are approximately twenty-five kilometers south of Kongola along the Namibia-Zimbabwe border."

"Roger, your position," said Dave, "We will be at your location in one hour. Do your best to narrow the search area."

"Roger wilco," came the reply.

Dave turned to Dan. "That sounds like confirmation to me," said Dave. "We now have two returns in the same general area."

Dan said nothing. He just bowed his head for a moment of silent prayer and then looked, misty-eyed, out the side window at the vast African terrain below. It would still be like finding a needle in a haystack.

Dan was back on the Flying Doves communication channel instructing pilots flying other bearings to modify their courses. Only three of the other seven responded. The other four were apparently out of range even at this altitude.

It seemed to Dan like a long time, but it was less than an hour, as they approached the Kongola area. Dan watched the radio closely for a return acknowledgment from Callie's cell phone. They continued to fly the 277-degree heading and were now in Angolan airspace. There were no return acknowledgments as they approached three hundred kilometers from Victoria Falls.

"What do you think?" asked Dave.

"Let's turn back and go higher," said Dan.

Dave began a wide sweeping turn and climbed higher in altitude.

The radio channel came alive "We have a return at 12,000 feet. Our position is over the Ngonye Falls on the Zambezi River about thirty kilometers north of Sioma Ngwezi Park," reported one of the Flying Dove's pilots.

"That's nearly two hundred kilometers northeast of here," said Dave. "We must be too far south."

Another plane reported, "We have a return at 8,000 feet near Luiana along the Cuando River. We are following the river headed southeast."

"Luiana is perhaps seventy kilometers north," said Dave

"The first plane near Kongola reported again. "We lost the return when we dropped below 2,000 feet approximately forty kilometers southwest of Kongola."

Dave pointed out the reported positions of the planes as Dan studied the map. "Why the hell haven't we picked it up?" exclaimed Dan. "We should be close enough."

"I can increase altitude until we get it," said Dave.

"No, it's the low wings that are the problem," said Dan. "Start doing 360s in as steep a bank to the right as you can."

Dan held the radio against the cockpit window as Dave did a steep 360 to the right. It wasn't long before there was a return, "Bingo!" exclaimed Dan.

"It's going to be inside Angola," said Dave. "There's the Portuguese connection for you." Over the next hour or so, the five planes active in the search area traded information over the radio and continually lowered their altitude. With each passing minute, the search area became smaller, as the Flying Doves coordinated their positions.

"I have a small clearing over here along the Cuando River on the Angolan side. There are several metal buildings and a dirt strip," announced one of the planes. "At 400 feet I am still getting a return."

"We will be there in just a few minutes," replied Dave.

Dave came in at 1,000 feet until he spotted the other plane, and then he circled the small clearing. He dropped down and circled very low. There were no signs of any activity.

"I am going in," said Dave, as he lined the plane up on the dirt runway. He kept the plane off the runway as long as he could. When he finally touched down, the stall horn was blaring and he came to a quick stop.

He radioed a request for a volunteer among the planes to land. He immediately received four responses agreeing to do so. Dave instructed two of the planes to return to Victoria Falls to refuel. He told one of the planes to remain in the area as a lookout, for as long as fuel allowed. He asked one of the planes to land.

Dan said, "Have them turn off the radios I gave them so that their interrogation signals won't interfere with ours."

Dave issued additional instructions, and soon, two of the planes were heading east toward Victoria Falls, and one plane circled at high altitude. In a few minutes, a Cessna 206 landed on the dirt strip. The co-pilot got out of the plane and walked toward Dave's plane. The pilot kept the engine running on the Cessna 206 and taxied to the other end of the runway.

"It's too dangerous for all of us to be here like this," said Dave. "We are sitting ducks. So, take whatever you must have out of your bag and leave the rest in the plane."

Dan understood. He removed his passport and camera from the bag. Dave killed the engines. They both got out. Dan brought his radio and Dave brought a hand-held aviation radio with him.

The co-pilot from the Cessna 206 hopped into Dave's plane and started the engines. As soon as the plane began to move, the Cessna 206 engines begin to rev up. In a few moments, he was traveling down the runway and was airborne. The Cessna 410 taxied into position and soon it was airborne.

"Well, it's just you and me, Kemo Sabe," said Dan.

They surveyed the area. There were several metal Quonset huts and a few old jeeps and military vehicles around the edge of the clearing. There were a couple of newer-looking bulldozers.

The two men searched the area, checking each hut and the surrounding grounds. They looked into several of the old military vehicles but found nothing.

"I am still getting a strong return on the radio, Callie's cell phone must be nearby," said Dan.

"There has been a lot of activity around here and very recently. There are hundreds of footprints, many of them small, many of them children," observed Dave.

"I can see that," said Dan.

"But it is what is not here that is more interesting," said Dave. "There is no rubbish, someone has gone to a great deal of effort to clean the place of all debris. One good rain and there will be no trace that anyone was here."

Dave looked into a several metal trash cans in front of the huts. "Even the bloody trash cans are empty," said Dave.

"Well, then we can use one," said Dan, as he picked one up and carried it to the center of the clearing and placed it on its side. It may have been empty, but it didn't smell like it. He held his breath and placed his radio well inside the can and waited for a few minutes. "Good," he said. "I have lost the return."

Every two minutes Dan rotated the opening of the can a few degrees, like a slow-moving radar antenna. Dave continued to search the area. After several attempts, he got a return. He continued rotating the trash can until the return disappeared. He split the difference between the return bearings and the opening of the can pointed directly at an old jeep sitting at the edge of the clearing.

Dan fished the radio out of the can and began walking toward the jeep. It had three flat tires and the hood was up. He unscrewed the antenna and removed it from the radio and waited. At the next cycle, he did not have a return. He walked up to the jeep and waited for the next cycle. He had a return.

He looked inside the jeep and immediately saw the wires of the cigarette lighter adapter dangling from the dash and disappearing under a burlap sack. He pulled back the sack to reveal a cell phone.

"Dave, Dave!" he yelled. "Come here."

Dave came running across the clearing to the jeep. "What do you have there, Dan?"

"It is Callie's cell phone," said Dan.

"Well, that's bloody ingenious what she did there Dan!" exclaimed Dave

Dan scrolled the cell phone's menu, there were dozens of "text alerts." There was only one that had been retrieved. He did some mental calculations. He knew when that alert had been sent. Callie's phone thought it was in a cell site and re-synced with the time source from the radio in the Learjet. After he thought about it, Dan said, "The time difference here is UTC+2, Callie was here around 7:43 a.m. local time."

Chapter 26

Dave once again surveyed the area. He carefully walked around studying the many footprints in the dirt. He walked to the edges of the compound and looked out at the surrounding terrain. It was an African savanna that Dave had flown over and walked in his entire life. Trees were spaced far enough apart that there was a canopy of leaves created by the sprawling limbs. It had been the dry season for many months, and the land was covered with brown grasses, quite tall in some areas. There were patches of green grasses and the landscape was punctuated with both brown and green bushes dotting the landscape. Not far away was a line of green bushes and grasses meandering through the savanna. The trees were greener and more closely together.

There was clearly a river nearby. Dave could see the river had withdrawn to a swampy marsh in many places. During the rainy season, the river could well have swollen to a size to place much of the area underwater. Dave knew his geography and he knew the climates well. It was difficult to be certain without a GPS, but Dave believed they were in southeastern

Angola near the Zambian border. He looked around for traces of recent human activity and found little except near the compound. He studied a dirt road going off the north. He knew there were few populated villages in this area.

Dan just stood silently watching Dave as Dave studied the area. Dan did not want to break the mood or risk interfering with Dave's observations. At times, Dan could clearly see that Dave was praying, as if asking for wisdom and guidance in his search for what had happened here.

Finally, Dave turned back toward the direction of the green tree line. He looked down at all the footprints again and said, "They went this way toward the river." Dave walked confidently toward the path leading through the grasses and the trees. The footprints were at times quite visible in the dirt, and at other times, the grasses hid any sign of footprints except the trampled grass itself. After a few minutes, they came to the bank of a slow-moving river meandering through the savannah. The shoreline itself often had dense green grasses, and you could not tell if there was an actual bank or the river had simply morphed into a swampy marsh.

The bank of the river had hundreds of fresh footprints many of them the small footprints of children. "They went downriver to the south," said Dave. "The Namibian border is not far from here."

Dave pulled out his radio and asked for the position of the nearest plane and of his Cessna 410. The Cessna 206 came back to him. "We are circling just inside Namibia, and we set your plane down at Lianshulu about sixty kilometers south of you."

"Okay," said Dave. "I need you to come up toward us and as you do study the terrain and look for any signs of where the girls could have been taken. We are along the shore of the Cuando River, and we can see where they were placed on boats that I believe they have been taken south. We believe they were here this morning.”

“Roger that,” came the voice from the radio.

“Okay, Dan, we are going to try and follow the river to the south.” Dave led the way through the grasses and trees and, at times, distanced himself from the river by a couple hundred feet as they headed south. It was difficult stepping through the grasses and sometimes they would come to a marshy area that forced them farther from the river. There were plenty of bugs and birds along the way. Often, they could get right up to the edge of the river and walk along the dry bank. Dave tried to stay as close to the river’s edge as he could whenever he could. Always he was studying the terrain and the river’s edge.

The whole trip seemed effortless for Dave but Dan was having difficulty keeping up. The hot sun was beating down on them and sweat was pouring off of Dan’s brow. Although it hadn’t been that long it seemed like an eternity. Suddenly, while walking along the bank, Dave stopped. There was a lone set of footprints in the dirt. Someone had come up to the river bank and then gone back into the grasses.

“These are fresh,” said Dave. “Look over here,” as he pointed to an area along the river bank that had been greatly disturbed.

“I see.” said Dan “It looks like whoever it was wallowed in the mud like a pig.”

“Strange, very strange,” said Dave. We can’t follow the tracks since they disappear into the grasses. Let’s just continue downstream and keep our eyes open.”

Dave brought the aviation radio to his lip and pressed the mike key, “Niner Niner Niner, this is the ground party.”

The radio jumped to life, “Ground Party, This is Niner Niner Niner.”

"We see some fresh tracks down here along the river bank. I need you to drop down lower near our position and scour the area for anything suspicious," instructed Dave.

"Roger that."

The two men continued their meandering trek to the south and soon they heard the sounds of the Cessna 206 flying overhead. It then began a series of sweeping S-turns along the river ahead of them.

It wasn't long before the radio silence was broken "Dave, we caught a glimpse of something orange in the grasses about one kilometer in front of you. Whatever it is, it hasn't moved."

The two men happened to be on the bank of the river when the radio call came in. "Dan," said Dave, "I need you to stay right here. I am going to go out and find whatever this is, and we can't afford to get separated on different tracks. If you stay right here, I can find you again without help from the plane. You must stay here. But be prepared for anything."

"I understand," said Dan.

Dave pulled an earpiece out of his pocket and plugged it into the radio.

And off Dave went, moving very fast now, much faster than they had been traveling before. Dan suddenly realized that he had been slowing Dave down. Dave moved at a quick pace through the grasses and disappeared within a few seconds.

The minutes ticked away. Dan could see the Cessna 206 circling in the air above them but at a fairly high altitude that made the sound of the engines barely audible.

Suddenly, Dan heard the rustling of the grasses and saw Dave heading straight for him carrying something covered in mud. It was a young white girl, her hair matted in mud and the mud spread all over her face. She was totally covered in mud except for a few places where her bright orange clothing showed through.

Dave carried her to the shore and set her down in the water and started cleaning her off. She was awake but seemed only half conscious.

"Where did you find her?" asked Dan.

"She wasn't moving," replied Dave. "They talked me right into her. She had hidden under a tree limb in the tall grass, but bits of her orange clothing could be seen from the air. Her face is sunburned and she has a lot of insect bites."

As the two men cleaned off the mud caked on her clothes and body, she opened her eyes and seemed to drift in out of consciousness. They cleaned all the mud out of her long blonde hair and off of her face and neck. After they had cleaned most of the mud off, they carried her to the edge of the grasses and placed her on a pile of grass below the shade of a tree. Dave took out his canteen and said, "She's dehydrated," as he poured the cool water on her lips.

Dan tried talking to her as she lay on the ground "What is your name? What is your name, Young Lady? Can you hear me? Do you speak English? What is your name?"

Her eyes opened, "My Torah, my Torah, where is my Torah?" she asked frantically as she felt along her abdomen. "Oh, good, here it is as she tried pulling the plastic bag from under her top.

"Are you an American?" she asked staring straight into Dan's eyes.

"Yes, yes," said Dan, "Who are you?"

"You have the same blue eyes," she said.

"Blue eyes?" said Dan. "Are you okay? What are you saying?"

"You have her eyes. You are Callie's dad?" she said as more of a word of knowledge than a question.

Both men looked stunned. They looked at each other in disbelief.

"Callie saved my Torah for me. My name is Ilsa and she said you would come."

"When, when, Ilsa? When did you see her? exclaimed Dan.

"This morning. This morning. She is fine but they're all gone now. I escaped from the boat." her voice trailed off and she either lost consciousness or fell asleep.

"Let her rest," said Dave. She can answer our questions later. We need to keep her out of the sun and let her rest. We need to get her someplace safe."

Dave picked up his radio and said, "Niner Niner Niner, this is Ground Party."

"We copy, Ground Party. Go ahead."

"We need ground transportation for the girl. What is the nearest airport where you can rent a vehicle and come and get us? And is there a road nearby that you can reach us?"

"Roger, Dave. We have already scoped out a ground path to you. The best airport is Lianshulu about fifty kilometers south. We will land there and get a vehicle to you. It will take two to three hours."

"Okay, do it. Get some blankets and medicine for insect bites and plenty of water for the girl at Lianshulu or Kongola on the way," said Dave.

"Roger, Dave. Hang tight and we will get back to you as soon as we can. Take care."

"Thanks," said Dave, "Ground Party out."

"No! No!" came Ilsa's weak voice. "You must try to find them, I can tell you things to help. I will be okay. Listen. We landed at a coastal city in the Oasis 747. They flew us deep into the jungle on four transport planes, where they held us for several days. I don't know how many. I have lost track of time. They kept us in three buildings and gave us water and shots and very little solid food to eat. This morning they transported us by motorized raft from upstream. It took a lot of trips. I was in one of the first boats to leave. I jumped overboard and escaped into the marsh. I covered myself in mud and snuck along the river bank to see where they were taking the rest of the girls. I watched as they brought boat after boat of the girls to a clearing along the river. They made the girls get into shipping containers. There must be eight or ten of them. They are white and on the back of a flatbed semi-trailer. The trucks are black and look new, and they headed downstream along the river. I can show you if you take me there. At first, we were held by black men in military garb and a few white men. All the white men spoke English and Arabic." Her voice grew weaker and began to trail off.

"The girls? What shape are the girls in?" quizzed Dan as he recorded her on his camera.

"They're all okay physically but emotionally most of them are a mess. They cry a lot. We have all been given shots they said to keep us healthy."

How many girls were with you?"

"Two-Hundred-Seventy-Five," she replied, and lifted her arm to show a wristband "They gave us all wristbands. They know our names and everything about us. Only the blondes, though. Only the blondes."

"What do you mean? Asked Dan.

"Only the blondes were with us. There were brunettes and other hair colors that were white. There were Black and Asian girls with us in the beginning, but we haven't seen them since Orlando. We all talked about it later. They were never on the Oasis plane with us." Her voice was getting weaker, "Miss Calloway too."

"Who is Miss Calloway?" asked Dan.

"She was the dance instructor in Orlando. She is a redhead. We saw her taken off the plane when they transferred us to the four transport planes, but she didn't get on with us and we never saw her after that."

Suddenly, the sound of the Cessna 206 engine was very loud. They looked up and saw it heading straight for them very low in the air as if on final approach. It banked right slightly and a package with a small parachute came floating down within one hundred feet of them. Dave ran to get it.

Dan had been recording Ilsa and stopped the recording.

The radio on the ground next to Ilsa came alive. "Ground Party, we have dropped you a medical kit and blanket and plenty of water."

In a moment, Dave was back with the package. He picked up the radio. "Thanks, Niner Niner Niner. Slight change in plans. How much fuel do you have?"

"Maybe two hours, plus reserve," came the reply.

"Okay," said Dave. "I want you to fly down along the river to Kongola and then fly along the Golden Highway straightaway to Livingstone. We believe the girls are being transported in a caravan of white shipping containers on flatbeds pulled by black trucks; at least eight, maybe ten of them. Once you get to Livingstone check the railways in case they are moved to rail. Check the train schedules. I think they are going to a seaport, and my best guess is Dar es Salaam.

"What about you?" asked the pilot.

"We can manage for a few hours with the supplies you dropped. Radio ahead and get another plane in the air to look for the container trucks, refuel and get to Lianshulu, and get the rental car to come get us."

"Roger, Dave. We will see you before sunset, Niner Niner Niner out."

Dave unwrapped the package to reveal a first aid kit, a shiny lightweight medical blanket and perhaps two dozen bottles of water. There was also some kind of nutrition bars.

"Ilsa, here drink this," said Dave, as he handed her a bottled water and opened a nutrition bar for her. "We need to get those muddy wet clothes off of you. We are going to spread this blanket over you so you can change out of them, and we will wash them thoroughly in the river and dry them."

Dave and Dan unfolded the blanket and spread it over Ilsa.

She was weak and wiggled a bit under the blanket and pulled out a plastic bag with a Bible in it. "Here, hold this she said to Dan. Your daughter saved it for me this morning and handed it to me before she got on the raft."

Dan accepted it in his hands as if it were a gift from God himself. In a moment of reflection, he prayed for the strength and wisdom to continue on. He took it out of the plastic bag and opened it.

"To Ilsa with Love. Enjoy your time in Jerusalem." It was dated and signed, "Father."

To think that Callie held it in her hands just a few hours earlier gave him great hope. He carefully returned it to the plastic bag and sealed it.

Ilsa was clearly weak and struggled to get her clothes off under the blanket. She handed out her pants first and then a few moments later her top. Dave turned them inside out. Both had quite a bit of mud on the inside. Dave gave Ilsa a cloth from the medical kits and told her to find any mud or residue and clean it off of her.

"Is there soap and shampoo in there, too?" she asked.

Dave searched, "Yes, there is."

She said, "Look, I can get up and get to the river. Twice today I have rolled in the mud to camouflage myself. I would love to have a real bath."

"Are you sure you are strong enough?" asked Dan.

"My great-grandmother was younger than me when she survived the Holocaust. What I have been through today would have been a good day for her."

She struggled to get up and wrap the blanket around her as Dan and Dave both turned their eyes from her. In a few moments, they heard a splash as Ilsa jumped into the river.

Dan kept his eyes looking away at all times.

"Let me know when you are ready to come out," said Dave, "I will glance around from time to time to make sure you are okay. But he didn't. He just backed closer to the edge of the water and listened. Dan could only imagine what Dave could hear that he could not.

She stayed in the water for a long time. She came back to the bank and put the blanket around her and said "Okay."

Dave turned around and picked her up in his arms as he had done when he found her. Dave took one of the cloths and cleaned the mud off her feet. There were some nasty bites on her legs and ankles.

Dave gently placed her in the shade on the grasses with the blanket wrapped around her.

He gave her a tube of skin ointment and said. "You need to check for any bites or abrasions and spread this cream on it." She took the ointment and did as he said. He pointed out some bites on her neck, face, lower legs and ankle that she could not see. After a little while, she drifted off to sleep.

Dave took her orange clothes, shoes and socks and the shampoo to the river and washed them. He hung them on the tree limb near her to dry in the hot African sun.

Dan and Dave opened a bottled water and a nutrition bar and sat there under the shade of the tree and waited.

Chapter 27

The radio blared out, "Ground Party, this is Land Cruiser."

Dave hurriedly picked up the radio and replied, "This is Ground Party."

"Are you in the same location where we dropped the supplies?"

"Yes," replied Dave.

"Good. We are parked very close. I will be there in a few minutes."

"Okay," said Dave.

Dave turned to Dan and said, "Let's wake the girl and get her ready."

Dan gently touched the girl's shoulder, "Ilsa. Ilsa, wake up. It's time to go."

She awoke, startled trying to get her bearing. "What? what? What did you say?" she mumbled softly.

"Here, these are dry. Put these on," said Dan, as he handed her the orange clothes.

She took the clothes under the blanket and fumbled for a while, trying to get them on. Finally, she threw off the blanket and sat on it as she put on her shoes and socks.

It wasn't long before a voice could be heard coming through the grasses along the river, "Hey, Mate," a booming voice said as a man in khakis emerged from the tall grass. He was dressed in the same safari-type, khaki shirt and pants that Dave wore.

"Johnny," said Dave, "You are a site for sore eyes."

Dan recognized the voice from the radio and the man as one of the Flying Dove pilots he had seen at Victoria Falls.

"Here," said Dave, as he handed the man the blanket and supplies that had been air dropped.

Dave looked into Ilsa's eyes. "How are you feeling, Young Lady? He asked.

Ilsa shook her head a little and said "Not so good."

Dave placed his hand on her forehead. "You have a slight fever," he said, "and you have a lot of insect bites. We need to get you someplace where we can take care of you," and he swooped down and picked her up in his arms, carrying her as he had before. "Lead the way," he said to Johnny.

Johnny headed back into the tall grasses. Dave followed, carrying Ilsa, and Dan followed behind. In less than ten minutes they came to a dirt road where a beige Toyota Land Cruiser was parked.

There was another fellow waiting by the car. As soon as he saw the group emerge from the grasses, he ran to help Johnny with the things he was carrying. The men piled into the Land Cruiser, with Ilsa placed in the back seat between Dan and Dave. The Land Cruiser started down the dirt road a short distance before turning right on to a slightly better dirt road.

"Stop!" Ilsa cried out, "This is the place."

"What?" said Dan.

"This is the place they made the girls get into the containers. I hid over here," she said as she pointed to an area to the left. They stopped the Toyota and got out. Dave quickly scanned the area. He could see there had recently been a great deal of activity in the area. In the dirt there were dozens of tire tracks belonging to a large truck. There were hundreds of footprints, many of them small as if made by children. He followed some of the footprints that lead to the other side of the road to a clearing.

"They have used this area as a latrine," said Dave.

Dan had followed him and was able to see as well. He thought for a moment and said, "This is a goldmine of DNA, if we could just bag it and send it to a lab."

Dave looked at him with a strange expression on his face. "What did you say?" he asked

Dan continued "They must have told the girls to use the bathroom before loading them into the containers. Think about it. They have been giving them liquids but very little solid food. They are doing that to keep the waste down as they transport the girls to wherever they are being taken. The dirt here is covered with the DNA of a lot of the girls. Sure, it would be difficult to sort it all out, but a good lab could do it. If they had any DNA from any of the girls, they could match it and ID the girls that were here."

"Well," said Dave, "I hear you but there is nothing we can do about it now. We have no way to collect it or transport it, but if it is that important, I have an idea. We can come back first thing in the morning prepared to collect samples. But right now, we need to get to Kongola before night falls."

They all got back in the Land Cruiser and proceeded down the dirt road. Occasionally, they could see the Cuando River to the right, as the sun was setting in the west. They occasionally passed crude dwellings. After about an hour they came to a nice highway and turned left onto it.

"This is the B8," said Dave, "the Golden Highway that connects the Atlantic with the Indian Ocean. To the right Is Windhoek Harbor in Namibia, and to the left is the road to Livingstone and then through Zambia to Tanzania and, finally, to a port city such as Dar es Salaam on the Indian Ocean."

"Do you think that is where they are taking the girls?" asked Dan.

"Yes, it would make no sense for them to go to all this trouble to get the girls to the southeast corner of Angola. They could have just got them on board a ship in Luanda. It may not be Dar es Salaam, but it is most certainly a seaport on the east coast."

Ilsa had been trying to stay awake, and was clearly exhausted, but she managed to speak. "You have to find them soon. It is the white slave trade. They were taking us to some Arab country to be used as sex slaves. That's why they just took blondes. If the ship sets sail on the Indian Ocean, you will never find out where they are."

It shocked the men to hear Ilsa speak so candidly about what they all had been thinking.

The ride was so much smoother now and, in just a few minutes, they came up to an intersection with some homes and businesses. It was a shopping center of some kind with a petrol station. It was the closest thing that Dan had seen to civilization in a while.

Dave directed Johnny to pull into a driveway of one of the houses. Dave went up to the door and knocked. An older distinguished man came to the door. They spoke for a few minutes and then Dave came back to the car.

"We are going to stay here tonight," said Dave. "This is Pastor Adams. He is the Pastor of the local Adventist Church.

Dave carried Ilsa in his arms, as before, as the other two men followed. The old man was dressed in a white pullover shirt that hung down well below his waist, and he wore white pants with shiny black shoes. He motioned Dave into a bedroom. Dave carefully pulled back the cover, placed Ilsa on the bed, and covered her up with a thin blanket. He pulled down a mosquito net hanging from the ceiling and tucked it in around the bed to protect Ilsa. He then turned on the fan. Ilsa looked up and smiled. Dan watched the scene from the hall and caught Ilsa's eye "Nighty night Ilsa" said Dan. Ilsa smiled and then spoke softly and said "Nighty night."

The men gathered outside in the courtyard and sat around the table and discussed the day's events.

"We have to decide on a course of action here," said Dave. We could take Ilsa to the Lianshulu airport in the morning and fly back to Harare. The problem is when we land, we must check in with Immigration and we have no passport for her. It is too risky to try and sneak her across the border. And the other thing is Dan you mentioned DNA. There is a DNA lab about one hundred kilometers from here at Katima Mutillo. If you are serious about collecting DNA samples, I can have someone here in the morning to go with us to the site."

"Seriously," quizzed Dan, "You have a DNA lab here in the middle of Africa."

"Yes," said Dave. "They are affiliated with a global DNA company out of the States."

"On the one hand, "began Dan, "No one may believe what we have to say, even when we produce Ilsa. She is just one girl and people may think we have a crazy conspiracy theory. But if we had the DNA of some of the other girls, it could be matched later with the families. That could be a strong piece of evidence if we have to persuade the authorities of our story. But there is a chain-of-custody concern with regard to legal issues."

"No, Dan, there is not," said Dave. "If I get the right person from the lab to come in the morning, she is qualified in Namibia to establish a chain of custody in the collection and the preparation of the samples. That's the best we can do."

"I hate to take the time," said Dan. "We have to continue the search. We can't afford to lose a day finding the containers."

"We don't have to," said Dave. "The Flying Doves can be in the air first thing in the morning searching from Livingstone to Lusaka along the main roads and the rail routes to the Indian Ocean. We can be in the air ourselves by early afternoon if they find anything."

"Maybe we should just call the authorities now and tell them what we know. We need help fast." said Dan.

Pastor Adams had been listening intently to the discussion and interrupted "That, my friend, is not a good idea. The local authorities are not going to believe you without a lot more proof than you have, plus you have a young girl with you in the country illegally, without a passport, that is not your daughter. It just doesn't look good and it is not believable. I don't even know if I believe it, but I trust Pastor Doyle and I trust Dave. You must wait and be wise in your decisions."

He was right, of course, and Dan knew that, but the pastor's comments gave Dan an idea. "I can get my daughter's passport sent to us from Indiana. They're about the same age, blonde, blue eyes and I think they look enough alike that we can get away with it."

Pastor Adams smiled. "I cannot condone such an action," he said, "Ilsa can stay here for the next few days, until you have an appropriate passport. Quite frankly, she needs the anonymity for a while to rest and gather her thoughts."

"Do you have Internet?" asked Dan "I need to send Annie, my other daughter, the instructions to send an appropriate passport."

Dave said, "Have her send it to Pastor Doyle's church in Harare. We don't want to involve Pastor Adams or his ministry in this. Pastor, may I use your phone to call my lab contact in Kutimo Mutillo?"

"Yes, of course," replied Pastor Adams, "the phone and computer are in my office." He pointed to the door of his office. "You're welcome to use them as much as you want. Your quarters for the night are across the courtyard. Pick whichever ones you want. As for me, I will check in on Ilsa and then retire for the night. It was a pleasure meeting you, Dan. I only wish it had been under better circumstances, but I am confident that the Lord will take care of the matter for you."

The old pastor labored to get up from his chair and returned to the main house.

Dave and Dan entered Pastor Adams' office and found the light. Dave found the phone as Dan sat down at the computer. Dan signed on to his e-mail service and began a message to Annie. "What's the church address?" asked Dan.

As Dave recited the address, Dan typed it in the e-mail. Dan had to be careful about what he told Annie. He could not reveal the existence of Ilsa yet. It was too big a secret to expect anyone to keep. He simply said in this e-mail that he knew with certainty that the Oasis plane did not crash off the Florida coast and that the girls, who have been recovered, were never on the plane. He told Annie that, at some point, he would ask her go to Florida and discreetly investigate how the girls and their luggage were transported from the hotel to the terminal. He told her it would be good experience for her career in journalism. He told her where to find the American Express credit card, issued in her name, which he kept for emergencies.

Dave had completed his phone call and waited for Dan to finish. The two men walked across the courtyard and found their quarters to retire for the evening.

The night passed quickly with Dan getting his first good night of sleep since the ordeal had begun. He was awakened from a deep sleep by the sounds of a woman laughing loudly in the courtyard. He quickly got up and peeked out the door to see a short heavy-set woman sitting with Dave and Pastor Adams at breakfast.

Dave noticed him and said, "Dan, this is Nellie Bates." He motioned toward the woman. "We will be ready to go as soon as you get dressed and grab a bit of breakfast." Nellie tipped her glass of orange juice to him as if it were a glass of wine. "Hurry up," she said, "We want to beat the mid-day sun at the collection site."

"Okay," shouted Dan. He quickly showered and dressed, and in only a few minutes, emerged from his door.

"Where's Ilsa?" asked Dan.

"She's still sound asleep and probably will be for a while," replied Dave, "Dan, This is Nellie Bates with the DNA Collection Lab at Katima Mutillo."

"Nellie," said Dan, as he reached out to shake her hand, "Pleased to meet you."

"No, you're not, Dan, you need me for some reason of which our friend Dave refuses to totally tell me about, but he has promised me it is not illegal. So, let's get the hell on the way. Every minute the DNA is exposed to the elements, the vermin and the hot sun is another minute the samples degrade."

"Okay, fair enough," said Dan. He grabbed a couple of bagels, hard-boiled eggs and a paper cup of orange juice from the breakfast table and said, "Let's go."

The three headed out beyond the courtyard to a Toyota pickup truck with some equipment, tools and two silver fifty-five gallon drums in the back. Two Black men were in the front seat. The three jumped into the Land Cruiser and Dan hopped in the back. Nellie motioned the men in the truck to follow.

Dan scarfed down his food, as Dave and Nellie talked about old times and people Dan did not know or care about. All Dan could think about was Callie. Twenty-four hours ago, she was here and now headed off to who knows where to the east, and here Dan was going on this mission of questionable importance. Yet, he knew there was nothing better for him to do. The Flying Doves were in the air, and if one of them found anything he and Dave could get to the Cessna 410 in Lianshulu in an hour and a half and be in the air. If this DNA is viable it will prove the missing girls were in Africa and corroborate an otherwise unbelievable story.

Finally, as they were nearing the collection site, Dan blurted out "Nellie, Do you know why we are here?"

She turned around to look at him.

"Truth, you need to know all the truth and it is not credible," said Dan.

"Go on," she said.

"My daughter, Callie and 275 girls were kidnapped over Florida on the way to the Super Bowl. Their 747 was actually flown to Luanda. The girls were transferred to some other planes and set down in southeastern Angola. A few days later, they were taken down the Cuando River to a site where they were loaded into shipping containers on semis headed east on the Caprivi Strip. We are going to a place where we know many of them used the bathroom yesterday morning," Dan paused.

"You're shittin' me," said Nellie. He couldn't tell if she believed him, or if that was a statement of skepticism. As he listened to the words he had just uttered, he wasn't sure he could believe it himself. Yet, they had Ilsa.

"Holy crap!" I heard about this on the shortwave, but not this angle. Don't they think all those girls died?" Then she realized she was speaking of Dan's daughter "I'm sorry," she said.

"Prove me to be a liar. I want you to because, when the time comes, the evidence you collect today is going to prove to the world I'm not a crazy father!"

"This is the place," interrupted Dave, as he came to the junction of the old dirt road. The three got out. Nellie motioned to the two men in the pickup to remain where they were when they got out of the truck.

Nellie had her camera out and began taking dozens of pictures of the footprints, the human waste, and the hundreds of small pieces of tissue paper strewn around and trapped by the wind against the plants in the area. She went to the pickup and came back with a pack of equipment. She began to place dozens of small orange flags with numbers all over the area and then took more pictures.

After a few minutes, she spoke to the two Black men in another language. Before long they had removed the two drums from the pickup with a dolly and positioned them in the middle of the flagged area. They began scooping up the entire area several inches deep around the flags and placing the dirt into small plastic bags with the flag. This included pile after pile of fly-covered human excrement, as well as areas covered with urine and flies and other small insects. The insects were brushed off as much as possible and the plastic bags were thrown into the fifty-five gallon drums until they both were full.

The two men struggled with the now-heavy drums to get them into the back of the pickup. They had a hydraulic jack to assist them.

"Mr. Grainger," began Nellie, "I don't know if I believe your fanciful tale or not, but I can tell you, from what I have seen so far, that several hundred young girls, most likely not of this continent, were here recently. We need to get these two-hundred-liter drums back to my lab as soon as possible and into refrigeration to preserve what we have. It is a gold mine of DNA, even in its degraded condition."

"Thank you, Nellie," said Dave.

"Yes, thank you," said Dan.

"Time is of the essence," Nellie replied, as she headed toward the pickup. She took the driver's seat and one man got in the front. The other hopped in the back with the precious cargo of human waste. The Toyota turned around and headed back down the dirt road.

Dan looked around at the area full of pot holes. He still could see occasional remnants of tissue paper clinging to some of the plants. He stopped to pray for a moment, and Dave gave him the space to take his time. With each passing minute, he feared Callie was getting farther and farther away from his grasp. Yet, he had to remind himself that he had been led to this place and he had no reason to believe that guidance and protection would not continue to bless his search.

Dan was a very practical man. Whoever perpetrated this hoax had not done a very good job. The hoax was only designed to fool people for a short time. There would eventually be questions. No wreckage would be found in the shallow waters of the Atlantic. No black box signal would ever be ever received. No more bodies would be recovered. Serial numbers from the recovered plane debris would not match maintenance records.

The people who devised this plan would become impossible to find if they saw their hoax exposed too soon. The girls would disappear forever. Dan had to find the girls before the story unraveled.

For the first time, Dan had irrefutable DNA evidence that the girls had been abducted. Dan knew that if he failed in his mission to find and save Callie himself, the DNA evidence and other circumstantial evidence he was compiling would allow Annie and Mike to proceed if anything happened to him.

Dave was in the Land Cruiser watching Dan. He didn't know if Dan was praying or was just lost in thought. Finally, Dan opened the door and slipped into the front seat.

"We'll find her Dan," said Dave softly. The Land Cruiser had no sooner started down the road than they were surrounded by a small contingency of armed men in military garb, with automatic weapons.

Dave stopped the car, as the leader of the group shouted commands to them in another language. Dan couldn't understand. "What's happening?" he said.

"It's Portuguese," said Dave calmly. "They're Angolan military."

"I thought we were across the border in Namibia!" Dan said, incredulously.

"We are, but try telling them that."

The two men were forced out of the car and forced to march toward the river.

"What are we going to do? We gotta find Callie!" exclaimed Dan. He was not even thinking of the consequences for himself or Dave "What are we going to do? No one is going to know where we are."

Dave motioned slightly and nodded his head upward toward the sky. Dan cautiously looked upward to see the Cessna 206 floating silently overhead. The sound of the engines was being carried by the wind to the southwest.

Dave looked straight into Dan's eyes and whispered, "Trust in the Lord."